THE BETTER PART OF WORSE

Also by Denise-Marie Martin

Tangled Violets: A Novel of Redemption

ADVANCED PRAISE

"An affecting, decades-spanning tale of love and mental illness."
— *Kirkus Reviews*

"Martin keeps the pace humming with heart-breaking plot twists and resonant emotional moments, transforming the narrative into a powerful rendering of the 'true meaning of love.'"
— *BookLife Reviews*

"In this engaging and evocative historical novel, Denise-Marie Martin explores the far-reaching impact of severe mental illness on individuals and families through a lens of deep faith—and without sugarcoating the struggles or ignoring the wreckage left in the illness's wake. *The Better Part of Worse* is a story about the true nature of love, which is never easy but always redemptive. Highly recommended!"
— *Rhonda Ortiz,*
Award-winning author of the Molly Chase *series*

"*The Better Part of Worse* is a love story, a historical fiction novel, and a mystery wrapped up perfectly. The novel emphasizes the resilience of love and the enduring hope that can flourish even amidst the challenges of mental illness, while celebrating the loving choice of adoption. A powerful line from the novel: *'God brings good out of even the hardest things,'* captures this beautifully. With every page, I felt drawn deeper into the characters' lives, brought to life through Martin's meticulous research and heartfelt storytelling. I simply couldn't put it down."
— *Leigh Ebberwein,*
Award-winning author of the Saints of Savannah *series*

"Denise-Marie Martin has woven a heart-breaking yet beautiful tale in her historical novel *The Better Part of Worse*. This post–World War I story of family bonds, oaths to God, and desperate clinging to goodness in the midst of mental illness evokes deep emotions the whole way through. I wasn't too far in before I could barely set it aside. I fell in love with the characters and found myself wanting them all to triumph over whatever was holding them back. Martin stays true to what we've come to expect from her—excellent research of topic, splendid character development, and writing that spans the gamut of emotions. I am proud to give my endorsement and highly recommend this unforgettable novel."

— *Mary Jo Thayer,*
Three-time award-winning author of Close to the Soul

"I absolutely loved this book. The characters are well-developed, the setting and time period well-represented and well-researched and the story is compelling. It's not an easy read, but it's an important one that defines the uniqueness and the irreplaceability of every human being, no matter how they were conceived. If I could give it more than five stars, I would. Highly recommend!"

— *Ellen Gable,*
Award-winning author of more than ten novels

THE BETTER PART OF WORSE
A Novel of Hope

Denise-Marie Martin

Misericordia Publishing

COPYRIGHTS

DEDICATION

For Carole

You don't choose your family. They are God's gift to you, as you are to them.
~Desmond Tutu
(1931 - 2021)

EPIGRAPH

The art of God is drawing good out of evil.
~Fr. Reginald Garrigou-Lagrange, O.P.
(1877-1964)

And we know that for those who love God all things work together for good, for those who are called according to his purpose. (Romans, 8:28)

PART ONE – FAMILY BONDS
(1927-1929)

ONE

For the lucky ones, twenty-one is an age of boundless possibilities and unbridled optimism. Jamie Murphy counted himself lucky, though not all seemed possible on his twenty-first birthday. Yet, he was alive, healthy, well-loved, and led a comfortable life—blessings he never took for granted, for Jamie was well-acquainted with the harsh realities of loss.

Jamie was only four when his seemingly healthy baby brother, Marty, died in his sleep. He didn't remember Marty well, but he never forgot the sound of his mother's wailing upon finding her lifeless infant in the crib. When Jamie was thirteen, his older brother Danny's draft number, 253, was the first to be drawn in the 1917 military draft lottery. Danny never made it home, his remains forever buried in a foxhole in France. Three summers later, Jamie's father, John, died suddenly of a heart attack at the dinner table, falling face-first into his meatloaf and potatoes.

Despite the Murphy family's share of tragedies, Jamie's mother, Peggy Murphy, cushioned their sorrows with her optimism, fortitude, resourcefulness, and unshakable faith in a provident God. If John Murphy's cup was half-empty, Peggy's was always half-full. His mom lacked both the temperament and the time to wallow in grief, with five children depending on her—Gracie, the eldest at nineteen; Jamie, then seventeen; Annie, twelve; Thomas, ten; and little Robert, only four—and a small farm to manage when his father had died.

But Jamie realized the Murphy family had been fortunate, too—some would say blessed. His father had the foresight and the finances to purchase a life insurance policy, though still uncommon at the time. That money, which his mother managed with frugal care, kept the family secure in their Tarrytown home and allowed them to hire a foreman to handle the day-to-day farm operations.

His parents had "discerned" a vocation *for* Jamie to the priesthood long before he had completed elementary school. "God has placed a special call on your life," his father would say as if it were the gospel itself, leaving no room for doubt. On John Murphy's New York Life insurance policy certificate, he had even scrawled a note: "In the event of my death, please set aside sufficient funds for Jamie's seminary schooling."

Though not particularly pious, Jamie was an obedient and exceedingly bright lad, often singled out for his academic achievements. Unlike his siblings, he never complained about praying the Rosary each night after dinner, though he found it hard on the knees and wretchedly boring. Jamie became an altar boy and took a quiet satisfaction in assisting the priest at Mass.

By all rights, the future-priest designation should have landed squarely on Danny's shoulders as the eldest son. However, like his father, Danny had loved the feel of the light, loamy soil in his hands— a passion shared by generations of Murphys, who had once been tenant farmers in Ireland before the potato blight of 1845. Danny's true calling was to work and manage the 130 acres of farmland alongside John.

Jamie, being more bookish, took after his mother's side of the family. The Gleasons proudly claimed several Jesuits, including his mother's brother, who taught philosophy at Fordham University. Fr. Jim, Jamie's namesake, had been a regular fixture in the Murphy household since Jamie's childhood.

Jamie's parents invested in a top-notch education to cultivate and solidify Jamie's imputed vocation. While there were several good schools for boys in Tarrytown, none were Catholic. So, they enrolled Jamie in Fordham Preparatory School, adjacent to Fordham University in the Bronx. He boarded there throughout his high school years, making it his home away from home.

When Jamie's adolescent hormones coursed through his body, plaguing his waking and dreaming hours with unbidden fantasies of the opposite sex, he might have questioned his call to the priesthood— if he had allowed himself that freedom. While other boys were navigating the mysteries of womanhood through observation, social interactions, and "hands-on" experience, Jamie inhabited an all-male universe, engaging in food fights, studying Latin and Greek, and spending much time in the confessional.

After high school, Jamie's priestly formation continued at St. Joseph's Seminary in the Dunwoodie neighborhood of Yonkers, where he was slated to study for six years. The seminary, set on forty picturesque acres atop Valentine Hill, was only seven miles from the family home. Whenever he had a free weekend or holiday, Jamie would ride the train back to Tarrytown. He was a model seminarian, consistently at the top of his class. Jamie had never consciously envisioned himself as anything other than the priest his parents had intended him to be.

Around Jamie's twenty-first birthday, halfway through the six-year formation, the color began to drain from his world. For the first time in his life, studying became a struggle. Sleep eluded him, and when he did manage to nod off for an hour or two, he'd wake up in a cold sweat, haunted by dreams of lying cruciform on the floor during his ordination.

Jamie's vocational anxiety gained momentum and magnitude, like a snowball rolling down a snow-covered hill in a blizzard of doubt. He lamented ever entering St. Joseph's Seminary and going through with the Rite of Candidacy. He begged God to set his heart ablaze for the priesthood, the vocation everyone else believed was perfect for him. But Jamie's heart did not change. God remained strangely silent and aloof in his hour of need.

He began a forty-day fast, allowing himself only water and one small meatless meal daily. He prayed with increasing fervor. His tall, sturdy frame grew emaciated, his handsome, chiseled features became sharper, and the mischievous sparkle in his dark brown eyes dimmed. But as his body grew leaner, Jamie's mental clarity increased. By the end of forty days, with the racket of his ego silenced and the clutter surrounding his vocation swept away, he knew what he must do.

During the regular academic year, Jamie and Fr. Jim had a standing tradition of meeting at Fordham on the second Monday of each month. Jamie had canceled their last two meetings, offering various excuses—demanding coursework, papers, comprehensive exams— though only the fatigue from his fasting was real. With his energy waning due to the rigorous fasting, he had to ration what remained between the essentials of seminary life and his studies.

~*~

The eleventh of June 1927 dawned as a pleasant day: warm but not yet suffocatingly hot and humid, with the sky a cloudless canopy of robin's egg blue. Jamie, however, was oblivious to the day's perfection. With a growing sense of urgency, Jamie hurried to meet his uncle, Fr. Jim Gleason—or "Unc," as Jamie and his siblings called him—before Unc left for a year's sabbatical in Rome.

Clad in his black cassock and Roman collar, Jamie disembarked at the train station on East Fordham Road, turned left onto 3rd Avenue, followed old Elm Road, and arrived at the edge of the 85-acre campus.

Despite his gaunt cheeks and thin frame, which made him appear even taller than his six feet two inches, Jamie still cut a dashing figure as he passed the ivy-covered, two-story brick Cunniffe House on his right and the statue of Archbishop Hughes on his left. Irish-born Hughes had purchased the 100-acre Rose Hill Farm in what was once a farming village in Westchester County—now part of the Bronx— with the bold dream of creating a university as a stepping stone for immigrants to become first-class citizens in their new country.

Jamie trudged along the tree-lined walkways and turned left onto Edgar Allan Poe Way, finally arriving at his destination. Collins Hall, one of the many stately Gothic buildings on campus, housed the philosophy department.

After scaling the fifteen steps to the porch, he entered through a heavy wooden door, passing beneath the ornate cartouche emblazoned with a cross and the IHS Christogram. Ascending two flights of stairs, taking them two steps at a time, Jamie paused just outside his uncle's office to catch his breath. A brass plate to the left of the open door read "Fr. James Gleason, S.J."

His uncle was writing comments in red ink on what appeared to be a student essay. The stocky priest removed his pince-nez spectacles, rubbed his eyes, and returned the glasses to his narrow nose. Unnoticed, Jamie finally rapped softly on the door jamb. Fr. Jim looked up, his smile fading as he took in the changes in his nephew's appearance since their last meeting.

"Lord God Almighty," Fr. Jim murmured. Pushing his chair back from the desk, he stood immediately. Taking Jamie by the arm, he pulled him into the office and closed the door. "What on earth is going on, dear boy? And don't tell me, 'Nothing.' Your mother must be worried sick." The priest pulled a wooden chair close to his own, its legs screeching across the tiled floor. "Sit, sit, sit, my son," he urged, removing his spectacles once again, his face growing ruddy.

Jamie plopped into the chair. "I haven't been home to see Mom for months." Beads of sweat formed above his upper lip. "I've made a terrible mistake, Unc." Jamie ran his hand through his thick, dark hair, his breath hitching as if he were bracing himself for a tidal wave. "I tried, I really did, but I just can't do this."

Fr. Jim's brow furrowed with concern. "Help me out here, Jamie. What are we talking about?"

What began as a trickle swelled into a confessional tsunami of shame and regret pouring from Jamie's heart. He laid everything bare before his uncle. Yes, he had honored his deceased father's and widowed mother's wishes, lived up to the academic expectations of his teachers and professors, and earned the respect of his peers. Yet his pride had silently fed on their praise and admiration. And no, he didn't need a leave of absence from the seminary to sort this out. He was absolutely certain.

"I've failed myself above all, trapping myself in a self-imposed prison under the guise of being a good son and devout seminarian. I've been a coward. I'm done with the charade. I've discerned that I have no true vocation to the priesthood. I'm ready to take responsibility for my own life—no matter how painful or humiliating it may be."

Fr. Jim's gaze softened with concern as he listened without interruption, Jamie's words punctuated by tears and gasps for breath. Jamie finished in deflated silence.

"Anything else, son?" Fr. Jim asked kindly and calmly.

"No, that's pretty much the mess of it." Did a hint of a smile flicker across Unc's face?

"Well, judging by the state of you, this has been weighing on you for quite some time. You may feel like a failure, Jamie, but I believe you're exactly where God wants you to be. One of the hardest steps toward manhood is being brutally honest with oneself. If we lie to ourselves, we can't be honest with God. And without honesty, we can't have the authentic relationship He desires with us.

"We aren't God; we all make mistakes. Owning and correcting those mistakes sows humility—the cornerstone of all virtue—in our souls. God has given you many gifts, Jamie, but remember, your greatest strengths can also be your greatest weaknesses. With academic gifts like yours, it's easy to fall into the quicksand of perfectionism—a prideful place that goes well beyond good stewardship of the Lord's gifts. We put ourselves on a pedestal, living in fear of failure and disappointing others, and in doing so, we block our chance for real growth in Christ. And that, dear Jamie, is your true vocation, above all others. Mine, too."

Fr. Jim stood up, pacing a few steps in his office, his index finger pressed thoughtfully to his lips. After a moment, he sat back down, his gaze steady on Jamie. "How do you see yourself five years from now, Jamie?"

"I see myself as a husband and father, working as a businessman. I'll finish college, but this time with a business degree. And I plan to repay Mom and the seminary for all the expenses from the last three years."

"That sounds like a solid plan. You can transfer from St. Joe's to Fordham—plenty have done it before, and plenty will after you. But keep in mind, all those philosophy and theology classes won't count for much toward upper-class standing in the School of Business. You'll likely need an extra couple of years to catch up."

Jamie exhaled loudly through pursed lips, his muscles relaxing. Simultaneously, exhausted and energized, he wiped tears of relief onto the sleeve of his cassock.

"You know, Jamie, there's nothing easy about any vocation this side of the grave. Marriage and family life come with big sacrifices. Being a good husband and father is hard—maybe even harder than being a priest. That two-becoming-one business isn't for the faint of heart. But becoming a priest just to make your mother happy and honor your father's dream—without a true calling—isn't what God wants for you. Now that you've admitted that to yourself, I have no doubt you'll tie up the loose ends and forge a new path for your life."

Fr. Jim smiled, raising one bushy white eyebrow. "Your battle with yourself isn't over, Jamie. In some ways, it's just beginning. God's got plans to make a saint out of you, one way or another. All you have to do is cooperate with Him—and survive telling your mother," he added, his blue eyes crinkling at the corners.

"Now, how about an early dinner, my boy? I'm buying. We never did celebrate your birthday, did we?"

"Thanks, that'd be grand, Unc. You're on."

Jamie felt like a new man—albeit a hungry one—ready to begin the next chapter of his life.

~*~

Jamie slipped through the front door like a cat stalking a mouse. He hadn't been home in two months. Leaving his suitcase in the parlor, he tiptoed into the kitchen, drawn by the sound of his mother humming. Mom stood with her back to him, her hands submerged in soap suds up to her elbows in the white-enamel cast-iron sink.

From the back, she could have passed for a much younger woman if not for the prominent streaks of gray in her brunette hair, tied back with a red bandana. Despite her fifty-one years and the toll of carrying seven full-term babies, her figure remained youthful and attractive.

She peered out the open window above the sink, watching her two youngest children. Fifteen-year-old Thomas patiently pushed his younger brother, Robert, on a swing made from two strands of heavy rope threaded through a wooden board suspended from a massive branch of a white oak tree. Nine-year-old Robert squealed with delight, pumping his legs in the air.

Gone were Jamie's cassock and Roman collar, replaced by a white shirt with sleeves rolled up to his elbows and high-waisted, tapered beige trousers held up by a pair of brown suspenders—now a necessity. He crept up behind his mother and gently placed a hand over each of her eyes.

"Guess who?"

Startled, his mother jumped, then squealed with delight as she recognized Jamie's deep, familiar voice. She turned to him, hands still dripping with suds.

"For the love of God, what happened to you? You look awful."

"Thanks, Mom," Jamie replied, lifting her off the floor in a bear hug.

"You know what I mean. You're still my gorgeous Jamie, but you're skin and bones."

"Well, I'm home now. Your good cooking will fix that in no time." Jamie smiled.

Jamie's complete honesty, combined with the familiar sights, smells, and sounds of home, would be the anointing leading to his healing.

"We need to talk, Mom..."

Their conversation unfolded much differently than Jamie had imagined (and feared). Perhaps Fr. Jim had smoothed the way by calling his sister or visiting her beforehand. After all, there had been plenty of time during the week between Jamie's withdrawal from the seminary and his registration for Fordham's fall quarter.

Jamie's mother, a woman usually full of words, had few that day. "I want you to follow God's will, Jamie—whether it's as a priest or in whatever way He calls you. At some point, a parent has to let go. It's time for you to live your own life." Standing up, she rubbed her hands against her apron, signaling the end of the conversation. "Now, it's time you earned your keep. Starting tomorrow, you can take over the accounting and financial oversight for the farm," she said with her characteristic no-nonsense tone, softened by a warm smile.

"I look forward to that, Mom."

"Well, now that that's settled, what do you want for dinner? We need to get some meat back on those bones of yours."

On June 15, 1927, Jamie Murphy became the architect of his destiny. For the first time in his life, all things felt possible. He was a lucky man indeed.

TWO

Mid-June 1927

Through an open window, the song of a yellow warbler floated into Jamie's bedroom, serenading him into consciousness. Sitting up in the lower bunk that had once been his oldest brother Danny's bed, he yawned with a constrained stretch. Standing, he pushed back the gauzy curtains that danced on the gentle breeze, drenching the room with bright morning sunlight.

A plump, butter-yellow bird surveyed the new day from its perch, a nearby hawthorn tree bearing the last of its white five-petaled flowers. The male bird then darted away, displaying the black stripes on his wings. His father, John Murphy, had taught Jamie the names of the birds in the Lower Hudson Valley and how to recognize their calls.

Father. Jamie had good years to remember John Murphy, unlike young Robert, who had no memories of his father at all to draw upon. *Danny.* Gone. *Marty.* Gone. "Each day was a gift, never to be taken for granted. Tomorrow, never to be assumed"—one of Unc's many adages came to mind.

Jamie fell to his knees, remembering those in his family who were no longer on earth and offered the same prayer as always at the beginning of each day. "O my God, I offer You my day. I offer You my prayers, thoughts, words, actions, joys, and sufferings ..." After finishing, he made the Sign of the Cross and rose from the hardwood floor. It was good to be home—wholly open to whatever the new day held—with the luxury and freedom to create his own future.

He found his work clothes, laundered and folded neatly, in the same oak chest of drawers he and Danny had once shared. He pulled out a pair of overalls and a long-sleeve cotton shirt—too warm for the early summer day but offering needed protection from the sun and the labor ahead. After dressing, he donned his worn but still serviceable leather work boots. Then, making his bed and giving the room a quick once-over, he felt satisfied. He wasn't one to be a slouch, having inherited his mother's penchant for orderliness.

His mother was already up. Although Jamie couldn't hear her puttering around downstairs, the enticing commingling of bacon and cinnamon wafted up to the second floor, testifying to her morning activities. He stood at the open doorway to his mother's room, the largest of the four upstairs bedrooms and opposite his room. He'd never entered the bedroom his parents had shared for most of their marriage.

After his father's death, his mother had painted the room yellow. "The color of hope," she had said. A quilt appliquéd with yellow and orange sunflowers, their brown faces turned upward, basked in the light of a bright yellow sun near the top of the double bed's coverlet. She refused to be governed by grief under a dark cloud of loss.

Thomas and Robert, though six years apart, now shared a room next to the master bedroom. Annie had a room on the same side of the hallway as Jamie, with the stairwell in between. Both bedroom doors were closed, a sure sign his siblings were still asleep. Since school was out for the summer, this was Annie, Thomas, and Robert's first day to sleep in, and apparently, Mom was allowing it, at least for now.

Since Gracie had married two years ago, Annie enjoyed having a room to herself. Gracie lived with her husband and toddler in Tarrytown, less than a half mile away.

There was another possible room in the attic, with a gable window that overlooked the front yard, and another in the Dutch hip, facing the carriage house where his father's 1918 Chevrolet Series 490 truck, with its half-ton bed, was parked. Jamie remembered the drive home from the North Tarrytown Chevy assembly plant with his father, not long after Danny had been deployed to Europe. As a boy, Jamie had imagined claiming that attic room, with its pull-down ladder, as his bedroom one day. That had proved unnecessary since the Great War had snatched Danny away, leaving his brother's room available as the number of siblings grew.

Jamie followed his nose downstairs. He peered into the mirror of the only bathroom in the house, located on the main floor between the stairwell and the kitchen. After combing his hair, he decided a shave could wait until after breakfast, and he walked through a narrow hallway to the kitchen. His mom bustled about in a yellow-dotted Swiss cotton housedress and her ever-present apron, her hair gathered in a loose topknot.

"Morning, Jamie. Did you sleep well?" She said, taking a pan of cinnamon rolls out of the oven and setting them on a wire rack to cool, their sweet and spicy aroma permeating the room. "Eggs?" she asked, pointing to the basket of eggs she'd collected from the backyard chicken coop before Jamie had even opened his eyes.

"Yes, and yes. Wow, those rolls look amazing!" Jamie hovered over the piping hot golden-brown rolls, he salivated as he grabbed a few slices of thick, crispy bacon from a nearby plate to placate his instantly ravenous appetite. While he'd never met a cinnamon roll he didn't like, his mother's were over the top. He impatiently waited the few minutes required before his mother would flip the pan over—that precise moment when the caramel, formed from butter, brown sugar, and cream at the bottom of the pan, congealed just enough to release the rolls, crowning them in gooey goodness.

"How about you, Mom? Did you sleep well? Looks like you've been up for a couple of hours." Jamie leaned against the wooden trestle table that worked double duty as a kitchen work table and breakfast table. Two long benches fit underneath the table and out of the way when not needed for seating.

"Slept grand." She reached for the Hills Brothers coffee tin from the cupboard. She held up the red can with its signature yellow-robed, turban-wearing Arab, silently asking her son if he wanted some.

"Yes, please. I'd love coffee. Thanks for making my favorite breakfast." Jamie walked over to his mother, bent down, and kissed the top of her head. "I'll set the table for us. Annie and the boys were still asleep when I came down." Jamie pulled the benches out from under the table.

"I'll give them another hour. That gives us some private time to talk before you drive out to the farm this morning." His mother nodded toward the canvas-covered ledger on top of the local newspaper at one end of the table.

By the time Jamie had retrieved the bottle of cream for their coffee from the basement icebox, the coffee was boiling on the stovetop, and the cinnamon rolls were freed from their pan, ready to be devoured. She plated two for Jamie and one for herself and poured them each a cup of coffee.

After consuming a third roll and another cup of coffee, Jamie cleared the dishes from the table and wiped off the red and white checked oilcloth. While she poured herself another cup of coffee, Jamie moved to the same side of the oblong table as his mother. As she sat down, she pushed the ledger between them, rubbing the lines etched above her brow.

She had retained overall responsibility for the Murphy farm as bookkeeper, just as she had when her husband was alive. Jamie's dad had recognized that his wife possessed many skills beyond those of a traditional homemaker. She had a head for facts and figures that he did not, and he was never too proud to rely on her intelligence.

Jamie's grandfather, his mother's progressive-thinking father, had nurtured his daughter's business acumen and natural talents. Ahead of his time, he believed that women should have expanded educational opportunities, just like men, if they desired them. He also felt that women should have the right to vote in all states, not just in Wyoming.

~*~

Peggy's mother died when she was fourteen. By then, her older brother Jimmy had entered the seminary. Her father, the owner of the Old Flour Mill two miles southeast of Tarrytown, began taking her to work with him when she was sixteen. Peggy loved being her father's assistant, and with her photographic memory and knack for numbers, she soon became his de facto assistant and eventually the bookkeeper for the entire flour mill operation until she married.

The men who worked at the mill or did business there might have complained about a woman working there. But she was, after all, the owner's daughter. She met and fell for the tall, brawny, dark-haired John Murphy, one of the farmers who supplied wheat berries to the mill. John was the kind of handsome that could steal a woman's breath away, invade her dreams, and rewrite her life plans. And those dimples when he smiled were irresistible to Peggy.

When she finally accepted John Murphy's marriage proposal (after turning down two others), she responded with one of her own. "I'm no farmer's wife, John Murphy, but I can't imagine my life with anyone else now. Look what you've done to me—can't live with you and can't live without you. Just promise me we can move back into town once our first child is of school age. I want my children to have access to good schools." John had agreed, probably figuring he could change Peggy's mind.

By Danny's fifth birthday, the Murphys had moved from the farm into a starter home near Broadway and Bedford on the eastern edge of Tarrytown, just two miles from the farm. When Peggy's father passed away, he left the Gleason family home on Elizabeth Street to both his son and daughter. However, Jimmy, being a priest, deeded his share to Peggy with only one request: "That I'm always welcome at your table," a winking Fr. Jim had said. He claimed his place at their table as often as possible, much to the delight of his sister, nieces, and nephews, especially after John's unexpected death.

After her husband's death, Peggy hired Lukyas de Vries, who owned the neighboring farm, to cultivate and harvest the Murphy's 130 acres of wheat along with his larger adjacent farm of 500 acres. The Murphy family's lawyer in White Plains had suggested sharecropping as the best option to protect her assets and continue generating some income rather than selling the land.

With thirteen children, including ten sons, Lukyas eagerly accepted her offer, and Peggy was grateful. Jan de Vries, the oldest of the thirteen, and his family had lived on the Murphy property as renters since John and Peggy had moved into Tarrytown. As part of the sharecropping agreement, Jan would live in the farmhouse rent-free, overseeing day-to-day operations, while Peggy would receive fifty percent of the harvest.

~*~

His mother's voice took on a serious tone. "Jamie, the farm has been in financial trouble since after the war. A New York City developer has offered me a tidy sum for the farmland and buildings, and I was hoping you could help me decide whether to sell. The offer is valid until this fall before we plant next year's crop, but there are some things you need to know. For now, please don't mention that I'm considering selling to Lukyas or Jan—I don't want to upset them. If we decide to sell, the de Vries family would have the first right of refusal, of course, but surely they must be struggling, too."

Peggy opened the canvas-covered ledger. She turned to the "Outstanding Federal Loans" section and then moved the thin crimson ribbon to the "Balance Sheets" section.

"During the war, government loans and subsidies encouraged

wheat production to feed our allies in Europe, as their farmland was largely abandoned. We took advantage of those loans and reached peak production during those years. Profits were at their highest. We bought the truck and went in with the de Vries family on a gasoline-powered combine. Once the war ended, demand fell off, but production remained high for us and all the other wheat farmers. Consequently, prices for wheat, corn, rye, oats, hogs, and everything else plummeted.

"To make matters worse, the government stopped subsidizing wheat five years ago. The price per bushel dropped from a guaranteed $2.26 to as low as $0.50 and never went higher than $1.50 for the next few years." She had charted the price per bushel of wheat since her marriage to his father and traced the trend with her index finger as she spoke to her son. "All my numbers and projections were based on the subsidized price."

Jamie listened intently and made sure he understood everything his mother shared. They reviewed the profits and losses for the last seven years, going back and forth in discussion. After a while, Mom closed the ledger stoically.

"Your father's life insurance money has kept us afloat," she said.

"Why didn't you talk to me about this before, Mom? I knew you and Dad sacrificed to send me to prep school and seminary, but I had no idea how much," Jamie said, feeling a mix of guilt, awe, and gratitude.

"What could you have done, Jamie? We were already in 'hot water' financially before your father died. Sometimes, I wonder if the farm caused his heart attack. Worry takes its toll on a man with a family to support."

"I'm home now, Mom. I'll do everything I can to help on the farm." Jamie wondered if he should continue his studies at Fordham in the fall. But that was a conversation for another day once he had time to digest everything his mother had shared.

"I'm really at a crossroads, Jamie. Farming is a way of life that your father and Danny loved. The Ireland our ancestors left was rural, not industrial. In the two waves of Irish emigration to America—before and after the Potato Blight of the mid-1840s—farming was what they knew. The first wave was mainly men hoping to improve their lot in life. That included your great-great-grandfather, who purchased the 130 acres that we're still farming and trying to eke out a living from.

"The Murphy farm represents generations of hard work and the realization of your forefathers' dreams. But sometimes, we have to let go of the past to embrace future opportunities. Farming is changing, and I can see it. Adapting to industrial innovation and education will be the keys to success in the future."

She grabbed the *Tarrytown Daily* from the end of the table. "I read this newspaper every day, and the world's changing, Jamie. The future is industry. With the improvement of farm machinery, I see big farms—not small ones like ours, where we just scrape by year to year. I don't see you as a farmer. Not Thomas either; he says he wants to build cars."

She opened the newspaper, flipped to the third and fourth pages, and set it down in front of Jamie. "Half of this newspaper is devoted to cars. Why not have a steady job from one month to the next? Did you know Gracie's husband now sells cars at Cayton Motors?" Jamie didn't have a chance to answer as his mother's monologue motored along without stopping for gas.

"Annie says she'll never marry a farmer. Ha! I said that, too, before I met your father. Love has a way of rewriting our dreams and desires." Mom paused to take a deep breath. "Who knows what Robert will want when he grows up? He always has his nose stuck in a book—so different from Danny and John—and hardly seems like the farming type."

His mother sighed. "I pray that God will light the path forward and provide for this family. What's best for us now might be different from when your father was alive. May his soul rest in peace." She made the Sign of the Cross, stood up, and wiped her hands on her apron.

THREE

Late July 1927

Jamie loaded the last of the wooden crates into the back of the truck, carefully stacking them three high and placing boards between them to prevent sliding. He braced the crates against the removable white pine panels he installed in the stake pockets along the top edges of the truck bed. The panels extended up to the height of the truck's cab. Once everything was secure, he tied down the stacks of crates with a web of rope.

Mom had carefully packed everything into the crates: a giant sack of potatoes, a large canister of lard, flour, butter, sugar, and a basket of Montmorency cherries—enough for several large pans of cobbler. Other crates held jars of creamed corn and green beans, the last of what she had put up the previous summer, and three dozen baking powder biscuits she had made early that morning.

Once prepared, the food would feed a hungry, hardworking crew their hearty midday meal on the last day of the Murphy farm's wheat harvest. Tonight, they'd bring back the extra pans, cooking utensils, buckets, and kitchen towels they'd taken to the farm for food preparation.

"Anything else, Mom?" Jamie hollered as his mother herded Annie, Thomas, and Robert, moving them out the back door like the last bits of molasses clinging stubbornly to a downturned jar.

"Nope, that's it. Just this motley crew." His mother closed the door, leaving it unlocked. No one locked their doors in Tarrytown.

As Jamie gave one final tug, the sun broke over the horizon, painting the cloudless sky with bands of pink, violet, and azure that resembled long, easy strokes of watercolor blending on heavy cotton paper.

Jamie had been up early to wring the necks of four Rhode Island Reds. He had used a broom handle to perform the cervical dislocation, but the plucking and butchering would wait until they arrived at the farm. He had placed the crate containing the dead chickens behind the other crates to stave off Annie's likely complaints. Sometimes, Jamie pitied the man who would marry his sister, although that was a long way off.

Fourteen-year-old Thomas, all legs and arms, and sixteen-year-old Annie, short and full-figured, squeezed into the back of the truck bed between the crates and the tailgate. They sat with their backs against the side rails, facing each other.

"Move your legs over, Thomas," Annie groused, flipping a thick, dark braid over her shoulder.

Jamie recognized that Thomas was the most easygoing of the Murphy progeny. Annie's uneven temperament never fazed him in the slightest.

There was no place for Robert except in the cab, sitting on his mother's lap, which didn't have enough padding to be comfortable. But the farm was less than six miles away, and Robert would likely fall back asleep en route. Today was the last day of the harvest, and it would be the longest. They had harvested thirty acres in each of the two previous days. Forty acres remained.

Jamie backed the truck out of the carriage house, turned right onto Elizabeth Street, then left onto Broadway. He drove north through the still-slumbering town. Beyond Main Street, Broadway laced between what, three generations ago, had been farms owned by the Motts, Purdys, Gilberts, and Blakes—impressive homes with large pastures and livery stables where Percheron, Belgian, Clydesdale, and Shire horses had once lazily grazed. Most of the land had been sold off, and multiple smaller homes had been built. Only the Gilbert estate remained with its pastureland and a few horses, a sign of the times.

Jamie had seen firsthand the growth in car and railway transportation pulsating through the arteries connecting Tarrytown to nearby White Plains and New York City. The automotive manufacturing plant in north Tarrytown, which had been producing Chevrolets for the last ten years, had brought many new blue-collar jobs to the area since opening at the turn of the century. New York City's middle class was migrating north to Westchester County, settling in Tarrytown and White Plains and commuting into the city for work.

So Jamie understood that the Murphy's farmland was valuable for purposes other than crops.

After the better part of a mile, Jamie turned northeast onto Bedford Road. As they left Tarrytown behind, the road wound between copses of red maples, white oaks, poplars, and elms. Smatterings of sumacs, black birches, dogwoods, and hackberries popped up here and there like delicate seasoning, imparting an appetizing complexity to a hearty landscape soup. The trees provided welcome summer shade to both man and animal and draped the landscape in glorious greens, yellows, oranges, and reds in the fall. Except for the dirt road, the land retained its virginal character, untouched by 400 years of European descendants who had settled and transformed the wild grasses and woods into wheat and dairy farms and orchards.

Jamie veered left onto Sleepy Hollow Road, following the snake-like curves of the dirt road for three and a half miles. To the left and right, they passed small to medium farms laid out like patchwork on the flat terrain. To the east rose the Pocantico Hills, with the Rockefellers' Kykuit Estate perched at the highest point, providing sweeping views of the Hudson River. The 3,400-acre estate's name, Kykuit (meaning lookout in Dutch), honored the region's Dutch heritage and continued presence since the seventeenth century.

"I'd like to be a bird for an hour and fly over Kykuit to take it all in. They say the gardens, terraces, and statues are amazing," Mom remarked. "But I remember reading in the *Daily* that no sooner had John Sr. finished work on the estate and the grounds than John Jr. and his wife had remodeled, redecorated, and changed things up, inside and outside, to suit their taste."

"Just imagine having that kind of money. I wonder how many C-notes they dropped redoing things that were perfectly fine," Jamie said, shaking his head.

~*~

Jamie pulled up close to the farmhouse to unload the food supplies. A short distance away, Jan de Vries and another man led the last two horses of the eight-horse team to their positions in the jerk line. The horses were harnessed in tandem and, together under the direction of the teamster, would pull the 1918-manufactured Holt combine and wagon. The cutting-edge machine combined reaping, threshing, and winnowing into a single process, thus reducing manpower requirements for harvesting wheat by three-quarters. John Murphy had carried thirty percent of the loan, and Lukyas de Vries seventy percent, during the early days of the Great War when demand for wheat had hit record levels, and the government made generous loans.

Because the Murphy farmland was flat and the Holt combine was gasoline-powered, eight horses were able to pull the fourteen-foot sickle bar and the wagon, even as it filled up with kernels of wheat and carried the workers: a mechanic, a header man, two sackers, and a sack sewer.

The wagon was hitched directly behind the team of horses while the combine sat to the wagon's left. After the combine separated the wheat kernel from the head, husk, and straw, the wagon would be filled with grain ready to be bagged, sewn, and ejected from the wagon's chute in groups of six.

Jamie and Pieter, Jan de Vries's son, had hefted the 140-pound sacks of wheat onto a horse-drawn wagon and stacked them over the last two weeks, first harvesting the de Vries crop and now the Murphys'. Jamie's lean, tall frame had filled out with solid muscle from his six weeks of heavy manual labor on the Murphy and de Vries neighboring farms. His square-jawed face, neck, forearms, and hands had acquired a healthy golden glow and, coupled with the effects of his mother's good cooking, were chiseled to perfection as if crafted by a master sculptor.

Downwind from the farmhouse, Lukyas de Vries, Jan's father, stood by the barn with the hired hands, smoking cigarettes as they waited to harvest the remaining acres of hard red winter wheat. Lukyas had employed the same men, for $3 a day, to bring in his wheat crop the previous week and a half. Assuming they finished the last forty acres of the Murphy land today, Jamie, Pieter, and Lukyas de Vries would transport the sacked grain to market tomorrow.

Like many men of pure Dutch ancestry, Lukyas and Jan were tall, well beyond Jamie's six-plus feet. Jamie looked up to the de Vries men—not only literally but also because he admired their work ethic.

Lukyas, although serious-minded and reserved, possessed a smile that transformed his stern, weathered face into the picture of affability. Jan was more congenial than his father. Pieter, Jan's son, and Jamie were becoming fast friends. Though still single and a year younger than Jamie, Pieter considered himself an expert on the opposite sex. Though inexperienced, Jamie was an eager student, and Pieter took on the role of a diligent teacher.

Jamie turned the truck off, exited the vehicle, and approached the passenger side to open the door for his mother and Robert.

Lukyas waved to Jamie. *"Goedemorgen,"* he hollered.

Jamie waved back. *"Goedemorgen,* yourself, Lukyas. Perfect day to finish up."

"Ja." Lukyas nodded in agreement and held his arms up to the sky, echoing Jamie's sentiments.

Thomas had jumped out of the back of the truck once it stopped. He unlatched the tailgate and helped his sister down. Around so many men, Annie might have been embarrassed to be seen in what she probably thought was a juvenile-looking blue calico dress with an attached off-white muslin apron—a hand-me-down from Gracie. However, there was no one here to impress, only a bunch of farmhands who would be caked with dirt and chaff as the day wore on.

His mother roused Robert. He emerged from the passenger side door, stretching and yawning. He would spend the day with Jan's two youngest sons. Anders was nine, like Robert, and Erik was three years older. The boys would haul water in buckets for the men and horses and carry steam-rolled oats to feed the horses while still finding ample time to play and roughhouse.

Annie's day would begin and end in the kitchen, doing whatever Peggy and Jan's wife, Freda, ordered her to do. Her only "escape" would be changing diapers and entertaining Freda and Jan's two youngest children—finally girls after all those boys—so that Freda could cook and serve.

Jamie surveyed the remaining stalks of wheat, glowing golden brown in the sun. A breeze set the stalks swinging and singing their rustling sound of plenty. The stalks from the previous day lay in the field, drying out. Thomas would spread out any clumps to facilitate their drying before bundling the straw days later.

Thomas and Jamie set about unloading the truck. Jamie handed Annie the crate of dead chickens. "Today's your lucky day. You start plucking the chickens, and I'll join you in a minute." Annie rolled her eyes but took the crate and headed to the back of the house, where Jamie would use the wide tree stump to butcher the chickens.

~*~

Peggy removed the bubbling cherry cobbler from the Glenwood cast-iron cooking stove and set it aside to cool alongside the other. Nearby, Freda dipped the last pieces of chicken in a buttermilk bath and dredged them in a mixture of flour, salt, and pepper, dividing them between two cast iron skillets, sizzling hot with shallow pools of melted lard.

Working with Freda was a pleasure for Peggy. Freda, a sturdy, quiet, and pleasant woman about ten years her junior, had passed along her flaxen hair and light blue eyes to all her children. Freda and Jan were part of the Old Dutch Reformed Church, as were many farmers nearby.

The kitchen was sweltering, as it had been since mid-morning. The remaining task for the workers' midday meal was to make white flour gravy from the fried chicken drippings for the mashed potatoes and biscuits. After checking the cook stove's fire, Peggy added another piece of wood from the firebox to the interior cavity, mindful of the hot water they'd need for cleanup. She stepped outside to watch the men working for a moment. It was cooler outside than in the kitchen; the breeze helped some, too. She entered the living room to check on Freda's little ones. It had grown awfully hushed in the next room.

Just as Peggy entered the main room, Annie stood up from the armless rocker, a snoozing infant in her arms. Annie gently placed the baby girl into the rocking pine cradle that featured a heart carved out in the headpiece. Her other charge, a towheaded toddler, slept soundly on a wedding-ring-patterned quilt near the open window.

"Finally, both asleep," Annie whispered, dramatically dropping her head and shoulders as if casting off a heavy burden.

"Has watching the girls been that taxing, Annie?" Peggy smiled, putting her arm around her teenage daughter's shoulders and escorting her into the kitchen.

"No, but my arm is asleep," Annie said, rubbing and shaking her left arm. "Geez, it's hot as Hades in here."

"See, you did have the easy job, Annie. Take a short break and stretch your legs. I'm going to grab some water for the dishes before things get crazy at lunchtime." Peggy headed for the back of the house with an empty 8.5-quart aluminum soup pot. The outside air felt cool on her face compared to the kitchen's stifling heat. She wiped her forehead with her apron.

As Peggy walked to the back of the farmhouse to fetch some water, she remembered living on the farm in the early days of her marriage without indoor plumbing—and not fondly. Hauling water for every little thing had felt like an endless chore back then, and even now, her back ached at the memory. Things hadn't changed.

She headed toward the hand pump near the well on the opposite side of the house from the outhouse. She might as well pay it a visit, too. That old privy had seemed so far away in the winter and too close in the summer.

The farmhouse still had no electricity, like the other nearby farms. Tarrytown may have been a small town, but compared to the farm, it was worlds away in comforts and amenities. Visiting during the harvest was more than enough for Peggy.

As she approached the pump, she spotted Erik bolting from the privy like the devil himself was chasing him.

"Hey, Erik. What's the big hurry?" she hollered as he zoomed past.

He didn't answer or even look back. Peggy raised a hand to shield her eyes from the near-noonday sun, watching him disappear behind the barn. *That tired old barn needs a few well-placed nails and a fresh coat of red paint*, she thought, shaking her head. *Not likely to happen anytime soon.*

~*~

Robert saw Erik run into the barn. His curiosity piqued, he grabbed Anders, and the two of them snuck in after him. They found Erik hiding behind a "wall" of stacked bags filled with wheat kernels harvested two days before. He sat on a pile of dry straw, looking like he owned the place.

Thirteen-year-old Erik pulled a half-full pack of Lucky Strike cigarettes from his front overall pocket and waved them in front of the two younger boys with a smirk.

"Where'd ya get those?" Anders asked, his mouth hanging open.

"In the outhouse. Found these, too." Erik held up a matchbook, flipping it over to show a picture of a barely clothed woman on the back.

"Bet you're too chicken to smoke one," Erik challenged, lighting up with a practiced ease.

Robert craned his neck, watching with wide-eyed amazement as Erik puffed out white rings of smoke by forming an "O" with his lips, poking his puffed-out cheeks with his index finger, and sending white smoke rings into the air. Robert tried to spear the floating "donuts" with his finger before they dissipated.

"Papa and *Opa* say you're never supposed to smoke in the barn," Anders said, puffing his chest out, trying to sound important.

"And who's gonna tell them?" Erik shot back, jabbing Anders hard in the chest with his free hand.

Robert watched, torn between fear and wonder. He'd never seen anyone make those magical white rings, but he knew smoking in the barn was forbidden. He stepped back, glancing nervously at the barn door, half wanting to run but feeling stuck, like Brer Rabbit with the Tar-Baby.

"Gimme one. I ain't no chicken," Anders protested.

"Here ya go, baby." Erik handed his brother a cigarette and the matchbook. It took Anders two tries before the match lit. When he finally took a draw, he sputtered and coughed, and Erik laughed hysterically.

Just then, the thrumming of the combine stopped. "Erik! Anders!" Mr. de Vries's booming voice echoed from outside. "Where are you, boys? The horses need to be fed and watered!"

Robert's heart leaped. He turned and bolted from the barn as fast as his scrawny legs could carry him. In his panic, he slammed straight into Mr. de Vries as he entered the barn.

"Sorry, Mr. de Vries," Robert mumbled, eyes wide with guilt.

"Whoa there, *jongen*, watch where you're going," Mr. de Vries said, his big hand steadying Robert for a moment.

Seconds later, Anders and Erik strolled out of the barn, cool as can be, no cigarettes in sight.

"You boys take care of the horses while the men eat. There'll be plenty left when you finish up."

~*~

Jamie joined his brother Thomas, Jan, Pieter, Lukyas, and the hired hands under the canopy of a giant elm tree. They sat on the ground or upside-down crates, eating the meal the women had prepared. The women bustled about, ensuring the men had their fill, knowing they and the children would eat afterward.

As his mother carried out the cobbler, a massive explosion shattered the calm. Orange and yellow flames erupted through the barn roof, sending fireballs spiraling into the sky. She dropped the pan.

Jamie's heart raced as he struggled to absorb the unfolding chaos. He could see Anders and Erik with the horses in the field—but where was Robert?

"Robert!" Mom screamed, sprinting toward the barn.

Jamie shot up from the ground, tearing after her. He grabbed her around the waist before she could get any closer. "No, Mom. You stay here. I'll find him."

He glanced back, yelling, "Thomas! Hold onto Mom! Keep her away from the barn!"

Without a second thought, Jamie ripped off his shirt, wrapped it around his nose and mouth, and ran into the inferno. Flames roared through the barn, devouring the freshly harvested bags of wheat. The fire sucked oxygen through the hole in the roof, making it burn hotter and faster.

Smoke stung his eyes and seared his lungs with every breath. But there—lying motionless on the dirt floor—was Robert, surrounded by scattered wheat kernels from the burning bags. Fire crawled toward him like molten lava. Jamie's heart clenched when he saw his little brother's left arm, charred black, the flesh like roasted meat. An empty feed bag lay near Robert's right hand.

Without hesitation, Jamie scooped up Robert, draping his shirt over the burnt arm, and sprinted out of the barn, coughing through the thick smoke. He ran past the house, heading for the protective shade of the furthest elm tree, away from the direction the wind carried the smoke.

In the shade, Jamie laid Robert on his unburned right side. Miraculously, the fire had spared his back and face. Moments later, his mother appeared, kneeling at Robert's side, her hands pushing Jamie aside as she bent over her injured son.

~*~

"Robert, breathe. Breathe," Peggy pleaded, striking Robert's back between his shoulders as if she could somehow dislodge the smoke or whatever was preventing him from breathing. *Not another one of my babies—you can't have him. No more, Lord.* Her body shook with silent sobs.

Her mind flashed back to the painful fullness in her breasts that morning—how they had screamed to feed baby Martin. It was the first time little Marty had let her sleep through the night. He had been such an easy baby, the picture of health, with such a vigorous appetite. But not that morning.

She had found him on his back, reddish-purple splotches covering his cold skin. Still wrapped in his blanket, she had picked him up and crumpled to the floor, his lifeless body in her arms. She'd held him to her chest, rocking back and forth, wailing, "No, God, no. Don't take him," over and over.

After several more blows to Robert's back, he coughed. Peggy pulled him into her lap, cradling her injured son. Her eyes closed as she prayed aloud, tears streaming down her face, "Thank you, Lord. Thank you, thank you."

"Jamie, go help the men salvage what they can. I'm taking him to the hospital. Annie can take me. No arguments," Peggy barked, adrenaline pushing her forward. She sprang to her feet, Robert in her arms, and headed for the truck.

"Annie, get my purse. You're driving us to the hospital," Peggy ordered, her voice sharp with urgency.

They got into the vehicle, Peggy cradling Robert as gently as possible. Screeching noises and the sound of trucks drew her glance back to the fire. Men from the surrounding farms were already arriving to help, drawn by the billowing curls of white and gray smoke and neighborly charity. Buckets in hand, they joined the line of men passing water, trying to quench the insatiable, fiery tempest that cracked and spit. *Farm be damned*, she thought. *Save my son, Lord!*

Once Annie began driving, Peggy turned her full attention to Robert, weakly moaning in her lap. Her heart pounded as she examined his burns—severe, far beyond what home remedies of ice and butter could handle. When she pulled his eyelids open, she noticed one pupil was larger than the other. But he was breathing—that was something.

~*~

Peggy's decision to take Robert to White Plains General Hospital was an easy one. With a population four and a half times that of Tarrytown, she reasoned that either of the two hospitals in White Plains would be better staffed and provide more up-to-date care than Tarrytown's small hospital.

Annie turned off Post Road and pulled into the U-shaped entrance of the hospital, a red-brick, modern-looking building.

"Just let us out here," Peggy said, cradling Robert in the crook of her left arm as she opened the passenger side door with her right.

Annie set the brake, exited the truck, and hurried ahead to open the hospital's main entrance doors for her mother, who was using both arms to carry Robert's limp form.

"Find someplace to park the truck around back and meet me inside. Don't forget to bring my purse, okay?"

"Sure. But where will you be? This hospital is a big place."

"Wherever they send me. Just ask at the front desk," Peggy said, nodding towards the woman sitting at the front desk directly inside the doors. "They'll know."

Once inside, Peggy waited as the woman at the front desk phoned for help. "I'm sending a burn victim your way—a child." She pointed Peggy down the hall as she hung up the phone. "Follow the signs to acute care services. Someone will meet you on the way."

Peggy nearly ran, navigating her way through a labyrinth of pale green halls and black-and-white tile floors. An orderly pushing a gurney soon met her, placing Robert on the gurney. The orderly moved quickly, with Peggy following close behind.

Robert was taken back immediately after Peggy explained to an intake nurse what had happened. She was then left to fill out paperwork in the white-walled waiting area, furnished with two green upholstered chairs, two long oak benches with backs, and a matching coffee table. Peggy's mind was too rattled to focus on the paperwork, so she paced the room, praying that Robert would recover.

There was no clock in the room. A few glass-framed prints hung on the otherwise sterile walls—rural landscapes and the same two photographic prints that adorned Peggy's bedroom at home, *Cupid Awake* and *Cupid Asleep* by Morris Burke Parkinson, iconic images of tranquility and innocence.

A pay phone booth was tucked in one corner of the room, but the farm had no phone service. Even if it did, what was there to say? She knew nothing about Robert and didn't want to hear anything about the barn.

Fifteen minutes later, as Peggy reached for the clipboard of paperwork on the table nearby, she felt a hand on her shoulder.

"Any news, Mom?" Annie set her mother's purse on the table.

"Not a word."

"Are you okay? Can I help you with the paperwork?" Annie asked with genuine concern, squatting beside Peggy and touching her mother's arm.

"Thanks, Annie, I'll be okay." Peggy squeezed her daughter's hand.

When would they hear something? Peggy had lost track of time, but Robert's paperwork had long been completed and turned in.

Finally, a matronly nurse emerged, wearing a stiff white hat pinned to her short, wavy brown hair. Her white bibbed apron covered the front of a light blue dress that hung nearly to her ankles.

Peggy rose immediately. "How's my son, Robert Murphy?"

"Your son has sustained a concussion and has suffered serious burns on his lower arm and upper hand. Most of the burns are second-degree, but there are some third-degree burns as well. The doctor will need to debride the third-degree burns by removing the damaged and dead skin so they'll heal better. We'll administer ether so he won't feel or remember anything during the procedure. However, he'll experience significant pain afterward, followed by intense itching as the healing process begins."

"So ... he'll be all right. Thank the Lord." Peggy placed her hand over her heart as a wave of relief and gratitude washed over her.

"The doctor will talk to you soon, Mrs. Murphy, and answer all your questions. But you must keep him down for a few weeks due to the concussion, and you must keep the burns absolutely clean. Your biggest concern with his burns is to prevent any infection. Force fluids—get him to drink as much as possible. The wounds will seep and crust over, and there will likely be scarring."

The nurse handed Peggy a sheet of paper covered with mostly legible script. "Here are instructions for your son's home care. But in a nutshell, rest for the concussion, dress and clean the burn wounds, and manage his pain and itching.

"Use Dakin's solution—a five percent sodium hypochlorite solution—to clean the wounds. Any pharmacist at an apothecary can mix it, or you can take it to the chemist at the hospital, and he can prepare it while you wait. We'll keep your son here for a bit after the procedure, but not overnight. Also, pick up some Bayer aspirin. Visit your doctor in Tarrytown in two days; he can prescribe laudanum if needed, but be cautious with its use."

"Thank you," Peggy said, her shoulders sagging and limbs growing heavy as the adrenaline that had kept her moving drained away.

She knew then—there would be no more farmers in the Murphy family.

FOUR

August 1927

A line of parked cars, mostly black Model-Ts, flanked both sides of Williams Street in downtown White Plains. Jamie found an inconspicuous but convenient spot to park the truck a block away from the Lawyers Building, which housed two of their stops today: Kennedy's legal offices and County Title & Trust. Once his mother signed the paperwork for the farm's sale, it was only a short walk in the opposite direction to deposit the check at the Central Bank of Westchester County on Main Street, where the Murphy family did their banking.

Brendan Kennedy had handled the paperwork for the farm and other legal matters after his father's death. His mother had trusted Mr. Kennedy to broker the sale of the Murphy farm to Siegal & Sons Development Company, ensuring she got the best deal. He had also drawn up the contract for Lukyas de Vries to buy out their interest in the farm equipment by simply taking over the federal loan payments.

Multiple-story buildings hugged each other tightly, cutting an uneven pattern against the sky: a bookstore, a savings and loan, a jewelry store, a deli, a clothing store for men, a shoe store, a U.S. post office, an ice-cream parlor, and several restaurants. The buildings had apartments above them, rented out to those who preferred or had no choice but to live in the heart of the city. White Plains was indeed a thriving metropolis compared to sleepy Tarrytown.

Directly across the street from the Lawyers Building was the large Revue Hall, where theatrical and musical productions were held, and singers performed after finishing their stints in the "Big Apple." Red, white, and blue banners, gathered into semicircles, hung beneath the marquee.

~*~

Jamie blew out a whistle of admiration as he spotted a navy blue Packard town car, a four-seater, parked directly in front of Revue Hall. "Beauty and the Beast," he thought, comparing the sleek lines of the Packard to the Murphy family "car"—a truck that seated two inside and everyone else in the truck bed, making for a cold, wet ride for those outside the cab for much of the year.

"You don't see many of those beauties," Jamie remarked to his mother, pointing to the luxurious Packard. His eyes traveled up to read the marquee. "I wonder who Irene Bordoni is? Somebody with lots of money, I bet, if that's her car.

"I betcha Gracie's husband would make you a deal you can't refuse when you're ready to drive a car instead of a truck," Jamie said with a grin.

"One thing at a time, Jamie. Selling the farm is plenty to deal with for now." Mom snapped shut the cover on the Elgin timepiece—her last gift to John the Christmas before he died—and stowed it back into her purse. "Fifteen minutes early," she said, exhaling audibly and dabbing her eyes with a lacy handkerchief.

Jamie had worn his Sunday best at his mother's insistence: a blue and white striped band collar dress shirt, gray trousers, and black oxfords. "Seems like wearing overalls and boots might be more fitting—one last hurrah and all for the farm," he'd said earlier that day. But his mother, too nervous and emotional, had obviously failed to find any humor in her son's droll comment.

She'd been distracted all day, burning the toast and forgetting to add the coffee grounds to the boiling water for coffee at breakfast. When Jamie had insisted on driving his mother to her appointment, she took him up on his offer without hesitation.

"Sorry this is such a hard day for you," Jamie said, watching her apply red lipstick and adjust her hat, killing time before her appointment and delaying the inevitable signing away of the farm.

"If your father can see things down here, I hope he isn't terribly disappointed in me."

"I'm sure Dad's fully occupied where he's at and completely detached from the farm. He would only want what's best for you and his children. Dad never lived through the times we are living through. I think you've made the right decision."

"Thanks, son. I appreciate your support." She reached over and squeezed Jamie's hand.

In contrast, Jamie was relieved that they were getting out from under the loans and debts incurred by the farm. The family would have sufficient money to live better than they had been with the proceeds from the sale. Although Jamie was now the primary wage earner for his mother and younger siblings, that bothered him very little; in fact, it energized and motivated him. He saw it as a way to repay all his parents had done for him. He just needed to find a woman willing to move into the house on Elizabeth Street once they were married and not mind being part of a ready-made family with a live-in mother-in-law.

Yes, there was much to be thankful for since the fire. Robert was healing well and bravely enduring his pain and itching as his burnt skin healed, though he was a bit withdrawn and not eating as usual. His mother dismissed Robert's sullenness, saying, "It's a lot for a nine-year-old boy to deal with," when Jamie mentioned his little brother's moodiness.

Jamie learned that the developers from New York had planned to demolish the buildings on the Murphy property anyway, so their offer wasn't reduced by the fire that destroyed the barn. The word circulating was that Siegel & Sons imagined another "Millionaire's Colony" in the western shadow of the Pocantico Hills, where the cluster of small farms was situated. Other farmers in the area were considering similar offers from Siegel, but the Murphys were the first to sell out. The stubborn de Vries family would likely be the last to sell, and only if they were down to their last dollar, with starvation and bill collectors knocking at their door.

Jamie walked around to the truck's passenger side and opened the door for his mother.

~*~

Jamie followed his mother into Mr. Kennedy's legal office. She had overdressed for the occasion, at least in his opinion. But he had to admit, it was a momentous day. What did he know about these things anyway? She looked pretty classy, even if the collar of her drop-waisted, brown-and-white checkered dress reminded him of a sailor's uniform. And, of course, Mom wore one of those hats she seemed to love—a straw bucket tied up tight with a brown ribbon.

A young woman sat at a large oak desk in the center of a rectangular-shaped room, its sage-green, ten-foot walls trimmed with wide, flaxen-colored crown molding. The tinkling bells as they entered prompted her welcoming smile. Her striking face was framed by waves of light auburn hair shaped in a loose, side-parted bob that hit just below her prominent cheekbones.

"Good afternoon. I'm Peggy Murphy, and this is my son, Jamie. I have a two o'clock meeting with Mr. Kennedy."

"Very nice to meet both of you. I'm Katie." The young woman stood up and extended her hand to Jamie and his mother. "Mr. Kennedy is just finishing up with another client; he'll be with you shortly. May I bring you a cup of tea or some lemonade while you wait?"

"Not for me," Mom answered.

"No, thank you," Jamie said. "You're fine ... I mean, I'm fine." Jamie felt his ears burn in embarrassment. But he had spoken the truth. This young woman was fine, indeed. Katie—a stranger, really—had utterly unnerved him. Her presence generated a physical attraction so strong that it straddled the border between torture and pleasure.

Katie's cheeks grew pink in response to Jamie's gaffe, minimizing the faint smattering of peach-colored freckles on her otherwise porcelain skin. His mom raised one eyebrow, a hint of amusement playing on her lips as she glanced at her son.

"Please have a seat and make yourselves comfortable," Katie said, sweeping her hand toward the seating options in the waiting area. Mom took one of the two russet brown Morris chairs, separated by a Mission-style end table. Jamie sat opposite his mother on a coordinating Mission-style cubic slat loveseat adjacent to an oak hall tree.

Jamie surveyed the layout of the legal office, occasionally stealing glances at Katie. Behind her desk, an open space led to three doors. A partially open door on the back wall, facing the front entrance, revealed an oak pedestal table and chairs. On the adjoining side walls, two office doors faced each other across the reception area, their half-windows covered with frosted glass.

An office door opened, and a stocky man with olive-toned skin, dark hair, and thick eyebrows resembling two caterpillars approached Katie's desk.

"*Mia cara*, could you type up this invoice for Mr. Esposito and mail it before the post office closes today?"

"No problem, Frankie," Katie replied, her stunning cerulean blue eyes briefly glancing at Jamie before she resumed working.

Frankie patted Katie affectionately on the head before returning to his office, and Katie didn't seem to mind.

That Frankie fellow has to be almost forty—way too old for her, Jamie thought, *and touching her like that was far too intimate for a boss. God forbid he's her husband!*

Jamie needed to see if Katie was wearing a wedding ring. He stood up and sauntered to the front window, his back to her, completely unaware of the people and cars passing by on Williams Street as he hatched his plan of action. He abruptly turned on his heels and planted himself in front of Katie's desk just as she rolled a piece of paper into her Remington typewriter. He waited for her to notice him.

"Is it too late to change my mind about that lemonade?"

"No, of course not. I'll be right back with it." She held his gaze longer than necessary. This was all the evidence Jamie needed—she wanted him as much as he wanted her.

Jamie glanced at her left hand. No ring.

"Thank you. I'll wait here." Of course, he'd wait here. *Where else would I wait? Out on the street? Get yourself together, man*, he told himself.

He watched Katie walk away and disappear into the back room. Her bias-cut dress draped nicely over her hips, emphasizing her tiny waist. Older than Annie but younger than Gracie, he decided. *Maybe this is the one*, he thought. *How nice it would be to come home to someone like that at the end of the day.*

"No need to see me out. I'll be in touch soon, Brendan," came a voice as an office door opened opposite Frankie's office. A thin, elderly gentleman exited, leaning on a lion's-head walking stick and moving stiffly to the hall tree. He placed a straw boater hat on his bald head. Before heading out the door, he nodded to Jamie's mother. "Good day, ma'am."

A minute later, a bespectacled, middle-aged gentleman emerged, wearing a beige linen vest with matching trousers and a brown tie loosened around his thick neck. "Mrs. Murphy, sorry to keep you waiting. Please come in."

The gentleman eyed Jamie, still standing at Katie's desk. He extended his hand in a vigorous greeting. "You must be Jamie, the eldest son. And, I dare say, the spitting image of your father, John. God rest his soul."

The sleeves of Mr. Kennedy's white shirt were rolled up to his elbows, revealing surprisingly muscular forearms for a lawyer.

"Brendan Kennedy here."

Jamie grasped the outstretched hand firmly. "Pleased to meet you, sir."

Katie returned with the lemonade, placed the tall glass on her desk, and sat down, unwilling to interrupt the conversation.

"Will Jamie be joining us?" Mr. Kennedy asked, looking directly at his mother.

"That's up to Jamie. It's not really necessary, is it?" Mom said.

"All that is required are your signatures," Mr. Kennedy replied.

"If you don't need me, Mom, I'll wait out here." Jamie glanced from his mother to Mr. Kennedy and then to Katie as if she were somehow part of the conversation.

Mom gave Jamie a knowing wink as she turned into the office, just ahead of Mr. Kennedy, who closed the door behind them.

Katie walked to the front of her desk and handed Jamie a glass of lemonade and a coaster. "Here you go," she said.

Jamie liked the soft timbre of her voice. As he took the glass, his eyes moved from her wide-set, impossibly large eyes, fringed with long lashes, past her pert nose and settled on her full lips.

"Thank you, Katie," he said before downing half its contents. "Ahh. Just hits the spot."

Katie sat back down at her desk and began typing. Jamie remained in place, conspicuously watching her every move.

He finished his drink, holding the empty glass as he strategized how to ask her for a date. He didn't have much time. How long could it take to sign a few papers and accept the check from Siegel & Sons?

Clack, clack, clack, shift, clack, clack, ping, zip, went the typewriter. *Clack, clack, clack, shift, clack, clack, ping, zip, clack, clack, shift, clack, clack.*

"So, how long have you worked here?" Jamie asked.

Katie stopped typing. "Excuse me, Mr. Murphy?"

"Have you worked here long?"

"Not long. I'm only filling in temporarily this summer until I start college this fall. My brother-in-law, Frankie, got me the job."

Frankie's her brother-in-law—it all makes sense now. "Which college?"

"Marymount in Tarrytown."

"Marymount. Well, that's convenient."

"How so?" Katie cocked her head to the side.

"I live in Tarrytown. We'll have lots of opportunities to get to know each other," Jamie said with a mischievous smile.

"Here, let me take your glass," Katie said, fighting a smile and reaching out to take the empty glass from Jamie's hands. But he didn't let go, their fingers nearly touching.

The sound of chairs screeching came from Mr. Kennedy's office. Jamie had to move fast.

"How do you feel about marriage, Katie?" Jamie asked, forcing a straight face.

"How about a date first?" Katie said, her face breaking into a full smile.

Her shoulders began shaking as she tried to control her laughter. Jamie laughed too, his feeble attempts at flirting exposed for what they were: obvious and hilarious.

"Yes, a first date is sensible. I accept your offer," Jamie said. "Perhaps you should tell me your last name now that I've agreed to a date with you."

"Are you crazy?"

"Maybe." Jamie's brown eyes twinkled. "I'll need your address and phone number. Oh, and how about your last name?"

"Houlihan. Aren't you a clever dog, Jamie Murphy?"

"I'm trying. How am I doing?"

Katie shook her head, still giggling. "You get an A for effort and an F for smooth-talking. Are you sure you're safe? Well, maybe if we're out in public." She rested her chin on her hand, her index finger over her mouth as she sized him up head to toe. "You're cute; I'll give you that. But I can't decide if you're weird or charmingly naive."

"Cute is good, and I vote for charming. Rest assured, I'm completely safe." He winked at her, adding, "Especially since you'll be my first date. Ever."

"Right. I doubt that."

"Houlihan—Catholic, right?"

"Of course, with a name like Kathleen Mary Houlihan, could I be anything else?"

"Well, Miss Kathleen Mary Houlihan, if you're nervous about a date with a smooth-talking, suave, sophisticated, and debonair man like me, why don't I pick you up for Mass Sunday morning and take you out for breakfast afterward? Mass and breakfast—all very public."

"I can't believe I'm doing this," Katie said, taking out a small notepad. Jamie watched as she wrote her address and phone number: 44 Lake Street, WP-4649.

"White Plains, right?"

"Yes. I live with my sister, Eileen, and her husband, Frankie. We go to the 8:30 morning Mass at St. John the Evangelist. I'll see you at eight. I can introduce you to my family, and we'll all ride to church together. Now, if you'll excuse me, I have a letter to type—unless you need more lemonade," she said.

"Nope. Everything's just ducky. I've never been so excited to attend Mass in my entire life, Miss Houlihan. I'll be counting the hours."

As if on cue, his mother and Mr. Kennedy emerged from the office.

~*~

"How does it feel to have all the loose ends tied up and the proceeds from the farm sale deposited in the bank?" Jamie asked as they drove home.

"Better than I thought it would," Mom said.

With the farm sale behind them, Jamie felt the weight of responsibility settle more heavily on his shoulders. His voice was steady and certain, as he turned to reassure his mother. "I hope you know I'll always take care of you, Annie, Thomas, and Robert. You don't have to worry about money ever again."

"Jamie, someday you'll have a wife and your own family to support and worry about. There's no need to saddle yourself with concerns about the kids and me."

"My family will always include you and my siblings."

"You have a good heart, Jamie. You are a dream son."

"I need to ask you a big favor and an important question."

"Okay, shoot. Favor first, important question second."

"Can I borrow the truck Sunday morning? It means you and the kids would have to walk to Mass."

"Of course you can. You know we always walk to church in the summer. It's a crime to drive when the weather is nice, and we can get to Transfiguration in ten minutes. Do you have other plans on Sunday morning that require a truck?"

Jamie tried to conceal his excitement and failed. "I do. I'm taking Katie to Mass at St. John's in White Plains and then out to breakfast afterward."

"Katie? The young lady we met today at Mr. Kennedy's office?" His mother's eyebrows lifted and her smile grew wide. "I could tell you were smitten with her the moment you laid eyes on her."

"That's the one. She's as nice as she is pretty. She lives with her sister and brother-in-law in White Plains and plans to attend Marymount in September."

"Well done, my boy. Making up for lost time, I see. A college girl, no less. I like that."

"Now, what's the important question?"

"Everything is set for me to begin classes at Fordham this fall. I had planned to commute daily on the train. But do you think I should still go in the fall, given how things have shaken out this summer with the fire and all? I can find work if you'd prefer me to hold off on college or quit altogether."

"Do you still want to attend, Jamie?"

"I do, but I'll defer to your wishes. I don't want you worrying about money or anything else."

"Of course, you'll finish college. There is no reason not to. You have the Gleason academic gifts, and I'll not see them wasted."

"Thanks, Mom, that's what I needed to hear."

"Maybe we should stop by Cayton Motors and visit my son-in-law, Chuck. I'd hate for some woman to marry you just because you drive this fancy truck." His mother laughed aloud.

"You got that right, Mom," Jamie said, winking at her.

FIVE

"*S*oon, *Sorellina*, you'll start college. Are you more nervous or more excited?" Frankie asked as he and Katie drove to the White Plains train station to meet Eileen at the end of the workday. Eileen rode the Harlem Line to and from work on Millinery Row in lower Manhattan every Tuesday through Saturday.

Eileen had been making hats since she was eighteen, starting in the Bronx manufacturing district. Her creative talent eventually landed her a better-paying job as a designer in the Manhattan fashion district, at one of the many millinery shops between Houston and Grand Streets. There, she designed the latest couture, with many hats selling for as much as twenty-five dollars (or more) to New York's high-society fashion mavens.

"A little nervous, I guess, but a whole lot excited. How about you, Frankie? Excited to get back to teaching?" Katie pursed her lips, suppressing a teasing grin.

Katie couldn't deny the impact Frankie had on her decision to become a teacher. His commitment, practicality, and humility were qualities she greatly admired. He'd been teaching math for a decade, starting in the Bronx and now at White Plains High School.

The pay wasn't great—she knew that—but it never seemed to bother him. Frankie had found a way to make ends meet by moonlighting at Kennedy's law office during the summers, filing taxes for late clients. She was impressed by how he managed it all, especially after he and Eileen bought their home on Lake Street four years ago.

To Frankie, teaching was more than just a job—at least, that's how Katie saw it. It was a calling. She remembered him talking about his own high school math teacher and football coach, the man who had made such a difference in his life back in the Bronx. Growing up in a tough, working-class neighborhood, Frankie had always been determined to give back, to help his students the way he had been helped.

The story of how Frankie had met Eileen was one Katie never tired of hearing. He had been a sophomore at Morris High School, and Eileen, a nervous freshman. Coeducation was still new at Morris at the time, something that had intimidated Eileen at first, though she quickly adjusted. Morris had been the pride of the neighborhood back then, with its grand Gothic architecture and stained-glass windows. Even Katie had taken pride in the school's beauty during her freshman year, feeling both awed and comforted by the same grand halls that had once welcomed Frankie and Eileen.

Katie often thought about how hard life had been for her sister Eileen at fourteen, riding the rattling trolley seven miles to Morris High School from their poor Irish neighborhood in the North Bronx. Eileen had excelled in school, but after Mam's death, she had little choice but to drop out at sixteen. She became the woman of the house, taking care of their twin brothers, Finn and Sean, and looking after Katie, not yet four at the time. Eileen had practically raised her, all while managing Da, whose drinking had worsened after Mam's passing.

At only three, Katie had no memories of Mam, except for the ones Eileen had stitched together through stories. Katie sometimes wondered if her resemblance to Mam—especially her red hair, a vivid, untamable hue in their otherwise brown-haired family—was why Da seemed to resent her. Katie often wondered if every time Da looked at her, he saw the wife he'd lost, or maybe he irrationally blamed her for Mam's death.

Katie had seen Frankie's dedication firsthand over the years. Though she wasn't the best math student herself, she knew how well-loved he was at White Plains, both in the classroom and on the football field where he coached. Frankie downplayed his role, often shrugging and saying, "Another day, another dollar," but Katie knew better.

Frankie was more like an older brother than a brother-in-law to Katie. He had been a part of Eileen's world for as long as she could remember and, by extension, a part of hers. His good-natured personality and warmth had helped dispel the darker times in the Houlihan home. Amidst the storms, Frankie was the anchor—always there, always steady. Even the Great War, which had scarred so many, had left Frankie untouched, ineligible for the draft due to his flat feet.

As Frankie pulled the car up to the railway station, the train screeched to a metal-on-metal stop, releasing a loud puff of gray exhaust with a shrill whistle. Moments later, a steady stream of men and women, completing the return leg of their daily commute between White Plains and New York City, poured out of the passenger cars. Eileen emerged mid-stream, stepping out onto the platform.

"Eileen, over here!" Katie shouted, exuberantly waving while standing on the Ford sedan's running board. Eileen made eye contact and waved back, quickening her pace.

As usual, her sister looked like she'd stepped out of the storefront window of Macy's flagship department store in Herald Square. She wore a semi-fitted, brown and white daisy-patterned voile dress, its wispy, asymmetrical hemline catching on the breeze. Eileen never went anywhere without a hat, usually of her own design. Today's was a simple woven hat with a turned rim, accented by a wide brown ribbon and a white silk gerbera daisy on the side.

Eileen's creative skills weren't limited to hats. She designed and made her own dresses, skirts, and blouses. Katie thought her sister should start her own line of clothing, a modest flapper style without plunging necklines, never sleeveless, and not too short. "Too much upfront capital and competition," Eileen had responded, thanking Katie for her confidence in her abilities.

Katie marveled at how her sister always managed to look so elegant despite the long hours she spent on her feet in her T-strap two-inch heels—the kind Katie could never imagine wearing for more than an hour or two at most. Eileen's job required her to interact with customers and direct the less experienced milliners in the construction room, with what seemed to Katie to be an endless supply of energy and creativity.

When Eileen reached the car, the two sisters exchanged a warm hug before Katie moved to the bench in the backseat.

"I'm glad to be home. Today felt like it would never end," Eileen said, removing her hat and running her fingers through her Dutch-cut bob.

"Two hours on the train each day—ten hours a week. That's a whole workday," Frankie said, shaking his head. "You could get a job in White Plains anytime you want out of the rat race, *amore mio*." He leaned over and kissed his wife softly on the lips.

Katie hungered for a relationship like Eileen had with Frankie. She wanted to feel safe and cherished, not like a burden. But so far, she'd never had a steady boyfriend. She'd kissed a few guys good night on the cheek after a first date but never agreed to a second. There was no hurry. Katie was going to be a career woman—a teacher. She'd spent the first year after high school working to save money for college. Yet Katie had felt something different when Jamie Murphy walked into the office today. Even thinking about him made her feel warm all over.

"It doesn't seem like the right time to quit yet, Frankie. I'd love a good reason to quit altogether," Eileen's voice faltered.

"I know, *cuore mio*, it will happen ..."

Katie wasn't sure how much responsibility she bore for her sister and brother-in-law waiting so long to marry or how much of the delay was Da's fault. But within two weeks of Da's burial, Eileen, nearly twenty-eight years old, and Frankie finally married. That was five years ago. At the end of the 1920-21 school year, Frankie had bought the house on Lake Street and moved "his girls"—Katie and Eileen were a package deal—to White Plains, far away from their sad memories and with plenty of room for babies.

~*~

Katie had already changed her outfit twice, carelessly tossing the rejects onto her bed. Why did her previously acceptable wardrobe suddenly seem so drab? The dresses were perfectly fine for Mass but not for her first date with Jamie Murphy, who was due to arrive in minutes.

Katie stuck her head out her bedroom door and shouted, "Eileen, I need your help!"

"Be there in a second. I'm downstairs."

The rhythmic sound of Eileen's footsteps on the wooden staircase calmed Katie. After a quick knock on the door, Eileen let herself in.

With flushed cheeks, Katie stood facing her wardrobe in her white cotton petticoat.

"I can't decide what to wear. Nothing seems right this morning," Katie moaned.

"This Jamie Murphy must really be something. I've never known you to have trouble deciding what to wear to Mass before—or anything else."

"I know it's stupid; I know nothing about him. Can you please pick something for me? Pretty please." Katie folded her hands together in exaggerated supplication.

Eileen picked up the dresses on the bed, holding them up, one by one, to Katie.

"Anything you wear will look fine. Honestly, even a flour sack would look lovely on you. He's twenty-one years old, right?"

Katie nodded, chewing her lip.

"He probably won't even notice what you're wearing."

Eileen sorted through the wardrobe and pulled out the Mary-Brooks-Picken "one-hour dress" that Katie had made earlier that summer with her help. "I like this one; it brings out the blue in your eyes," Eileen said, holding up a short-sleeved teal cotton dress. It was chemise style to the hip, then fell into a two-tiered, slightly gathered skirt.

"What hat should I wear?"

"Goodness gracious, you're fit to be tied." Eileen shook her head in disbelief. "Here, this works."

Eileen pulled out a straw-colored basin hat with an adjustable brim, the crown shaped like a bucket. "I have the perfect scarf to tie around it. Now go finish getting ready, you goofy girl. Your date will be here any minute."

"Thanks, Eileen. You're the best."

~*~

Jamie parked his truck a few houses down from the address Katie had given him. Arriving ten minutes early, he used the brass knocker, shaped like an elephant's trunk, to announce his arrival with a solid knock.

Frankie answered the door. "Jamie?"

"Yes, Jamie Murphy. I hope you don't mind me tagging along for Mass this morning."

"Not at all. I'm Frankie Caruso, Katie's brother-in-law." They shook hands.

"Come on in and take a load off. The ladies will be down shortly."

Jamie stepped off the braided rug in the entryway and settled onto an overstuffed green tapestry davenport in the living room.

"Here we are," a woman not much taller than Katie but significantly older—perhaps in her mid-thirties—said with a lilt in her voice, following Katie down the staircase, hat in hand.

Jamie stood as the two sisters joined him. Both women were attractive, but Katie was the pick of the litter. Every cell in his body responded to her presence.

"Hi, Jamie." Katie smiled brightly.

"Good morning, Katie, you look lovely this morning." And she did.

"That's kind of you to say. I see you met Frankie. He teaches at White Plains High School and coaches the football team."

Jamie nodded approvingly, though he still wondered about Frankie Caruso's job at Kennedy's law office.

"This is Eileen, my sister and best friend."

Eileen held out her hand to Jamie. "Very nice to meet you, Jamie."

"The pleasure is all mine," Jamie said, shaking her hand. He then turned to Katie. "It's a gorgeous day. What do you say about walking to St. John the Evangelist for Mass? If we leave now, we can get there on time."

Katie glanced down at her feet at her T-strap heels. "Um... sure," she said, her voice sounding a bit off, but Jamie brushed it aside, too focused on the thought of spending the next few hours with her.

"I think it is a grand idea," Eileen said. "We'll see you on the way. If you change your mind—it *is* a mile—we can give you a lift for the rest of it." Eileen winked at Katie.

"That works. I may take you up on that," Katie said.

"See you there," Eileen said, gently shooing them out the door with a wave.

"I thought we'd all go together," Frankie said, his forehead knit in confusion.

"Yes, but they hardly know each other, darling. This gives them a little time alone to get acquainted." She gave him a peck on the cheek and headed back upstairs.

After the front door closed, Jamie said, "We don't have to walk; I have the truck." He pointed to where he'd parked, and Katie's eyes followed.

"I can drive us to Mass, or we can go with your brother-in-law and sister, as you probably assumed. I just thought it might be nice to learn a bit about each other without an audience. Your family seems great, and I want to become better acquainted. But you are my first real date, and I'd like to get to know you without distractions."

~*~

Katie couldn't hide her surprise when Jamie revealed his time in the seminary and his reasons for leaving. As she listened, she pictured Jamie Murphy in a black cassock, though she had never known a handsome priest before. The pastors at St. Barnabas Church in Woodlawn, where she grew up, and at St. John the Evangelist on Hamilton Avenue, where she now attended Mass, were kind but far from attractive. While she knew a handsome man could be a priest, it seemed like such a waste in Jamie's case, especially since he seemed to long for a family.

They walked in silence for a moment as Katie absorbed Jamie's words, erasing her mental image of Fr. Jamie Murphy. "Well, I'm honored to be your first date, Jamie Murphy." Katie turned her face, framed by her hat, toward Jamie. Taking his hand, she wondered what it would be like to share his first kiss.

Jamie beamed at Katie's gentle smile, which radiated warmth and acceptance.

"You're not my first date, but I've never been on a second date with anyone," Katie confessed.

"That's hard to believe. You're gorgeous. Why no second dates?"

Suddenly, she understood why. "I've never met anyone I could see myself with for more than an hour or two. I mean, why date someone if you can't imagine a future with them?" *Those other guys were boring, immature clods and never made me feel the way you do just by being with you*, she thought.

"Will I get a second date, Kathleen Mary Houlihan?" Jamie asked, his face open, honest, and confident.

"Only if you ask me, Jamie Murphy," Katie teased.

Aaoogha, aaoogha, blared the horn as Frankie and Eileen pulled up alongside them when they were halfway to St. John's.

"Still want to walk, you two?" Eileen hollered out the window.

"It's your call," Jamie said to Katie.

"Do you mind? I think breakfast will taste better without blisters on my heels," Katie giggled.

Jamie opened the back passenger door and helped Katie inside the car. They rode the rest of the way together with Frankie and Eileen.

~*~

After Mass, Katie and Jamie rode back to the house with Frankie and Eileen. As Jamie and Frankie exchanged handshakes and the usual pleasantries, Katie watched, feeling a mix of nerves and excitement building inside her. When Jamie turned to help her into his truck, his hand warm and steady in hers, she felt a slight flutter in her chest. She smiled, settling into the passenger seat, stealing a glance at him as they pulled away.

As they drove around downtown White Plains, Katie noticed that no restaurants were open for at least another hour, except for hotels with live-in boarders. Since the start of Prohibition several years ago, restaurants were encouraged to open on Sundays as long as their hours didn't deter people from attending church services and they didn't serve alcohol. Katie now realized they were too early for breakfast.

Katie shifted in the passenger seat, wondering how this was going to play out. Surely Jamie had noticed that nothing was open, too—but what was he thinking?

Jamie cleared his throat. "How do you feel about going to a hotel with me on our first date?" He appeared to be trying to keep a straight face, though his dimples gave him away.

"I'm sure Eileen would be happy to feed us breakfast, but they're probably enjoying some time alone for once on a Sunday," Katie replied, amused by Jamie's humorous double meaning.

"Or we could drive to Tarrytown and have breakfast with my family. My sister Gracie and her husband might be there; they sometimes stop by after Mass. That's twenty more minutes for you to tell me about yourself."

Katie hesitated, her nose crinkling slightly as her voice softened with uncertainty. "Would your mom mind if we just showed up?"

"Nah, she'd love to meet you again. She's used to extra people showing up. You might have to endure Annie's cross-examination or Thomas and Robert staring since I've never brought a girl home before. They walked to the nine o'clock Mass, so we'll get there shortly before they do. If you're nervous, we can wait outside until they arrive."

"You made them walk?" Katie asked, surprised.

"We always walk in the summer; it's barely a half-mile."

"Is there a phone at your house, Jamie?"

"Of course."

"Okay, if you're sure your mom won't mind, I'd love to have breakfast with your family. I can call Eileen and Frankie once we get there."

"I like your flexible attitude and adventurous spirit." Jamie made a U-turn at the next intersection and headed northwest toward Tarrytown Road. "You seem really close to your sister and Frankie. How long have you lived with them?"

"I've always lived with Eileen. Mam died before I turned four, and Da died ten years later. I was part of the package when Eileen and Frankie got married five years ago."

"I'm sorry about your parents, especially your mom dying when you were so young. My dad died several years ago. It's been hard on the family; he was a great guy."

"I never knew my mother, Jamie. The doctor discovered her breast cancer around the time she became pregnant with me. Mam had hidden her cancer from everyone, according to my sister, for as long as she could. She'd been unwilling to submit to 'mutilation,' as she called her only treatment option.

"Eileen took care of me and Mam both. But after Mam died, I had to stay with Mrs. Mowry in the apartment next door when Eileen was at school until I started school myself.

"After Mam died, Da took to the bottle. Eileen and my twin brothers, Sean and Finn, quit school at sixteen—as soon as it was legal—and went to work to pay rent and keep food on the table. Something Da couldn't seem to manage."

"You have twin brothers?"

"Had. They were more than willing to answer President Wilson's call to 'make the world safe for democracy.' By then, they only came home to sleep. Both had enlisted in the Army, together, of course. Finn was a casualty of war, and Sean, a casualty of the second wave of influenza, sweeping through Army training camps and everyplace else, stateside.

"After my brothers died, Da just kept spiraling down and crashed. Four days before Armistice Day, he was dead."

Katie closed her eyes, remembering the day she and Eileen found out Da had died; she'd been fourteen. Back in the Bronx, Katie relived sitting on the stoop of the crumbling brownstone on E. 233rd Street, unable to muster even a sliver of sadness to mourn the end of her father's drunken tirades. No more Da throwing things about the house. No more Da drinking up his pay. No more hateful glares at Katie, as if all his troubles were her fault. Instead, an overwhelming wave of relief had washed over her.

Then there were the whispers at Da's funeral: "He couldn't take any more heartache ... Losing his wife, then both his boys ... He lost the will to live ... How much can a man take?" they said, shaking their heads not so much in judgment but genuine pity.

Sure, it had been an accident: a laborer falling off a scaffold as the story went. But Katie knew many had suspected his death was intentional. Either that, or he was drunk and lost his footing. Eileen and Katie hadn't been enough reason for Da to live.

After Da was buried, Eileen finally told Katie how Da had provided the deadly mixture that ended Mam's pain for good. Sixteen-year-old Eileen had found the whiskey bottle and the two empty double-strength laudanum bottles in her parents' bedroom when she checked to see if Mam could eat anything that morning before school. She'd found Mam cold and lifeless, her eyes staring wide at nothing.

Eileen had found Da passed out, head and arms sprawled on the kitchen table, along with an empty Jameson whiskey bottle and overturned empty glass on the kitchen table. At first, she thought Da was dead, too.

"I think what Da did ate away at him, Katie, and destroyed any semblance of the father that you never had a chance to know," Eileen had said. "I know it's hard, but try to pray for him. Mam, too. Da was as sick as Mam—not in body—but in his mind and soul."

Jamie's voice pulled Katie back to the present as he turned onto Benedict Avenue.

"What did you just say? Sorry, I got lost in thought for a minute."

Jamie reached over and squeezed Katie's hand briefly. "We all have our ghosts." His touch felt accepting and reassuring to her. His brown eyes reflected understanding, reaching a place deep inside her that she'd never allowed entry to anyone else to access. Eileen had come the closest.

Katie thought Jamie would have made an excellent priest but an even better husband for some lucky girl.

They sat in comfortable silence for a few miles until Jamie turned onto Broadway, and they entered the city limits of Tarrytown.

As she studied his profile—straight nose, full lips, and a strong jawline—he glanced over at her. "I lost two brothers, too: Danny and Marty. Danny was four-and-a-half years older than me; he died in the war. Marty died when he was just a baby, and I was four."

"I'm sorry, Jamie. That must have been hard to lose your brothers. Especially your older brother." Katie hadn't been that close to her brothers, but she couldn't imagine life without her big sister, Eileen.

"It was. Danny and I shared a room for many years. We had different interests. Like my dad, Danny was a farmer at heart, but I idolized him. Marty's death was tough on Mom, but I was so young; it didn't affect me the same way as when Danny died."

"Somehow, I can't picture you as a farmer, Jamie."

"Before we sold the farm, I could do a decent impression. Hey, and what about these fancy wheels? Not just any beautiful young woman gets to ride around in a truck like this."

"Nope. A total mismatch—you and the truck. I see you more as the roadster type."

"I'll take that as a compliment, Miss Houlihan." Jamie turned onto Elizabeth Street. "And here we are."

Katie loved the Murphys' house, a Dutch colonial revival style with a gambrel roof. A screened-in porch had been added. Jamie pulled up to the carriage house and turned off the car. He opened the door for Katie and offered his hand.

"We can sit on the porch if Mom and the kids aren't back yet."

"That sounds perfect." Katie sat on the bench, hoping no one was home and Jamie would sit beside her.

SIX

After calling Eileen to inform her of the change in their breakfast plans, Katie joined Jamie on the screened-in front porch to await the Murphy family's return from Mass. Her stomach was doing cartwheels—she wanted so much for Jamie's family to like her.

Jamie sat at one end of the wooden swing that hung from rusted chains attached to a sturdy overhead beam. The swing was simple yet charming, crafted from weathered oak darkened with age, its seat just wide enough for two people to sit comfortably with a respectful distance between them.

"Won't you join me, Katie? I promise I don't bite." Jamie's teasing smile helped Katie relax a little. "The family should be arriving any moment now."

As she sat down beside him, careful not to sit too close—although she would have preferred otherwise, the sound of a car engine caught her attention. A shiny, new 1927 Chevrolet Superior Series F Touring rolled to a stop in front of the house.

"Now that's the kind of car I picture you in," Katie said, eyeing the snazzy car.

"Here's the first installment of the Murphy clan," Jamie said, standing up and reaching out his hand to escort Katie down the porch steps for the introductions. "Ready to be the toast of the town? They'll love you, Katie."

Katie smiled, though her heart skipped a beat. Would they really? Jamie's confidence felt encouraging to her; she hoped he was right.

A young boy of around nine or ten was the first to exit the vehicle, his arm and hand still wrapped in gauze. He scurried up the porch stairs like a mouse after cheese. The other three—a man and woman in the front seat, and a teenage girl in the back—remained in the car with its convertible top folded down.

The boy rushed past Jamie with downcast eyes, not noticing Katie until his older brother gently stopped him with a hand on his shoulder.

"Hey, buddy, slow down. I want to introduce you to someone special." He gently turned Robert to face Katie.

"This is my friend Katie. We went to Mass together this morning at her church in White Plains, and she's going to join us for breakfast. Katie, this is my youngest brother, Robert."

Shyly, Robert looked down at the ground after making brief eye contact with Katie. His dark eyes were fringed with impossibly long lashes, and he had a single dimple on one cheek. He looked like a mini version of Jamie, minus one dimple.

"Hi, Robert, it's so nice to meet you. Jamie has told me how brave you've been since the fire. I hope you are healing well." She extended her hand toward the nine-year-old, who only responded with a barely perceptible nod.

Robert went into the house wordlessly, leaving the door open.

Katie's bubbly personality concealed an undercurrent of turbulence, like a gurgling brook flowing through jagged terrain, washing over rough rocks midstream. She was especially perceptive of others' emotions, particularly when they were troubled, sad, or critical of her. "What did I say wrong?" she asked, grimacing as she turned to Jamie.

"Nothing. I need to spend some time with Robert one-on-one; he's been off since the fire. Something is bothering him."

Jamie led her down the walkway towards the car, along a path worn by foot traffic on the lawn. A brief surge of anxiety quickened Katie's breathing. *Will they like me? Don't borrow trouble*, she told herself, focusing on the gorgeous man with his hand resting on the small of her back.

Two women, one older than Katie and one younger, stood by the car. A man behind the steering wheel, wearing a brown and olive-patterned flat cap, fiddled with something under the dashboard.

"What a nice surprise. I'm Gracie, Jamie's *very big* sister, and this is my husband, Chuck. You must be Katie. Annie's told us about you," she said with a welcoming smile.

Katie stole a glance at Jamie, who put on his best I-know-nothing look. The comely woman, with dark hair and eyes, held out her hand to Katie.

Chuck tipped his hat to Katie from the driver's seat, nodding and winking at Jamie with evident approval.

"Very big at the moment," she said, placing her hands over her hugely pregnant belly. She nodded toward her husband, who was now revving the motor. "Chuck is doing his Peter DePaolo impersonation right now."

"Oh, that hurts, Gracie," Chuck said, holding his hand over his heart.

"DePaolo won the Indy 500 this year," Jamie said softly, providing context for Katie. "Chuck loves cars and racing just as much as my brother Thomas."

"Oh, I know about DePaolo. My Uncle Frankie is Italian-American and follows his racing career. He was a fan of his uncle, Ralph DePalma, too," Katie said confidently.

Jamie gave Katie a wink.

"Chuck and Gracie live in town, up by Patriots Park, not far from here," Jamie added.

Leaning against the car in her pink straight-line dress, hat and gloves in hand, the teenage girl seemed to be giving Katie a thorough once-over. She was a good six inches taller and chunkier than Katie.

Stepping toward Katie, she said, "I'm Annie. Jamie thinks you're the bee's knees." She looked from Katie to Jamie impishly.

"Guilty," Jamie said. "But don't tell Katie all my secrets, Annie. I want her to like me."

Katie empathized with Annie's social awkwardness and sensed her insecurity. Thankfully, Jamie had rescued what could have been an uncomfortable moment with his irrepressible charm.

"Annie, so wonderful to meet you. I've been looking forward to it." Katie crossed her fingers behind her back, wanting Annie to feel special and accepted, just as she desired for herself.

Clearly, Gracie and Annie were sisters, about the same height, with amber eyes and dark hair, but their differences outweighed their similarities. While Gracie's short, dark hair framed an attractive, open countenance, her easy smile graced by perfectly aligned teeth, Annie's long hair framed a plain face, just shy of homely and marked by teenage acne. Overlapping front teeth punctuated Annie's tentative smile— poor Annie, the ugly duckling in the shadow of Gracie, the swan.

Katie had never gone through an ugly duckling phase; she knew that men found her attractive. Over the last year, through Eileen's connections in Manhattan's fashion district, Katie had earned a better-than-good wage doing nothing more than standing still in Macy's windows as a live mannequin. She modeled clothing from the store and hats on consignment that were created by the shop where Eileen worked.

The window shoppers' gawking and staring weren't enjoyable, but the money was too good to turn down. Katie refused to let Eileen and Frankie pay for her college. For her, self-sufficiency was a matter of principle. She had one last gig as a window mannequin before starting at Marymount, an all-women's Catholic college, in September.

She wouldn't miss the modeling work, but she would miss the paychecks. She had saved enough money for her first year of college and half of the second year. Many school districts still hired teachers with only two years of college, but that was changing in the bigger cities. Even Tarrytown's Marymount College had been offering a four-year baccalaureate degree to its students since 1924.

Just then, a middle-aged woman and a tall, gawky young man rounded the corner from Broadway onto Elizabeth Street. Annie ran to join them, calling out loudly, "Jamie's Katie is here! Can she have breakfast with us this morning?"

"Of course, darling. We always have room at our table," said the woman, placing her arm around Annie's shoulder. The woman's pleasant face broke into a smile, sweeping over the crowd gathered in front of the house, finally resting on Katie like a butterfly.

The young man, who had to be Thomas, tucked his shirt back into his trousers and straightened his tie. He smoothed his hand through his dark pompadour-style cut, taming any potential vagrant hairs—though there were none.

While Katie had never seen a picture of Mam or had any direct memories, she'd created an image in her mind. It was not so very different from this woman, with her silver-streaked brown hair peeking out beneath her brown bucket hat—except Mam's hair would have been red. Mrs. Murphy's classy outfit, a pin-tucked white blouse and brown pleated mid-calf skirt, would have hung on a shorter frame—like Katie's. Of course, Mam's eyes would have been blue. Still, something about this woman awakened a sense of familiarity and longing in Katie.

"What a delightful surprise! We'd be happy to have you join us for breakfast this morning," Mrs. Murphy said, taking Katie's hands.

"Thank you, Mrs. Murphy. I'd love to do that. Jamie suggested we come here because the restaurants hadn't opened up yet after the early Mass."

"Their loss and our good fortune," Jamie's mother replied.

Jamie introduced Katie to Thomas, who shared Jamie's height and easy demeanor. Everyone, including Chuck, headed into the house.

It was a perfect late August morning, with blue skies and spun-sugar clouds. Even the birdsong echoed the joy swelling in Katie's heart. She felt like twirling around, letting the wonder of the day and the pleasure of being part of the Murphy family seep into her pores. She had yearned to be part of a normal family for so long. How nice it would be to be part of this one.

Katie was utterly enamored with the Murphy clan, and she had only just met them.

~*~

Katie insisted on helping Jamie's mother prepare breakfast, determined to make a good impression and to be a help, not a hindrance. She admired the way Jamie's mother had everything under control, from the cinnamon-swirl sour cream coffee cake sitting on the countertop to the sizzling bacon in the pan.

"Next time you come, I'll make you my famous cinnamon rolls—Jamie's favorite," Mrs. Murphy said.

Katie's heart warmed at the thought of being invited back. She was already beginning to feel welcome here. "That sounds delicious," Katie replied. She was wearing one of Mrs. Murphy's aprons as she flipped sizzling bacon in a cast iron skillet on the stovetop while keeping an eye on the bread toasting in the oven.

Jamie's mother sent him out to the coop to gather any remaining fresh eggs she might have missed earlier, leaving Katie and Mrs. Murphy alone to work side by side in the kitchen.

"Jamie says you'll start at Marymount College in September. Make sure he gives you our phone number if you ever need anything. We're only half a mile by foot if you cut across the field at Hamilton and Neperan Road. No more than a mile by car," Mrs. Murphy said, cracking the eggs she had in hand into the bowl and scrambling them.

Were mothers always so nice? Katie wondered. What a wonderful mother-in-law Mrs. Murphy would make. As attracted as she was to Jamie, she felt an equally strong, albeit different, connection to his mother.

Jamie hovered nearby, claiming he was "under the hypnotic spell of cinnamon and brown sugar." Katie glanced over and smiled as he nursed a cup of coffee, watching her and his mother interact comfortably, a pleased look on his face. He seemed to grow more attractive by the minute, almost taking her breath away—and setting her adrift in uncharted territory.

Gracie waddled into the kitchen and straddled the end of the long bench Jamie had pulled out for her from underneath the trestle table. She rubbed her back. "Only two more weeks. I'm counting down the days."

"You never can tell, Gracie. Sometimes, the first one is stubborn and can take longer. Danny was two weeks overdue; you were a week late," the older woman said. "Jamie, over there, came early, ready to say, 'Hello, world.' Every baby is different."

"Chuck and Thomas are in the living room talking about the newest cars rolling off the Chevy assembly line at the North Tarrytown plant," Gracie said. "By the way, Mom, Chuck says he can get you a good deal if you want to trade in the truck."

"Jamie and the other kids are after me to do that, too. I'm almost ready," Mrs. Murphy said, winking at Jamie.

"I'm ready to offer my assistance if you want any second opinions or chauffeuring," Jamie said, winking back.

Aha, Katie thought, *that's where Jamie gets the wink that leaves me feeling so weak in the knees.*

"Jamie, do you mind hollering for Annie and Robert to come downstairs? Tell Annie to set the table in the dining room. We're just minutes away from eating," Mrs. Murphy said. "Let Chuck and Thomas know, too, please."

As soon as Jamie left the room, Gracie began pummeling Katie with questions.

"So, what do you think of my brother? You know, you're the first girl he's ever brought home."

"What kind of question is that, Gracie? Good heavens, they only just met," the older woman said, looking at Katie apologetically. "You know how nosy women can be."

Katie did know. Her frequent interactions with Frankie's enormous Italian family, from childhood to the present as Eileen's tag-along sister, had taught her that a thick skin was required to survive in large families and that sisters could be very protective of their brothers. Giving each other playful grief was a preferred form of entertainment. Katie took no offense to Gracie's question and recognized that asking personal questions was a form of female bonding—and testing.

"Gracie, I do know that I'm the first. From what I've heard, they frown on dating in the seminary." Katie giggled, recalling how Jamie had mentioned this when he asked her out earlier in the week. "I'm just getting to know Jamie, but what I do know so far, I like very much."

~*~

After breakfast, Annie cleared the dining room table while Thomas swept the floor. Jamie insisted on doing the dishes, and Katie happily volunteered to dry them. There were no leftovers—always a good sign—so once Jamie's mother stacked the dishes and shooed Annie out of the kitchen, Jamie and Katie found themselves alone, filling Katie with a flutter of excitement.

Katie tied on Mrs. Murphy's extra apron again. When she looked up, Jamie had pulled a large brown kangaroo-style apron over his head, embroidered with the words *Handsome Men Cook & Clean Up*. She suppressed a laugh—it was so Jamie, perfectly blending his charm and playfulness.

"Nice apron," Katie said, unable to hold back her grin.

"It was Dad's, but he rarely wore it. How is it working for me?"

"It doesn't hurt," Katie teased.

"When would you like to head back home?" Jamie set a clean plate in the basin of rinse water. "I'd hate for Eileen and Frankie to be upset with me on our first date. Speaking of which, I think I need more practice to get this dating thing down. Would you be open to being my teacher? Maybe on a second date. I'm in need of a lot of tutoring."

Could she say no to Jamie Murphy? That smile, those dimples, and the way his eyes made her feel so cherished by him. She was completely at ease with him, more than she'd ever felt with anyone, more than she'd ever felt with anyone besides her sister and brother-in-law.

"Do you always ask two questions at once?" Katie bantered, returning his smile and the inviting look in his eyes.

"Only with you," Jamie replied. The warmth of his gaze made Katie feel like she was melting from the inside out.

"I don't have a specific time to go home as long as I keep Eileen informed. As for that tutoring business, Jamie Murphy, I've never been on a second date, so we're on equal footing there. But I'd be happy for us to learn together."

"Then, regarding that second date..." Jamie said, drawing out his words.

For the first time in her life, Katie felt overwhelmed by physical desire. It surprised her, but at the same time, it felt completely right. Without worrying about who might walk into the kitchen, she stood on her tiptoes, wrapped her dish towel around Jamie's neck, and pulled his lips to hers. He responded immediately, bending down to meet her in a kiss that was soft, warm, and full of an unspoken yes.

"Could we try that again? I'm a slow learner," Jamie murmured.

Katie marveled at her own boldness, though she wasn't sorry. If anything, it scared her a little—how easily this man could stir something inside her that she had never felt before. For the first time, she understood how love—if that's what this was—could blur the line between caution and desire, dissolving one's better judgment.

May God have mercy on me, she thought.

SEVEN

J amie was nearly home before the euphoric glow from his time with Katie began to dim. Only then did the growl of his empty stomach register, pouncing like a hungry lion circling its prey. He glanced at his watch. Late afternoon—he had missed lunch entirely.

Walking into the entryway, he hung his canvas newsboy cap on the hall tree, passed the stairs in the narrow hallway, and headed straight to the kitchen to make a sandwich.

Mom was seated at the trestle table, looking up from her notepad as she composed her grocery list. The radio played the happy, jazzy sounds of "Whispering" by Paul Whiteman's band. Jamie began whistling with the chorus, foxtrotting with an imaginary partner—two steps forward, two quick steps left, then repeating, dancing his way to the cupboard.

"You look mighty happy, son. Does this have anything to do with a pert little redhead?"

"Not hiding it very well, am I?"

"No reason to hide it. Katie seems like a lovely girl."

"I really like her. A lot." Jamie glided to the bread box, taking out what remained of an unsliced loaf of his mother's homemade bread and retrieving a serrated knife from the nearby knife block.

"Obviously," she said with a grin. "Where did you learn to dance like that?"

"Mom, I was in the seminary—I wasn't dead," he said playfully, his deep dimples amplifying his broad smile. He continued his graceful, rhythmic moves over to where Mom sat, momentarily dumbfounded, before dancing back to the counter.

"How long after you and Dad met did he propose?" Jamie asked, cutting two generous slices of bread and slathering them with peanut butter and honey.

She laid down her pen, pausing as if lost in thought for a moment. "Your dad used to tease me every time he came into the mill, always good-natured, of course," she said with a soft smile. "Once we started dating, it didn't take long before he proposed. Honestly, I wasn't even sure I wanted to get married back then." She chuckled lightly. "But it was the best decision I ever made."

Jamie filled a glass with water at the sink, then joined her at the table and took a bite of his sandwich.

"How did you know Dad was the one?"

Mom shook her head and smiled. "People often talk about knowing for sure that this or that person is 'the one,' as if there's no other. A better question is: Are both parties willing to commit one hundred percent to each other for better or worse, no matter what the future holds?

"If they can't make that commitment before God and to each other, then they're not ready to marry. Love is a decision, much more than a romantic feeling. Feelings can be mercurial, but marital love is unconditional, sacrificial, and rewarding—though hard work! Spouses don't always agree. Especially when it comes to raising kids, there needs to be a unified front."

Jamie finished his sandwich and washed it down with the rest of his water. His mother retrieved the cookie tin from the pantry and set it on the table before Jamie, who removed an oatmeal-raisin cookie.

"Jamie, you're young. Take your time. There's no hurry."

"Thanks for the advice, Mom." He planted a quick kiss on her cheek and headed upstairs, taking two stairs at a time to change out of his church clothes.

Looking out his bedroom window, he spied Robert playing marbles in the side yard. Robert had drawn a large circle in the dirt and scattered the marbles inside its circumference. It was time Jamie talked with Robert. Enough was enough—Robert had been rude to Katie.

Jamie pulled out a shoe box from under the bottom bunk. He opened the lid and removed a small cowhide bag laced shut with a thin piece of leather. The bag was filled with marbles that had once belonged to Danny. Jamie went downstairs and exited the back door, dressed in a cotton shirt and blue dungarees, to join Robert.

Squatting down in the dirt, Jamie watched Robert prepare for a shot. With his shooter in hand, Robert knocked two marbles outside the perimeter of the circle he had drawn in the sand while keeping his red, white, and blue shooter inside.

"Yes!" Robert said, celebrating his shot.

"How about we play a game of Bull's Eye or Knock Out?" Jamie held up the cowhide pouch of marbles.

"Sure," Robert said with excitement. "Can we play for keeps?"

"Why not?"

Jamie had held onto those marbles for seven years—a tangible memory of good times with Danny. He had clutched them in his hands like rosary beads during the early months after Danny's death when the pain of missing his big brother throbbed like a toothache. Today was the day that he would pass them on to Robert.

In the first game, Jamie let Robert win by fumbling the necessary number of shots to make his loss convincing. Robert relaxed into his early victory.

"What did you think of my friend Katie?"

"She was fine, I guess."

"You weren't very friendly, Robert. Taking her hand when she offered it would have been the polite thing to do."

Robert said nothing, tracing his fingers in the dirt and avoiding Jamie's gaze.

"Something is troubling you. I wish you would talk to me about whatever it is."

Robert swiped at the stream of tears trickling down his face, leaving a trail of dirty brown marks. "It's my fault," he said, his voice catching.

"What's your fault, buddy?"

"The fire," he shouted, as if angry with the world. "Mom having to sell the farm." Robert's body trembled, his words breaking into sobs as he struggled to speak. "If I'd told on them ... but I didn't want to tattle ... I wanted them to like me."

"Do you mean Erik and Anders?"

Robert nodded, wiping his nose and leaving behind a grimy mustache of dirt and snot.

"They were smoking in the barn. I didn't, but I watched them and didn't say anything. I ran out of the barn when Mr. de Vries yelled for us to tend to the horses. I should have told him right then. I went back in a little later to check on things, but ..." Robert's breath came in jagged spurts as he tried to swallow his sobs.

Jamie gently guided Robert's chin upwards. "Robert, please look at me."

Robert slowly raised his eyes to Jamie, who recognized the pain in his little brother's brown eyes. Jamie wished he could carry the weight of Robert's pain for him, but he knew some things couldn't be taken away that easily. Still, he couldn't ignore the consequences of Robert's silence.

"I'm glad that you told me what happened, Robert. Not because I needed to know but because you needed to tell someone.

"A week after the fire, Mom and I drove out to the farm and offered to sell it to Lukyas de Vries. He told us that his grandsons, Erik and Anders, had confessed to smoking in the barn several days after the fire started. They were clear that you hadn't participated. Now, if the gasoline cans hadn't been in the barn (which they shouldn't have been), there might not have been an explosion or near the same destruction.

"And while it may be true that by telling Mr. de Vries immediately, the fire might have been prevented, we'll never know. But one thing I do know for sure: There'll be times in your life, Robert, when you can intervene and prevent harm. It'll take courage to do the right thing, even if it means facing possible rejection from others."

"I'm so sorry, Jamie," Robert croaked, his lower lip shaking. "What can I do?"

Jamie squeezed Robert's shoulder, feeling the weight of his brother's guilt. He'd been there before—grappling with things he couldn't control, wishing he could change the past. But he knew that this was part of growing up, learning how to bear the weight of your choices.

"You can learn from your mistakes. We all have to do that. I've made my share of mistakes, and unfortunately, I'll continue making them—hopefully, less and less as I grow older."

Robert's voice wavered. "So, Mom already knows? Is she mad at me?"

"No, she isn't angry with you—not like you mean. But she is worried about you and has been waiting for you to talk with her about this. She was giving you the time you needed to heal, both on the outside and the inside.

"Admitting our mistakes is hard, Robert. I'm not sure it ever gets any easier. The important thing is to never give up trying to do better."

"I'm sorry I wasn't very nice to Katie. I promise to be polite and nice if she comes over again."

"You'll have many opportunities to be nice to Katie if it's up to me." Jamie hoped there would be many more times.

"Katie is real pretty," Robert said.

"She sure is. Both on the outside and the inside."

~*~

September 1927 (Two weeks later)

Katie stood motionless, frozen in place with two other female models in the storefront window of the Herald Square Macy's. The display was one of four along the Palladian façade on W. 34th Street, each featuring three young women dressed in the store's finest apparel and accessories. Although her body was trained to mimic a mannequin, Katie could sense the shoppers outside, some pointing, others rushing by.

The frenetic throngs of midtown shoppers and a few curious men reminded Katie of bees swarming honeysuckle nectar. From her glass-front stage, muffled street-side conversations filtered in, a buzzing hive of sound punctuated by the occasional sting of a car horn. It wasn't always this busy on Saturdays, but today was Labor Day weekend—thirty-three years after Grover Cleveland made it a legal holiday.

Few onlookers could imagine the coordination and behind-the-scenes effort that went into the shows. But that was the point: to make it appear flawless and seamless—the work of Jillian, the modeling coordinator (and taskmaster), an eccentric woman whom Katie admired. Jillian always stayed calm, even when things went wrong—as they sometimes did behind the scenes. Katie wished she could be more like that.

When exhaustion began to creep in, as it did now, Katie would remind herself of Jillian's words, spoken before each show: *You must cast a vision so that each woman, young or old, sees herself transformed by the fashions you wear.*

Katie fixed her gaze above the flow of foot traffic, just as her high school speech teacher had taught: *Look above their heads—they'll think you're looking right at them, but you won't see them at all.* It helped her keep the illusion intact, but even after three years of modeling, she still found it difficult to ignore the stares of those who stopped to point or critique. They weren't just judging the fashion—they were judging her. Katie didn't need to see them to feel it.

She couldn't risk looking for Jamie. If she saw him, she'd smile, and the mannequin illusion would be shattered. He was meeting her at five, after her last show. The ache in her legs and feet told her it must be close to four-thirty—the end of the fifth and final half-hour show of the day.

The day had begun much earlier. At half-past seven, Katie and Eileen had boarded the train at White Plains, arriving at Grand Central Station an hour later. They had walked to the millinery shop where her sister worked. Katie savored the crisp fall air as they made their way through the city. She loved the coolness of the morning and had wished she could store it away for later when the hot lights of the storefront would make her sweat.

When she arrived at Macy's 34th Street entrance, a man with slicked-back hair, dressed in a snappy double-breasted linen suit, was just opening the door for the crowd that had gathered. "Welcome to Macy's," he said, stepping back to avoid being trampled as the flood of customers surged inside.

Her gaze drifted upward as she waited for the crowd to pass. Four beaux-arts marble statues stood "watch" in pairs between a gilded clock one story up. The hands pointed to ten o'clock—a full hour before she was due to check in. She let her eyes wander further, past the eleventh floor, until they rested on the cerulean blue sky dotted with cottony cumulus clouds.

Katie stepped inside, feeling a surge of excitement as she walked through the bustling store toward the staging area to check in with Jillian.

Arriving ahead of schedule gave her plenty of time to relax and try on the outfits Jillian had selected. The racks of clothing—five changes for each of the twelve models—were neatly organized by name. Once Katie ensured her ensembles were the right size or could be made so with small adjustments by a well-placed pin, she checked in with Jillian.

Katie stood before Jillian's makeshift desk—a small table and chair from the furniture department, nine floors up—waiting for her to look up.

"There you are, Katie, early as usual. I wish all my girls were as prompt as you," Jillian said, her tone more businesslike than friendly. Katie understood the pressure Jillian was under to deliver a flawless show, one that would ultimately be measured in women's wear department sales.

Jillian, a tall, exotic-looking woman in her forties, wore her jet-black hair parted down the middle and gathered in a rolled bun at her neck. The giant spit curl in the middle of her forehead, along with her dark charcoal eyeliner and red lipstick, made Katie think of a cross between a flamenco dancer and a flapper. Her red georgette blouse, tucked into a black kick-pleated skirt, black silk stockings, and two-inch Mary Jane heels only reinforced the image.

"Everything fits fine, Jillian," Katie said.

Reaching for a clipboard, Jillian nodded. "Excellent. Let's see here. Nellie will assist you today."

Katie smiled. Nellie was as meticulous as she was conscientious, and they worked well together.

The assistant dressed the model, made sure no hair was out of place, and touched up her makeup. She brought each outfit's coordinating shoes, purse, hat, gloves, and silk stockings to the dressing room before each wardrobe change.

It was a carefully coordinated fashion symphony: Jillian selected the scores, the dressing assistant was the conductor, and the model was the instrument without which the "music" could not be heard. Every player was critical to the success of the performance.

Katie studied the sketches in the dressing room and chatted with Nellie, who had brought her first wardrobe change. Soon, she heard Jillian's alto voice announce, "It's time, girls," as she always did ten minutes before each hour, accompanied by a double clap of her hands.

Imitating a mannequin made for a long, dull day, but thirty-five cents an hour was nothing to sneeze at.

During Katie's five shifts, Jamie consumed her thoughts. She relived every soft touch of his hand, the hungry look in his eyes before he kissed her, and the warm invitation of his lips. Feelings and sensations she had never experienced but had heard other girls whisper about in high school had taken hold of her. There was a pleasant aching—a confusing sensation she didn't know was possible.

The twenty-five days since their first meeting had flown by; they had been the best days of her life. Tomorrow, she would go to Mass at Resurrection with his family—her second time at church in Tarrytown with Jamie. She pictured him helping her move into the dormitory after Mass. Eileen and Frankie had planned to help her, but she'd insisted Jamie be the one.

Katie had been preparing for college by working hard to earn good grades and saving money from babysitting and modeling. Now, it was finally upon her—a new stage of life. Yet her anticipation was tinged with sadness. She and Jamie would have less time together with college starting for both of them. Jamie would commute to Fordham during the week, and with his new part-time job at the grocery store on Saturdays, how would he find time for her? And then there were the demands of their coursework. Katie knew how long hours of study were needed to keep her grades up.

A double clap echoed through the air, followed by, "That's it, ladies." It was four-thirty. Finally, the best part of her day was about to begin. In unison, she and the two other girls in her window smiled at the crowd and waved goodbye, causing a few onlookers to jump and then laugh.

She stepped down from the storefront window using the movable stairs. Famished and thirsty, she returned to the dressing area. As she waited for Nellie, Katie studied herself in the long mirror, admiring the dress she had just modeled, fantasizing about wearing it on her date with Jamie tonight.

"That's such a cute outfit on you, especially with your red hair," Nellie said as she unzipped the crepe de chine A-line dress.

The gray tunic top had a black sailor-style scarf looped below the scoop neckline. The bodice met the black skirt at her hipline, the skirt falling just below her knees. The two pieces came together in a repeating triangular pattern that reminded Katie of eight jack-o-lantern teeth. Its three-quarter-length cuffed sleeves were sheer. But it wasn't just the dress—everything had been perfectly coordinated: gray ankle-strap heels, a gray purse, and a gray bucket hat, each with contrasting black bands.

Katie glanced at the price tag: $22.95—tucked out of view for the show. That was about what Eileen earned in a week and more than ten times what Katie had made for her six hours today at thirty-five cents an hour. Everything, including the black lace gloves she carefully removed finger by finger, would return to the sales floor for some lucky customer to purchase.

"I really love it too," Katie said wistfully, imagining Jamie's admiring gaze. Everything had changed since she met Jamie Murphy. Clothing, which had meant little to her before, now carried a new importance. She wanted Jamie to be as proud to be seen with her as she was to be with him.

"Oh well, for someone else." Katie shrugged and slipped back into the same clothes she'd worn on the train ride that morning with Eileen—a serviceable poplin day dress, sensible walking shoes, and a tunic-length sweater, all from the Sears catalog. The eye makeup, rouge, and lipstick from the show still adorned her face. Using her fingers as a comb, she lifted and smoothed the waves in her hair. She wasn't sure if Jamie would like her cosmetically accentuated look, but she would soon find out.

Grabbing her purse, Katie headed for the perfume counter, where she and Jamie had agreed to meet. "If you have any change in plans," she'd told him on the phone last night, "don't worry. I'll walk to the shop where Eileen works and ride the train home with her."

Still, she prayed that Jamie wouldn't decide he wanted someone better—someone more refined, classier. If he ever saw the dump she grew up in, or worse, met Da, he might not even give her the time of day. A nagging voice in the back of her mind insisted that someone like Jamie couldn't really love someone like her. That was why she always gave him an "out." But the evidence said otherwise. Jamie Murphy seemed as daft about her as she was about him.

The click of her heels echoed on the tiled floor as she hurried to the perfume counter, hoping to beat Jamie there. Like most large department stores, Macy's had strategically placed the counter near the front door to mask the street's smells. Now, the mingling of exotic fragrances smothered the scent of car exhaust.

Katie found the tester for Chanel No. 5 just as a saleswoman approached.

"*Bon choix.* Chanel No. 5 is one of our most *populaires* fragrances," the clerk said, using the glass stopper to daub a tiny bit of the golden liquid on Katie's wrists. "It takes about five minutes for the diverse notes to emerge. The *parfum* smells slightly *différent* on each person."

Katie waved her arms to dry the perfume. Suddenly, she felt something akin to a gentle breeze—as if a warm but insistent breath caressed the back of her neck.

"You already smell yummy enough," Jamie whispered in her ear, melting her heart like butter under a noonday sun.

Her face flushed with excitement at the sound of Jamie's voice. He wrapped his arms loosely around her waist, his warmth spreading through her as she leaned back into his embrace.

"Thank you," Katie said to the saleswoman, who seemed to enjoy the scene unfolding in front of her.

"*Je vous en prie*," the saleswoman said with a nod. *You're welcome.* "*La joie du jeune amour.*" *The joy of young love.*

Katie turned to face Jamie, her wide smile returning his own, made even more endearing by his dimples. Indeed, the joy of young love floated in the air like a sweet, delicate fragrance.

"Do you mind if we run up to the second floor to get something to eat and drink before the picture show starts?" Katie asked.

"That's perfect. Unfortunately, I had to get tickets for the six-thirty show; the later one was sold out. We don't have time for a fancy dinner, and I don't have the budget as a poor college student," he said, winking as he pulled his front trouser pockets inside out, making Katie laugh.

"Just teasing, Katie. I've got everything covered," he added, patting the wallet in the back pocket of his slacks. "If Macy's restaurant is already closed, we should be able to find something in the twelve blocks between here and the Embassy Theatre."

"By the way, you looked ravishing in that last gray and black outfit."

"How long were you out there watching me?"

"Long enough to know I'm the luckiest man in New York."

"When I graduate from college and get a decent job, that dress will be your reward for putting up with me." Jamie winked at her. That wink—so dangerous—it would be the end of her. She was a goner.

"And what makes you think I'll still be interested in you in two years, Jamie Murphy?"

"Because, Kathleen Mary Houlihan, we were made for each other."

EIGHT

Late March 1928

Katie waited to use the telephone in the lobby of Sacre Coeur Hall—a donated, one-time Victorian mansion. She lived in one of the two newer wings of Sacre Coeur that the college had added for first-year students in 1920. Though small, the spartan dorm room she shared with another studious young woman suited her perfectly, as did her roommate's introverted personality. Even in St. John's Hall, the brand-new dormitory, the individual dorm rooms were still without telephones. Regardless of class standing, all students had to live on campus unless their families resided in Tarrytown (and most did not).

Next in the queue, Katie toyed with a nickel, ready to feed the payphone. She shifted impatiently on an oak settee, watching the big hand of a nearby round-faced wall clock tick off the minutes; she'd been waiting seventeen minutes already. At freshman orientation, the young women had been instructed to limit their phone calls to ten minutes out of "charitable consideration for others" when there was a line.

As had become their routine, Katie called Jamie on Thursday evenings as close to seven-thirty as possible. Initially, he'd tried calling her at the payphone's number (Spring 4649) to solidify their weekend plans. However, due to the phone's high usage, he rarely got through. So, Katie now called him.

Spending time together was more complicated than Katie had imagined. While she and Jamie now lived in the same town, their time together was stretched thin. He commuted to the Fordham Bronx campus by train every weekday, an hour each way, and worked on

Saturdays at the Corner Grocery until six p.m. Plus, they both had demanding coursework.

She chided herself for not bringing her history textbook down to keep her company. Her last final exam for the quarter was tomorrow.

The settee, with its well-worn bench and vertical back slats, leaned against the wall just beyond the phone booth. Girls waiting in line readily overheard ongoing conversations emanating from the doorless phone booth. Katie suspected that the lack of privacy was intentional—meant to discourage long or inappropriate calls.

Marian Hall was the only other building on campus besides the two dormitories. It housed classrooms, administrative offices, living quarters for the religious sisters who operated and taught at the college, the Chapel of the Sacred Heart, and the refectory where the women ate their meals. Marian Hall was the heart of the campus.

The college had grown from a boarding and day school with six young girls in 1907 to a four-year high school with two additional post-high-school years in 1918, then to a provisional college in 1919, and finally to a fully accredited institution offering liberal arts baccalaureate degrees in 1924. Before the 19th Amendment granted women the right to vote, Marymount College offered classes to women in philosophy, history, modern languages, chemistry, political science, and law. The Tarrytown campus was home to the first of several Marymount colleges started by the Religious of the Sacred Heart of Mary (RSHM), a French order.

Katie stood, turning to read the framed, now-yellowed, eleven-year-old newspaper clipping that hung on the beige-plastered wall behind the settee. The advertisement for Marymount College had run in *The New York Sun* the same year that America entered The Great War.

> *The time has gone by when to be feminine meant to be helpless.*
> *The world has never needed womanly intelligence and sympathy*
> *so much as it does today.*
>
> *~Mother Marie Joseph Butler, RSHM*
> *Founder, Marymount College, Tarrytown*

Seven months ago, during freshman orientation, Katie heard Mother Butler, the president of Marymount, speak for the first time. She challenged the young women in ways Katie had never considered before. "My dream," the sixty-seven-year-old, charismatic Irish-born dynamo had said, "is to prepare you for leadership through education and equip you to create positive change in the world." Katie's own dreams suddenly felt minuscule compared to Mother Butler's vision.

Katie aimed to earn a two-year degree to teach in public schools—a path to independence and self-sufficiency. With marketable skills, Katie could always take care of herself no matter what the future held. She would never be a burden to anyone else, as she had been to Eileen. She could forget her tattered past and face the future with self-pride, confidence, and less anxiety.

Next to the framed advertisement, Katie studied the sepia-toned photograph of Father Jean Gailhac surrounded by six RSHM sisters. Fr. Gailhac had founded the order in 1849. The sisters on campus still wore the same black floor-length habits and veils with white coif, guimpe, and wimple.

Mother Butler told the incoming freshmen in her delightful French accent how Fr. Gailhac had a special ministry to the most destitute and marginalized women in Béziers, France. "He had come to understand that these poor, desperate women had turned to prostitution as the only means to support themselves and their children," she had said. "He also had a special ministry to orphans. Eventually, his ministry led him to start our order, the Religious of the Sacred Heart of Mary. We remain passionate and committed to women's education. Through education, women are empowered."

Would the young woman, tying up the only phone, ever finish her call? Didn't she understand they were supposed to limit their calls to ten minutes? Katie was losing her patience; Jamie was expecting her call.

She paced past the phone booth several times, ensuring the heels of her shoes clicked loudly on the black-and-white tiled floor. The brunette, her hair in a low chignon, faced the wall, not seeming to notice the show of impatience Katie enacted for her benefit.

Katie continued walking toward the mailroom, tucked in a recessed corner of the lobby. A half-wall and dark-stained oak countertop separated and secured the mailroom. Her eyes roamed to slot number thirty-seven—her mail cubby—one of many three-by-six-inch wooden slots. Each week, Katie looked forward to the short notes Jamie wrote her. While only half a page long, the half-dozen sentences kept her heart tightly tethered to him. Each ended with an *I love you, Jamie.*

Katie returned to the settee, her fingers fidgeting with the buttons on her blouse as she counted the square tiles on the path back. Every step felt like it stretched time.

Just then, another freshman exited the stairwell and sat down on the opposite end of the settee. Her shoulder-length, wavy blond hair bounced as she checked out the phone booth before sitting down next to Katie. Her finely tailored clothing and expensive shoes screamed refinement and money.

A bubble of envy percolated through Katie, fleeting but sharp. She glanced at the young woman's elegant outfit and manicured nails, knowing that world was out of reach for her, no matter how much she wished otherwise. But the feeling passed—she had her own treasure—now. Jamie.

"She's been on for a while," Katie said with a note of exasperation, giving a slight nod toward the phone booth. "Hopefully, she'll be off soon."

"Let's hope so," the blond woman sniffed.

Katie often noticed the young woman in the dorm and even shared a couple of classes with her. Her designer clothes, including several striking Coco Chanel outfits, commanded attention. Katie thought about introducing herself but held back. She was a common mutt seated next to a French poodle. Katie knew her place in the pecking order of the world of wealth and refinement—in the chicken coop.

Finally, the brunette gabber hung up. "Sorry the call lasted so long," she said, passing by Katie and the blond.

"My call will be short," Katie said as she rose and hurried to the booth.

Katie's heart soared like a bird taking flight as she dialed the Murphys' residence. She hoped Peggy wouldn't answer the phone. Calling Jamie felt so forward.

"Hello. Murphy residence."

"Hi, Annie. May I speak with Jamie?"

"Sure. I'll get him, Katie." Annie's voice clanged like a loud bell next to Katie's ear, making her flinch and pull the receiver away slightly. She pressed it back against her ear, bracing herself for more of Annie's hollering.

In the background, she heard Jamie's muffled voice. "I've got it, Annie. You can go now. C'mon, skedaddle now. Get."

After another couple of moments, Jamie spoke softly. "Is this the woman of my dreams?"

Katie closed her eyes and visualized his face. "I certainly hope so. Is this the man of my dreams?" she whispered, her pulse quickening at the sound of his voice.

"It'd better be. I can't wait to see you. A whole week off classes. I do have to work at the grocery, but that will seem like a vacation by comparison."

"My last exam is at one tomorrow," Katie said. "When do you finish up?"

"Ten, tomorrow. I'll be back in Tarrytown by the time you're done. I'll be in the lobby, waiting for you. Either with the car or walking."

Katie felt a surge of desire at his words. Although it had only been five days, it seemed like an eternity since she'd seen Jamie.

"I love you, Katie Houlihan, and I can't wait to get my arms around you."

"Same here, Jamie Murphy. Now go study hard." Then, cupping her hand around the phone's mouthpiece to cover it, she whispered, "And I'll try to concentrate on ancient history instead of imagining the feel of your arms around me—making modern history."

~*~

Jamie's steps quickened with excitement as he practically ran to the Harlem Line platform behind the university, eager to head home. The hypnotic thrumming of the steel wheels might have lulled him to sleep, his body finally feeling the weight of exhaustion from a long quarter had it been any other day.

Well past Yonkers, his view from the passenger car window shifted from urban to pastoral. The train tracks hugged the Hudson River to the west and the undulating hills of Westchester County to the east, sprinkled with farmland. Fields of winter wheat, now in their tillering phase, sprouted tufts of green crowning brown furrows. Occasionally, large estates owned by the wealthy popped into view.

In the distance, spring exhibited her artistry in riots of color and form. Wild dogwoods unfurled their four-petaled flowers in rosy pinks and snowy whites. Redbud trees, still absent their leaves, stood regally adorned with their tiny, orchid-like blossoms in fuchsia pinks. The earth had yawned awake from its winter sleep, heralding new beginnings and the kiss of promises to come.

Jamie reached into his coat pocket. His fingers closed around the small, blue velveteen ring box. A steady determination settled over him as he thought about what it represented. He could hardly wait to see Katie.

~*~

Jamie waited in the lobby of Sacre Coeur, facing the main entryway. Long sidelight windows on each side of the door afforded him a view of the porch. Over the door hung a crucifix, and below it, a parchment scroll in a narrow shadow box read *Ut Vitam Habeant.* "That They May Have Life," Jamie translated automatically. After his seminary years, reading Latin was second nature to him.

Several austere sofas and armchairs formed a seating area to the left of the main entry. Jamie had tried them all in the last half-hour, a futile effort to expend nervous energy. He stood and stretched again, making a visual check to the mailroom behind. *Good,* he thought. *Sister Louise is still there. Surely, she'll remember what I've asked her to do.* He sat back down and felt inside his coat pocket once again. *Everything's ready; now I just need Katie.*

The instant Katie appeared on the porch of Sacre Coeur, Jamie shot up from the oak spindle-back chair. She rushed through the door straight into his open arms. The women nearby paused their conversation, their smiles catching the joy radiating from Katie and Jamie.

"Ugh, glad that's over." Katie slumped her shoulders, exhaling dramatically like a deflating balloon. "A whole week off—I need it!"

"How was it?" Jamie's eyes devoured Katie, head to toe, settling back on her lips. He barely registered her comments on her history exam; his thoughts were elsewhere.

"Let's just say... it's over. All essay questions. My hand cramped up by the end."

Jamie took her right hand in his and massaged it gently with his thumbs. Without breaking eye contact, he brought the palm of her hand to his mouth and kissed it. "Better now?"

"Much better." Katie felt her body tingle. "I need to run upstairs to grab a few things. I'll be right back down."

"Okay, I'll be here. Check your mailbox on your way upstairs," he called after her, his gaze following her as she moved. "Katie, we'll be outside for a good bit and walking, too."

"Thanks for the warning," she hollered back, walking backward toward the mailroom and stairs, blowing him a kiss as she went.

From where he stood, Jamie kept an eye on Sister Louise Marie at the mailroom counter as Katie closed the distance. He'd recruited the ruddy-faced, jolly sister for his plan earlier that day.

Katie walked up to the counter. He watched as Sister Louise greeted her warmly, her gestures animated as they appeared to exchange words. A flicker of electric excitement coursed through him, knowing what was about to happen now—and later.

Sister Louise reached beneath the counter and pulled out a white florist box tied with a red ribbon, just as he'd arranged. He imagined Katie's surprise as she accepted the box. Her back was to him now. He pictured her removing the tiny envelope tucked beneath the ribbon, her fingers lingering over his note—*My love for you will bloom forever.* He could almost feel the moment—the scent of roses reaching Katie—a sensual prelude to what was to come.

~*~

Katie nestled close to Jamie, careful not to interfere with the stick shift. Though she wasn't a fanatic about cars like Thomas and Chuck, she preferred the Murphys' new Superior K Touring over the old crank-start farm truck. Just before the fall chill settled over the Hudson Valley last year, Peggy had finally traded in the old truck for a sleek cobalt blue Chevy sedan.

"I love the corsage," Katie said, inhaling its heady fragrance and touching the velvety petals of the spray of red rosebuds gracing her petite left wrist.

"Is there some special occasion that I don't know about?" She counted out the months since their first meeting in August on her fingers. "Our seven-month anniversary of meeting?"

"We're a few days short of that," Jamie replied, his smile teasing but holding back something else.

"My birthday isn't until next month." She placed her chin in her hand, her brows raised in curiosity. "I give up."

"You'll just have to wait and see."

Katie's mind whirled. What could it be? She wasn't sure what Jamie had planned, but the corsage and the picnic basket in the back seat hinted at something special. After seven months of courting, she had learned that Jamie Murphy delighted in surprising her. The idea of a picnic felt romantic, but there was something more behind his quiet excitement.

The car's electric ignition started with a happy rumble. Before shifting into drive, Jamie leaned over and kissed her softly, and then, with more urgency. Katie responded, her heart racing, dizzy with the feel of him. In these moments, nothing else existed—Jamie was her whole world. She felt herself melt into him, her sense of self dissolving in the depth of her love for him.

As they rode north on Broadway, the silence between them felt comfortable, like an old married couple who didn't need words to communicate. Katie glanced out the window, noticing the familiar sight of the Old Dutch Reformed Church. Its fieldstone exterior hadn't changed since its construction at the end of the 16th century, a reminder of the timelessness around her. Jamie turned left onto Palmer Avenue, and as they drove over a bridge, she glanced down at the train tracks below.

The breeze off the river nudged the clouds eastward as the day warmed, leaving the land to bask under a clear sky and the sun's gentle warmth.

"We're going to that new park beyond the lighthouse, aren't we?" Katie asked, already knowing the answer but enjoying the thought of it.

"Yes, Kingsland Point." Jamie said, smiling at her.

Katie loved the idea. The eighteen-acre park had become one of her favorite places. Situated on the eastern shore of the Hudson River, at the mouth of the Pocantico River, Kingsland Point was a ten-minute drive from Marymount College or a picturesque, forty-five-minute walk approaching from the south along the river's edge, passing by the red and white lighthouse at the halfway mark.

As the car approached the park, the crunch of gravel under the tires signaled their arrival. "Let's take a walk first. We can come back for the blanket and basket," Jamie said, taking her hand.

They walked along a path that followed the natural coastline. Between them and the river stood a three-foot stone wall. They strolled hand in hand until they reached the park's southwestern edge, which presented an unobstructed view of the lighthouse yet was sheltered from prying eyes.

She loved this peacefulness, this quiet intimacy with Jamie.

Everything felt right.

Jamie turned toward Katie and asked, "Do you love me?" His voice was soft but serious, "If so, I need to hear it."

Katie's heart pounded in her chest. Of course, she loved him. How could he doubt her? But his question, so direct, startled her. She had never said the words outright. She always deflected with a "Me too" or "Same," afraid of the vulnerability those words carried.

Jamie's gaze was steady, and Katie felt the sting of tears in her eyes. She tried to blink them away, but they spilled over, blurring her vision like raindrops on a windowpane.

"Jamie, please forgive me. I've been afraid to say it... even though I do. Desperately so."

"Why are you afraid, Katie?" Jamie's hand gently touched her face, his tenderness calming her. "I want to spend my whole life with you. I want to marry you, make a life with you."

Katie's tears fell harder now, her emotions a tangled mess. Her body ached with the intensity of her love for him. She wanted everything he offered—marriage, a future—but the fear of losing herself, of giving up her independence, gnawed at her.

"Those are the things I want, too! A million times over! But how does my life make sense if I admit how deeply I love you?"

"Why wouldn't your life make sense? Help me understand."

"My goal, ever since I can remember, has been to take care of myself. It's been why I've saved every dime and why I'm a student at Marymount. Men can always dig ditches, but what I have is my mind, not muscles, to earn a decent living. No school board will hire me unless I'm single, and if I get married, I'll lose my job.

"I never imagined falling in love would force me to choose between you and my education—essentially, between you and myself."

"Oh, my sweet Katie," Jamie said, embracing her softly. He gently lifted her chin and gazed into her glistening blue eyes. "Is it so crucial to earn your credentials to teach?"

"Not teaching, exactly, but having a way to support myself and not be a burden on anyone, like..." Tears trickled down her cheeks as she choked out her words, "...like I've been to Eileen ever since the day I was born."

Jamie removed a white handkerchief from the back pocket of his slacks and wiped her tears. "You are a precious gift to me. You could never be a burden. Please, believe me."

He led her to a metal park bench formed by black-enameled arabesque flourishes. They sat beneath the gnarly branches of a weeping willow, its emerging chartreuse leaves hanging like tiny green tears.

"Katie, talk to me."

Oh, if only I could tell you everything, Jamie. But then you wouldn't want me.

Katie felt like a spray-drenched, listing sloop tossed about on a stormy sea of emotions. She wanted a life with Jamie so badly that her body ached when they were apart, yet she feared both rejection and losing control over her life if she professed her love for him.

"At Marymount, all these highly accomplished women challenge me to make the world a better place and develop my full potential. But, Jamie, all I think about is being married to you."

A sense of failure washed over Katie, as if she had climbed a mountain only to realize, just steps from the summit, that it had all been a mistake—that she wasn't meant to climb mountains after all.

"Love has a way of reshaping one's priorities; my mother told me that once. Loving you has made me a better person. I believe that together, we can be the best versions of ourselves," Jamie said.

"I'm not sure I'm enough for you."

"Katie-love, look at me. Not only are you enough for me—you are everything that I desire, have hoped for, and prayed for."

I'm so unworthy of this man, Katie thought, feeling her heart swell with an overwhelming love that almost hurt.

Jamie reached into his pocket and, taking out the small box, removed the white-gold engagement ring. The solitaire wasn't a single diamond but five small diamonds centered around a sixth, forming a flower-like cluster.

"Kathleen Mary Houlihan, will you marry me?"

Katie lifted her chin, tears gathering in her eyes. "Seriously?" she asked, wiping her nose with her hand and sniffing. Her countenance transformed from dusk to sunrise, her smile a sudden beam of sunlight.

"I was hoping for a 'yes,'" Jamie said with a measured grin.

How could she refuse him? Without him, her listing sloop would have no mooring, no shelter from the stormy seas.

"Yes, of course, I'll marry you!"

Jamie slid the ring onto Katie's finger.

"Oh, my goodness, how could you afford this? It's exquisite!"

"Big diamonds are the expensive ones, not these small ones. Why do you think I've been working at the grocery store?"

"But how can we marry? We're both in college. We have no money."

"Well, Katie-love, your man has a plan."

NINE

The Next Day

“It's your decision, Jamie, but does getting married this summer really make sense? Neither you nor Katie have finished college,” his mother said, leaning against the kitchen sink. Mom kept her expression calm, though Jamie detected the worry behind her faint smile.

Jamie stood nearby, still in his church clothes, a cup of coffee in hand. The family had finished breakfast, and now it was just the two of them. Annie was at a friend's house; Robert and Thomas were upstairs. Katie hadn't joined them for Mass this morning. She had gone with Eileen and Frankie, and he would meet her at their place for lunch later.

“It depends on how you look at it, Mom. Financially, it makes sense. Katie doesn't have enough money for her tuition plus room and board for her last year. She could live here with us in Tarrytown if we were married—if you were agreeable, of course.

“This year, her costs for room and board were \$380, books \$30, and tuition was \$400. She's saved up half of what she needs for her second year, but if room and board go away, everything's Jake.”

“I suppose having her share a room with Annie is off the table? That solves the financial issue without marriage.”

“No doubt, Annie would think that's a grand idea, but it would be torture for Katie and me. I'm ready to marry Katie,” Jamie said with firm conviction.

“Naturally, you are both welcome to live here. But you won't have much privacy. And what if Katie gets pregnant?”

"Katie is open to children; we both are. Even if they come fast and furious, we'd rather be together than apart." Jamie flashed a grin. "You're not opposed to being a grandma, are you?"

"No, you know I enjoy being a grandmother. But true love stands the test of time, and marriage is a big responsibility. Are you sure you want to saddle yourself with that right now?"

"Yes, I do. Being married to Katie is more important than finishing college—but I plan to do that, too."

Mom hesitated for a moment, then spoke, almost as if convincing herself as much as Jamie. "You know, when I was your age, my father didn't think John was good enough for me. I was nearly twenty-five, and still, he worried. But in the end, he gave his blessing, and I never regretted marrying your father for a second." She smiled, the memories softening her face. "Katie's a wonderful young woman, and seeing how happy she makes you... well, that's all I need to know. I've never seen you this happy."

"Katie makes me happier than I ever dreamed possible. I'm a total goner, Mom—she's the one."

"If you're sure, then you have my blessing. You two may as well live here until you finish college. You haven't even been home from the seminary for ten months; I'm not ready to be rid of you yet."

His mother turned to the sink, wetting a dishcloth to wipe the crumbs from the table. Jamie thought he saw her lips quiver—just for a moment. She seemed to be holding something back, maybe tears. She hesitated, and Jamie wondered if she was thinking of that old Shakespeare line she liked to quote about love being blind.

"Jimmy will be back from Rome at the end of June," his mother said. "I know he'd love to marry you two."

"That's my plan. I intend to write to Unc, informing him of my engagement and upcoming wedding as soon as the details are finalized."

She tossed the dishcloth aside, giving up on cleaning the table. "Come here, you crazy kid," she said with a smile. His mother pulled Jamie into a hug, but before she could finish, he lifted her off the ground, twirling her around. She let out a laugh, her mock protests drowned by their shared laughter.

As he set his mother down, she wiped the tears from her face. "Congratulations, son. Katie is a lovely young woman. May you both find great happiness together."

~*~

June 25, 1928 (Three months later)

Katie knew she should be elated. The day was perfect—clear skies, a gentle breeze carrying the sweet scent of linden trees in full bloom. Birds sang from the branches as sunlight danced on the heart-shaped leaves and delicate yellow-white flowers in the churchyard of White Plains' oldest Catholic church.

Katie's sister, Eileen, cracked open the storage room door just off the vestibule and squeezed into the cramped space.

"Ready? Everyone's here. We just need the bride," Eileen, the matron of honor, said with near-giddy excitement. She wore a drop-waist dress of her own design in lavender georgette, paired with a matching minimalist turban-style hat.

Katie jumped, startled out of her thoughts. She had been absentmindedly chewing her thumbnail down to the quick when Eileen's voice broke through.

"Yes! It can't happen soon enough." Katie's hand flew back to her mouth, finishing the last of her pre-nuptial manicure.

"Stop it! You'll make your fingers bleed." Her sister said, and in a maternal gesture, guided Katie's hand down from her mouth, squeezing it affectionately. "Some things never change. I'd have imagined you'd outgrown that nasty habit by age twenty!"

"I'm waiting until I'm twenty-one to stop," Katie replied, feigning offense.

With a teasing shake of her head, her sister tapped one of Katie's hands with a pair of lacy white gloves. "Here, put these on. It's time to make your grand entrance. Let's get your veil on."

Eileen reached for the tiny hat with its attached cage veil from the nearby table, the only piece of furniture not piled high with hymnals and boxes.

She secured the headpiece slightly off to one side on Katie's head, as was the fashion, and clipped it into Katie's short, wavy hair—the color of sun-ripened apricots. Then, she arranged the veil's tulle fabric to fall just below Katie's lips. A few loops of satin ribbon and a rhinestone brooch artfully anchored a profusion of small white feathers, framing Katie's heart-shaped face.

"You're simply beautiful," her sister clucked, like a mother hen. She stepped back to admire Katie and the hat she had crafted just for this occasion.

Katie smoothed the back of her chemise-style ecru velveteen dress, overlaid with off-white gossamer silk, which fell just below her knees. The dress had been a generous gift, costing several months of her sister's wages.

Her hand inched to her lower abdomen, feeling for what she hoped was an inconspicuous curve. The style of her dress helped conceal her thickening waist and fuller breasts. Jamie hadn't noticed the small changes in her body—she'd made sure of that.

They hadn't meant for things to go so far that evening after his proposal—the one and only time. They had promised each other it wouldn't happen again. And it hadn't. She should have resisted, but it had felt so right. She blamed herself, and Jamie blamed himself.

Guilt and a prompt confession had kept Katie from breaking their promise. The old Irish priest had told her, "Our feelings are excellent companions but poor guides." She had been lucky—her nausea had only dulled her appetite, never progressing to the telltale vomiting that would have alerted the girls in the dormitory bathroom.

Jamie still didn't know. She had been too afraid to tell him, and now, she wondered if that had been a mistake. By the time she knew for sure, their wedding plans were already made. How would it have changed things, anyway?

If only Jamie hadn't insisted on waiting for his uncle to return from his sabbatical in Rome. They could have married two months ago before she knew for sure. But even that made no sense—they were both still in school. She caught herself daydreaming of ways to mask the effects of something that never should have happened.

Finally, she had told her sister, carefully leaving out the part about Jamie still not knowing. She hadn't *exactly* lied to him—he just hadn't asked.

Her sister held up a mirror so Katie could see herself in the hat and veil. "What do you think? Should I angle it a bit more?"

"No, no, it's perfect. How can I ever thank you for everything you've done, Eileen? You're the best big sister in the whole wide world." Katie's blue eyes brimmed with tears of gratitude. "I hope you're not ashamed of me."

"Now you listen to me, Kathleen Mary Houlihan. Stop talking nonsense—this should be the happiest day of your life. Whether this baby comes after five months of marriage, nine months, or even five years, a baby and a husband who loves you to the moon and back are always a blessing," her sister said, pulling Katie into a tight embrace.

"The Murphys are good people. And besides, what's not to love?" Her sister's words soothed Katie but also deepened her guilt. Eileen, who'd been married for over six years, had never been able to conceive.

The two sisters exited the storage room and joined Eileen's husband. Frankie waited in the narthex, hands clasped behind his back, ready to walk Katie down the aisle. He wolf-whistled as Katie and Eileen approached. "*Bellissima!* A feast for sore eyes." Winking at Eileen, he pulled a cascading bouquet of coral-orange and lavender roses, white daisies, and green bells of Ireland from behind his back, presenting them to Katie.

Katie reached for the flowers, overcome with emotion, her eyes once again bleary. "This is too much, Frankie."

"Nothing is too good for my favorite *sorellina*." With outstretched arms, Frankie admired Katie cradling her bridal bouquet like a priceless work of art. Frankie kissed his fingertips with a flourish, then extended his hand outward in a sweeping motion. "*Perfetta!*"

"Thank you, Frankie," Katie said, swatting at her tears. She was grateful Frankie was walking her down the aisle instead of Da, who would have surely made a fool of both of them. She hoped for a marriage as perfect as Eileen and Frankie's, even though she already felt she had messed things up.

On cue, Katie stood at the back of the church, positioning herself to walk down the aisle. She held onto Frankie's proffered arm and clutched her cascading bouquet. As the organist began the bridal march, all heads turned toward Katie.

A frisson of fear shot through her at the thought of becoming a wife, a mother, and part of the Murphy picture-postcard family. Katie pushed the fear aside, pulling her shoulders back. She flashed her best smile at Jamie and imagined herself floating down the aisle like a dandelion's fuzzy seed on the breeze.

As Katie neared the altar, she stopped suddenly, staring at the empty pew on the left-hand side, one row back from where the Caruso family sat.

Later, Jamie would ask her about the awkward moment she paused on the way down the aisle. "Were you having misgivings, Katie?" he'd ask. She'd answer, "No, no, Jamie. I just felt light-headed."

She'd had no misgivings, just a moment of confusion—disoriented by the sound of breaking glass and sudden darkness. Then Da appeared, sitting in the pew. He glared at her, shaking his head in shame. Or was it anger? Maybe both.

Frankie whispered, "*Sorellina,*" and then, poof, Da was gone—the pew empty once more. Katie snapped back to the present, the center of attention at her wedding. Her alabaster skin flushed as she continued down the aisle.

She was determined to make this the best day of her life. Nothing would spoil this precious day, not even the ghost of Da showing up— uninvited. Yet it had seemed so real.

~*~

Jamie was grateful to his new sister-in-law, Eileen, and her husband, Frankie, for hosting the reception at their White Plains home for the small group who attended the wedding. In the dining room, a three-tiered white cake with buttercream frosting took center stage on the oblong table draped in a white tablecloth. Nearby, dishes of butter mints and mixed nuts added to the spread. Eileen had borrowed a crystal bowl for the fruity virgin punch, and a silver serving set from Frankie's mother held the coffee, cream, and sugar.

Frankie had arranged the six dining chairs between the dining and living rooms, away from the table, providing extra seating options for the guests. However, most guests preferred to stand around chatting, offering their best wishes, and gushing about what a handsome couple Katie and Jamie made.

Jamie agreed wholeheartedly as Katie's soft laughter drew his gaze. She looked especially beautiful today. He couldn't quite put his finger on it, but she almost seemed to glow. The reception was lovely, but punch, cake, and nuts could only go so far—all Jamie wanted was to be alone with his wife. A sense of anticipation swelled within him.

Once the guests had left—including the Murphy clan, Fr. Jim Gleason, Frankie's extended family, Jan de Vries and his family, and Katie's roommate from Marymount—Frankie dropped Jamie and Katie off at the Ferris Ave train station. After an hour's ride south on the Harlem Railway Line, the couple disembarked at Grand Central Station.

Jamie carried their two small overnight bags the few blocks along Fifth Avenue to 33rd Street. Most guests of the Waldorf-Astoria Hotel did not arrive on foot, carrying their own bags. But if the doorman, dressed in his smart black suit, billed cap, and white gloves, was scandalized by the plebeian scene, he gave no indication. Here, they would stay for two nights, a stark contrast to their new life in Tarrytown: sharing a home with four others—Mom, Thomas, Annie, and Robert—and a flock of chickens roosting in the backyard coop.

Exiting the elevator, the bellhop placed their two overnight bags just inside the door and handed Jamie a brass skeleton key with 612 stamped on the bow. The bellhop's attire, though unusual, matched the opulent Art Deco style of the hotel. His black, long-sleeved jacket, fastened with a single closure at the neck, was cut in an inverted V pattern, revealing a white vest beneath. Gold trim, matching the detailing on his epaulets, ran down the leg of his pants and encircled the sleeves of his jacket.

Jamie discreetly tipped the bellhop, a man not much older than himself, with protruding ears and dark, friendly eyes. "Thank you," the man replied, closing his hand around the silver half-dollar piece.

"Dial zero to let the front desk know if you need anything," the bellhop said, pointing to the cream-colored telephone on an antique Louis XV writing desk. The phone was no less a piece of art, with its tall, swan-like neck and top-mounted mouthpiece shaped like a stylized daffodil. A bell-shaped earpiece hung off a golden hook midway down the neck, and a newfangled rotary dial graced the rounded, elongated base.

"Congratulations, Mr. and Mrs. Murphy," he said with a smile, quick to take his leave.

"Thank you," Katie and Jamie replied together.

Jamie picked Katie up, carried her inside the hotel room, and closed the door with his foot.

Little did Jamie notice the champagne sitting on the bedside table, cooling in a silver bucket with a note from Frankie and Eileen. He felt, rather than consciously perceived, the elegance of the room—its classic Aubusson rug, brass headboard, hanging chandeliers, European antique furniture, coffered ceiling with pink roses and blue ribbons painted around the edges above the crown molding, velveteen-flocked burgundy wallpaper, and crystal wall sconces etched with tiny flowers.

Finally, he was free to love Katie in all the ways that he so desired from this day forward. And they began undressing one another with the uninhibited, passionate hunger of young lovers.

~*~

Katie propped her head up with her hand and forearm, resting on one elbow. Her free hand gently stroked Jamie's face as she admired his long, dark lashes and the soft curls of his hair, still damp from the evening's warmth and the energy of their lovemaking. His breathing was barely discernible.

"So much better than the back seat of a car," Katie whispered, her voice soft as the sun's last light set their bodies aglow. The lacey, floor-length curtains, drawn over the west-facing, nearly floor-to-ceiling windows, cast a textured play of shadows on the wall opposite. Jamie lay on his back, eyes closed.

Jamie opened one eye in her direction, a faint smile tugging at his lips. "So much better now that we are married. All the pleasure and none of the guilt."

"Agreed," Katie said, her smile warm but burdened. She knew that she had to tell Jamie about the baby, but she didn't want to spoil the moment. But when would be the right time? How would she know? She needed a sign. *Please, God help me know*, she prayed silently.

"I love you, Mrs. Murphy," he said, rolling onto his side and reaching for her again.

"And I love you, Mr. Murphy." Once Katie's emotional spillway had been breached and the dam had thunderously burst, she found it hard not to tell Jamie constantly how much she loved and adored him.

"The face of an angel and the body of a goddess," he murmured, his hand tracing the curves of her torso as she lay on her side, facing him. "A perfect figure eight."

And there it was. She drew a deep breath—the moment had arrived.

"Enjoy it while you can," she said. "My body is going to change. We're having a baby." Her worry over the secret she had kept for the past six weeks condensed into a single tear that glided down her cheek.

"Yes, of course, we'll have babies. Someday."

"That someday is upon us, Jamie. About six months from now."

Her words hung in the air for a moment, her heart pounding.

"You mean that one time? But I didn't even…"

"Well, apparently you did… because I'm carrying our child." Now, that single tear became a waterfall.

Jamie's half-lidded eyes opened widely. "Why didn't you tell me?"

Katie couldn't quite decipher the emotions in his voice—was it confusion, concern, joy, or anger?

"I didn't want to tell you because I didn't want you to feel that you had to marry me," she choked out.

"But I'd already asked you to marry me. It wouldn't have changed anything."

"I know, but you might have changed your mind. I couldn't be sure."

"Oh, Katie-love. You didn't have to go through this alone."

"I didn't completely. I told my sister when I missed my second monthly. She insisted I go to the doctor, who confirmed the pregnancy six weeks ago."

"Are you okay?"

"I'm fine. I've lost some weight because food hasn't been my best friend lately."

Jamie sat up on the edge of the bed, facing away from Katie, running a hand through his hair.

Katie moved to his side and sat beside him, pulling the tangled bedsheet around her. Worry and shame spread over her like warm molasses.

"Are you angry with me?" Katie asked.

"I'm angry with myself. I should never have put us in this situation. I knew it was wrong." He wrapped an arm around her. "You don't have to hide anything from me. We're an us now."

Katie started sobbing into the sheet. It wasn't because her time at Marymount would end or because of the baby, although she knew nothing about babies. She cried because she had disappointed Jamie, her failure etched in his hunched shoulders and tightly pressed lips.

"Are you upset about the baby, Jamie? Because I'm not. I love our baby already."

"No, Katie, love makes babies. And obviously, we make them pretty easily." He smiled and shook his head, his facial expression softening. "It's just…"

"Just what?" she asked. Her heart fluttered like a hummingbird trapped in her chest.

"I'll need to let Mom and Uncle Jim know. I don't want them to think that I hid the pregnancy from them."

"Do we have to tell them?"

"Yes, Katie. Absolutely. With the baby coming, Mom may want to reconsider the living arrangements. Although, I think it won't take her long to warm up to the idea of a grandbaby in the house."

"Well, then, we'll tell them together since I'm the one who kept the pregnancy from you. I can't have you taking the blame for not telling them."

Jamie exhaled loudly. "I have to think this over."

"Can you forgive me?" she asked, fiddling with the wedding band beneath her engagement ring.

"Done. That's easier than forgiving myself. Can you forgive me?"

"Of course, Jamie."

"We'll not let this ruin our honeymoon or life together. All babies are a gift from God. We just have a head start, Katie."

TEN

Katie didn't say much as she and Jamie rode the train back to Tarrytown after their two-night stay at the Waldorf-Astoria. Her mind raced like a thoroughbred, imagining the worst possible outcomes when Jamie told his mother she was pregnant. Together, they walked the same ten-minute route from the train station at 1 Depot Plaza to the house on Elizabeth Street that Jamie took each weekday when commuting to and from Fordham.

As they turned from John Street onto Elizabeth, Katie's head began pounding. Thoughts of Peggy's judgment—and really that of the whole Murphy family—pressed upon her. She quietly prayed that all would go well and that her mother-in-law would still look upon her favorably.

"Don't fret, Katie. Everything'll be okay in the long run, even if there are some initial bumps," Jamie said as if sensing her distress. "No pun intended." He winked at her and patted her abdomen. She couldn't help but return his broad, dimple-laden smile.

Red and purple petunias, yellow snapdragons, and white daisies bordered the front of the house, welcoming the couple home. Jamie opened the screen door for his wife and set their two bags on the porch. The forest green front door was wide open. Jamie swept Katie up in his arms, kissed the tip of her nose, and carried her over the threshold into the reception hall.

Jamie placed Katie on the parquet flooring as Peggy appeared on the second-floor staircase landing.

Peggy. Katie's heart clenched. *Will she look at me the same way once she knows about the baby? Will she reject me, after all?*

"Welcome home, you two lovebirds," she said, continuing down the stairs and into the reception hall. "How was the Waldorf-Astoria?"

"It was great," Jamie said, pulling Peggy into a one-arm hug and kissing her cheek.

"Our home is your home now," Peggy said, drawing Katie into a three-way hug.

"Thank you, Mrs. Murphy."

"Katie, you are part of the family. No need for formalities—Peggy is fine, or Mom would be lovely someday when it feels right." Peggy's warm, inviting smile did not insist; it simply extended an offer. Katie released a soft sigh, trying to quell her anxiety and relax a bit.

Mom would be lovely, Katie thought. After Jamie had proposed, Katie had teased him that she would have married him solely to have Peggy as her mother-in-law. Perhaps it wasn't true, but it could have been. She loved mother and son dearly and hoped Peggy would still accept her once she learned about the baby.

"Where's everybody?" Jamie asked.

"Out and about. Too gorgeous a day to be young and inside," she replied. "Even if it's only to hang out laundry, which I'm about to do."

"Can the laundry wait for a few minutes? Katie and I need to talk to you about something important."

"Of course." Peggy's eyes traveled from Jamie's face to Katie's as Katie reached for Jamie's hand.

"Do you mind if we go to your room upstairs to talk? I don't want the kids walking in on us," Jamie added.

"Let's go," Peggy replied.

The newlyweds followed Peggy upstairs to the largest bedroom in the house. Once everyone entered the cheerful yellow room, Jamie closed the door behind them.

He moved the T-backed walnut desk chair from the secretary desk to face the end of the double bed, where Katie sat, chewing her fingernails.

"Here, Mom, please sit," Jamie said, holding the back of the chair as Peggy sat down. Jamie then joined Katie, taking her hand in his.

Jamie explained to his mother that Katie was pregnant, three months along. He had first learned of the pregnancy when Katie told him at the hotel, having found out six weeks before. And, yes, they were sure of the date—it only happened once.

He took complete responsibility for the lapse in judgment and apologized for the shame that his actions would bring upon the family, especially to his mother.

Katie felt that Jamie shouldn't be taking all the blame. Guilt, gratitude, and awe coursed through her as she watched her husband for any hint of regret that he had married her. But she saw none. Instead, as he spoke, he clutched her hand tighter. Katie interpreted this as reassurance of his love, which she needed desperately at this very moment.

Peggy's face was without expression during the telling, her eyes fixed on Jamie until Katie interrupted.

"Mrs. Murphy—I mean, Peggy—I didn't want Jamie to feel like he had to marry me. I realize now that I should have told him. Truly, he wasn't hiding my pregnancy; he didn't know. Please don't be angry with him, be angry with *me*."

Katie held her breath, praying for some sign of acceptance from Jamie's mother.

Peggy sighed. "I'm not angry with you or Jamie. While having a child right away is not the easiest way to start a marriage, I don't doubt you two will make your marriage work. And, clearly," she cleared her throat, "your love is fruitful. Shall we call this an early Irish blessing?"

"Thanks, Mom. Katie and I needed to hear that." Katie noticed a subtle shift in Jamie's posture as he exhaled deeply. She realized then that he'd been more nervous than she'd thought.

"We'd like to remodel the attic into a bedroom and nursery if you're agreeable. Katie has offered her remaining college funds for that," Jamie said.

Katie noticed a slight furrow in Peggy's brow. "Are you sure about depleting your college funds, dear?"

"Yes, I am. Jamie has asked me the same thing many times over the last day and a half. College was the way to create security for myself as a single woman. I didn't want to depend on Eileen and Frankie forever. I had no idea I would meet Jamie, that I could ever love anyone as much as I do your son, or that anyone could love me the way he does. What I really wanted was a family of my own. Jamie has given me that."

Katie squeezed Jamie's hand, and he brought her hand to his lips and kissed it. Was it possible to love anyone more than she loved Jamie? She doubted it.

"Well, if you're sure and have thought this through..." Peggy said, pausing. "From my end, I see no problem building out the attic. But you better get on it. The baby will be here before you know it. Until then, I want you two to move into this room. I'll move across the hall to Jamie's old bedroom."

"That is extremely generous, Mom, but it's unnecessary."

"There you are wrong, son. Trust me, you'll need the sanctuary of my room and the privacy it affords in the coming months. Many in the community will judge you harshly for your lapse in judgment. I do not, although it does set a bad example for the younger children. I'll leave it to you to share your news with Gracie, Annie, Thomas, and Robert as you see fit. Sex before marriage is not so unusual these days, although it still works best the other way around—according to God's plan.

"When the attic rooms are finished, you can move into them, and I'll move back into my room. I can then move Thomas into your old room. He's too old to share with Robert, anyway.

"Have no doubt I love you both. And my new grandbaby. Your baby will be a year and a half younger than Gracie's little boy—future playmates."

Katie burst into tears at that point. Peggy's acceptance spun a warm cocoon around her fluttering, insecure heart. She loved this woman seemingly as much as she loved Jamie, though differently.

Her love for Jamie was an insatiable, passionate, bottomless love that melded two hearts into one—a safe harbor through the storms of life. Her love for Peggy germinated from an arid desert place within her heart, now showered with spring rains. In Peggy, Katie found a maternal love that still called a spade a spade but looked beyond wrongdoings. An unconditional love that wordlessly communicated, "I know you, and you are mine." It was exactly how Katie would love her baby.

~*~

Katie had never been involved in a construction project before and found overseeing the conversion of the attic into a bona fide living space thrilling. The first step had been to build a flight of stairs from the second floor, at the end of the hallway by Annie's room, up to the attic.

Over the next five months, as her body completely changed shape, she watched the attic's exposed beams, uninsulated plywood walls, and bare two-by-fours transform into a cozy bedroom and nursery, separated by a small bathroom. She didn't disturb the workers during the day, but as soon as they left, she couldn't resist climbing the stairs to see their progress. Each day, the space felt homier and more beautiful to her. The nursery and bedroom centered around the dormers, and she was delighted when the old windows were replaced with ones that slid up to let fresh air inside. *Jamie had thought of everything!*

Katie grew closer to her mother-in-law over the months. It wasn't difficult. Peggy had generously covered the costs for the plumbing, electrical wiring, and the addition of radiant heat, using some of the proceeds from the sale of the farm.

With the addition of the attic rooms, Katie felt more at ease knowing that when Meggie Mae (short for Margaret, Peggy's name, and Mae, for Mam) or John Patrick (named after Jamie's father) cried during the night, the baby wouldn't wake the whole household. Katie would work hard to keep the baby from crying, but she knew some crying was inevitable. She had no experience with newborns, but at least that much she was sure of.

Opening the door to the stairwell leading up to the attic rooms, Katie stepped inside. She locked the door behind her, even though everyone was out of the house. Light filtered down from the dormer window into the stairwell, guiding her as she climbed the steep stairs. Katie held onto the wooden handrail with one hand and supported her eight-month-pregnant belly with the other.

She paused at the sturdy, decorative wooden railing that enclosed the stairwell as it opened into the attic bedroom. The locking gate mechanism required adult strength and dexterity to operate, ensuring that no accidental falls—whether child or adult—would occur.

Unlatching the gate at the top of the stairs, Katie stepped onto the newly laid attic flooring: embossed linoleum that resembled sienna-brown tile with dark brown grout. It had been quick to lay and far less expensive than even a roughhewn pine floor. A deep sense of home filled her as her eyes swept over the once-lath-and-plaster walls, now covered in thick gypsum plaster. She would have loved to have the money to paint or hang wallpaper, but like the millwork, that would have to wait until Jamie graduated from college.

Katie held her arms out and twirled slowly, taking in the bedroom's "expectant" emptiness, envisioning how she would fill the space and make it her own. Her nesting instinct was in full throttle now. There was enough left from her college fund for a new double bed, headboard and footboard, and a wooden rocker for the nursery.

All the other furnishings that Jamie and Thomas would soon move from the garage to their new attic home were either free or inexpensive second-hand pieces. Frankie had salvaged an old pine teacher's desk and chair from the high school in White Plains, and Katie thought it would be the perfect spot for Jamie to study. Once the bed arrived— any day now—Katie and Jamie would move upstairs. She couldn't wait; it would be their own home within a home.

Katie had the energy of a momma chickadee, readying and feathering her nest in anticipation of her little hatchling. And finally, Peggy could move back into her own bedroom, which helped assuage Katie's guilt at displacing her mother-in-law.

Jamie's oldest sister, Gracie, had been very generous too, lending them the rocking cradle her fifteen-month-old son had outgrown ages ago, along with all his newborn clothing and receiving blankets. Her sister Eileen had given them oodles of diapers and had sewn lovely maternity clothes that concealed Katie's pregnancy for quite some time, expanding as needed.

Walking over to the bedroom's dormer, Katie pulled the lower window pane up while kneeling on the window seat she'd had the builder add. November's cold, cleansing air blasted into the room. She admired the tufted cushion on the window seat and the matching pull-up fabric blinds she had made with Peggy's help. While working on Peggy's treadle Singer sewing machine, Katie realized she enjoyed sewing far more than studying and didn't miss college one bit. It was only the idea of college she missed—the clout it might have afforded her.

Katie treasured the time she spent with Peggy, nurturing the closeness she had longed for from the first day they met. Her mother-in-law taught her how to bake bread and Jamie's favorite cinnamon rolls. While Jamie worked at the Corner Grocer during the summer, Peggy even taught Katie how to drive the Chevy sedan. Katie now had her operator's license, which had cost two dollars but required no written exam or driving test.

Everything would be all right after all. Her sister had been right about the Murphys—they were good people. Katie believed she had found perfect happiness as Mrs. Jamie Murphy and as Peggy's daughter-in-law. She had not just married Jamie; she had married a family.

Gracie, Thomas, and Robert had warmed to Katie right away. Annie had been the most challenging, but Katie's persistent kindness had even won over the mercurial Annie. She wasn't yet able to call Fr. Jim 'Unc,' as Jamie did, but his visits were a pure delight for her.

Katie loved them all and felt well-loved in return by the entire Murphy clan.

~*~

Katie was beginning to think she would be pregnant forever. She'd been having contractions off and on for weeks. Her belly would tighten like a drum and then let up—uncomfortable but not exactly painful. "Those are practice contractions helping your body get ready to have the baby," Peggy had reassured her.

Since Mam had died when Katie was a wee child, and Eileen had never been pregnant, the mystery and fear of impending childbirth had further bonded mother-in-law and daughter-in-law. One day, Katie began calling Peggy "Mom," just as Jamie did. She couldn't remember exactly when. If Peggy had noticed the change, she hadn't said anything. Katie was happy and content, sucking up the love surrounding her like a nursing babe.

"Mom, would you stay with me when the baby is born?" Katie had asked her one afternoon.

"Of course, Katie dear. Nothing would make me happier. After having seven babies myself, I'd love to watch the process," Peggy had answered. "However, you must decide where to have your baby—at home or in the hospital. That determines who, if anyone, can be with you during your labor and baby's birth. Gracie had her baby in the hospital, and I wasn't allowed in.

"Things have changed so much. You have choices now, Katie. When my babies were born, labor and delivery were home-based events with female family members or midwives attending. I delivered my babies at home with the help of a wonderful midwife. Heddy had immigrated from Germany, where she'd trained and had far more experience than the first doctors who began offering maternity and delivery services in this country."

Katie appreciated Peggy's perspective and gathered the facts to make her decision. Jamie had allowed her the choice.

Between Tarrytown and White Plains hospitals, the latter was larger and seemingly more advanced. The price tags were about the same: $160, which included a two-week mandated stay. The midwife Peggy had used, Hedwig "Heddy" Mueller, still practiced in Tarrytown and charged a flat $10. The hospital charge represented three-quarters of the cost for a whole year's tuition for Jamie at Fordham. Katie figured that if women had done it all these years without hospitals and male doctors, she could do the same.

Katie appreciated that she had a choice, but her desire for Peggy—Mom—to be with her and the financial consideration made for any easy decision. Home it would be!

~*~

Katie slipped out of bed early on Friday morning, a week after her due date. This time, she knew that practice was over; these contractions were the real deal. There was no reason to wake Jamie or anyone else in the household—the pains were still far apart. Dressed in her nightgown, robe, and slippers, she crept down the staircase, quiet as falling snow.

After flipping on the kitchen light, she found a pencil and paper. Katie jotted down the time on the kitchen wall clock: 2:25. Then she walked room to room, waiting for her next pain—kitchen to dining room to living room to reception hall, through the hallway passing by the bathroom... *ad infinitum*, or so it seemed. The hands of the clock moved in slow motion.

When her pains came, she returned to the kitchen, braced herself against the wall, timed them, and made a note. Sometimes, she raced to the bathroom, not knowing which end was calling. After several hours, her contractions were lasting a minute and radiated through to her lower back.

Many thoughts jockeyed for position in her mind, like chickens squabbling for feed, pushing each other away. She welcomed their diversion except for those that warned of things that could go wrong: maternal hemorrhage, childbed fever, and stillbirth. At least the baby was still active—Katie could feel its movements and the occasional kick—so there was nothing to worry about on that front.

When dark thoughts came to roost, Katie imagined a cheery scenario instead. Jamie would go to class as usual, arriving home to find a radiant Katie, their beautiful baby nestled in her arms, and Peggy bragging, "What a brave girl Katie was today." Jamie would be so proud of her. Or maybe, if she wasn't so brave, Jamie would have been lucky enough to miss it all.

An hour later, her contractions were coming regularly, ten minutes apart. The last one sent Katie running to the bathroom once again. But before stepping inside, her water broke. Katie wiped up the pink-tinged fluid as best she could. The character of Katie's contractions changed, becoming waves of cramping, like every monthly she'd ever experienced rolled into one. The pressure in her lower back felt like an elephant was stepping on her. Her contractions were now fast and furious, eight minutes apart, lasting almost a minute.

Katie knocked softly on Peggy's bedroom door, her courage dissipating. When she didn't answer, Katie let herself in. The bright moonlight, streaming through the gauzy layers of drapery, guided Katie to Peggy's bedside. Peggy's dark eyes fluttered open when Katie touched her gently on her shoulder. She sat up quickly. "The baby?"

"Yes, my water broke."

~*~

Bent over with a contraction, Katie gripped the edge of the desk in their attic bedroom. Peggy stood beside her, holding her hand and rubbing her back. Katie barely registered Jamie's presence as he brought the midwife upstairs. When the pain subsided, she saw Jamie standing at the top of the stairs, peering back into their bedroom as he made his way out. The pained expression on his face told her he'd witnessed her last contraction.

"I'm okay, Jamie," Katie said, trying to reassure both him and herself. "But it's not fun," she added with a small, strained smile.

"Jamie, first babies can take a long time. Or not," Peggy said, her voice gently reassuring. "Try not to worry; Katie's in good hands—Heddy delivered you."

"Well, holler if you need anything," Jamie said, then added with a grimace, "Although I have no idea how to help."

"Jamie, if you could get the kids up for school and get breakfast going, that would be most helpful," Peggy said.

"Sure, Mom," he replied.

"We'll call you if we need you, Jamie," Heddy said, not unkindly but with an air that left no room for negotiation.

Peggy sent Jamie back down the stairwell and closed the door behind him.

Katie almost felt sorry for Jamie. Almost, but not quite. She knew he hated to see her suffer, but as her next contraction hit, any empathy she had for him vanished under the grinding force of the pain. After all, he was *intimately* connected with her labor pains.

As the contraction ebbed, Katie watched Heddy screw the legs into the odd-looking wooden three-legged stool. "What's that thing?" she asked. The stool stood about twenty inches tall, with a broad, toilet-like seat that seemed to be missing the entire front half. It had side handles and a curved back support about eight inches high.

"It's a birthing stool," said Heddy, speaking with a slight German accent but otherwise perfect English. The sturdy, well-rounded woman had a full head of white hair puffed out and pulled up in a Gibson Girl style.

"You sit on the stool and grab the handles when it's time to push the baby out. Delivery in a vertical position works with gravity," Heddy said, projecting confidence.

"Women have used some version of these stools or sat on the knees of other women since the beginning of recorded history to deliver their babies. It is easier than squatting when you're all worn out from labor or, God forbid, lying on your back to give birth like in the hospital. The Egyptians used birthing stools, and the Book of Genesis mentions them too." As she spoke, Heddy pulled out several items from her black leather bag.

"That looks like the same stool I sat on to deliver my babies," Peggy said.

"It is. You can't improve upon perfection." Heddy's amber eyes twinkled as she nodded, looking from Peggy to Katie. Her face, deeply lined with wrinkles, was softened by the smile lines around her mouth.

"Katie, you don't have to use it, but I believe it'll help us both," Heddy said, rolling up the sleeves of her belted brown cotton dress that reached the top of her lace-up brown boots.

The midwife's smooth, deliberate movements filled Katie with trust and imparted a sense of calm into the room. "You can think about it, Kaite, while I go wash my hands," Heddy added.

Turning to Peggy next, Heddy said, "My dear, would you please spread these sheets out on the bed? The rubber sheet goes down first."

When Heddy returned from washing her hands, she pulled a spotless white apron over her head. Katie noticed how Heddy's apron covered the front and back of her dress and tying neatly at the sides as her next contraction began.

Just as her next pain waned, Peggy finished laying an old bed sheet atop a half-rubber sheet spread on the double bed. Heddy moved a stack of clean, though worn, towels—ones Peggy had brought up earlier that morning—closer to the birthing stool.

"I must check your progress and listen for the baby's heart. You can lie on the bed or sit on the birthing stool. Your choice, my dear."

Weighing her choices, Katie decided that spreading her legs on the bed seemed less appealing than sitting on the birthing stool. The stool option seemed more modest. She still felt in control and was reticent to bare all—at this stage of labor.

Heddy used a pinard, a wooden horn-shaped device, to listen to the baby's heartbeat. "Baby's heartbeat is strong," she said.

Six hours later, Katie's contractions were five minutes apart and lasting about a minute and a half. Her bleeding had become more pronounced as labor progressed, and she was certain she had seen Peggy and Heddy exchange worried glances over the past several hours.

"Is there supposed to be this much blood?" Katie asked. She lay on the bed, watching as Heddy replaced the bloody folded towel with a fresh one. The sight of yet another blood-soaked towel sent intensified her panic. "Not always," Heddy said.

"Bleeding can happen for several reasons," Heddy said evenly. "If the placenta attaches low in the uterus, close to the cervix, then as the cervix opens, there can be bleeding. Once your baby is born, and you deliver the placenta, and the babe starts suckling, the uterus will start contracting, and I trust that the bleeding will stop."

A half-hour later, Katie's pains came like violent, pounding waves with no break between. She cried out, "I have to push. Mary, Mother of God, help me."

"Try to blow away the urge to push while I check you—hopefully for the last time," Heddy said as she and Peggy helped position Katie on the birthing stool.

"The baby is in perfect position, and your cervix is fully open," Heddy said. "Now, channel all your energy into pushing that baby out.

Let's have this baby!"

Katie began to buckle under the weight of her exhaustion. Peggy rushed behind the birthing stool, instinctively placing her arms under Katie's armpits, giving her daughter-in-law strength and balance.

Heddy felt the next contraction tighten across Katie's belly. "Take a deep breath, hold it, and push with all your might. Now."

Katie leaned forward, squeezing her eyes shut, and pushed with all her might. A guttural sound tore from her throat, as if she were moving heaven and earth.

"Excellent. The baby's head is crowned. Just a few more pushes and your baby will be here." Katie peered into Heddy's eyes with absolute trust. The urge to push overtook any lingering fear. Her world narrowed into a single focus—birthing this child.

"You're doing wonderfully, Katie dear. The baby is almost here," Peggy said, brushing Katie's wet hair off her forehead.

"With your next contraction, inhale deeply, and then bear down hard for the entire length of the contraction," Heddy said, her voice calm but firm, echoing years of experience.

As Katie delivered her child, a burning, stinging pain ripped through her, like hornets piercing her flesh. Yet amidst the excruciating pain, there was relief—it was finally happening.

"You're doing great, Katie," Peggy said between the animal-like shrieks that echoed off the bedroom walls. She wiped Katie's forehead, holding back her damp hair.

After one final push, Heddy announced, "What a fine little girl." She presented the bloody, vernix-covered newborn to an exhausted and emotionally drained Katie. Moments later, Heddy held the baby upside down and gently slapped her tiny butt. Only then did Meggie Mae's strong cry announce that she had made the journey safely from the warmth of her mother's womb to the outside world.

Heddy wrapped the baby in a clean towel, wiping her little button nose.

"She's just beautiful, Katie. Just perfect," Peggy said, taking the baby from Heddy's arms.

Katie watched the twisty, blue umbilical cord pulsate. Heddy tied it off a minute later, and then Katie felt her body begin to shake uncontrollably. The last thing Katie remembered was a full head of black hair, slightly bigger than a grapefruit but not nearly so round.

ELEVEN

January 1929 (One month later)

Jamie walked downstairs to the kitchen with Meggie in his arms. Katie was still upstairs and, Jamie hoped, sound asleep on this cold and dreary Saturday morning. He planned to wake her a half-hour before leaving for work. He joined his mother, who sat at the kitchen table, still in her bathrobe, reading the newspaper and enjoying her morning coffee.

"Seems like Katie and the baby had another rough night," Mom said. "I heard the baby a couple of times. Poor little thing."

"Yeah. I can sleep through the ruckus mostly, but Katie was up with her a lot last night. How long do babies have colic, anyway?"

"I've heard it can last as long as six months; I can't say for sure, though. I was lucky. All you kids were easy babies."

"She's an angel now. Fast asleep." He took in Meggie's cupid's bow upper lip busily making sucking motions, her alabaster skin and dark long lashes. "We'll see how long that lasts," Jamie said, pouring himself a cup of coffee with his free hand.

"Here, let me take her while you grab some breakfast."

Jamie transferred the sleeping infant, wrapped tightly in a blue receiving blanket, into his mother's waiting arms.

Meggie squirmed and opened her eyes briefly. Mom gazed down at her, wearing that fond expression Jamie had come to recognize.

"Meggie really takes after you, Jamie. She has the Murphy dark hair, and I suspect she'll probably inherit your brown eyes, too. They seem to be getting darker."

"Katie's having a hard time, Mom. I don't know what to do. She refuses to let me help by walking Meggie when she cries during the night." He ran his hands through his unkempt hair, sighing in exasperation. "It's like Katie's either angry or sad."

"She's just tired, son, and likely overwhelmed. Don't take it personally. Remember, she came close to hemorrhaging after Meggie was born. She's still recovering. It's only been a month. Things will get easier."

"I hope so." Jamie wished things between him and Katie weren't so strained and wondered what he could do to make them better.

"Nursing for first-time mothers is no picnic for the first week or two, even when everything goes according to plan. Katie had her hands full just dealing with her own recovery. It didn't help matters when Meggie had trouble latching on, and Katie developed mastitis in both breasts. That's something I never had to deal with," his mother said, taking another sip of coffee.

"Katie feels that it's her fault that Meggie has colic because she gave up on nursing," Jamie replied.

After the baby had begun losing weight, the doctor recommended that Katie switch Meggie to a homemade mixture of 13 oz. of evaporated milk diluted with 19 oz. of water and sweetened with two tablespoons of corn syrup. It took extra work, boiling the glass nursing bottles and nipples and storing the filled bottles in the basement icebox.

They'd even tried expensive infant formulas like Horlick's and Nestlé's. Still, the result was the same: red-faced, inconsolable crying after her feedings, tightly clenched fists, legs pulled up to her tummy, and a rigid, arched back. However, despite her colic, Meggie was now gaining weight and growing. No one was overly worried—except Katie, whose nerves were frayed like the ends of a rope.

"Any advice, Mom? I think Katie is losing her confidence." Jamie wondered where the happy, teasing Katie had gone. And if she'd ever come back.

"Tell Katie you're proud of her and that she is a good mother. Reassure her that you love her and still find her beautiful. Keep asking if there is anything you can do for her. Patience and understanding are the keys. Doc Collins says it's not uncommon for some women to experience bouts of melancholy after giving birth."

"Yes, but he said the crying and anxiety should've passed by now. It was only supposed to last a couple of weeks."

"Well, doctors don't know everything about women and babies. Each woman is different, and babies are, too." His mother reached over to pat Jamie's hand. "This too shall pass. Trust me."

~*~

February 1929

Katie got up slowly from the rolled seat of the wooden oak rocker in the attic nursery. Little Meggie was soundly asleep on her shoulder. Late evening moonlight reached its silvery fingers through the dormer window, guiding her steps along the multicolored braided rug to the crib, its white-enameled steel side already down. She gently placed the sleeping infant in the crib, patting her back. Meggie squirmed briefly, then settled. Katie covered her with a baby blanket, feeling a small sense of relief—a brief respite before the next demanding outburst.

She picked up the empty nursing bottle from the side table by the rocker, tiptoed out of the nursery, and quietly shut the door behind her. Katie exhaled, wishing that she could similarly expel the exhaustion, darkness, and hopelessness—her constant companions since the second week after Meggie's birth. The baby was now six weeks old, and there had been no change in Meggie's sleep or colic, nor any improvement in Katie's mental outlook despite all the liver and onions she had consumed, as Doc Collins had prescribed, to boost her iron stores.

Jamie sat at his desk, just to the right of the bedroom dormer, studying with the aid of an old desk lamp. The double bed on the opposite side of the room called to Katie. All she wanted to do was crawl under the covers and hibernate forever. Instead, she lowered the dormer curtain and sat on the window seat, watching her husband's eyes move from his textbook to the paper he was composing. The shadow play between the lamp's yellow light and the room's darkness outlined his strikingly handsome profile.

He reached out his hand to Katie, and she took it. He then pulled her onto his lap, tucking her small, delicate body under his chin and stroking her face gently as if she were made of blown glass.

"I've missed you, Katie," he whispered, laying down his pen, running his hands through the copper waves of her hair, and gazing into her distant, listless eyes.

Katie was silent. She missed him, too, but she missed herself even more. Except for the nightly colic fits, everything else was perfect in her life, yet Katie could find no way to enjoy it. What had happened to her? she lamented. Was she like Da after all?

Jamie lifted her chin and kissed her full lips with a gentle passion. Katie felt empty. She went through the motions as best she could, she hoped. Jamie deserved that much—and more.

"I'm sorry you are so exhausted and sad. What can I do for you?"

"Just love me... don't give up on me," Katie forced a smile. "Meggie's asleep. I'm going to get ready and crawl into bed."

"May I join you?"

Katie knew what this meant. She recognized the hunger and longing in his eyes. It had been six weeks since Meggie was born; she wasn't nursing, and her menses had resumed a week ago.

"I'll never tell you no, but we can conceive again, Jamie."

"Already?"

"Yes, Jamie."

"Don't fret, Katie-love; I just need to feel your body next to mine."

~*~

Mid-April 1929

Eventually, Meggie's colic lessened, and the baby began sleeping for three hours at a time. Katie was more receptive to Jamie's advances. Two months later, Katie could again appreciate the beauty of a blue sky, the soft touch of her husband's seeking lips, and the downy feel of Meggie's fine hair. She was infused with the glow of gratitude for many things: a handsome and devoted husband; a darling and healthy baby girl; acceptance by the entire Murphy clan (especially Peggy, whom she worshipped); a safe, warm home; and the continued love and support of Frankie and Eileen.

Something had changed within Katie. Her appetite was back. She savored the delicious promise of life itself. Colors became vibrant again. She delighted in the birth of spring: the yellow narcissus blowing kisses in the breeze; the pink, blue, and white Spanish bells tinkling, "Arise," and bright red tulips, having braved the winter months, shouting, "All is new!"

It was the tingling and tenderness in her breasts that first tipped Katie off to the delay in her monthlies. She consulted the calendar on Jamie's desk. Three weeks late—she was pregnant. The timing was not optimal. Jamie still had nearly two years left of college, and that assumed he would be attending classes this summer at Fordham.

According to her calculations, this baby would be due around Christmas, just as Meggie had been. They would be "Irish twins."

Her nausea confirmed the pregnancy for Katie. She would gladly take nausea and pregnancy over the emotional prison that had robbed her of joy in those early months after Meggie's birth. Any fear or apprehension of another difficult delivery was inconsequential compared to her deliverance from the previous confining and impenetrable cloud of darkness.

She said nothing to Jamie that evening. When he turned out his study lamp and crawled into bed, Katie awaited him. Her body tingled in anticipation of their union. She reached out to him, initiating their lovemaking with a torrent of passion.

They had only come together twice since Meggie's birth; neither time had been planned. Katie had never felt anything physically or emotionally during either of those encounters. Yet tonight had been different. Katie had craved their physical intimacy and was filled with desire for her husband. She had risen from the dead.

Afterward, she whispered into his ear, "We are pregnant again." Jamie was already asleep. She would tell him soon.

~*~

June 1929

"Thank you for picking Meggie and me up this afternoon, Eileen. I needed a change of scenery," Katie said as she put a diaper bag in the back seat of the Caruso's Model T. "Are you sure you don't mind?"

"Are you kidding? There's nothing I'd rather do on my day off than spend it with you and my little goddaughter," Eileen replied, adjusting her wide-brimmed straw hat, topped with a profusion of red and white silk flowers, in the rearview mirror.

Meggie sat on Katie's lap, facing Eileen, with her fat little fingers exploring her mouth and her giant brown eyes fixed on Katie's sister with curiosity.

The two sisters dressed in their summery best for their outing and picnic. Eileen wore a light blue linen, drop-waist dress, and Katie wore a loose-fitting, floral print dress with pleats below the bodice and a sailor-type collar. Katie had dressed Meggie in a pink and white gingham-check creeper, with its rounded collar trimmed in lace that matched the trim on the pink bonnet tied beneath her dimpled chin.

Her sister grabbed one of Meggie's chubby bare feet and pretended to loudly gobble it up, eliciting irresistible laughter from the six-month-old baby. She had Jamie's adorable dimples.

"What a pretty little girl you are. Yes, you are." Her sister spoke in an exaggerated, high-pitched voice and shook her head, prompting coos and slobbery smiles from Meggie. Long gone were Meggie's painful, soul-curdling colicky cries.

"I finally feel like myself again." Katie's voice broke as she remembered the agony of those first months. "I'm afraid I've not been much of a sister since Meggie was born. But I've been even a worse wife and mother."

"Oh, Katie, don't be so hard on yourself."

Her sister started the car and began the short drive north and then east to Tarrytown Lakes Park, the community's water reservoir. Eileen had packed a picnic basket for them. Afterward, Katie hoped they would stroll along the wooden walkway bordering the lake, as they had done many times before when a family outing consisted of Eileen, Frankie, and herself after moving to White Plains from the Bronx in her early teen years. Life was simpler then, although she hadn't appreciated it at the time.

"I can't explain what was wrong with me, Eileen. It was like I was dead inside, unable to feel anything at all. I was trapped in an awful place." Katie thought, *Hell could not be much worse.*

Katie tried not to think about the nightmare of the first months after Meggie's birth—the horrible things she'd never told another soul, not even Jamie. Those agonizingly long, lonely nights when it seemed Meggie would never stop crying, and Katie felt she was losing her sanity. One night stood out in Katie's memory as the absolute worst, the nadir of the oppressive darkness. The baby had been crying for hours on end and had refused to take the bottle. Katie couldn't comfort her. Mother and baby were both drenched in sweat, the baby from continuous crying and Katie from anxiety, panic, and frazzled nerves.

Her nerves had been coiled like a snake ready to strike when she screamed at Meggie, "I hate you. I wish you had never been born." After her venomous outburst, the baby had shrieked even louder. Katie had begun shaking and had laid the inconsolable crying baby in her crib. She had opened the nursery door and entered the small bathroom separating the bedroom and nursery. After splashing water on her face, she looked into the mirror and didn't see herself; instead, a monster flashed before her eyes—a hideous, distorted face with flashing red eyes and horns. The very thing she had become.

Katie shuddered at the memory, one she would never share with another soul.

"I feared that I would never love Meggie. I thank God that those horrible feelings of desperation finally passed." Katie's eyes glistened with unshed tears.

"Of course, you always loved Meggie," Eileen reassured, squeezing Katie's hand.

"I pray that doesn't happen this time around," Katie said. "Yes, I'm pregnant again—about three months along."

"Oh, Katie, I don't know what to say." Eileen's mouth trembled ever so slightly.

Katie knew how much Eileen and Frankie had wanted a child. Why had God made it so easy for her to conceive and impossible for her beloved sister? Who could understand the ways of the Almighty? It was clear to Katie that she did not. Why were God's blessings so often braided together with threads of sorrow and strands of suffering?

~*~

Jamie enrolled in classes at Fordham that summer. Fewer students were on campus than during the regular school year. The dress was more casual; jackets weren't even required for the all-male student body.

He scaled the steps to Collins Hall to meet up with Unc, seeking his guidance and wisdom on a "personal matter." Having already shared the topic with Fr. Jim ahead of time, Jamie wanted—"needed" was his exact word—to know if there was any "church-sanctioned method of birth control."

Two years ago, almost to the day, Jamie had entered Collins Hall wearing a black cassock, his heart burdened and ready to confess his lack of vocation to the priesthood. Today, he entered the building as a married man with a gorgeous wife, a darling daughter now crawling around the house, and another child on the way around Christmastime. Jamie had much responsibility, but he was content. Still, he was concerned about his and Katie's incredible fertility. He wanted more children, just not until he was out of college.

As Jamie stepped onto the third floor, he saw Fr. Jim pacing the marble-floored hallway outside his office, his arms moving as if having a debate with himself. His uncle walked toward the window at the end of the hallway, pausing to take in the green and lush view of the campus grounds. Jamie felt a deep respect and affection for the genial, wise priest. There was something timeless about the man.

Jamie approached his uncle's office and leaned against the doorway. Fr. Jim, deep in thought, passed by his nephew without noticing him.

"Do you have time for lunch, Unc? You seem awfully deep in thought," Jamie called out.

At the sound of Jamie's voice, Fr. Jim looked up, his broad smile reflected in the twinkling of his dark eyes. "Ah, Jamie, my boy." The priest walked toward Jamie with an outstretched hand. Their energetic handshake morphed into a quick, manly hug and slaps on the back. "Yes, I was just thinking about the topic you wanted to discuss. Come on in. Take a load off."

Jamie followed Fr. Jim into his office and sat down. Fr. Jim's desk seemed more orderly than usual. Several books lay open, and a white legal pad was half-covered with scribbled notes. His fountain pen lay capped next to his spectacles.

"How's the family? I need to crash Peggy's Sunday dinner soon. I think I'm losing weight." Fr. Jim patted his belly. Clearly, he was *not* losing weight.

"The family is thriving and growing. Katie is feeling better than she has in months. As I mentioned on the phone, she is expecting again. Meggie is finally sleeping through the night and has grown out of her colic. Mom is busy, as always. Katie and Mom have adopted each other. Annie has a babysitting job this summer and is dating a pleasant, down-to-earth young man who works at the Chevy plant. He got Thomas a summer job working at the plant, and Thomas hopes for a full-time position in engine assembly in the fall.

"I think Robert will turn out to be the family's scholar. It's too bad Mom and Dad wasted their money on me. I'd bet Robert is the one with a vocation. How many fourteen-year-old kids read *The Imitation of Christ* when no one makes them? Since school has been out this summer, he gets up every weekday to serve at morning Mass. I was a heathen compared to Robert at that age. Come to think of it, maybe I still am." Jamie winked at his uncle.

"That all sounds good, except you are doing a lousy job at the heathen part, Jamie. You are trying to obey God's plan for the family and sexual love. Not many heathens ask if there is any church-approved method of birth control. Well, I'm not sure you'll like my answer."

"Nothing, I guess then?"

"Well, nothing that blocks or interferes with the reproductive aspect of married sexual love. However, if there are natural periods of female fertility and infertility in a woman's cycle, a couple could practice periodic abstinence during her fertile periods for serious reasons to delay childbearing. Of course, my expertise is ethics, not the mysterious workings of female reproduction.

"After consulting with a professor in the biology department, I learned of independent discoveries by several biologists—one Dutch, one Japanese, and another German—indicating that such periods exist for women. However, there is much variability, and the possibility of conception can never be a hundred percent ruled out. Since this information has only come out in the last twenty years, it will take a while for the Church to give direct guidance.

"As far back as 1853 and then again in 1880, ethical questions on this exact topic have been addressed to the Sacred Penitentiary."

"Unc, isn't the Sacred Penitentiary the arm of the Church that provides guidance on matters of conscience and living out one's faith in a manner consistent with Church teaching?"

"That's it, more or less. Anyway, the Sacred Penitentiary ruled that there was nothing objectionable to periodic abstinence during a woman's infertile cycle, so long as the spouses were both agreeable and did nothing to impede conception during sexual intercourse. The problem is that scientists don't yet know how to predict a woman's fertility or infertility. There are some theories, of course, but that's all they are.

"The big thing, son, is that God is the author and creator of life—He owns all human life. He is in control; we are not. Yes, we are charged to make the best decisions possible, even though we are selfish creatures with imperfect faith, trust, and love. It's easy to get blindsided by our own desires.

"Have you ever considered that the love between a husband and wife images the communion of love within the Trinity? Just think of it, Jamie. The love between the Father and the Son is so boundless and fruitful that it generates a third person—the Holy Ghost. On a human level, this is mirrored in your family: the relationship between you and Katie and your children.

"But remember, as I've often said, the primary role of each spouse isn't for perfect happiness on earth—it's to help one another reach heaven. You and Katie have chosen each other to journey hand in hand toward God. Trust that He who has brought you together will give you the grace to make the journey home to Him."

PART TWO – SHADOWS & SILENCE (1929-1941)

TWELVE

Late 1929

Despite more women choosing hospital births for their supposed safety, Katie insisted on having her second baby at home. She overrode Jamie's objections by repeating Heddy's words, as much to reassure herself as to convince him: "Where the placenta attaches inside the uterus differs for each pregnancy, so what happened the first time is unlikely to occur on your second delivery."

The recent stock market panic gave Katie another reason to insist on a home birth. With the Murphy family's investments from the farm's sale halved, it seemed not only practical but mandatory to save money where they could.

Katie tried to project confidence, but inside, her anxiety grew like wild buckthorn, invading the soil of her existence. Her anxiety had nothing to do with the potential complications of labor and delivery, though she wasn't blind to them. What Katie feared was a repeat of the months of emotional darkness that had followed little Meggie's birth, choking out her *joie de vivre*.

In Katie's mind, bottle feeding had caused Meggie's colic, which, in turn, had snowballed into months of unremitting sadness. This time would be different. There would be no blocked milk ducts, mastitis, or bottle feedings.

On December 17, just before dawn, Katie finally held Patricia Mary in her arms. Patsy had a full head of dark hair and alert, curious eyes that locked immediately onto her own. She could have passed for Meggie's identical twin if not for being born a year apart. Peggy remarked once again, "This little one could be my own. She looks so much like her daddy did when he was born."

Heddy's delivery fee remained at ten dollars, and Peggy was there to encourage the laboring Katie. This time, Katie's labor and delivery, from start to finish, were under six hours. There was no unusual blood loss. It was textbook perfect, with no extraordinary drama.

~*~

Katie listened for the sound of Jamie's steady breathing. Once she was sure he was asleep, she threw off the covers and quietly slipped out of their shared bed. She paced back and forth, pressing her temples as if to silence the thoughts racing through her mind like thoroughbreds.

She felt her breasts, still soft—no milk. Why hadn't her milk come in yet? She had been holding Patsy at her breast every waking moment. She hadn't slept since Patsy was born—it was now the third night. On the first night, Katie would nod off and then awaken almost immediately with a start, her heart pounding.

December's cold moonlight guided her to the nursery. The golden stripes in the floral-and-vine-patterned wallpaper reflected the soft, ethereal light, almost as if beckoning to her. She remembered when Peggy had found the clearance-priced wallcovering and convinced Jamie to hang it, hoping to lift her spirits during those difficult months after Meggie's birth. Katie shuddered, recalling the long, lonely hours she had spent in the attic rooms back then.

She sat in the rocking chair next to Gracie's loaner wooden cradle, which they were still using. Katie waited for the infant to awaken. After a few minutes, fearing that Patsy was dead, she stroked her soft, downy face, causing the baby to squirm. Uttering a prayer of relief, she picked up the baby, carried her into the bathroom, and switched on the overhead light. After unwrapping Patsy on a small walnut table, she changed her diaper, rinsed it in the toilet, added it to the diaper pail, and washed her hands. The baby, now fully awake, cried in protest.

Katie lowered the toilet seat cover and, once seated, offered one breast to the baby and then the other. Absent was the rush of first milk to her breasts. Present only was the initial pain of Patsy's latching on and the cramping of her uterus as the baby sucked. How long had it taken before with Meggie? She couldn't recall exactly, but this was the third day. Where was her milk?

Katie returned to the nursery, holding Patsy over her shoulder and patting her back. As she settled back into the rocking chair, a sense of euphoria descended upon her, like the descent of the Holy Ghost.

A sudden, overwhelming realization washed over her—hidden knowledge now revealed—she had been there with the apostles and the Virgin Mary in the upstairs room at Pentecost.

The moonlight seeping through the dormer window coalesced into a single ray, piercing her heart and communicating a secret message—one she didn't hear but sensed viscerally: God had called her to be a prophetess. Although she didn't know the details of her divine appointment yet, she perceived that her family's safety depended on her executing this sacred mission correctly.

After placing Patsy back in her cradle, she moved to the crib, where Meggie lay fast asleep, thumb in mouth as usual. Her hair formed a loose halo of black curls framing her cherubic face.

Katie was still in the nursery when Jamie got up, her rosary beads in her hands as the morning light began to filter in.

"There you are. How did you sleep last night?" Jamie asked, still in his pajamas.

Katie remained silent.

"Katie?" Jamie waved his hand in front of her face. "Katie, are you all right?"

"My milk hasn't come in."

"It took a while last time, too. There's nothing to worry about. You didn't sleep last night, did you?"

"I don't think so. But I understand what I need to do. Everything's clear now. I understand my life's work."

"What is clear is that you need to sleep. And eat. Come downstairs with me. The girls are both asleep. I'm going to fix you breakfast."

"Please, Jamie, let me eat up here. I can't leave the baby." Her voice trembled, and tears welled in Katie's pleading eyes as she reached for his hand.

"Okay, just this once. But you can't keep on like this. I'm going to call Doc Collins if you don't take a nap today."

"I *will* sleep. I need to bed down right here beside Patsy. That's the problem—I can't leave her."

~*~

Katie nibbled at the toast and scrambled eggs Jamie had brought her but gulped down the milk, hoping it would stimulate the onset of her breast milk. When he returned for the breakfast tray, she had already

117

dressed and combed her chin-length copper waves of hair. Meggie sat on her lap, finishing the last of Katie's breakfast.

"You'll feel better now that you've eaten something," Jamie said.

"Yes, I suppose so."

As her eyes met Jamie's, a surge of electrifying terror shot through her—this was not the real Jamie. This imposter looked and sounded exactly like the real Jamie, but it wasn't him. How had she not noticed before?

"Thank you for fixing my breakfast and bringing it up to me," she said, trying to keep her voice steady and not betray the fear sparked by her new insight.

Meggie reached out her arms towards the false Jamie, smiling and laughing. "Dada," she said eagerly.

He tried to scoop Meggie up in his arms, but Katie panicked and held onto her tightly. No, she couldn't let this imposter touch Meggie.

"Let me dress her first, and then I'll bring her downstairs after I change and feed Patsy," Katie said, buying time.

"Why don't I dress her, Katie, and you can focus on the baby."

"No!" Katie replied sharply. "Please," she added, her voice softening.

The imposter exhaled loudly, barely masking his frustration and concern. He rolled his shoulders, shook his head, picked up the dirty dishes, and headed downstairs.

Katie's face was awash in tears as she carried Meggie back to the nursery. She changed her diaper and put clean rubber pants on her. After dressing her in warm tights and a long-sleeved dress with smocking across the bodice, she set Meggie back in her crib with a few toys.

She couldn't remember when she'd last changed or fed Patsy, but she woke the baby to start the process anew. Settling in the rocking chair, she clutched Patsy to her breasts. Both felt firmer now. After the initial pinch and sting when Patsy latched on, Katie felt the tell-tale rush of new milk into her breasts. Her letdown reflex followed.

Closing her eyes in relief, Katie uttered a prayer of thanksgiving. When she opened them, Patsy stared back with piercing, demon-like eyes. Katie recoiled, her gaze snapping away. It was a trick—Satan was trying to fool her, to keep her from doing her work as a prophetess of

God.

Meggie stood in her crib, gripping the metal railing and fussing. She wanted her morning bottle and to be out of the crib, but she would have to wait a bit longer. Once Patsy finished nursing, Katie placed her back in the cradle, picked Meggie up, and headed down the attic stairs to find Peggy.

With Meggie in her arms, Katie nearly ran into Annie in the upstairs hallway. Annie's face was distorted and elongated, and the cadence of her morning greeting didn't match the movements of her mouth. Panicked, Katie rushed past her, gripping Meggie so tightly that the child began to cry.

Peggy wasn't in her bedroom. Katie rushed through the living room, her breath quickening—Thomas and Robert were there, their eyes fixed on the radio, but they didn't notice her. Why weren't they helping? Why wasn't anyone helping?

Katie stopped when she heard the announcer say, "This cannot continue. We must stop her." *Dear God*, she thought, *they are telling everyone about me.*

Thomas and Robert's heads swiveled impossibly, their eyes hanging out of their sockets. Smiling grotesquely. They knew. Everyone knew. Terrified, she ran into the kitchen, where the false Jamie sat at the table.

"Where's Mom?" Katie demanded, her voice ringing with desperation over Meggie's frantic wailing.

"At Mass." The false Jamie stood, dropping the newspaper on the kitchen table. He slowly reached to take Meggie from Katie's arms.

Katie clutched Meggie tighter in protest, causing Meggie to shriek even louder.

"No, she has to come home. I need her to help me." Katie was sobbing hysterically and screaming.

The false Jamie looked at the clock on the wall. Worry was etched on his face. He should be worried—Katie knew the truth; he wasn't the real Jamie. This man, whoever he was, was evil. She could see it in his eyes, shifting nervously.

"Mom will be home in fifteen minutes," the imposter said. "You're not acting like yourself. Please, calm down. You need to sleep. Lack of sleep makes anyone irrational and emotional."

"How dare you say that to me? You're not Jamie. You've taken over his body. You are an evil imposter!" Katie screamed, in concert with

Meggie's howling.

He reached for Meggie, but Katie held her tighter, her heart racing. The man was trying to rip Meggie out of her arms. He wasn't her father. She had to protect Meggie.

Out of the corner of her eye, she saw Annie, Thomas, and Robert watching. Why weren't they helping her? They were in on it, too!

"Thomas, Robert, Annie, help me with Katie. She's not well. We need to get Meggie out of her arms without hurting either of them."

Katie thrashed wildly, trying to hold onto Meggie, but they forced her to the floor. The false Jamie and Thomas were holding her down, but all Katie could focus on was Meggie's cries, louder than ever now that she had been torn from her arms.

Through Katie's blurred vision, she saw Annie cradling Meggie, patting her back gently. Katie tried to reach out, but her body refused to move. Meggie's tiny sobs were muffled as she buried her face in Annie's shoulder, turning away from the bottle Robert offered her.

"Annie," the imposter said, "please take Meggie upstairs to the nursery. Lock the door to the attic rooms, and don't open it until I tell you."

Just then Katie heard the front door open and saw Mom walk in and Robert run to her. He leaned in and whispered something to her, though Katie couldn't hear what Robert said. Whatever it was, Mom dropped her coat and hat onto the floor, made the Sign of the Cross, and ran into the kitchen.

Katie was sitting on the kitchen floor, moaning and rocking back and forth. "It's the end. They know. It's over. I have failed."

The imposter sat nearby on the floor, his mouth moving, but his words jumbled. Katie leaned away from him as Mom stepped closer and knelt beside her. "I'm home," she chirped as if everything were perfectly normal. But they weren't.

"Oh, Mom, you have to help me," a sobbing Katie pleaded, collapsing into Mom's arms.

"Do you want to go upstairs to my bedroom and tell me what's wrong?" Mom asked gently.

"No, we have to go to the nursery, Mom. Patsy's all alone." In a whisper, but loud enough for the imposter to hear, Katie pointed to him and said, "He's not the real Jamie."

~*~

After Mom went upstairs with Katie, Jamie dialed Doc Collins, the family physician, his hands trembling as he fumbled with the phone. Doc Collins was the kindly doctor who had cared for Robert after he was badly burned in the barn fire several years back.

"I can't recommend anything to help Katie sleep unless you can convince her to stop nursing, at least for a while. Irish whiskey or laudanum has been used to help women settle their nerves after childbirth when they suffer ongoing insomnia like this. But both pass into the breast milk and are very dangerous for the baby. And, frankly, neither is guaranteed to work. Sleep is the only cure," Doc Collins explained to Jamie over the phone.

"I doubt I can convince her to stop nursing, Doc. She's completely obsessed with it, confused, and not thinking straight."

Not thinking straight was a *mild* way to describe Katie's bizarre behavior. He explained to the doctor how Katie refused to come downstairs to eat or take a break from her hypervigilant watch, even after she had just nursed Patsy and the baby was sleeping soundly.

"That makes it hard, Jamie." Doc Collins paused briefly. "If things get worse, you may have to hospitalize her."

"I'm not sure how things could get much worse. Katie thinks I'm an imposter—not her real husband. She's completely unreasonable, like she's out of her mind."

"If she becomes a danger to herself or anyone else, including the baby, or if she becomes impossible to control—God forbid—then we must get help for her sake and for your family's safety." Doc Collins' voice was serious and full of warning.

"I'd recommend Harlem Valley State Hospital in Wingdale. It's a little over an hour away in Dutchess County," Doc Collins said.

"Couldn't I take her to the hospital in Tarrytown or White Plains?"

"No, they aren't equipped to help her. Harlem Valley is a mental hospital."

"Good God, an insane asylum?" The words hit Jamie like a punch to the gut.

"No, nothing like that—more like a home away from home, where she can get well. It's a beautiful facility, only about six years old, with a good reputation. You could also take her to New York City, to the New York State Psychiatric Institute. It's an older facility, and the atmosphere is not as pleasant. The doctors are excellent there, too, but it feels more institutional. If it takes Katie a while to respond to treatment, you want a place that feels more like home. One can't predict the progression of these things.

"Call me Sunday night or Monday morning to let me know how things are going. If need be, I can call ahead to let the facility of your choice know you are bringing her in. As you might expect, the baby would stay behind."

"...then Katie wouldn't be able to nurse Patsy, anyway," Jamie said.

"I'm afraid not. But Jamie, with Christmas this coming Wednesday, we want to get her settled immediately. Let's hope it doesn't come to that, and Katie will consider a temporary reprieve from nursing so that you can try less drastic measures."

~*~

"It's been six days since Patsy was born, and you still haven't slept. Katie, I promise you, nobody is trying to poison you or the baby," Eileen said, drawing a cross over her heart with her index finger, just as she had done when Katie was a child.

Katie narrowed her wild, frightened eyes, clutching Patsy tighter. "You don't care if Patsy starves!" she shouted, her heart racing as Eileen's soothing tone felt like a threat.

"She won't starve. We'll bottle-feed Patsy, just like we did with Meggie. Do you remember that, Katie?"

"Who are you? I don't know you. What did you do with the real Eileen?" Katie's voice trembled as she backed away. The woman in front of her wore Eileen's face, but Katie wasn't fooled. She didn't trust her. She didn't trust anyone.

Katie's thoughts whirled in a fog of fear and confusion. She felt like a shell of her former self, barely holding onto Patsy's care while something darker tugged at the edges of her mind. The suggestion of bottle feeding made no sense to her—her breasts were full of milk. Patsy would only be safe as long as she nursed her. The strange looks from those around her confirmed what Katie already knew: they were all part of a plan to derail her divine mission.

She remembered caring for Meggie, but now she could barely bring herself to touch her. When Meggie crawled toward her, reaching up with chubby hands, Katie froze, paralyzed by a suffocating dread.

Katie couldn't meet Patsy's gaze. Those eyes—terrifying, flaming pupils—glared back at her with a malevolent stare. No, she couldn't look. She sat in the nursery rocker, her eyes fixed on the wallpaper, the delicate floral pattern blurring into a haze. She was trapped, imprisoned in her mind, waiting for further direction from above to complete her divine mission.

~*~

Mom, Jamie, and Eileen talked among themselves Sunday evening. Katie wasn't improving. She was no longer speaking or responding coherently to their direct questions. Eileen and his mom were adamant that Katie needed hospitalization.

Jamie struggled against this conclusion, unwilling to accept that it had come to this, especially since Katie didn't seem a risk to herself, the baby, or anyone else in her current state of near stupor. He thought back to the alarming incident when he and his siblings had wrested Patsy from Katie's arms in the kitchen. That terrifying burst of 'excitability' had been short-lived and never repeated. He desperately wanted to believe it was a one-time incident and that she would get better. Wasn't she better off at home, surrounded by people who loved her?

Finally, he nodded, acquiescing to his mother's and Eileen's assessment of the situation—it was two against one. They were likely more objective, but they had less to lose, too. He couldn't shake the feeling that he was failing Katie by sending her away. All she needed was a couple of good night's sleep. That would cure everything, Jamie thought. How hard could that be? She had to be exhausted.

When Doc Collins called Sunday night, Jamie asked him to make the necessary arrangements for Monday morning. Afterward, they prayed for a miraculous recovery during the night. But if no miracle came, Eileen had already decided to take the day off from the millinery shop to accompany her sister to Wingdale, along with Mom and Jamie.

~*~

Dawn's first light filtered through the dormer window Monday morning. Katie sat immobile in the rocking chair in the nursery, a prisoner in the cell of her self-imposed exile. She held sleeping Patsy, with a full tummy of breast milk, while little Meggie slept soundly in her crib on the opposite side of the room.

As the sunlight crept in, Katie remained focused, deciphering the secret messages embedded within the wallpaper. Suddenly, the stripes in the wallpaper peeled off the wall, encircling Katie within their vertical bars of gold. A profound sense of revelation and understanding filled her—everything made sense now. All the mysteries of the universe lay bare before her. She saw patterns, dangers, signs in everything.

Katie heard a loud voice say, "You and the baby are not safe; you must flee to safety." It was God's voice—unmistakable.

"Open the nursery window," the voice commanded. A brilliant light vibrated with each word, filling the attic nursery with dazzling brightness.

"They are trying to kill the child," boomed the voice again. "You must take the baby and flee to safety. They want to poison her."

Katie stood abruptly, pacing the room, clutching Patsy to her chest. *But where should I go?* she thought, panic taking hold.

"I shall send an angel to guide you to safety. You must escape out the window. My angel will catch you and the child and carry you to safety. But first, you must get a knife to protect yourself from those who wish to kill the child."

Suddenly, the orange trumpet flowers on the wallpaper withered before her eyes, falling to the floor in a lifeless heap. The vines, once decorative, slithered down, weaving an impenetrable thicket around her. She was trapped.

Katie felt herself being pulled downward, against her will, by a dark, evil force. The vines moved ominously toward her, grabbing her by the neck, arms, and ankles. Suddenly, everything went dark.

On the seventh day, Katie descended into hell...

The only light came from burning chasms of fire that smelled of sulfur and decaying flesh. Moans and screams echoed off the cavernous walls where demons tortured people who had failed—like Katie. Their fangs dripped with blood, and their eyes flashed like fire in snake-like heads. They walked upright on the back legs of their lizard-like bodies, jabbing people with sharp, red-hot pokers in all parts of their bodies.

Katie tried to run but found herself shackled and chained.

Satan swaggered toward her, cackling like a witch. The heat was unbearable, and her body began sweating profusely. Satan spat in her face and grabbed one of her arms. His touch sent searing pain through her body, burning her flesh.

"So, you think you are too good for me?" Satan said in her father's voice. His face melted off, as if wax, and became Da's face. Satan slapped her face, and her cheek burned in agony.

"Where is the child? She must be sacrificed. You have failed," Satan bellowed.

"Kill me, not the child," Katie screamed, trying to free her arm.

Then she understood: she had been sentenced to hell because she had failed her mission. But what was that mission? She didn't know, and now it was too late. Many would suffer because of her. She saw a stream of innocent people, bleating like lambs, washing into hell on a current of molten lava—Peggy, Eileen, and Jamie among them.

"It's my fault, it's my fault," she cried in horror, suffocating with guilt and remorse and laboring to draw breath.

She felt a stream of cool air on her face. She looked up to see an angel flying into the inferno toward her.

"I am Gabriel with a message for you," he said, his voice like the ringing of a crystal bell. "We must flee into Egypt, where the child will be safe."

The angel cradled Patsy in one iridescent wing and shielded his face with the other. He pulled on Katie's arm, but it tore loose from her body. A demon then came forward and gouged out her eyes. She screamed as all went dark.

~*~

From the bedroom, Jamie jolted awake at the sound of Katie's screams. His heart raced as he burst into the nursery, where Meggie and Patsy were both wailing.

"My God, Katie, what are you doing?" he shouted.

Katie had wrapped Patsy around her in a makeshift sling of baby blankets. She was naked except for her bloomers, her eyes unfocused as she brandished a black-handled butcher knife.

"Kill me instead!" she screamed.

"It's okay, Katie. No one is going to hurt you or Patsy," Jamie said softly, inching closer, his eyes fixed on the knife.

Katie collapsed to her knees. "Oh my God, I am heartily sorry for having offended thee," she whispered repeatedly, her voice thick with remorse.

Jamie knocked the knife from her hand, the metal clattering to the floor, and threw it out the window. He knelt beside her, pulling her close. This time, she didn't resist.

"Katie, my love, where have you gone? Please, come back to me," he sobbed.

THIRTEEN

January 1930 (Two weeks later)

The snowy landscape stretched out before Jamie, sparkling like diamonds beneath the brittle, cloudless sky as he drove north along Route 22 to Wingdale. Normally, he might delight in the beauty of his surroundings: random stands of conifers, their green branches bending beneath weighty clumps of unblemished snow, and merry black-capped chickadees feasting on plump, red holly berries. But today, he was blind to this beauty; his mood mirrored the bleak, skeletal deciduous trees bordering the road. Thoughts of Katie brought on the now-familiar tightness in his chest—a pain that crept through him like frost, piercing and unshakable.

He checked the time on his new wristwatch, a Christmas present from Katie, bought months before Patsy was born. Opening the gift on Christmas morning without her had brought a sting to his eyes and a lump to his throat. Now, a wave of grief washed over him as he reflected on those better times.

Dr. Albrecht Schuler, Katie's doctor—a psychiatrist, the receptionist had called him when setting the appointment—expected Jamie at Harlem Valley State Hospital at eleven. It would be his first chance to speak with the man since Katie's admission, and anxiety pressed heavily on his mind.

Surely, two weeks was sufficient time to observe and assess Katie's condition and to find a treatment that worked. What were reasonable expectations for Katie's recovery? Jamie had no idea. He needed to believe that she would recover. Why wouldn't she? She was young, healthy, and sharp-minded—it was all in her favor. The uncertainly gnawed at him.

Scenes from the nightmarish week after Patsy's birth flooded Jamie's mind like flotsam from a shipwreck, tossed helplessly on a sea of madness. The last time he had driven these roads, Eileen and Mom had sat with Katie between them in the backseat. When Patsy fussed, Katie had nursed her mechanically, her eyes vacant and distant, devoid of the tenderness of the Katie he had fallen in love with.

Katie had refused to release Patsy, clinging to her with a desperate strength that shook Jamie to his core. Two towering male orderlies had stepped in, and even the nurse, who, despite her starched white dress and cap, resembled a wrestler, had pried Patsy from Katie's arms and placed the infant in Mom's care. Katie's screams had pierced the air as the orderlies strapped her to the gurney, kicking and thrashing all the way inside.

Mercifully, her screams had faded as the orderlies wheeled the gurney away, somewhere that Jamie hadn't been allowed to follow.

With a shaking hand and a dirge in his heart, he had filled out the surprisingly few forms for Katie's admission. That the hospital hadn't requested much information regarding Katie's condition further upset Jamie. How could they treat her in a vacuum of pertinent details? He remembered watching his mother and Eileen in the waiting area, calming Patsy with a bottle of milk, tears spilling onto their cheeks, as he tried to calm himself enough to complete the minimal paperwork for Katie's admission.

Jamie parked the car in the lot to the left of the main building, the three-story red brick structure looming over the sprawling campus. He glanced at his watch—twenty minutes early for his meeting. Across the lot, a maintenance worker bundled against the cold shoveled a path to the building. They exchanged brief nods, but Jamie's face remained hard.

Pea gravel crunched underfoot as he made his way across the parking lot to the front entrance. He opened the heavy wooden door, the metal bars of its window forming a grid beneath a shallow, recessed archway.

Jamie stepped into a wide hallway, its sage-colored walls and pale yellow ceiling adorned with matching crown molding stretching high above him. The tessellated linoleum floor—a pattern of dark green diamonds and lighter green hexagons—led him forward, guiding him to the check-in area, where the hallway opened into a T.

A middle-aged, matronly woman sat behind a rounded wooden enclosure—half desk, half barrier—and looked up as Jamie entered. She stood immediately, smoothing her gray woolen dress, a shade darker than the gray streaks in her hair, which was pulled into a tight bun at the nape of her neck.

"Good afternoon," she said pleasantly. Her obsidian eyes, accented by high, thin brows, flicked over his face and upper body in a quick, appraising glance, though Jamie barely registered it today.

"I have a meeting with Dr. Schuler regarding my wife, Katie Murphy," Jamie said. "I'm early. The drive from Tarrytown didn't take as long as I thought it would."

"Please have a seat, and I'll let Dr. Schuler know you're here." She motioned to the two alcoves on either side of her desk. "Either side, it doesn't matter."

Each waiting area was a mirror image of the other: an overstuffed sofa with two matching chairs, a coffee table holding two small books, and a pair of end tables with lamps. Above the sofa hung an architectural rendering of the hospital, its design resembling a bat wing.

Though the facility was impressive in size and only six years old, the bars latticed across the windows made it clear this was no ordinary hospital. Jamie chose the alcove to his right and sank into the sofa. He reached for the nearest book on the coffee table, *Harlem Valley State Hospital: Kirkbride's Model for Healing the Insane*. He cringed at the word "insane" but flipped it open and began reading.

> *Harlem Valley State Hospital is a 900-acre facility located in a stunningly beautiful area of Dutchess County, New York. Originally, the state purchased the land for a prison but chose instead to construct a mental hospital according to the "Kirkbride" plan.*
>
> *In this architectural plan, multiple floors of patient rooms fan out in a "V" shape from the main entrance and central administrative offices, with men on one side and women on the other. The staggered arrangement of patient rooms, or "pavilions," ensures that every room receives maximum airflow, sunlight, and an unobstructed view of the serene, park-like surroundings.*

> *Each pavilion is organized into a ward or "family" unit with approximately twenty patients. Patients in each ward take their meals together in the company of the charge nurse and, ideally, the treating psychiatrist.*
>
> *The wards for patients requiring the most care are located at the ends of each floor. As patients progress, they move to pavilions closer to the hospital's center and, consequently, to the exit— which is the goal of treatment.*

Jamie leafed through the pages, studying the pictures and reading their captions. He soon realized that Harlem Valley State Hospital was like a small city, complete with its own power plant, sprawling agricultural fields, dairy farm, ice cream parlor, bowling alley, golf course, bakery, and even a cemetery, "providing opportunities for patients to engage in meaningful activities." There was also an infirmary, a small hospital within the hospital, where patients could be treated for illnesses, injuries, or surgeries beyond their psychiatric care. There were dentist offices, too.

A train platform connected Harlem Valley State Hospital to Manhattan. Though many of the staff lived on-site in housing built for that purpose, the facility still couldn't accommodate everyone needed to care for the nearly 1600 patients and manage its massive operations.

Jamie glanced at his watch again. The doctor was running late. He put the first book back on the table and picked up the second. Opening its aged, brown leather cover, he flipped to the title page: *On the Construction, Organization, and General Arrangements of Hospitals for the Insane: With Some Remarks on Insanity and Its Treatment*, by Thomas S. Kirkbride, M.D., second edition, 1880. The book was as old as the worn cover suggested.

Jamie skimmed the first several pages. This Kirkbride fellow had spent forty years as Chief Physician at the Pennsylvania Hospital for the Insane. This experience led him to believe that the architectural design and physical environment of asylums and hospitals were critical for the recovery of the insane. Jamie read: *"With proper custody, in fully funded state institutions, and with appropriate treatment provided by strangers rather than the family, recovery is achievable for more than 80% of the insane."*

Jamie needed to believe in that eighty percent. He reasoned that if Dr. Kirkbride had written those words fifty years ago, cures would be even higher now. The New York State Legislature had agreed with

Kirkbride's ideas, as there had been no mention of payment when Jamie had checked Katie into Harlem Valley State Hospital.

"Mr. Murphy," the receptionist called from her desk.

Jamie was so absorbed in the book that he didn't hear her the first time. Even when she called his name again, it barely registered.

"Mr. Murphy, Dr. Schuler will see you now," she repeated, standing in front of him, her tone more insistent. Jamie quickly closed the book and stood, feeling a sense of encouragement as he followed her to the second floor.

~*~

"Good morning, Mr. Murphy. I'm Dr. Al Schuler, your wife's psychiatrist. I'm glad you could make it today."

Jamie took in the doctor's appearance: a short, stocky man with a pale complexion and dishwater blond hair. Round, dark-framed eyeglasses framed his serious, gray eyes. His mouth bent into a tight smile beneath a well-trimmed mustache, thin as a caterpillar. Confidence and formality radiated from the man, and Jamie guessed he was in his forties or fifties.

"A small break in the weather helped," Jamie said, extending his hand to meet the psychiatrist's lukewarm handshake.

The doctor motioned to one of the walnut Art Deco-style armchairs facing his desk. Between them was a small walnut table with a notepad and pen.

Jamie glanced around the office. A tall wooden bookcase, overflowing with books, covered the entire wall behind Jamie. Dr. Schuler reclined in his swivel chair behind a large walnut desk. The window in his office faced onto what appeared to be a small town, though Jamie now understood it was part of the facility. He noted the absence of bars on the window and spotted a large barn and smokestack exuding curly white smoke in the distance.

Dr. Schuler wiped his needle-thin nose with a white and brown plaid handkerchief, still folded. "Just getting over a cold," he explained, sniffing. He stuffed it back into the coat pocket of his brown, well-tailored three-piece suit.

Jamie read the diploma on the wall behind Dr. Schuler's desk. "You studied in Germany at the University of Munich?" he asked.

"Yes, before the war." Dr. Schuler quickly added, "But only for my medical studies. I returned to the United States in 1908. I studied under

Professor Emil Kraepelin, which is why I went to Munich. Have you heard of him?"

"No, I've never had a reason to follow in this new field of psychiatry, that is, until Katie's recent troubles."

"Kraepelin has done much to advance the understanding of patients suffering symptoms like those your wife is currently experiencing. He died four years ago, but I have kept up with his research and clinical findings." As he spoke, Dr. Schuler waved toward several open books on his desk.

Jamie sat expectantly, waiting for the doctor to continue. He felt a bit overwhelmed by the immensity of the facility, his ignorance of mental disorders, and the realization of how important this man might be in helping Katie get well as soon as possible.

"I have your wife's file here." Dr. Schuler tapped an open folder on his desk. "I've met with her twice since she was admitted, most recently yesterday. Additionally, I've spoken with the head nurse in her ward, reviewed all the daily notes, and observed her at mealtimes when I joined her group for lunch."

"Then perhaps you can help me understand what's wrong with my wife. How can she be perfectly fine for her whole life and then, days after giving birth, experience a devastating nervous breakdown?" Jamie leaned forward, inching closer to the doctor.

"It is early in your wife's hospitalization, and I don't yet have a final diagnosis. But based on my clinical observations and years of experience, I think she is suffering either from dementia praecox or manic depression. Eugen Bleuler, a European psychiatrist, used the term *schizophrenia* for dementia praecox. But I use the more accepted terminology, dementia praecox, as I believe it is more descriptive of the eventual outcome."

From Jamie's years of studying Latin in seminary, he knew that *dementia praecox* meant premature dementia. A wave of dread washed over him, submerging his optimism.

"It can be tricky to differentiate between dementia praecox and manic depression. The symptoms overlap considerably in the acute or subacute phase of dementia praecox and the hypermania or psychosis phase of manic depression. The primary difference is in the progression and outlook for the two diagnoses.

"In dementia praecox, the internal connections within the brain and psychic personality are destroyed as the disease progresses. A loss of mental activity and an inevitable poverty of thought generally follow. Many patients may eventually become mute and completely withdrawn.

"Consequently, the outlook for dementia praecox is quite dismal, while manic-depressive individuals can have long periods of remission and do not experience the complete disintegration of personality. The treatment, however, remains the same for both.

"Your wife has not had any episodes of extreme excitability beyond when she was first admitted, but there has been little change in her condition. She remains passive and withdrawn. In addition, we are treating her for a mild case of mastitis, which sometimes happens when a woman stops nursing abruptly."

"You mentioned that the treatment is the same. What exactly is the treatment, doctor?"

"You are an educated man, Mr. Murphy. I noted that you have several years of college education on Katie's admitting paperwork, so I'll speak bluntly. The primary treatment is the passage of time and the facility itself, which provides a safe and humane environment for the brain to heal if it can. Should Katie become unduly agitated, I will prescribe potassium bromide to help calm any behavioral seizures or hydrotherapy, which consists of restrained water baths. Failing that, there are times we must resort to a straitjacket—although this is far from my preference."

"Sadly, there is no medication to heal either malady: dementia praecox or manic depression. Potassium bromide is not without its difficulties. Yes, it is calming, but it further impairs the patient's memory with long-term use."

"But she is so young. How could this happen? She was perfectly fine before this."

"Regarding age at first hospitalization, let me show you something." Dr. Schuler pulled a book from the stack on his desk, opening it to the first bookmark and handing it to Jamie. "You are studying economics, again information I gleaned from your wife's admission paperwork, so you are familiar with data and charts."

Jamie nodded.

"We don't know what causes dementia praecox or manic-depressive insanity—be it organic or genetic—but I believe the root is biological. I'm an empiricist, as was my mentor Kraepelin. I have nothing but disdain for Freud's psychoanalytic methods." Dr. Schuler grimaced at his mention of Freud's name. "But to your question, note on the bar chart that seventy percent of the cases of dementia praecox occur between the ages of twenty and thirty."

"But you said that you aren't sure if Katie has dementia praecox or manic depression," Jamie objected.

"True. However, I want you to temper your expectations. Unfortunately, it may take many months, possibly years, to diagnose confidently. The primary importance of a diagnosis is to set realistic expectations for recovery. Every patient is different, and the symptoms of both diseases can vary even within the same patient and may wax and wane over time. But with dementia praecox, the spiral is ultimately downward."

Jamie closed the red leather-covered book and was ready to hand it back.

"Not yet," Dr. Schuler said, holding his palm out. "Go to the second bookmark." He waited for Jamie to do so. "On page 242, begin reading at the second full paragraph. To yourself, please."

When Jamie finished, he turned to the title page: *Dementia Praecox and Paraphrenia* by Professor Emil Kraepelin, Munich, publication date 1919.

"As you just read, Kraepelin documented that for about twenty-five percent of women he observed—among thousands of cases—the onset of dementia praecox was triggered by pregnancy, childbirth, in childbed, after a miscarriage, and—this is the part I wish to emphasize—sometimes during the period of lactation, as was your wife's experience.

"I believe the changes caused by the work of reproduction in a woman's body can trigger changes in the brain that may lead to either manic depression or dementia praecox. Only time will tell in your wife's case."

Jamie struggled against the anger-tinged desperation welling up inside him, fighting to retain his initial optimism like a starving man grasping at bread crumbs. Despite Dr. Schuler's extensive education, intelligence, and clinical experience, he didn't know Katie like Jamie did. She was a fighter. She would get better.

"May I see my wife today?" There was an urgency, almost a

demand, in Jamie's voice.

"We should be able to look in on her briefly, assuming she isn't agitated."

"Of course. I only want what is … best for Katie." Jamie heard the break in his voice, his discouragement dissolving into grief. He wanted the best for himself, too, and for their two daughters, Meggie and Patsy. What was happening now was the worst for everyone.

"She is eating lunch now. While we allow Mrs. Murphy to finish, I would like to ask you some questions since Katie was either non-communicative or unable to answer my questions comprehensibly. Is that all right?"

Jamie nodded slowly, struggling to maintain his composure.

"As I previously stated, I believe there is a biological root to Mrs. Murphy's mental state. However, emotional and physical stress can trigger biological vulnerabilities in the mind. I hope you won't take offense at any of my questions. I'm not trying to psychoanalyze—that's useless nonsense—but I do need context when working with her should she begin speaking again."

The psychiatrist's questions were comprehensive: *How long had Jamie known Katie? What was her life like growing up? What was her relationship with her parents and siblings? Was there a family history of mental illness? How had she performed in school? Did she attend college? Had there been any grave disappointments, worries, or guilt that burdened Katie? Any extenuating circumstances when they married? How long after they were married was the first child born? Any mental or physical health issues before or after the first child was born? When did the problems begin with the second child? Had she seemed upset by the stock market collapse and runs on the financial institutions? Had Katie ever heard voices or seen things that other people didn't? Was she a happy person?* And so it went.

Finally, Jamie described everything from the seven days leading up to her hospitalization, stopping at times to swallow the anguish that threatened to consume him.

It took over an hour to get through all the doctor's questions and ensuing discussion. Dr. Schuler took copious notes, nodding and actively listening, occasionally probing deeper with follow-up questions. Jamie couldn't help but feel that Katie was in good hands. The doctor's thoroughness restored a fragile sense of hope despite everything.

"I'll summarize what I think I heard, Mr. Murphy. If you think of anything else while I'm summarizing, please jot it down—or if you need to correct anything, please note that too. There's a pencil and paper on the table for you."

Jamie had to give the psychiatrist credit. Dr. Schuler had listened and transcribed carefully.

"Would you like to add anything?" Dr. Schuler asked when he finished, his gray eyes intent.

"My wife and I were very happily married. I love Katie more than life itself and want her back home as soon as possible." Jamie's voice caught, thick with emotion.

"I empathize with you, Mr. Murphy. I'm a married man with a family, too. Your wife is a beautiful woman who should be enjoying the best years of her life with her family. Rest assured that I want nothing more than her recovery as well." Dr. Schuler laid down his pen and notepad. "Katie's ward will have finished lunch by now. Shall we go, then?"

As they walked to Katie's ward, Dr. Schuler explained how things operated there. "Normal visiting hours are in the afternoon, between one and four. I suggest calling beforehand to ensure your wife is doing well enough to accept visitors that day. The fewer visitors, the better. There is a specific room set aside for visitation in each ward."

"Today's visit will be slightly irregular, but I think you may be comforted to see where your wife is living, given her current symptoms," Dr. Schuler told Jamie as they left his office.

They took the stairs to the third floor, turned left, and made their way down a long hallway to the end.

The doctor unlocked a wooden door with a grated window, leading them into another hallway and then a train-like succession of pavilions, each set back slightly from the last. Narrow passageways with doors connected the pavilions. Each pavilion was a complete ward which, as Dr. Schuler explained, "has its own dining room, recreation room, shower area with therapy room, and a visitation room, in addition to the patient rooms."

They finally entered Katie's ward, passing by rooms on either side of the hallway where the women slept. Each private bedroom contained a twin-sized bed, a small wooden desk and chair, a recessed nook with a toilet and sink, and a window with an outside view. Jamie noticed one patient lying on her bed, motionless.

Dr. Schuler stopped suddenly. "Well, here we are," he announced. "This is the recreation room, where we encourage the women to gather after lunch," Dr. Schuler told Jamie as he led him inside.

Katie stood in front of the large picture window at one end of the spartan room, her back to Jamie and Dr. Schuler as they entered. Her copper hair caught and reflected the sunlight off the snow through the glass. She wore the same slipper shoes, socks, and shapeless cotton shift as the other women, though the fabric varied. Katie was not the youngest, but nearly so. A white cotton sweater hung loosely from her narrow shoulders. Jamie's heart leaped at the sight of her and then sank as he studied the other women in the room.

Several women sat alone at tables with two chairs, doodling on foolscap paper with Binney & Smith chalk-based crayons. Others wandered around the room aimlessly, while still others held dolls with bisque faces and soft, stuffed bodies dressed as babies. Some paged through picture books. One woman conversed with herself, standing up, slapping each leg rhythmically, laughing aloud, sitting back down, and then repeating the process. Several women, seated alone, stared blankly.

A young, sturdy woman with a kind face, dressed in a blue smock with a white apron and nurse's hat, walked toward Dr. Schuler and Jamie. Another patient, a wizened woman with short gray hair, walked up to Jamie, inspecting him from head to toe and circling around him. None of the other women seemed disturbed or even aware of Jamie's presence.

"It's okay, Gladys. Why don't you find a book for me to read to you? I'll join you shortly after I talk with Dr. Schuler," the nurse said, pointing to a small bookcase in the room. She gently but firmly squeezed the thin woman's wrinkled hand.

Gladys's lower lip pushed out in an exaggerated pout, but she did as the nurse suggested.

"Nurse James," Dr. Schuler said, "this is Mr. Murphy, Katie Murphy's husband. He wants to say hello to his wife before returning home to Tarrytown."

"Nice to meet you, Mr. Murphy." Nurse James smiled, but her eyebrows drew together in confusion.

With a calming motion of his hands and a nod that seemed to say,

"It's okay, and yes, I know this is irregular," Dr. Schuler reassured Nurse James. She nodded in understanding and joined Gladys, who had selected a child's book and was waiting at a table.

Dr. Schuler motioned for Jamie to follow him to where Katie stood.

"Katie, your husband is here to see you. Can you say hello?" Dr. Schuler said.

"Hi, Katie-love," Jamie said with a forced, joyful lilt. "I've missed you. Patsy and Meggie are doing fine. Mom and Eileen send their love."

Katie didn't respond, stepping further away from the two men without turning around or casting even the tiniest glance in their direction.

Jamie watched Katie move away, denying him even the slightest note of recognition. His heart ached, and he felt a raging anger toward God for the first time in his twenty-five years.

He felt Dr. Schuler's hand on his elbow.

"It's still early, Mr. Murphy. Give her time." He added softly, with slight hesitation, "One of the first manifestations of dementia praecox is a complete reversal of the patient's emotional relationships, where former feelings of affection for those closest to the patient are often replaced with aversion."

~*~

Dr. Schuler returned to his office after escorting Jamie back to the reception area. He sat at his desk, ruminating. Although it was highly irregular to allow a family member into the "bowels" of the facility, he wanted Mr. Murphy to see where his wife's condition would likely progress. He strongly suspected that Kathleen Murphy was in the acute phase of dementia praecox and that her prognosis was likely hopeless.

Why had her case touched him so deeply? Schuler hated to think it was due to her natural beauty, which, even burdened with insanity, blossomed like a single rose amongst a field of weeds. After twenty years of working with the insane, mostly with women, he had never become personally involved or even been tempted. Yet twenty-two-year-old Kathleen Murphy had somehow crawled beneath his tough professional skin. Barring any physical affliction, she would likely live a long, meaningless life in this very mental institution—such a waste.

She had already brought two babies into the world. What awaited them and their descendants? He wondered if Kathleen's mental illness would have taken root if she'd never given birth.

Like most men in the American Association for the Study of the Feeble-Minded, he firmly believed in compulsory sterilization laws. Without the judicious use of sterilization, it was impossible to cope with the problem of feeblemindedness and the financial drain on society that their custody and care posed.

New York State allowed for the involuntary sterilization of patients with mental illnesses, developmental disabilities, or other hereditary defects, as did twenty-nine other states. Dr. Schuler was proud that the operating room at Harlem Valley State Hospital now performed salpingectomies (removal of the fallopian tubes) as well as vasectomies or castrations for males when deemed essential by the treating doctor or psychiatrist. Eugenic sterilization, he believed, was essential to preserve the genetic integrity of America's people, and such measures within a state mental institution did not require spousal or parental consent.

Kathleen's illness, like that of several other women he had treated over the years, seemed to be tied to reproduction. He followed the new science on hormones carefully, particularly the work of American researchers Edgar Allan and Edward Doisy and that of German Adolf Butenandt, who had isolated a substance in the urine of pregnant women called estrone.

Dr. Schuler wondered if this hormone might have applications in treating mental illness in women like Kathleen, whose insanity was triggered after the birth of a child. Could such a hormone trick a woman's brain into a hormonal state of false pregnancy, thereby reversing her mental decline brought about after childbirth?

He would need to bide his time carefully, waiting at least eighteen months or longer. If Kathleen Murphy showed no improvement or her condition further degenerated, he would initiate his experiment. By then, he expected her husband's visits to taper off. Schuler had seen this happen routinely. As the ravages of the disease drained their hopes for recovery, family members, especially spouses, stopped coming. "She doesn't know who I am; why bother? I must continue with my life," they reasoned, to endure their grief and loss of hope. Schuler didn't blame them.

Yes, he would need to wait. But eventually, Kathleen Murphy's life could at least advance the cause of science, even if she never experienced a cure.

FOURTEEN

October 1932 (Two years, nine months later)

"I'm taking the train to see Katie after classes today, so I'll be late getting home, Mom. Do you want me to ask Gracie or Annie to watch the girls? It'll make for a long day without me here to help out," Jamie said.

"No, no. I'll be fine." His mother shifted her weight slightly, as though trying to ease the ache in her fifty-six-year-old lower back from lugging around Meggie and Patsy for almost two years, acting more like a mother than a grandmother. "Gracie has plenty on her hands with her two youngsters and a third on the way. Besides, Annie and Bill are packing up their apartment and moving in with his parents today."

"What?" Jamie looked up with raised eyebrows and set down his mug of coffee before taking his first sip. Thomas and Robert jerked their heads up, breaking their focus from their plates of bacon, eggs, and toast.

"Annie called last night very upset after all of you were in bed. Bill got laid off at the Chevy plant yesterday. I feel so bad for them—this is not the easiest time to begin married life. No one's protected from the downturn in the economy. When will it end?" Mom said, her look drifting out the kitchen window into the backyard.

Like the front yard, the Murphys had replaced the back lawn with a vegetable garden. They always had eggs, thanks to the backyard chicken coop, and now they enjoyed plentiful vegetables in the summer and early fall. Any excess was canned and stored for the winter months. Although the vegetable garden came at the sacrifice of the lawn and Mom's rose and flower gardens, hard times made such choices easy.

When half the money from the farm sale evaporated overnight, it seemed like a devastating loss. Jamie knew Mom felt blessed and grateful for the half they still had. She often said many folks had it much worse. Even Katie's hospitalization and care at Harlem Valley hadn't cost the family a penny. Things were far from perfect, especially for Jamie, but his mother was a spot of sunshine on even the darkest days.

Patsy rested on Mom's left hip, balanced by her grandmother's embracing arm. With her free hand, Mom leaned over to grab a bib from a kitchen drawer. "At least Annie and Bill's lease was month-to-month," she said, pushing up the tray of the oak high chair. She placed Patsy in the seat of the high chair, pulled the tray back down over her head, and tied the bib around her neck. Mom handed Patsy a piece of jelly toast.

"Yum, toe-th," she said.

"Rats, that's too bad Bill lost his job," Jamie said. "I can't say I'm surprised, though. Demand for automobiles has fallen by three-quarters compared to the years before the market crashed, and unemployment is still climbing. Who has money for new cars when people are just trying to feed their families? God only knows what jobs there will be when I graduate from law school in June." Given the pitiful state of the job market, Jamie had stayed on at Fordham University for his Juris Doctor, specializing in contract law, after finishing his bachelor's degree in business and economics two years ago.

"I sure wish I could help Bill out. I owe him one," said twenty-year-old Thomas, who had been rustling up odd automotive repair jobs since being laid off over a year ago. "Without him, I'd never have gotten my foot in the door at the Chevy plant. If only he had some hands-on mechanical car skills. Sometimes, it pays to be the common laborer instead of a manager pushing numbers at a desk."

Meggie sat between Jamie and her uncle Robert as the family finished breakfast. She quietly poured milk over the remainder of her eggs and toast.

"I'll watch Meggie and Patsy when I get home from football practice today," Robert said. The athletic and thoughtful fifteen-year-old carried his breakfast dishes to the sink, tickling Patsy's bare feet on the way.

Mom cleared her throat. "I'm glad you are finally going to see Katie. You haven't gone to see her for over two months. She's still your wife and your daughters' mother," Mom said, a chiding edge to her voice. But she was right—he'd stayed away too long. "We can't give up hope, son," she said more softly.

The sadness of dashed hopes resided in Jamie's wide-set dark eyes, his once sunny disposition replaced by a swirling storm that built in force and never cleared. He had weathered the first year of Katie's illness and hospitalization as well as any husband could have. But everything changed nine months ago when he brought home her final diagnosis: dementia praecox.

Jamie's trips to Wingdale began to dwindle after that—from weekly to twice monthly, to monthly, or even longer. It had been his way of coping, though it didn't excuse his absences.

He could see the pain in his mother's eyes when their eyes met— the burden of his loss weighing on her as well. Jamie knew his mother was doing her best to fill in for Katie with Meggie and Patsy, but there was little she could do to diminish the loss of his beloved Katie.

"I know, Mom. But it's so hard. She has no idea who I am. It's almost worse than if she were dead. At least there would be closure instead of waiting for a miracle that never happens."

Jamie glanced down, noticing the mess Meggie was making as she splashed milk on his arm. "No, Meggie, don't make a mess," he said sharply, taking her glass of milk away but missing the soupy mix of eggs and toast on her plate.

"Eileen saw Katie last month and said she seemed like she was gaining some weight, but she was still as confused and vacant as ever," Jamie said.

"I'm praying for a miracle every day for Katie," Robert said as he hefted his book bag over his broad shoulders.

"Thanks, buddy. That means a lot," Jamie said, his lips parting into a weak smile.

"Grammy, me all done," Meggie interjected in her sweet, high-pitched voice as she patted her hands into the milky mix of half-finished scrambled eggs and jelly toast. "Me getting down now," Meggie announced.

"Meggie, let's wash your sticky hands and face first before you get down to play," Mom said. "Jamie, please keep her at the table while I get a warm cloth."

Jamie put down his fork and distractedly pulled Meggie up onto his lap. After his mother wiped her hands and face, he set Meggie down, kissed the top of her head, and finished eating the scrambled eggs swimming in milk from his daughter's plate. No one wasted food in the Murphy household.

"I need to ring the hospital to let them know I plan to visit Katie today. Excuse me," Jamie said, pushing away from the table.

Jamie stepped into the hallway where the telephone hung on the wall and placed a long-distance call to Harlem Valley State Hospital. As he listened, his voice grew loud, irritated, and angry as the conversation progressed. Mom came to the hallway and wiped her hands on her apron. Her face tightened with alarm.

He waited, gripping the receiver tightly.

"You get a message to Dr. Schuler that if anyone touches my wife, I'll make sure he never practices medicine again. Do you hear me?" Jamie's voice sharpened. As a third-year law student, he had acquired a certain cockiness.

"I'm driving to the hospital as soon as I hang up. Tell Dr. Schuler to expect me in an hour, and I intend to see my wife. There is to be no procedure—whatsoever—unless I say so. Do you hear me?"

Jamie slammed the phone down, cutting off the call.

"What's wrong? Is Katie sick?" Mom asked, suddenly at his side.

"I don't know. The person I usually check in with transferred me to a nurse who told me I couldn't visit today or for two days because Katie was scheduled for some medical procedure this morning. Something isn't right." Jamie exhaled loudly, his mind racing. "May I use the car to drive to Wingdale? There's no time to take the train."

"Of course, take the car. I know you're upset, but please drive carefully, Jamie."

~*~

Jamie stormed into Dr. Schuler's office without waiting for the receptionist's escort. The psychiatrist's gray eyes remained placid, as if an angry man rushing into his office were a daily occurrence. He stood up from behind his desk and offered his hand to Jamie, but Jamie refused to shake it.

"What procedure did you authorize on Katie this morning without my consent?" Jamie railed, standing in front of Dr. Schuler's desk, his body shaking with anger.

"Please, sit down, Mr. Murphy. Try to calm yourself, and I'll explain everything," Dr. Schuler said, closing the office door.

Dr. Schuler raised his hands in a placating gesture. "Please, Mr. Murphy, be seated."

Jamie sat in the chair closest to the door, directly in front of the desk where the psychiatrist now sat.

"First of all, the procedure did not take place—yet. The hospital is authorized by the state of New York to perform a salpingectomy for the insane without your approval."

"What on God's earth is a salpingectomy?" Jamie demanded, his eyes narrowing.

"It's a procedure that removes the middle section of the fallopian tubes to prevent any future pregnancies."

"You mean to permanently sterilize my wife and make her unable to conceive any future children, even if she makes a miraculous recovery?" Jamie seethed.

"Yes, but there was a snag. When Mrs. Murphy was examined by the surgeon this morning, around the time you phoned to say you were planning to visit, she was found to be about three months pregnant," Dr. Schuler calmly explained.

"Pregnant? Are you kidding me?" Jamie shouted, wanting to hit someone. "How could that happen under your care?" His hands balled into fists, adrenaline shooting through his veins like a speeding train. As if the situation with Katie couldn't get any worse, it just had.

"I can't give you a specific answer, except to say that sexual relations between staff and patients, or between patients, should never happen. There is absolutely no excuse for it. We have rules and safeguards to protect against this. The most likely explanation is that a man on staff took advantage of your wife."

"You mean like a doctor?"

"It's possible, but more likely a male orderly or another employee. Nurses often call for male assistance when dealing with out-of-control female patients. While we have strict protocols in place to prevent inappropriate sexual contact, there has been an inexcusable breach in your wife's case—for which I'm deeply sorry.

"Without minimizing the gravity of the situation, the country's severely depressed economy has significantly reduced funding for state asylums like ours. We rely entirely on state appropriations to provide the fee-free care Katie receives. However, staff reductions have strained us, and we now care for over a thousand more patients than when you committed your wife."

Jamie was keenly aware of the budget cuts. He followed the news diligently, as did his mother. Still, a crime had been committed against his defenseless wife, and someone had to pay. But it wasn't that simple. Any litigation would only fuel negative publicity for his family and complicate the plight of the baby.

"Of course, we will take every reasonable step to find the culprit, although we may never know if Katie can't tell us. But now that Mrs. Murphy is in this most unfortunate situation, we must determine the best course of action while we still have options."

Jamie held his head in his hands, fighting back tears, praying this was just a bad dream. How could a good God allow this to happen? The thought of another man violating Katie infuriated and sickened him. "What do you mean by options?"

"We can surgically terminate the pregnancy, as she's not too far along, and ensure it never happens again with a salpingectomy."

"You mean abort the baby Katie is carrying and permanently sterilize her because you couldn't protect her?" Jamie stared at Dr. Schuler in disbelief.

"Well, yes, although that's the most negative way to frame it."

"While your solution may sweep this horrendous situation under the rug for the hospital—and your ward, specifically, Dr. Schuler—it doesn't solve or change anything. And let's not forget you're talking about snuffing out an innocent life. You do know abortion is illegal, right?"

"Right now, only three people know about your wife's pregnancy: you, me, and the surgeon scheduled to perform the salpingectomy. There's no written record of her condition. If we're all in agreement, the abortion can be performed confidentially, along with the salpingectomy."

"I do *not* give my permission. Even though we both know the baby growing in Katie's womb isn't mine, I'm her husband, and that makes the child legally mine—whether or not I'm the biological father, and regardless of Katie's mental state."

"But think of the child, Mr. Murphy. No one will adopt a baby with a double stigma: a mother with dementia praecox and the product of a rape. The child will end up in an orphanage, living a horrible life without the benefit of a loving family."

"You and I don't know that. And you call yourself a doctor! 'First, do no harm'—I believe that's an oath you took."

"There are different kinds of harm, Mr. Murphy."

"Yes, there are, Dr. Schuler. But we don't get to play God. He allowed that poor child to be conceived, and though I may wish He hadn't, the fact remains that He did."

"But think of the burden this pregnancy will place on your wife's physical and mental health—"

"I'm fully aware of that, doctor. But this child's right to be born isn't diminished by the horrific way its life began. God allowed conception to occur and infused a soul at that moment. You'll be hearing from my attorney, Mr. Kennedy, who will document the manner of conception and demand that this baby be given every chance at life!"

Dr. Schuler sniffed indignantly and gave a slight bow. "As you wish."

"Now, if you don't mind, arrange for me to see my wife in the visiting room. Immediately."

When Jamie entered the visitation room, Katie was already there, dressed in a shapeless blue smock and slippers. Her hair was cut short, unfashionably so, as if someone had snipped around a bowl placed on her head. Yet her remaining wavy locks, like a shimmering golden-orange crown, still accentuated her delicate features.

She stood facing the picture window, which overlooked the lawn and three pyramid-shaped linden trees, their now-yellow heart-shaped leaves clinging to the last of autumn.

A female staff member sat quietly in one of the chairs in the corners of the room. "I'll leave you two alone, Mr. Murphy. When you're done, just ring for me," she said, pointing to a buzzer on the wall before slipping out of the room.

Jamie moved closer to Katie and whispered, "Hello, Katie. It's me, Jamie." He reached out to touch her upper arm. She looked at his hand but did not pull away. Gently, he turned her to face him and studied her features. He recognized the familiar signs of early pregnancy. Just as with Meggie and Patsy, her cheeks had a warm glow. Her breasts, hips, and abdomen were a bit fuller—more rounded. He'd always thought Katie wore this stage of pregnancy beautifully.

When he placed her hand gently on her abdomen, she didn't resist. He imagined another man's hands on her body, and his mind swirled with questions. Had she fought the vile man's touch? Had she been aware of the attack?

"Katie, you are carrying a baby," he said, searching her eyes for some sign of recognition, but there was none. "I'm not sure how we'll get through this, but somehow, we will. God help us all."

How could the staff not have known? The women who helped Katie shower must have seen the signs. At that moment, Jamie trusted no one—neither Dr. Schuler nor anyone else at Harlem Valley State Hospital, whether patient, staff, or physician.

Had he not called this morning, Jamie was certain Katie's baby— for that is how he must think of the child to preserve his sanity, not as the child of some nameless, perverted man—would have been aborted. Katie would have been sterilized in the name of eugenics, and he would have been none the wiser.

He gently gathered Katie into his arms. She didn't resist, but neither did she relax. It felt like he was hugging a statue.

"Please, Katie, come back to me. I need you."

~*~

Jamie drove straight from Wingdale to the Fordham campus. He waited outside the classroom in Collins Hall, where his uncle, Fr. Jim, was finishing his eleven o'clock ethics class. Leaning against the wall, out of Unc's line of sight, he listened to his deep, commanding voice.

"An act remains intrinsically evil by its object alone. Neither the motive nor the circumstances make an inherently evil act morally acceptable. However, some actions have a double effect: good and evil. Is it morally permissible to pursue a good end while fully aware of the evil that will also result? Aquinas provided four guidelines to evaluate the morality of such actions."

As noisy students began spilling out of nearby classrooms, Jamie saw Unc glance at his watch.

"All right, it's almost noon. We'll pick up from here tomorrow. Class dismissed."

Jamie stepped back from the doorway as Unc's students exited the classroom like a stampede of wild horses. Most of the young men weren't philosophy majors; he knew they took his uncle's class to fulfill a graduation requirement.

Stepping into the classroom, Jamie silently watched Unc erase the blackboard and slap the yellow chalk from the sleeves of his black cassock. Unc gathered his belongings from the square, oaken desk at the front of the room. Jamie had never needed his uncle's love and wisdom more than he did today. Unc turned toward the windows that spanned the entire wall opposite the doorway, showcasing a cluster of sugar maples in riotous reds, their leafy branches stretching up to the second-floor classroom. A surge of desperation washed over Jamie as Unc turned to face him.

"What a nice surprise, Jamie, my boy. I thought you had class at noon," Fr. Jim said, tilting his head slightly.

"I do. I cut class today, Unc."

"That doesn't sound like you," Fr. Jim said with a grimace. "Is something wrong?"

"You mean besides everything?"

"Let's get some lunch. We can talk things through."

Jamie let out a heavy sigh as his shoulders slumped in defeat. "Yes. Do you have time to talk?"

"All the time you need. I'm done teaching for the day. Follow me, son."

Instead of returning to his office or heading to the cafeteria, Unc led Jamie outside to the shade of an enormous sycamore tree, still clinging to its bright orange leaves, in the center of a grassy knoll in the commons. They sat on a wooden bench with peeling green paint. As they spoke, students scurried along the walkways under a canopy of bright midday sunshine, their steps vibrant, carefree, and hopeful—a distant memory, or so it seemed to Jamie, from another lifetime.

Jamie explained that Katie was almost three months pregnant with another man's child, along with what had nearly transpired at the hospital that morning, the conversation between Dr. Schuler and himself, and his time with Katie.

As Jamie spoke, their shared grief was reflected in Unc's tear-filled eyes. Unc listened, while Jamie maintained a stoic exterior, though inside, he was falling apart.

"So, Katie has made no progress toward recovery at all?" Unc asked.

"None. With a diagnosis of dementia praecox, the outlook is dismal. Absent a parting-of-the-Red-Sea-sized miracle, Katie will continue her mental decline and live out the rest of her life in a custodial hospital for the insane."

They sat silently for a few minutes, both men staring vacantly into the cloudless sky with troubled faces. Fr. Jim massaged his temples, then started to speak but stopped. Finally, he said, "Let's talk about the baby. What are your plans for the child?"

"God help me, I don't know. On my way here, I thought about Eileen and Frankie Caruso. Maybe they'd be open to adopting the baby. You know they've never been able to have children."

"Well, that might be a good option. Eileen is the biological aunt." Fr. Jim rubbed his chin and asked, "But do you think *you* could love the child, Jamie?"

"I just don't know." He brought his fist to his pursed lips and closed his eyes briefly. "If the baby were a girl, it might be easier. But if it's a boy—the son of the rapist—" Jamie paused, clenching his square jaw and raking his hair with his long, slender fingers. "—I wish I could say it doesn't matter, and maybe in time, it wouldn't, but right now, it's just too hard." Jamie hung his head. "For the first time in my life, I feel something akin to hatred for the man who did this to Katie—to me— to my family. I want to kill the scumbag who violated my Katie."

"Don't let that man take any more from you than he already has, son. Hatred will destroy your soul and cripple your capacity to experience joy. With time, Jamie, you must forgive, even the rapist."

"But why would God allow this to happen, Unc? Is He punishing Katie and me because Meggie was conceived before we were married?"

"God doesn't work that way, Jamie. Yes, our poor choices and sins have natural consequences, which God allows. Reaping what we sow is one of the ways God teaches us to learn from our mistakes. The rapist, even if never brought to justice, will suffer the dire spiritual consequences of his actions unless he repents and asks for forgiveness.

"Evil, pain, and suffering are stark realities in this life. For Christians, the answer to suffering lies in the incarnation of Christ. When the Son of God took on our flesh, He entered fully into our suffering—physically, emotionally, and spiritually. Jesus carried our suffering through His humanity into the divine 'embrace' between the Father and the Son.

"When we unite our suffering and death with Jesus's sacrificial suffering and death on the cross, we share in His resurrection. This doesn't lessen our pain, but it does give it purpose—uniting us with God.

"No one escapes suffering, just as no one escapes death. Suffering can either separate us from God or bring us closer to Him. God can use both our good and bad experiences, even our sins, to fulfill His good purposes for those who love Him. We must trust in His promises and divine plan.

"Life is hard, but without that trust, we cannot endure its disappointments and heartaches without losing hope. We must strive to turn the labor of our suffering into a labor of active prayer in and through Christ."

As Unc's words sank in, Jamie regretted what he'd said at the breakfast table—that it would be easier if Katie were dead. He had to confront the painful reality: his life would never get any easier, only harder. Somehow, he had to find a way through the muck pulling him into a pit of despair and anger.

"Do you believe in coincidences, Unc?"

"There are no coincidences; a divine hand is always at work. Why do you ask?"

"Because I haven't wanted to see Katie for months. But this morning, I felt compelled to see her. Had I not called this morning to arrange a visit, I would have never known about Katie's pregnancy— or the planned abortion and sterilization. Dr. Schuler would have carried out his plan without hindrance, and I would have been none the wiser."

"Jamie, God has big plans for all His children, including the baby Katie now carries, no matter how the child was conceived. Ask St. Brigid, the patron saint of newborns, to intercede for Katie's baby's health, safe delivery, and proper placement or adoption. Storm heaven with your prayers for wisdom, peace, forgiveness, and that giant-sized miracle for Katie's recovery. I'll do the same."

After an emotional parting, Jamie returned to the car, and once inside, he collapsed into the seat and sobbed inconsolably.

FIFTEEN

April 16, 1933

Jamie and Eileen sat quietly in the expectant father's waiting room at Danbury General Hospital. In the early hours of the morning, Katie had been transferred there by ambulance—a modified sedan that could accommodate a stretcher.

"Your wife is in active labor and doesn't understand what is happening. She is extremely agitated and uncooperative," the nurse had said when Jamie took the call earlier that morning. "Dr. Schuler has transferred your wife to Danbury General Hospital and ordered a cesarean section. He believes this will best protect your wife and baby from injury."

Jamie envisioned a very pregnant Katie in a straitjacket, twisting, turning, and fighting as she had when first admitted to Harlem Valley State Hospital. It had taken two male orderlies, a nurse, and a stretcher with leather straps to restrain her and pry the week-old Patsy from her arms.

He could have asked the nurse about the straitjacket when she called the house earlier that morning, but he didn't want to know. Instead, he inquired why Katie had been taken to Danbury across the New York-Connecticut state line.

"We send patients there when a procedure falls outside the norm or expertise of Harlem Valley's surgeons. Danbury's close by, only twenty-one miles northeast, and has a decent-sized maternity ward. We don't deliver many babies here—none that I can remember. I've been here since '24 when Harlem Valley opened," the nurse had said.

The fact that the baby's birth certificate would list the place of birth as Danbury, Connecticut, instead of Wingdale, New York, was a blessing. Everyone from miles around knew that the tiny township of Wingdale existed for one purpose alone: to support and sustain the Harlem Valley State Hospital for the Insane. Danbury, listed as the place of birth, would facilitate the baby's adoption should Frankie Caruso persist in his objection to Eileen's pleas to adopt.

"The baby has a better chance for a normal life if adopted by strangers," Frankie had argued. "The less known about the biological parents in an adoption, the better. You can't keep people from talking—even in my family. I wish it weren't true, but people are people. Nothing tickles the throats of gossips like scandal."

Jamie understood Frankie Caruso's logic. Adoption was shrouded in secrecy, and significant stigma was attached to adopted children, who were viewed only slightly better than those deemed mentally "defective" or insane. Adoptees often faced discrimination and were treated as inferior to biological children. Concerns about "bad blood" or hereditary traits were rampant. Katie's baby had three strikes against it before ever seeing the light of day: a mother diagnosed with dementia praecox, an unknown biological father, and conception through rape.

Eileen had already quit work and planned to care for the newborn as her child, confident that Frankie would fall in love with the infant (and fatherhood) once they had the baby at home. She had begged Jamie to give her a year with the baby to finalize the paperwork. Brendan Kennedy, Jamie's lawyer, had advised against it. "Infants are more readily adopted than even a year-old child," he'd warned. "Be prepared to raise the child as your own should you delay the adoption, Jamie. One cannot predict the future."

Jamie second-guessed himself. Perhaps he shouldn't have agreed to Eileen's plan, but she was the baby's closest adult living relative outside of Katie. It was impossible to know what the best course of action was.

A quiet young man had joined Eileen and him in the waiting room. Jamie wasn't sure exactly when; he'd lost track of the time. Just a kid, younger than Thomas, Jamie thought as he watched the fellow's pleated, high-waisted, baggy trousers flap like laundry in the wind as he paced back and forth. Other than a brief pause to unbutton and roll up the sleeves of his windowpane-checked shirt, the kid had been in perpetual motion, oblivious to the trails of ash the cigarette dangling from his mouth left on the floor.

Having smoked his last cigarette, Jamie was itching to bum one from the young fellow or snatch the one he was wasting to show him how to smoke it properly. Jamie had started smoking in law school while having a few drinks with his buddies on Fridays or after big exams. He could blame his classmate Colin Maddigan for those acquired vices. The guy was persuasive and ever the ebullient optimist. The mix of nicotine, whiskey, and camaraderie could almost make Jamie forget his woes, even if only for a short while. He never offered information about his wife, hiding the details of her illness and institutionalization. But when pressed, he only said she was "a gorgeous redhead, mother of my two girls."

"First baby?" Eileen asked.

"Yes, ma'am," he replied, then resumed his relentless pacing, which only aggravated Jamie's nerves.

Eileen and Jamie sat at opposite ends of the imitation leather sofa pushed against the wall. They exchanged glances—hers one of empathy for the young man, Jamie's one of irritation.

Jamie thought Eileen had lost weight since he'd last seen her. She appeared more petite than he remembered but still the stylish maven in her belted blue-gray poplin tea dress. He watched her rosary beads rhythmically slipping through her fingers as she prayed silently. He missed the comfort of prayer. His faith was at an all-time low, which he acknowledged. He saw himself as a "Job" but with a rotten attitude. But what did God expect after abandoning Katie and him?

He checked his wristwatch. How long did it take to deliver a baby by cesarean section, anyway? They'd been waiting for hours. Impatient, worried, and in dire need of distraction, he stood up, walked over to the tall, wood-framed window in the middle of the waiting room, and peered outside.

The sixth-floor view overlooked the gravel parking lot filled with cars: Fords, Chevrolets, Buicks, Chryslers, and Dodges of various shapes, sizes, and colors. In Jamie's short lifetime, he'd seen cars evolve from black boxes on wheels, rumbling along, to elegant and comfortable vehicles, purring down the streets—from alley cats to sleek panthers.

He spied a single Studebaker with its distinctive aerodynamic design. His brother Thomas had mentioned that Studebaker now offered automatic transmissions—a car that could almost drive itself. Who would have thought? Someone had parked their Packard away from the other vehicles. It was hard to miss with its bullet-nosed front end and maroon color among the predictable blacks, blues, grays, and greens. He wondered what it might be like to own a Packard: luxury and impeccable engineering, but with a price tag that could reach up to three grand. Who could afford that? Probably a surgeon, Jamie thought. Doctors felt the pinch of hard times, too, but surgeons were faring the best.

Money, money, money—Jamie had invested so much in his education, borrowing against the remaining farm sale cash. He owed plenty to his mother and was determined to repay it. Jamie thought about his graduation in two months and his subsequent bar exam. Some lawyers had made decent money over the last three-and-a-half years of economic desperation, but they specialized in bankruptcy, foreclosure, and corporate law.

His thoughts suddenly returned to his mother's words from six months ago: "This baby is the last part of Katie you may ever have to love, son. What if, by some miracle, she recovers? Do you think she would have wanted you to give her baby away? I know the situation is far from ideal, but this baby has two sisters and a family that would love her no matter how she was conceived."

He wasn't sure he could love this baby, some other man's child. Frankie's indecision and waffling had given Jamie more time to stew and worry about his mother's question: What would Katie want? Surely, Katie would want Eileen to raise her baby if she and Jamie could not.

Jamie's reverie was interrupted by quick, sure footsteps echoing down the terrazzo-tiled hallway. He turned from the window as Eileen stood expectantly while a nurse entered the room. The young man extinguished his cigarette in the ashtray and looked toward her.

"Mr. Brown?" The attractive nurse, with blonde hair pinned up beneath her round cap, searched both men's faces with an assuring, happy smile.

"That's me," the young man said with palpable excitement.

"You may see your wife and new son now," she said. "Both are doing well."

"Hot dog, a son! Dang!" A face-splitting smile spread across the man's narrow face.

Jamie extended his hand to Mr. Brown. "Congratulations," he said with a forced brightness. He remembered the joy when Meggie and

Patsy were born—a joy absent today.

Mr. Brown shook Jamie's hand enthusiastically.

"Can I see my son and wife now?" Mr. Brown asked.

"Yes, of course," she said, her rosy lips parting in a joyful smile to reveal perfectly shaped white teeth. "Follow me."

"We should be hearing something soon, don't you think, Jamie?" Eileen said. "I hope nothing's gone wrong."

It wasn't long before another set of quick steps reverberated down the hallway. A middle-aged man with swarthy features entered the waiting room. His knee-length white doctor's coat bore the embroidered name "Dr. Lombardi." He removed his surgical cap and stuffed it into his coat pocket. He stood a couple of inches shorter than Jamie, who immediately rose to his feet.

"Mr. Murphy?" he said, his eyes earnest but tired.

Jamie nodded and introduced his sister-in-law. As the three huddled together, Eileen's gentle face, previously tight with worry, now glimmered with hopeful anticipation.

"You have a healthy baby girl. Your wife is recovering well, with no complications after a forceps-assisted delivery and her 'twilight sleep' anesthesia," Dr. Lombardi said, exchanging handshakes with Jamie and Eileen.

The muscles in Jamie's body relaxed at the news of the baby's gender. Katie had birthed a baby girl, not another man's baby boy. A sigh of relief escaped Jamie's lips.

"I was able to avoid a cesarean delivery, or C-section as I prefer to call it, and general anesthesia, both of which would have complicated your wife's recovery, particularly given her mental state. We'll keep her here under light sedation to help manage her confusion and anxiety for a few days before we discharge her back to Harlem Valley State Hospital."

"Excuse my ignorance, but what exactly is 'twilight sleep'?" Jamie asked.

"It's a type of anesthesia for childbirth, using morphine for pain and scopolamine for sedation. Unlike ether, it has fewer risks and a faster recovery. Contractions still proceed, but the woman can't push, which is why I used forceps. Ether often causes nausea and vomiting, which is extremely painful after a C-section. I only do C-sections if absolutely necessary."

The doctor continued, "I understand that you plan to take the baby home with you as soon as possible, but we'll keep her here for a day or two in the nursery. If there are no issues, you may be able to pick her up as soon as tomorrow."

"Can we see the baby?" Eileen asked.

"Of course, although she is still quite sedated from the drugs we gave Mrs. Murphy. The nurses are cleaning her up in the nursery as we speak. With a full head of copper-colored hair, she is easy to spot. Ask the nurse to remove her cap if they have it on her. She is a beautiful baby, and I have seen many." The doctor added tentatively, "Mr. Murphy, I'm very sorry about your wife's illness. It's always such a tragedy—dementia praecox striking the young so mercilessly."

"Yes, it is." Jamie swallowed the lump in his throat. "May I see my wife before we leave?"

"Let's wait until you pick up the baby, Mr. Murphy. Then we can arrange a short visit if there are no complications."

As the doctor turned and walked away down the long hallway, Jamie turned to Eileen. "Well, what did you decide to name her?"

"Bridget Kathleen. Bridie for short," Eileen said, positively glowing. "Oh, Jamie, I'm so happy. A little redhead, just like Katie! I can't wait to see her. I hope you don't mind staying a bit longer so I can see the baby before heading home. I know it's been a long day for you."

It had been an excruciatingly long, tense day. Jamie had received the call before dawn and had picked Eileen up in White Plains an hour later. It was now past time for the evening meal, and Jamie's stomach complained.

"Bridget Kathleen," Jamie said, trying out the name. "Bridie—yes, I like the name very much. Of course, we can stay to see Katie's baby."

Just then, Jamie remembered that Unc had encouraged him to ask for the intercession of Saint Bridget, the patron saint of newborns. Although he hadn't followed his uncle's suggestion, it seemed Saint Bridget had already made a protective claim on this child.

They found their way to the nursery and peered through a large glass window. Six babies were wrapped in receiving blankets, four in pink and two in blue, lying in clear bassinets atop waist-high, rolling tables. One bassinet was empty. Jamie searched the name tags for the babies swaddled in pink. Bridie slept peacefully under a name tag proclaiming her a "Murphy," as she would be until she was adopted.

Eileen tapped on the window, pointed to the "Murphy" baby, and motioned for the nurse to wheel her bassinet closer to the glass where they stood.

The nurse nodded, rose from the rocker, and complied immediately. She placed her sleeping blue bundle in the empty bassinet. Eileen gestured for the nurse to remove baby Bridie's snug beige cap. As the nurse removed the cap, loose curls—the color of ripe apricots—surrounded the baby's tiny face, reflecting the overhead lights and sparkling like a halo. There was a slight molding of her head, a small bruise on her forehead, and a few marks on her face. But even so, this baby girl possessed an obvious delicate beauty.

Eileen spoke first. "She's the spitting image of Katie when she was born. I was the first to hold her. We always shared a room. I felt like Katie was more my baby than Mam's."

"I'm glad she looks like Katie," Jamie said, his voice breaking. He turned away from the viewing window, hiding his tears from his sister-in-law, overwhelmed by the miracle of new life even amidst tragedy.

SIXTEEN

Mid-October 1933

Eileen looked down at six-month-old Bridie, peacefully sleeping while sucking two fingers of her right hand. She was transported back to her early teen years, gazing not at Bridie but at Katie. Bridie possessed the same angelic perfection that Katie had at the same tender age.

Mam had been so weak after Katie had been born that Eileen had cared for her baby sister as if she were her own. Later, when Mam had become too sick to bathe herself, Eileen took over that task as well. She immediately discovered the cause of her mother's illness and the source of the fetid stench emanating from the small bedroom that Mam and Da had shared.

The ulceration in her mother's left breast had formed a weeping, necrotic protuberance. The entire breast had been red, hot, and tender to the touch, and the nipple had been inverted. The doctor had only confirmed what Mam had already told Eileen. "Nothing can be done for me, Eily. My own *máthair* died of the same thing—'tis the breast cancer," Mam had said with a pervading sense of resignation.

Eileen's fingers moved to the lump and the surrounding thickened tissue of her left breast. This lump was different from the sore, little marbles that had come and gone here and there with her monthlies. Frankie had brought the flattening of her left nipple to her attention several weeks ago, around the time Bridie had begun sleeping through the night, and their lovemaking had returned to its pre-Bridie tempo.

There had been no pain, no redness to alert Eileen to the change in her breast. Besides, she hadn't been in the habit of examining her body and probing for changes. No woman did that, for heaven's sake!

Getting up with Bridie all those nights for the past six months and dealing with a cough that had lingered from last winter had left Eileen tired and without self-focus.

~*~

Eileen checked in at the front desk and sat in the busy waiting room. Dr. Johnson shared a practice with another doctor who also specialized in women-only medicine. The other women were younger than Eileen, and several were visibly pregnant. Seeing a pregnant woman no longer caused Eileen a sense of envy or anguish. All those unsettling and unpleasant emotions had evaporated like a summer drizzle on a hot tin roof the instant she'd first held little Bridie in her arms. Katie's tragic circumstances had become Eileen's great blessing—the baby she'd so desperately wanted for the last fifteen years.

Her posture was tense, and her shoulders were slightly hunched as if bracing for impact. Despite her attempt at composure, the worry etched in the furrows of her brow and the occasional, involuntary quiver of her lips revealed her inner turmoil. Surely, God wouldn't allow the worst when little Bridie so needed a mother. Yet, the workings of God were beyond human understanding and scrutiny.

"Eileen Caruso," called the nurse with an air of calm detachment into the waiting room. Eileen sprang to her feet at the sound of her name. "Good afternoon," the nurse said, closing the door to the waiting room and leading Eileen down a long, narrow hallway.

The hemline of Eileen's summer dress swished as she followed the nurse's brisk steps past a bank of closed doors all the way to the last room, its door ajar. She had taken apart two dated dresses, one a multicolored floral print and the other a complementary solid, to create this "new" dress. Given the weight she had lost—she was down a whole size—it was easier to redesign and recreate this dress to match the newer styles: subtly padded shoulders, higher and belted waists, and narrower skirts with flared hemlines.

The nurse closed the door behind them as they entered the exam room. "Your chart says you are here to discuss a lump in your breast. Is that correct?" the nurse asked with cool efficiency.

"Yes." Eileen suddenly felt lightheaded and breathless, as if she had run and not walked down the hallway. She had provided the bare minimum of information when making the appointment.

"You'll need to remove your clothing, including undergarments so that the doctor can examine you." She handed Eileen a white hospital gown and a small sheet for her legs. "The opening of the gown faces frontward. The doctor will see you shortly; there's one patient ahead of you." On her way out the door, she turned back toward Eileen and, with a smile that reeked of pity, added, "Dr. Johnson is a very competent physician. You are in good hands."

Eileen reached up to remove her hat, only then realizing she was not wearing her summery Greta-Garbo-slouch hat. That was a first—leaving home without a hat! Between the nagging worry over the lump in her breast and trying to remember to pack everything in the diaper sack that Peggy might need while watching Bridie during her doctor's appointment, the hat had remained on the kitchen counter. It was far more complicated to leave the house nowadays, with the well-being of a little one to consider. Being a new mom at age forty-one was not easy. Lifelong routines were upended, and a good night's sleep was never guaranteed. Eileen had never felt so bone tired.

There was no window in the examination room, which was painted an earthy shade of taupe. A colored lithograph hung on the wall opposite the door, depicting an autumnal woodland scene with a river in the distance. Scattered stands of maples, royally arrayed in their fall splendor, had exchanged their green foliage for a fiery display of yellows, oranges, and reds. She stepped closer to read the engraved title plate on its wooden frame: "*Autumn on the Hudson (c. 1860), Jasper Francis Cropsey.*" A glint of sunlight broke through the painting's dark clouds, releasing subtle rays of prismatic color and lifting her thoughts heavenward. *Not like Mam. Please, Lord, not like Mam.*

Except for the painting, the furnishings in the room were strictly utilitarian: an exam table covered by a thin leather pad with removable metal stirrups, a rolling circular stool, a single wooden chair, and a waist-high metal storage cabinet.

Eileen wondered how often women were diagnosed with breast cancer and whether it ran in families. Eileen knew that women often concealed a breast cancer diagnosis, as Mam had, due to societal taboos and the stigma associated with the disease. A woman's value remained tied to her appearance and childbearing abilities. Breast cancer, a virtual death sentence, was hardly a subject for polite conversation.

As she began undressing, Eileen wondered if these fancy new gynecologists could have helped her conceive a baby over the past fifteen years. Their infertility had always been assumed to be her problem. Now, doctors finally understood that men could also play a role in infertility. However, it remained medical practice never to share this information with the husband, as it might lead to an inferiority complex or impotence.

The doctor, lean and tall, entered the exam room. His pleasant face still had a youthful appearance despite his brown, pencil-thin Errol Flynn-styled mustache. Eileen had already surmised that Dr. Johnson would be young, as his diploma from University and Bellevue Hospital Medical College bore a 1931 graduation date. But the man barely looked old enough to have a beer should the Twenty-First Amendment garner enough votes to pass and repeal Prohibition.

"Mrs. Caruso, I'm Dr. Ray Johnson. It is very nice to meet you," he said, bowing slightly. A single dimple and a deep cleft in his chin punctuated his reassuring smile. His demeanor projected an aura of confidence and professionalism.

"Please hop up on the examining table," he said, patting the side of the exam table.

Dr. Johnson kept each part of her body modestly covered when not being examined and explained each step before proceeding. After comparing and palpating her breasts, he said, "Go ahead and lie down now. I'm going to check for swollen lymph nodes."

Eileen coughed several times, covering her mouth with a lacy handkerchief she had ready in hand.

"How long have you had that nasty cough?" the doctor asked.

"I got a cold last fall, but the cough keeps hanging on."

Eileen closed her eyes while the doctor felt her neck, armpits, abdomen, and groin area.

In his calm voice, he continued asking questions. "When did you first notice your symptoms?"

"A few weeks ago," she answered.

As he felt the lump, he asked, "Is it painful?"

She said that it wasn't. "My mother and her mother died from breast cancer. Is breast cancer hereditary?"

"We suspect that heredity has a role in some cases, but we just don't know yet. The study of genes and their inheritance is in its infancy." He covered Eileen back up with her gown. "We're finished with the physical exam. Go ahead and get dressed, Mrs. Caruso. Please open the door when you're ready, and the nurse will show you to my office. We can finish our discussion there."

When Eileen finished dressing, the nurse escorted her to Dr. Johnson's office.

"Thank you, Helen. Please shut the door," Dr. Johnson said to the nurse. Turning to Eileen, he asked, "How are you feeling?"

"Very nervous. Worried. Okay, terrified," Eileen admitted.

"I'm not going to beat around the bush; the changes in your breast are worrisome. I'm referring you to Memorial Hospital in Manhattan, near Gramercy Park, for a breast biopsy. They specialize in the treatment of cancer and associated diseases."

"Will they cut a chunk out of my breast to do a biopsy?" Eileen asked, her voice trembling slightly.

"No, that's the beauty of this newer method. After a shot of novocaine, they make a small incision in the center of the lump, and then, using an 18-gauge needle attached to a syringe, they withdraw a sample using suction. Dr. Hayes Martin and Dr. Edward Ellis at Memorial have been using this procedure for several years with excellent results, both to diagnose cancers and avoid unnecessary scarring and surgery. They work closely with the pathology department to determine if suspect masses are cancerous, providing immediate results. If this lump turns out to be carcinoma, Memorial has the best surgeons."

"But what if it is cancer? Has the treatment evolved since my mother's time, when the treatment was removing the whole breast?"

"I'm afraid that a radical mastectomy is still the primary approach. And yes, that includes the removal of the entire breast, underlying chest muscles, and lymph nodes in the armpit. However, Memorial Hospital is fully equipped to provide the best care possible, including surgery and radiation therapy if needed. Should the lump prove to be cancer, Memorial will check to see if the cancer has spread elsewhere, for example, to the lungs, using radiography. Memorial has ongoing research in radiation therapy as an adjunct treatment for breast cancer, although it's not as far along as we'd like it to be.

"My office will make an appointment as soon as possible and contact you with the details. Do try to remain optimistic, Mrs. Caruso."

After the tests, Eileen received the devastating diagnosis of metastatic breast cancer that had spread to her lungs. Given the advanced stage of her cancer, the doctors gave her "no more than six months to live" and did not recommend surgery. Absent a miracle, no cure was possible. She submitted to experimental radiation therapy in the hope of extending her life.

When radiation failed to produce anything but burns, Eileen quickly passed through the initial stages of grief, clinging to her faith in God. Denial was short-lived, given that she'd nursed Mam through her last months of breast cancer. She steered clear of anger's devastation, having watched it destroy Da's life, transforming him into a frightening, drunken stranger. Bargaining with God was futile—her life was not hers; it had always been God's. She rejected depression's plan to steal the joy of her last few months with Bridie and Frankie. Ultimately, Eileen resigned herself to God's will and made peace with God's providential plan.

~*~

February 1934

Before her death, Eileen had prayed that Jamie would accept Bridie into his family as his own daughter, believing that Katie would have wanted this had she been in her right mind. In God's infinite mercy and wisdom, this was the miracle He granted—not Eileen's cure nor the restoration of Katie's mind, but the melting of Jamie's heart.

During her final meeting with Jamie, standing at her hospital bedside, neither spoke of the troubles brewing in the world or that Frankie hadn't been interested in being a single father. None of that mattered now as she held her brother-in-law's hand and they said their final goodbyes.

Even amidst the haze of her morphine-blunted pain, Eileen could see how Jamie's heart had opened to Bridie, who had already been living in the Murphy household for months during her illness. When the time came for Eileen to breathe her last, she did so with perfect resignation to God's plan.

~*~

And so it came to pass that Bridget Kathleen Murphy was "adopted" into the Murphy family, although no legal paperwork was required. As Kathleen Mary Houlihan's husband, Jamie had always been listed as the father on Bridie's birth certificate, even though the true father remained unknown.

Bridie's first word was "Dada." Though still burdened by Katie's physical and emotional absence, Jamie felt his heart stir with a quiet joy.

SEVENTEEN

Early April 1941 (Eight years later)

Jamie felt exhausted and numb. He sat at the trestle table in the kitchen with Thomas, Gracie's husband Chuck, and Annie's husband Bill—all of them nursing shots of Jameson whiskey. Everyone had finally left after Mom's wake. The house had been packed to the gills. Jamie knew how much Mom had meant to the Transfiguration parish and to the people of Tarrytown, but the size of the crowd at the wake had astonished him.

Gracie and Annie stood at the sink washing dishes, while Mom's eight grandchildren—Jamie's three, Annie's one, and Gracie's four— still had the energy to whoop and holler throughout the house, largely ignored by their grieving parents.

Memories of Mom lingered in every room, but nowhere more than the kitchen. Jamie almost expected her to walk in, take the dishtowel from pregnant Annie's hands, and order her off her feet. But she would never do that again. The Kelvinator, Mom's prized possession, which had replaced the ice box just four years ago, stood bursting with leftovers from the wake and seemed to whisper her name.

Every corner of the house was infused with her personality and love—not a haunting—but a painful reminder of her absence. After all, Mom had been born in this very house—as had he, Meggie, and Patsy—in the same master bedroom upstairs. Except for her first years of marriage on the farm with Dad (where Danny and Gracie were born), all but two of his brothers and sisters had been born here, too. His brother Marty had died here, just like Dad.

Jamie imagined St. Peter throwing open the pearly gates, with Dad, Danny, and Marty running to meet her. It was a comforting thought, but it didn't lessen his loss. Mom had been the mortar holding together the bricks of his life and that of his girls.

Unc had left about an hour ago, appearing more devastated than Jamie had ever seen him. He seemed to have aged ten years in a day and a half. With Fr. Kilian, Unc would celebrate her funeral Mass tomorrow. Jamie couldn't imagine what it must feel like to stand at the altar and say goodbye to his own sister. For that matter, how would Jamie get through Mom's funeral? He didn't know.

"There was so much about Mom I never knew," Annie said softly. "Did you know she helped her father run the flour mill across town?"

"Yes, but I didn't know how many suitors Mom had," Gracie said with a laugh. "But I can see why. She was gorgeous. I have no idea why she put away the wedding picture of her and Dad and those others taken of her before she got married."

"It was Meggie's idea, not mine," Gracie added. "She knew exactly where Mom kept her picture stash."

"I guess being a snoop runs in the family," Annie said with a grin.

"You ought to know, Annie," Gracie replied, gently nudging her younger sister.

"Snooping has its advantages," Annie shot back. "Who knows what treasures Mom has hidden away in this house?"

"It was a nice touch putting those old photos out," Jamie said. He'd been reflecting on how tempting it was to think of his mother as a mirror, simply reflecting his needs and wants. But she had a life independent of her family, although they were her number one priority. This was clear from the many stories her friends had shared at the wake.

"Mom told me once that, on the inside, she still felt twenty years old." A faint smile crossed Jamie's face as he thought back to the beautiful young woman in the wedding photo, remembering her humility and self-giving love. He preferred that image to how she had looked at the end.

Jamie keenly missed his "little" brother's presence at the kitchen table, though Robert was not so little anymore at twenty-six. Their eleven-year age difference, and Robert's generous, sensitive nature, had always stirred Jamie's paternal feelings toward him.

When Jamie had phoned Robert in Italy to tell him the dire news, Mom took the receiver and ordered him to stay in Rome. Even in her final days, Mom had been a force to be reckoned with. Jamie had overheard the entire conversation, her words still vivid in his mind.

"Look, Robert, getting from Rome to Tarrytown is no small feat. It'll cost a fortune, change nothing, and disrupt your doctoral studies. My time is short, and I'm at peace. Pray for me and for the whole family—especially Jamie," she had said.

Mom and Dad had been wrong about one thing—it was Robert who was cut out for the priesthood, not him. After high school, Robert had spent two intense years at the Jesuit novitiate of St. Andrew-on-Hudson in Poughkeepsie. He'd begun his scholastic formation at the Jesuit House on the Fordham campus, studying philosophy and theology, before transferring to the Pontifical Gregorian University in Rome.

Annie rubbed her aching back. "I have to sit down, Gracie. Sorry to abandon you."

"No worries, I'm almost done. Relax," Gracie said.

Jamie saw a lot of Mom in Gracie. Of all his brothers and sisters, he felt closest to her and Robert.

Annie sat down next to Bill as another wave of sorrow swept over her. "I just can't believe she's gone," she said, wiping her swollen eyes and taking a tiny sip of Bill's whiskey. "It happened so fast. Three months ago, Mom was just fine."

"But that's the thing, Annie—she wasn't just fine," Jamie said. "I could tell her back was bothering her for months, but—typical of Mom—she didn't complain and just kept working like a dog."

Gracie turned toward the table while drying a plate. "Mom had been losing weight for a while, but when I mentioned it to her, she just laughed and said, 'I could stand to lose a few pounds.'"

Jamie flicked a long cylinder of ash from the end of his cigarette into the empty coffee cup on the table and took a deep drag. "I can't help but feel it's partially my fault."

"For an educated person, you can be pretty stupid, Jamie," Thomas said, normally reticent but probably feeling the effects of his beer and whiskey. "How can it be your fault that Mom got cancer?" His narrow face and thin mouth twisted in restrained grief under the cover of impatience.

"Let's face it," Jamie said softly, glancing around to make sure Meggie, Patsy, and Bridie were out of earshot. "If Mom hadn't been so busy taking care of my girls, she might have paid more attention to her symptoms."

"And what if she had?" Chuck, Gracie's husband, replied. "There isn't much they can do about pancreatic cancer anyway, according to what Doc Collins told Gracie."

"That's true, Jamie. Most people—especially those as healthy as Mom—don't always have symptoms," Gracie said, recalling the doctor appointments she had attended with Mom. "Besides, you know darn well that Mom loved taking care of your girls."

Gracie tossed her dishtowel on the counter and walked over to Jamie, who sat with his back to her. She hugged his neck from behind, pressing her cheek affectionately against his.

Jamie reached up and squeezed Gracie's hands. "Thank you, Gracie. I needed that," he said, fighting tears.

"I can't fathom how the last dozen years would have unfolded without Mom," Jamie said, pouring another round of whiskey for the men. He stared into his glass for a moment. "She radiated hope—not just for Katie, but for this whole country during its darkest times. Mom was a tough-as-nails optimist."

"Our loss is heaven's gain," Chuck said, raising his glass. "To my sainted mother-in-law." The other men lifted their glasses in a quiet toast.

Bill grabbed the pack of Camels from across the table. Lighting up, he inhaled deeply and closed his eyes, savoring the warmth and calm. "Thank God the economy is finally turning around," Bill said, his voice carrying a hint of relief. "Say what you like, but in my book, FDR is the greatest president this country has ever seen."

Jamie nodded slightly. He couldn't deny that Westchester County, like most of the country, had benefited from Roosevelt's New Deal. He knew Thomas, Chuck, and Bill had all found work with the Works Progress Administration (WPA) during those bleak years. Their jobs had been grueling, often at the mercy of brutal winters and scorching summers, but the paycheck had meant food on the table and a roof over their families' heads.

Since the spring of 1935, the three men had been part of WPA crews that built trails at Bear Mountain State Park, just fifteen miles northwest of Tarrytown, ran electric lines to remote areas of the county, and constructed levees to control flooding from the Bronx

River. They'd even helped restore historic landmarks like the Old Dutch Church in North Tarrytown and the Jacob Purdy House in White Plains. Sleepy Hollow Cemetery had also gotten its share of attention, thanks to the men's work, making it more accessible for the curious drawn by Washington Irving's legend.

Now that automotive sales were rising again, Chuck had been rehired at Cahill Motors, back to selling cars. Bill and Thomas, too, had their sights set on returning to the Chevrolet production plant north of town before summer.

Nine months after Jamie graduated with his law degree, he landed a WPA job managing government contracts for the ten Hudson Valley counties. He oversaw contracts for supply materials and staffing requirements on numerous public works projects. Specializing in contract law had paid off. For a half-dozen years, Jamie commuted into New York City on weekdays. After all his years at Fordham, traveling by train into the city was second nature to him.

Occasionally, his work took him to Washington, D.C., for meetings. When Mom was alive, his absences hadn't been a problem, but now it was different. At least Meggie, now thirteen, had the maturity and temperament to keep her sisters in check. Bridie was no trouble, but Patsy was another matter. She reminded Jamie of Annie at that age— spirited and a handful.

He didn't dare admit to anyone but himself that, if it hadn't been for his mother's words—*"the last gift that Katie can give you"*—he might have given Bridie, now eight, up for adoption after Eileen's death.

Each day, Jamie thought Bridie looked more like Katie—a constant source of both joy and pain for him. Bridie's eyes were gray, unlike Katie's bright robin's egg blue, and her nose was a touch sharper than her mother's. She looked nothing like Meggie and Patsy, who had inherited Jamie's black Irish looks. Of the three girls, Bridie was the only one who always wanted to accompany him to Wingdale, despite Katie's lack of recognition and her inability—or reluctance—to communicate.

Jamie felt suffocated, existing but not truly living—a jaded, withered soul trapped in a thirty-seven-year-old body, longing for a life he could no longer have. Doomed to celibacy, he missed a woman's touch. If only he could start life all over again. But what would he do differently? Did he wish he'd never met Katie? The thought alone filled him with heartbreak and self-loathing.

Unlike his siblings, Jamie knew the terms of their mother's will. He had helped her draft it when she was fit as a fiddle. Staying in the house wouldn't be an option unless he decided to buy it—a decision he had no intention of making. The house on Elizabeth Street would have to go up for sale.

~*~

A week after his mother's funeral and the day before Jamie was set to meet with his siblings to discuss her will, he received a phone call from Colin Maddigan. Colin had been his closest friend and drinking buddy during law school. Both men had specialized in contract law and stayed in touch for a while, but Jamie hadn't heard from him in several years, not since Colin moved to California for a job. Despite their friendship, Colin knew nothing about Katie's illness; the shame of her mental condition was kept within the family.

Jamie immediately recognized Colin's velvety, smooth voice and confident tone. Colin had landed a job in contracts at Douglas Aircraft Company in Santa Monica, California. He needed help managing, negotiating, and drafting contracts with government agencies, suppliers, and subcontractors to produce aircraft and related equipment.

"An avalanche of government orders is coming in—quicker than I can process them," Colin said. "I need your help, pal, and I have an offer you can't refuse."

This time, Colin wasn't exaggerating as he was inclined to do. Jamie knew exactly what he was referring to. In March of 1941, Congress had passed the Lend-Lease Act, allowing the United States to lend or lease military equipment—like airplanes—to Allied nations, especially Britain, without demanding immediate payment. Douglas Aircraft had been flooded with orders from the government to produce bombers, fighters, and transport planes. The surge in contracts was expanding production at their Santa Monica facility, and Jamie could see why Colin needed an extra hand.

Colin was delighted when Jamie explained what he'd been doing for the WPA in government contracts.

"Your experience is exactly what we need here—assuring compliance with procurement regulations and contractual obligations," Colin said. "Say you want the job, Jamie, and the job is yours."

Jamie couldn't believe this job had just fallen into his lap. He could think of nothing better than getting as far away from Tarrytown—and Wingdale—as possible.

"I want the job, but I have some personal details to sort out. My mother recently passed away, and my three girls have two months of school left to finish."

"I'm sorry about your mother, buddy. I hate to sound callous, but I need you to start in two weeks—three at the most. Just leave the girls with your wife. There's no way I can hold this job for two months."

Jamie was conflicted but couldn't let the job pass. "Can you give me until tomorrow night to decide?"

"Sure thing. But I'm telling you, this place is awesome. Heaven on earth, my friend."

Katie's doctors had abandoned her treatment. God had refused to cure her. It was time for Jamie to move on.

~*~

Jamie continued reading from his mother's will, "I give the rest of my estate to those of my children who survive me, in equal shares, to be divided among them and the descendants of a deceased child of mine, to take their ancestor's share per stirpes."

"We can ignore the 'ancestor's share per stirpes' language," Jamie said, glancing at his siblings.

"Okay, but what does it mean?" Annie asked, her brow furrowed.

"It's easiest to understand with an example," Jamie explained. "Suppose I died before Mom's estate was liquidated, my share would be divided equally between Meggie, Patsy, and Bridie."

"But what about Robert's share?" Annie asked.

"What about it, Annie?" Jamie replied calmly.

"Well, he's not here, and Jesuits can't have any money."

"Geez, Annie," Bill said, exasperated, rolling his eyes at his wife's comment, which smacked of greed.

"He's got at least five years left before he's ordained. Jesuit formation is a long process, eleven to fifteen years. He can always change his mind." Jamie, speaking from experience, though Robert's vocation seemed an authentic calling. "It's his money to spend or donate however he sees fit until then."

Jamie glanced Bill's way. "It's good to ask questions. It's the best way to make sure there are no misunderstandings.”

“How much is Mom’s estate worth?” Thomas asked.

“It all depends on when we sell this house and for how much. That’s where the bulk of the value is. The house and its half-acre are estimated to be worth about ten thousand in today’s market, but that assumes we have a buyer. There’s about four thousand remains from the farm’s sale, and I owe the estate just under one grand remaining from my law school loans. So, roughly, I’d estimate fifteen thousand dollars, excluding the household furnishings and the car, to be divided equally.”

“Selling the house would mean you, the girls, and Thomas would have to move out. Are you okay with that?” Gracie asked, making eye contact with Jamie and then Thomas.

Jamie paused, waiting for Thomas to respond.

“I’m thirty years old, Gracie. I’m happy to get a place of my own, especially now that the economy seems to be bouncing back,” Thomas said.

All eyes now turned to Jamie.

“No one would have to move out until the house closes. But I’m ready to sell,” Jamie said. “I’ve accepted a job offer with Douglas Aircraft Corporation in Santa Monica, California.”

“What! California? You’ve never even been there!” Annie said, her mouth agape.

“You’re right, Annie. I’ve never been to California. But with the economy improving and people getting back to work, political pressure is mounting to cut WPA spending—or kill it altogether. My job is less secure every day. The position at Douglas Aircraft is stable, well-paying, and has room for advancement.”

“When?” Gracie asked, her eyes wide with shock. “And what about the girls?”

“Three weeks. And yes, the three-week, non-negotiable start date is a problem, especially for my girls. It’s hard enough they’ve just lost their grandmother, and now I’m leaving... But I don’t want to get too far off-topic since we’re here to discuss Mom’s will.”

“You can’t just drop a bomb like that and change the subject, Jamie,” Gracie said, digging in her heels, though not unkindly.

“Well, obviously, I’d like the girls to remain here in Tarrytown to finish the last two months of their school term, even if that means I have to hire a woman to live in the house to take care of them until the school term finishes."

"Come on, Jamie, surely you've got a better plan than that. What about Annie and me?" Gracie said. "What's family for if not to help each other out? We could keep the girls for two months. Right, Annie?"

Annie still looked stunned, her mouth hanging open in a deer-in-the-headlights expression. "Yeah, right," she sputtered, snapping back to attention when Bill gently elbowed her.

"I'll admit that I've thought about you and Annie. But it would be a big sacrifice for all of you." In truth, Jamie had thought of little else since calling Colin back to accept the job.

"And what are your thoughts?" Gracie pressed, holding firm. Jamie would get no wiggle room from his big sister.

"What if Annie and Bill moved out of Bill's parents' house and into Mom's house until it sells?" Jamie suggested. "Besides affording them more privacy, that would give Thomas time to scout around for his own place," Jamie said.

"Are you kidding me?" Annie's face lit with excitement. "Bill's parents would be overjoyed to have their place back to themselves. They love Johnny, but having a two-and-a-half-year-old in their house is a lot of chaos and mess, besides a soon-to-be crying newborn."

"You and Bill would have to decide that together, Annie. Same goes for Gracie and Chuck," Jamie said, glancing at both couples. "I'm afraid having all three girls here would be too much for you with the baby, Annie—or even you, Gracie. Since Meggie and Patsy fight like cats and dogs, they'll be better off separated. But I'd like to keep Meggie and Bridie together. Meggie's responsible and could help with the new baby, and Bridie loves babies too."

Annie shrugged. "Patsy's so independent. I think she'd be fine without her sisters if she stayed with Gracie and Chuck. You know Patsy—she can hold her own with Gracie's four boys."

Jamie nodded. "Once school is out, the girls would ride the train to Los Angeles. Meggie's thirteen going on thirty, conscientious, dependable, and responsible—a miniature version of her take-charge grandmother. Two months would give me time to settle in and find a place. I know it's a lot to ask."

Jamie looked directly at Bill and then Chuck. "If you're not able or interested in watching the girls, I can hire someone, like I said, to stay in the house with them temporarily. But, obviously, I'd rather pay you for the girls' room and board and have the peace of mind knowing family is watching over them."

~*~

Two weeks later

Jamie walked down the stairs, gripping the leather handles of his two suitcases. The yellow-beige cases, crafted from woven straw adhered to sturdy paperboard, contained all his personal effects, clothing, and shoes for his new life on the West Coast. He had packed the rest of his wardrobe into boxes and donated them to the ladies at the church for charitable distribution.

With each step, he felt himself moving further from the warmth of good memories—and the sting of painful ones. He knew this would likely be the last time he'd ever be in the house. His sisters and their husbands had agreed to the plan he'd proposed for the care of his daughters.

Annie and Bill had moved into Mom's old bedroom and would stay until the house went on the market and sold. Later in the day, Gracie would drive the short mile to pick up twelve-year-old Patsy, who would live with her family for the next two months. Patsy was the least troubled about Jamie's departure and most excited about all the changes that would come with the move to California. Meggie and Bridie would stay together at the house on Elizabeth Street in the attic bedrooms, where they'd been since birth.

Jamie wore the navy blue suit he'd bought off the bargain rack at Martin's Department Store in White Plains. The single-breasted, boxy jacket, with softly padded shoulders, hung just below his hip. The cuffs of his loose-fitting slacks brushed the tops of his black leather oxfords. A gray, navy blue, and white striped necktie, knotted in a four-in-hand style, was tucked beneath the collar of his light blue dress shirt. He hoped to blend in with the affluent business travelers who could afford the luxury of air travel.

Jamie had no idea how striking he looked. All he saw in the mirror were the flecks of gray at his temples and the lines etched deep from years of stress and heartache. The difficult years since Katie's illness had worn him down, leaving traces of both confidence and vulnerability in his face—qualities he never gave much thought to, though they quietly drew the attention of others, particularly women.

~*~

Bill stood at the front door, ready to give Jamie a lift to the Tarrytown train station. From there, Jamie would catch a train to Penn Station and then a bus to LaGuardia. His journey on American Airlines involved multiple plane changes. If everything went smoothly, it would take a full day to get to Los Angeles—longer if the planes were delayed. The Douglas Aircraft Company had purchased his one-way ticket for $800, a small fortune.

His three daughters stood near the front door, where Bill waited, dressed in a beige houndstooth sports coat and wide-legged slacks. The girls wore their school uniforms: solid green jumpers that fell below their knees, white shirts, and ankle socks. Meggie and Patsy wore black and white saddle shoes, while Bridie had on her Mary Janes. Meggie had braided her long, dark hair, tying white bows at the ends. Bridie's apricot curls were pulled into a ponytail—no doubt Meggie's handiwork—tied with a big green bow. Patsy's shoulder-length hair was neatly combed and curled.

Meggie's lips trembled as she fought to hold back her tears, while Bridie's small shoulders shook with barely stifled sobs.

"You look like a movie star, Daddy," Patsy said as Jamie reached the bottom of the stairs. "Do you know how far Santa Monica is from where they make movies?"

"Very close," Jamie said, wondering if Patsy would miss him at all and hoping Meggie and Bridie wouldn't miss him too much.

"Now, you girls, be good while I'm gone. In two short months, we'll be all together again."

Meggie stood a whole head taller than Patsy, although only a year older. Her fair skin was dotted with blotchy pink spots from earlier tears. "Daddy, I'm going to miss you so much," she said, her voice heavy with emotion, as Jamie pulled her into a hug.

"I'll miss you too, sweetheart. I'll write you, okay?" He gently wiped the tears from her face.

"You better," Meggie said. "And I'll write back."

"Patsy, now you mind Aunt Gracie and help out with your cousins. Meggie will be in charge when you take the train to Santa Monica, so don't argue about everything, all right?"

"I'll behave, Daddy, don't worry about me," Patsy said, standing on her tiptoes to hug him. "Get a house by the beach, okay?" she whispered in his ear.

"I'll do my best, Patsy."

Finally, he came to Bridie. He knew she was struggling terribly with the loss of her Grandma Peggy. And now, he was leaving her, too. "The time will go quickly, Bridie. Aunt Annie's baby will be born soon, and you'll have plenty to do to help. You'll be so busy, you won't even notice I'm gone."

The mention of the baby brought a brief smile to Bridie's face, but it quickly faded. "Daddy, are you sure Mommy can't come with us to California?"

"No, she can't, Bridie. We've talked about this. Her doctors are here. Your mother doesn't handle change well."

"But she'll be lonely without our visits. And she'll miss me brushing her hair."

Jamie had said his goodbye to Katie last week, though it hadn't felt like much of one. She was now a stranger in the body of the woman he had once dearly loved. His love for her had become a decision, not an emotion. It was hard work now. Bridie had, as always, come with him, lovingly brushing Katie's hair while chatting about school, calling her "Mommy," and expecting nothing in return.

To Jamie's astonishment, Katie made momentary eye contact with Bridie and said the word "Katie" aloud. Had she thought Bridie was her younger self? But just as quickly, Katie fell silent, her gaze vacant once again. In twelve years of institutionalization, it was one of the few words Jamie had ever heard her speak. One confused word was hardly enough to reignite hope or reclaim the years and dreams her shattered mind had stolen from them.

"Aunt Gracie promised to take you girls to Wingdale to say goodbye to your mother before you join me in California," Jamie said, looking from Bridie to Meggie and finally to Patsy. "I want you all to go." He knew Patsy would put up a fuss.

After one final hug to each daughter, Jamie left the house with Chuck and headed to the train station. He never looked back.

PART THREE – NEW HORIZONS
(1941-1956)

EIGHTEEN

Jamie jolted awake to the pale light of dawn. The lingering traces of a dream—his honeymoon at the Waldorf Astoria, making love with Katie in the double bed—flooded his mind. His body ached with the familiar pull of desire as he rubbed his eyes and stretched his tall, lean frame in the cramped space of the inner cabin. His neck was stiff, the window's hard edge having served as his pillow for the past four hours.

His journey on American Airlines had begun with a departure from LaGuardia Airport at noon the previous day. The total travel time was twenty-four hours, with five stops—Chicago, Kansas City, Dallas, Albuquerque, and Phoenix—before he'd finally land in Los Angeles.

Through that narrow window, Jamie had seen more of the country than he had ever dreamed possible. When the DC-3 ascended out of New York City, he caught glimpses of the Appalachian Mountains. Flying westward, he marveled at the patchwork of fields and rural areas sprawled lazily below, interrupted by the vast bodies of water—Lakes Erie and Michigan—he remembered from geography classes as a boy. Heading south, the Great Plains stretched out flat, punctuated by open prairies and occasional gently rolling terrain and river bottomlands.

Jamie worked the cramps out of his long legs during the extended layover at Dallas Love Field by walking from one end of the terminal to the other. He then boarded another DC-3 with a fresh flight crew. After Albuquerque, darkness swallowed the deserts below, and the humming in the cabin lulled him into a restless sleep after a long day of travel.

He didn't remember landing in Phoenix and was momentarily

confused by what he saw out the window. The Pacific Ocean? A deep blue mirror, shimmering with golden highlights—it had to be. As the aircraft leveled off for its eastward approach to Mines Field, a breathtaking view greeted Jamie. The sun was rising above the horizon, painting the sky with vibrant hues of orange, pink, and purple. The curvature of the earth was visible, and the spectacle filled him with a numinous awe. "Will you look at that," he murmured aloud.

"Breathtaking, isn't it?" said the stewardess, standing nearby. "It never gets old." Jamie's gaze briefly flicked to her knee-length navy blue uniform, which fit snugly over her trim, shapely figure. The matching hat, with its angled crown, tiny brim, and eagle insignia, rested neatly atop her chin-length platinum blond hair.

"What brings you to Los Angeles?" she asked. One of her light brown eyebrows arched over her almond-shaped, hazel eyes. Jamie noticed how her gaze lingered just a fraction too long, making her question feel a bit more personal than casual. But then, he knew the mirage of a man dying of thirst in a desert sees water where there is none. He absently rotated his wedding band, a habit he'd picked up in graduate school whenever his buddies asked about his wife or when he found himself talking to attractive women.

"A new job with Douglas Aircraft in the Santa Monica plant."

"Santa Monica is a great place. Being based in Los Angeles, I go to the beach there whenever I can." There was that eyebrow again. "We'll be landing shortly. Last chance for a cup of coffee. May I bring you anything?"

"Coffee would be fantastic."

"Cream or sugar?" she asked, flashing a lovely smile with dazzling white teeth.

"Both, thank you." Jamie smiled back at her, his eyes lingering on her full, "bee-sting" bottom lip. He watched her hips sway as she walked off to get his coffee and took a deep breath.

Once the plane landed, he retrieved his two suitcases, exited the terminal, and climbed into one of the yellow Plymouth taxis queued outside.

"Good morning. Where to?" the cabbie asked, placing his cap, emblazoned with the Yellow Cab Co insignia, back on his bald head. He stubbed out his cigarette in the ashtray, already overflowing with butts and ashes.

"Santa Monica, Miramar Hotel." Colin had suggested this hotel when Jamie called to accept the job.

"Ten miles. That'll cost ya two-and-a-half dollars."

"Make it an even three, and take me by Douglas Aircraft Park before dropping me off at the hotel."

"The L.A. plant or the Santa Monica plant?"

"Santa Monica."

"Three bucks it is then," the cabbie said, shifting into gear.

They headed northwest along Lincoln Boulevard toward Santa Monica, passing through industrial districts, commercial areas, and neighborhoods of apartment complexes and modest single-family homes.

Jamie rolled down the window in the back seat, relishing the comfortable early morning air and inhaling Southern California's fresh scent. Compared to New York, this new world of vegetation revealed all manner of palms swaying their fronds in the breeze. Citrus trees were shedding their last white blooms, while dark green oleander bushes burst into white, pink, and occasionally red blossoms. The narrow blue-green leaves of eucalyptus trees rustled, their smooth bark peeling in long strips, releasing a menthol-like fragrance.

As they neared Santa Monica, the Pacific Ocean lay calm and serene, a vast expanse of blue glass reflecting the soft morning light. The air felt charged with a unique energy. Gone were the bucolic green hills of New York's Westchester County, replaced by a different kind of beauty and allure—a seductive charm. Jamie found himself falling under its spell.

When the cabbie learned Jamie was moving from New York and probably had time to kill before checking in, he swung by the Santa Monica Pier at the northern end of Santa Monica's three-and-a-half-mile beach. "The beach is only a half mile from the hotel," he said.

By the time Jamie stepped out of the cab, the cabbie had shown him the nearest Catholic church to the hotel and given him a quick tour of the city, which had been expanding rapidly thanks to nearby aircraft industries like Douglas, North American Aviation, and Hughes. Metro-Goldwyn-Mayer Studios in neighboring Culver City had also contributed, but Jamie declined taking a side trip there when the cabbie suggested it.

Jamie handed the cabbie six dollars and thanked him for the tour.

The cabbie gave him a Yellow Cab Company card and scribbled his name on it. "Ask for Lou if you need a lift."

As Jamie stepped out of the cab, the hotel grounds felt like an oasis amid the burgeoning urban landscape. The main structure struck him as a modernistic, multi-storied concrete box, lacking the flourishes of the grand hotels in New York City.

Hungry and tired, he headed for the lobby. Since his room wasn't ready yet, he found a quiet spot to rest. As his wait dragged on, he ordered a pot of coffee and breakfast. He longed to get out of his suit and remove his necktie. A few early-bird guests roamed the fashionable lobby in shorts, T-shirts, and sundresses. People certainly dressed more casually in Southern California than in New York.

~*~

The Next Day

Jamie woke up early Sunday morning after sleeping away much of Saturday, still not fully adjusted to the time difference. As he pulled back the hotel room's curtains, the sunshine burst into the room, invigorating him with its warmth. The bright blue sky lifted his spirits, filling him with hopeful anticipation. Perhaps God hadn't completely abandoned him after all. How else could he explain the gift of this new beginning? Santa Monica felt like a place of healing, offering Jamie a chance to soothe his weary soul.

During the fifteen-minute walk from the hotel to St. Monica's Catholic Church, he listened to the chirps, trills, and whistles of the birds, trying to recognize their calls. He identified the long, jumbled warble of a finch and the cheerful song of a robin.

After Mass, Jamie stood outside on the steps of the Spanish Colonial Revival church, waiting for his turn to speak with the parish priest. Old Monsignor Conneally greeted his parishioners with lively handshakes and smiles as they exited after the last morning Mass.

Jamie checked his watch; it was now quarter to twelve. He had fasted since midnight and was hungry, kicking himself for not attending early Mass. He'd certainly been up early enough, with his body still on East Coast time.

From the priest's introductory prayers, Jamie picked up on his melodic lilt and figured him to be an Irish transplant—Connacht dialect, if he wasn't mistaken. He would have to let Unc know; perhaps his uncle knew Monsignor Conneally or his family. The Murphys had immigrated from Galway once upon a time.

Unc. The most difficult part of leaving Tarrytown and his old life was leaving his uncle behind. Unc was the one person Jamie couldn't hide his inner feelings from; his uncle knew him better than Jamie knew himself.

Jamie's eyes traveled above the heavy, double wooden doors to the semicircle transom in the recessed limestone arch. In relief, an artist had carved St. Monica with her arms extended to St. Augustine as a young child.

Mom. He'd never have left his mother to come out West, but God had called her home. Perhaps that was all part of a hidden, grand plan. He missed his girls, but that was a temporary ache. Missing Unc and his mother was of a deeper kind, one that felt permanent.

At thirty-seven years old, Jamie Murphy was on his own for the first time—no mother to pick up the slack, no Unc to impart wisdom and guidance, and the full responsibility of three daughters whose care he had left primarily to his mother. It felt like an enormous weight, too much to carry alone. He needed to get reacquainted with God.

"Monsignor, may I have a word with you?" Jamie asked as the older priest turned to go back inside, the stream of hand-shaking parishioners having dried up.

"Well, let's have it, then. You're standing between me and my lunch, young man," the priest replied, his clear blue eyes sparkling with mischief.

Jamie held out his hand to the priest. "Jamie Murphy, Monsignor. I'm new to the parish and Santa Monica. My daughters will join me once school lets out for the summer back in New York."

"Ah, Jamie Murphy, is it now? Welcome, welcome. Your daughters, you say?" He arched his wily, white eyebrows, which needed a good trim, reminding Jamie of the battered wings of a seagull in flight.

"Yes, three daughters, and I need to get them enrolled in school for the fall."

"The good Sisters of the Holy Names of Jesus and Mary can help you with that, sure enough. They run the elementary and high schools for the parish. Fine schools, they are."

Jamie knew that the campus was large—stretching a city block from Lincoln Boulevard to 7th Street—but it was reassuring to hear

Monsignor's assessment of the schools.

"What brings you here? The industry or the pictures?"

"Movies? Ha, hardly." Jamie laughed aloud. "A new job with the legal department at Douglas Aircraft."

"Oh, a barrister, are you? And no wife with you?"

"Yes, a wife. But she isn't well enough to travel." No one needed to know that his wife was insane or that she would never be joining him. The less said, the better. Word invariably got around, as it had at Transfiguration and in the neighborhood. He didn't want pity or people treating Meggie, Patsy, or Bridie like lepers. This was a new start for everyone... except Katie.

Poor Katie. Jamie's persistent longing for her felt like a gutting wound, and he mourned the life he was supposed should've had with her. He grieved a marriage to a woman whose mind was lost somewhere in a body he still desired and the vows that kept him permanently celibate.

Jamie took a circuitous route back to the hotel, keeping an eye out for signs advertising single rooms or houses for rent. He didn't find many, but one looked close enough for the girls to walk to school. As he wove through the neighborhoods near Lincoln Boulevard, he noted bus stop locations and made a mental note to ask for the schedule at the hotel desk. He planned to take a taxi to work for the first day or two but hoped to save money by riding the bus afterward.

During lunch, Jamie perused the *Santa Monica Evening Outlook* for both short-term and long-term rentals. He hoped to find a reasonably priced place that was near St. Monica's campus or his new job location. He found just one—at 726 Pier Ave. Returning to his room, Jamie immediately called the number listed in the ad.

Jamie asked about the house's location relative to his two main points of interest. The gentleman on the phone replied, "It's about two miles southeast of St. Monica Church and two miles southwest of the Douglas Aircraft Plant on Ocean Park Boulevard," where he would be starting work tomorrow.

"What about proximity to bus stops?" Jamie asked.

"The house is just a block from Lincoln Boulevard, so there's easy access to bus stops. Best of all," the man added, "it's less than a mile from the beach."

"Can I come by and look at the house this afternoon?"

"Can you make it here in an hour? My wife and I are heading out soon."

"Sure, no problem."

"What was your name again?"

"I didn't say, but it's Jamie Murphy. I'll see you within the hour."

As soon as Jamie hung up, he rode the elevator down to the lobby to speak to the concierge. Another couple had gotten there first: a short, overweight, balding man tightly clutched his companion—a taller, voluptuous woman half his age—as if she were on a short leash.

Once they left, Jamie approached the concierge with an air of urgency.

"Good afternoon. I trust your stay is going well," the gentleman said. "What can I do for you, young man?"

He pushed up his wire-rimmed glasses on his broad nose and smiled as Jamie sat down. His gray hair was combed over a bald spot, though it wasn't quite enough to do the job. Beneath his tan sports jacket, a red bow tie added a splash of color to his crisp white shirt.

"I have some questions about the area," Jamie said.

"I'd be glad to help you with that. I've lived in Santa Monica my whole life. I work here now that my wife is gone. I enjoy meeting people." The man pulled a picture of his wife from his desk drawer.

"Sorry about your wife," Jamie said, hoping the concierge wouldn't lose his job for pulling out the picture once too often in front of some heartless soul.

"Gone five years this June, but it seems like yesterday. We had a long, happy life together. No kids, though." A wispy cloud of sadness briefly passed over the man's caramel-brown eyes.

Jamie's spark of envy flickered but quickly died—a vice he struggled against when other men spoke of long, happy marriages. Nobody has everything, he reminded himself, no matter how it looks from the outside. Jamie might be wife-poor, but he was kid-rich. He needed to work on his gratitude. For that matter, he needed to work on a lot of things. Santa Monica felt like the perfect place to start.

"Do you have a map of Santa Monica I can keep? I have some questions about the different neighborhoods. Sounds like you're the expert on this."

"I do, indeed, the tool of my trade. I worked in real estate in my younger days." The concierge winked and pulled a map from the desk drawer. "Fire away, Mr. ...?"

"Murphy. But Jamie works best," Jamie replied with a smile.

"Pleased to meet you, Jamie. I'm Eddie to everyone and their dog." The two men exchanged a warm handshake, and Eddie opened up the map, flattening the folds with his hands.

"About where is 726 Pier Avenue on this map?"

"Right about here," Eddie marked a little X and circled it on the map. "This part of Santa Monica is called Ocean Park."

"Is it a good neighborhood? I have three daughters joining me from New York once school lets out for the summer."

"There aren't any bad neighborhoods here in Santa Monica. It's not like Los Angeles—yet, anyway. But our population has doubled in the last two years, pushing up home prices. The aircraft manufacturing industry has brought many people into the area, and there's no sign of it letting up. The movie industry, too. But honestly, with Santa Monica's beaches and the weather, I understand the attraction. What's not to love?"

"I'm one of the imports pushing up home prices. My first day at Douglas Aircraft is tomorrow. I'll be working in the legal department, overseeing government contracts."

"Congratulations. Sounds like a good job—and a secure one, too."

"I'm counting on it," Jamie said, smiling. "Is Ocean Park a good place to buy a home? And how do home prices compare to other neighborhoods in the city?"

"The growth in the job market has made housing, especially rentals, extremely difficult to find. Demand is driving up the cost of buying a place. It's a great time to invest in a home if a person can. Ocean Park is a mix of middle-class and working-class families. More affordable, too, compared to homes in upscale neighborhoods like NOMA."

"NOMA?"

"Sorry, North of Montana Avenue. NOMA has more upscale homes—tree-lined streets and more affluent residents, like people from the movie industry. More affordable neighborhoods include Pico, Sunset, and Midtown." He circled these areas on the map and jotted down their names. "But my favorite is Ocean Park. I wouldn't hesitate to buy something there, especially if it's an older home.

"Douglas Aircraft is building homes in these areas to support the influx of workers they're hiring. But these new homes aren't anywhere near the quality of the older homes. Some folks who've been there for years are packing up and moving out. Change is hard for some people, you know."

"Mr. Hodges, you just made my day. What days do you work?"

"Don't worry about that, Jamie." Eddie handed him a card after writing a phone number on the back. "I noticed you at Mass this morning at St. Monica's. I'm an usher. I'm glad to help in any way I can. Welcome to the area. By the way, I'm the old guy who caught you when you tripped on the kneeler coming out of the pew for Communion."

"Nice to know I can make memorable first impressions." Jamie studied the card. *Eddie Hodges.* "Thank you for your help today, Mr. Hodges. Both times." He winked back at Eddie.

Eddie stood and offered his hand. "Eddie, not Mr. Hodges," he said when Jamie shook his hand firmly.

"I have a feeling we'll be seeing more of each other." Something about Eddie Hodges reminded Jamie of Unc.

"I'd like that," Eddie said with a warm smile.

~*~

Jamie was running numbers for the house on Pier Avenue based on his new salary. The owner had mentioned he was open to selling the home to the right buyer. Jamie wasn't sure if the price to buy the house quoted by his new landlord was reasonable or what tuition would be for his three girls at St. Monica's.

Bridie would be in fourth grade and Patsy in seventh. This upcoming school term would be Meggie's last year before high school. He felt ill-equipped to raise three daughters without a woman to help. Perhaps he could hire someone initially to prepare dinner on weeknights. He would have to figure that into his budget. Hopefully, they could get by without a car for the first year. Colin had mentioned something about a housing allowance; he would ask him about that at dinner.

Then there was Katie's upkeep. After being hired by the WPA— Jamie's first and only job as a lawyer until now—he had made small monthly donations to Harlem Valley Hospital in Wingdale in Katie's name. Although not required by law and with no guarantee of better

189

care, he hoped these contributions helped Katie receive the best medical care possible, decent clothing and food, and ensured she wouldn't be relegated to some godforsaken ward for incurable, indigent cases. If nothing else, it made him feel like he hadn't completely abandoned her.

Jamie had already forked over the first and last month's rent for the house on Pier Avenue and could move in as early as May 15th, just two weeks away. The owner and his wife were moving to San Diego, where their son's family lived. Was Jamie interested in buying their twenty-year-old home—furniture and all? the owner wanted to know. Jamie assured them he was, but he needed to talk to his friend, Eddie Hodges, a longtime Santa Monica resident. Did the landlord know him? "Yes, everyone knows Eddie Hodges," he'd replied, "as good a fellow as they make 'em."

Once the house in Tarrytown sold, Jamie would have a sizeable down payment, even after repaying his college debt to his mother's estate. He explained the situation to the landlord; until then, he would pay rent.

The phone rang in his hotel room. He glanced at his watch: 6:10. He'd lost track of time and was supposed to meet Colin Maddigan, his new boss, downstairs ten minutes ago.

"Jamie, you coming down some time this year?" a big, buttery baritone voice asked.

"Sorry, Colin. Heading down right now." Jamie grabbed his jacket and tightened his necktie.

When the elevator door opened, Colin stood in the lobby, schmoozing with two attractive women—same old Colin. Jamie had lost a few pounds, while Colin had gained a few, but not enough to dampen his playboy appeal. He was an inch taller than Jamie, with dark auburn hair and striking green eyes.

In law school, Colin had been committed to eating, drinking, and being with as many "Marys" as possible while consistently performing at the top of his class. Eventually, the two men's friendship blossomed through their good-natured academic competition. Colin's infectious laughter and trust that tomorrow would only bring good things had helped Jamie forget his problems, temporarily lifting his spirits during a dark time when he had struggled to find joy in living.

The two men were opposites but had mutual respect for one

another. Jamie enjoyed Colin in small doses and knew that having him as a boss would be nothing short of an adventure.

The click of Jamie's oxfords on the travertine floor announced his arrival, and Colin turned briefly toward him.

"Ah, here's my friend now. You must excuse me, ladies. It was a pleasure meeting you," Colin said, bowing slightly and walking briskly toward Jamie.

"You're looking swell, my friend. Life must be treating you well," Colin said, giving Jamie a manly slap on the shoulder. He had dressed for an informal evening out: loafers, khaki trousers, a short-sleeved brown and white checked shirt, and a white cotton sweater draped over his shoulders and tied around his neck.

"I see you haven't changed," Jamie said, nodding toward the two ladies.

"We're going out to eat, not to work ... or to Mass," Colin said, eyeing Jamie's suit and tie.

"I haven't changed since Mass this morning. It's been quite the day."

"You can take the boy out of the seminary, but you can't take the seminary out of the boy," Colin smirked.

"Lose the tie, throw your jacket over your shoulder, and you'll be fine. We're heading to the Lobster Shack. Great view of the beach. Don't worry, they'll give you a bib."

"A bib? You really know how to hurt a guy," Jamie said, placing his hand over his heart and slumping dramatically.

"This ain't New York, my friend. Things are far more easygoing in SoCal. My car's just outside. I slipped the valet two bits to let me leave it out front."

Jamie followed Colin to a yellow Ford Deluxe coupe parked off to the side of the tree-lined drive, its convertible top rolled down and snapped under a matching leather cover.

"Nice wheels, Colin." Jamie whistled in appreciation.

"Hop in. Time's a-wastin'. We've got much to catch up on before you show up tomorrow."

NINETEEN

Early June 1941

"**M**eggie, Aunt Gracie is here. Let's get a move on it," Annie hollered up the stairs, her voice cutting through the air like a fog horn. She cradled her month-old baby girl in the crook of her arm while her toddler, Johnnie, pulled at her housedress for attention.

Gracie remembered feeling as frazzled and worn out as Annie looked now, with a pang of sympathy for her sister. She didn't miss those days.

"Mom's dress looks nice on you," Annie said, turning back toward Gracie, who stood in the front hallway beside a basket of bedding still to be washed.

Gracie wore a fitted summer dress, tiny white flowers scattered across a field of soft blue. It was one of several she had kept when she and Annie had sorted through their mother's closet last month. Whenever Gracie slipped into this dress—one of her mom's favorites—she imagined her mother's comforting arms enfolding her. Although Gracie was several inches taller than her mother, they wore the same dress size. Hems were shorter now, so Mom's dresses worked just as they were for Gracie. Not so with Annie, who had always struggled with her weight.

Glancing into the parlor, Gracie saw Johnnie's wooden blocks and toy metal cars and trucks strewn everywhere. A teddy bear and stuffed toy rabbit were positioned on the couch with books in their paws. Undoubtedly, the work of Bridie entertaining Johnnie, Gracie mused.

Now that the house was for sale, there was still so much work left to do. And who would do it if she didn't? Gracie had taken on the lead role in overseeing the house sale, but it was like herding cats trying to accomplish anything with her siblings still living there. Annie had her hands full with a toddler and a newborn. Besides, Annie was...well, Annie. Gracie had never figured out the secret to motivating her sister.

Annie and Thomas still hadn't made up their minds about which furniture they wanted to keep. It frustrated Gracie—time was running out, and they'd need to find a new place to rent once the house sold. But getting them to make decisions felt like pulling teeth.

No one seemed in any rush except Jamie, who was eager to buy the house he was renting in Santa Monica. Whatever was left behind would go into an estate sale, with the remainder donated to the St. Vincent de Paul Society. Once Meggie, Patsy, and Bridie joined their father, dealing with the house would become Gracie's top priority. She'd enlist her four boys—ages eighteen to ten—to help once school was out for the summer.

Bridie sat on the bottom step of the staircase, elbows on her knees, hands cupping her face. She appeared lost in thought. A dark green bow held her copper hair back from her heart-shaped face, likely tied by Meggie under Bridie's careful direction. Gracie smiled to herself, knowing how particular her niece could be about how things were done.

"Hi, Bridie," Gracie said.

Bridie lifted her chin. "Hi, Aunt Gracie. Thanks for taking us to see Mommy and tell her goodbye."

"Of course, Bridie, my pleasure," Gracie replied, watching as Bridie reached for the calico bag beside her. It looked like something Mom might've sewn from fabric scraps. Bridie carefully pulled out a mirror, a comb, a brush, and a book, as if double-checking to make sure she had everything.

"I'm not sure Meggie heard me," Annie said. "Bridie, can you go upstairs and hurry Meggie along? Tell her Gracie is here."

"Okay, Aunt Annie." Bridie replaced the items in the bag and darted up the stairs, the crinoline swishing beneath her green, polished cotton party dress.

"Bridie looks so cute, all dressed up to go visit her mother," Gracie said softly to Annie.

"That dress was Bridie's idea. I couldn't talk her out of it," Annie said, shaking her head.

"It's fine. I think it's sweet. Bridie loves her mother. It's quite remarkable, considering her mother shows no sign of recognition, from what Jamie has told me," Gracie said softly. "She's an extraordinary girl."

"Where's Patsy?" Annie asked.

"She's pouting out in the car. She didn't want to come, but I made her. For all we know, this could be the last time the girls see their mother," Gracie said. "Patsy's a handful—moody and stubborn as a mule." Gracie shot Annie a wry, knowing look and added, "She reminds me of someone else at that age." *Still does*, Gracie thought.

"Oh, come on, Gracie. I was never that temperamental. Jamie will have his hands full with Patsy, especially without Mom to tame the wild streak in her. Thirteen, but able to pass for seventeen, is another whole can of worms. Meggie didn't want to go either, but at least she didn't fight me about it."

"Jamie called last night," Gracie said. "He wants the girls to ride the train to Los Angeles the week after school ends. He's wiring me the money for their train tickets, enough to buy a trunk, a small carry-on for each girl, and other incidentals. We'll need to help the girls figure out what clothes to take, given the difference in the weather between here and there. He found a house in Santa Monica and hopes to buy it once Mom's house sells. By the way, have you had many people come by to look at the place?"

"A couple, but not many. Jamie called here a couple of days ago to talk to the girls. Meggie and Bridie sure miss him, especially Bridie." Annie looked upstairs and listened for Bridie and Meggie. All was quiet. She whispered, "Jamie's a better man than most, raising another man's child as—"

"Stop, Annie. Nothing good comes out of rehashing the past." *I hope to heaven that Annie hasn't been talking like this around the girls*, Gracie thought. Tact had never been Annie's strong suit.

Bridie came galloping down the stairs just as Gracie finished speaking. Meggie followed close behind, a book in hand. Meggie had shot up recently, now a head taller than Patsy, though still straight as a beanpole. While she hadn't filled out like Patsy, she was far more responsible, emotionally mature, and particularly maternal toward Bridie. Gracie saw a lot of herself in Meggie.

"Ready, girls? I made sandwiches to eat along the way. Patsy's already out in the car waiting."

Gracie walked over to Johnnie, scooped him up, kissed him on the cheek, and then set him back down. She hugged Annie, eyeing the sleeping infant in her sister's arms. "They're so darling when they're sleeping, aren't they? I'll have Meggie and Bridie back before dinner. We can talk later about the packing."

~*~

The party of four entered the hospital's front door. Gracie couldn't remember the last time she'd been to Harlem Valley State Hospital. Five years ago? Maybe longer. She'd only visited a couple of times in the many years Katie had lived there, and even then, it was to support her brother. Gracie found it just as difficult as Meggie and Patsy to visit Katie; the place gave her the willies.

After Gracie checked in at the front desk, they waited for their escort to whatever visitation room they would be assigned. A middle-aged woman of modest height, full figure, and glowing mocha-colored skin eventually arrived to guide them. The woman wore a white blouse tucked neatly into the waistband of her gray wrap-around skirt. Her dark eyes conveyed compassion, and her full lips parted in a gentle smile.

"We heva long ways ta walk," the woman said, leading the way. Gracie noticed that her heavy-set frame moved with surprising grace as they entered what felt like the "bowels" of the hospital. Gracie and Bridie followed closely behind, while Meggie and Patsy trailed further back.

"Are you a nurse?" Bridie asked, catching up to walk alongside the woman. Gracie moved closer to listen to Bridie's chatter—her way of putting things—never ceased to delight her.

"I'z an aide. See, no nursin' hat." The woman pointed to her shiny, straightened black hair, neatly bobby-pinned into a tiny roll at the back of her head.

"Do you take care of my mommy?"

"Sometimes, I do, chile. You look just like your momma, right purty."

Gracie, now a few steps behind Hattie and Bridie, was joined by Meggie and Patsy.

"Mommy's been sick since I was born. Daddy used to bring me to see her, but now he's in California. My sisters and I have to move there after school ends. I don't want to leave Mommy behind. We're here to tell her goodbye. When I grow up, I'm going to be a nurse and take care of Mommy in this hospital. I fix her hair when I visit so she knows I love her. She doesn't talk to me, but I know she understands."

"That mighta nice of you. You'z a good daughter."

"Thank you. My name's Bridget, but everyone calls me Bridie. What's your name?"

"Folks call me Hattie, short for Henrietta."

Patsy nudged Meggie with her elbow and whispered, "Bridie is so embarrassing."

"Only to you," Meggie whispered back.

Good for you, Meggie, Gracie thought.

Gracie turned to the girls beside her just in time to see Patsy cross her eyes and stick out her tongue at Meggie, who simply shook her head in response.

Finally, at the end of a maze of halls, Hattie unlocked the last steel, latticed door with her ring of jangling keys. "Well, we'z here," Hattie said. "Please wait here. I'll bring Missus Murphy roun' shortly." Hattie's gaze moved from Gracie to Meggie and Patsy in their casual summer shifts before resting on Bridie, dressed in her Sunday best.

The walls in the visiting room were a tranquil cerulean blue. A single picture hung on the wall: a framed copy of Norman Rockwell's Doctor and Doll. Gracie recognized it as the famous Saturday Evening Post cover from the same year Patsy was born, and Katie was institutionalized. The thought stirred memories, bittersweet and tangled.

Two card-sized tables with four chairs sat in the middle of the room. In the corner was a small bookcase. One of the shelves held board games: Checkers, Scrabble, and Monopoly, as well as a couple of well-worn books.

Patsy walked over to the board games. "Which game, Meggie?" she asked.

"I don't care; you pick." Meggie set the novel she'd brought from home on one of the tables and moved to the framed corkboard on the wall opposite the picture.

"It's such a lovely day; too bad we can't go outside with your mom for part of the time," Gracie said, gazing out the curtainless window that faced the grounds, where oaks and sycamores created dappled shade. Several patients were outside walking with a uniformed staff member. The window, covered with metal grid-like bars, was open, letting in fresh, warm air and a robin's cheery, flute-like song.

"It says here that you can go outside," Meggie pointed to one of the posted sheets, "but you have to arrange it ahead of time." She glanced at the paper again and then read aloud, "The assigned physician has to approve, and a staff member must accompany the patient with the visitor."

"Maybe we can go outside after I fix Mommy's hair," Bridie suggested.

Patsy rolled her eyes, exhaled loudly, and slumped her shoulders, making an ugly face again. Gracie shot her a warning glare.

Hattie returned, holding Katie's hand as she led her into the visiting room. "Lookie here, Missus Murphy. You have visitors."

Katie's loose-fitting, institutional cotton dress was a dingy, greige color. Her slipper-like shoes clip-clopped with each step. Her still-lovely face showed no recognition, happiness, or sadness—just a blank, empty stare.

"Come sit here, Mommy, so you can look out the window while I brush your hair," Bridie said.

Hattie guided Katie to the chair that Bridie had moved in front of the window. Katie complied and sat on the wooden chair, its stain and varnish had long since worn down to the straight, uniform grain of the poplar.

"Now, if you be needin' hep durin' your visit, just press this ahere buzzuh." Hattie pointed to the round red button mounted on the wall to the left of the doorway. "Or wen you ready to en' yo visit. I be the one escortin' you back to recepshun."

"Miss Hattie, can we take Mommy outside for a little walk today? It's such a nice day, and it's our last chance to be with her for a really long time." Bridie's voice broke, her eyes a stormy gray, like the churning Hudson on a cloudy day.

"Did you 'range for a staff member to 'company you outside wen you set up for this ahere visit?" Hattie asked Gracie.

"Normally, Katie's husband sets up the visits, but he's already moved to California for his job. I didn't know enough to ask. Is there any way to still arrange it?"

"Seeuns how it's Saturday, Missus Murphy's reg'lar doctor is off today. But there's a doctor on call from a diffrunt ward. I can ask 'n see what he sez, if y'all er not in a hurry."

Hattie took her leave, the clip of her shoes squeaking faintly under the weight of her stride and then fading away.

"Thanks, Bridie. Now we'll probably spend the whole day here," Patsy complained.

"Patsy, let's try to be a little less negative," Gracie said.

"How should I fix your hair today, Mommy?"

Katie's eyes blinked, meeting Bridie's eyes for a fleeting moment—as quick as the flap of a hummingbird's wing.

"Okay, I'll just brush it today," Bridie said, removing the hairbrush from her bag on the nearby table. Standing behind the chair, Bridie began stroking Katie's shoulder-length, wavy hair, identical in color to hers.

Bridie gently ran the soft boar hair bristles through her mother's golden-apricot locks. With each brush stroke, she ran her opposite hand along the section of hair she had just brushed. Gracie noticed how Katie closed her eyes with each touch of Bridie's hand.

Meggie and Patsy stopped playing Scrabble to watch their mother yield to Bridie's gentle touch. Patsy tilted her head and drew her eyebrows together while Meggie pursed her lips, her eyes shining.

Bridie chattered like a magpie about anything and everything that came to her mind as she ran the brush through her mother's hair: what grade she was going into in the fall (fourth); her easiest subject in school (math); her favorite class (reading); the book that she had brought to read to her mother after fixing her hair, a birthday gift from Daddy (Gertrude Chandler Warner's *The Boxcar Children*); where she was moving to join Daddy (Santa Monica, California); what she was going to be when she grew up (a nurse) to take care of her, and so on.

Twenty minutes later, Hattie still hadn't returned, but a short man wearing a white coat entered the room. He wore a badge around his neck that read, "Dr. Albrecht Schuler." His hair, or rather what remained of it, was a mix of light brown and gray. Since those first years that he was Katie Murphy's treating psychiatrist, he had gained a bit of girth and a few wrinkles.

Dr. Schuler surveyed the room, his gray eyes darkening behind his round glasses as his focus settled on Bridie. His light complexion flushed. Bridie, sitting in front of Katie, reading to her from the book she'd brought, stopped reading and looked up at the man.

He shifted his gaze from Bridie to Gracie, but it was slow, almost hesitant, as if he were dragging his attention away.

"Hello, I'm Dr. Schuler. I understand you'd like to walk outside with Mrs. Murphy today."

"Yes. I brought her daughters to tell her goodbye. They are moving to California to join their father. I apologize for not making arrangements ahead of time. I wasn't aware that this was a possibility," Gracie said apologetically.

"I'm somewhat familiar with Mrs. Murphy's case." His eyes wandered back to Bridie.

Bridie stood up and walked over to Dr. Schuler, staring up at him.

"And who do we have here?" Dr. Schuler said, crimson dots dappling his cheeks.

"I'm Bridget Kathleen—Kathleen for Mommy—but everybody calls me Bridie." She smiled at Dr. Schuler, his gaze sweeping over her like the beam of a lighthouse. "I turned eight in April. Meggie is thirteen, and Patsy is twelve," Bridie said, pointing out her big sisters. "That's my Aunt Gracie, Daddy's big sister. Do you know my daddy?"

"Yes, I...I believe I do know your father." Dr. Schuler coughed and cleared his throat. "It's nice to meet you all."

Gracie moved next to her niece to make her own impassioned plea for Bridie's sake but stopped short. She watched as Bridie took Dr. Schuler's hand. "Please, Dr. Schuler, say yes." Rules were rules, but how could the man refuse the child—her eyes now full of tears?

"I'll send Hattie to escort you outside. But no more than a half-hour, please." Dr. Schuler abruptly turned and left the room. Hattie was already waiting outside the doorway.

~*~

Dr. Schuler felt dizzy, as if the air had been sucked out of him. He hurried to the floor above, stopping several times to catch his breath on the stairwell.

He'd been captivated by Bridie's eyes—pools of silvery gray, precisely mirroring his own, though almond-shaped like her mother's. Dr. Schuler's two children, both sons of draft age, shared his wife's coffee-brown eyes. He'd noted that Bridie's nose was slightly thinner than Katie's—more refined, aristocratic, like his own. Bridget Kathleen Murphy was a beauty, just like her mother.

A maelstrom of emotions drew him to an upstairs window—guilt, smugness, and a certain wistfulness or loss. From there, he watched the small group moving about on the park-like grounds as Bridie danced and twirled, holding Katie's hand.

~*~

Over the next week, Gracie watched as Meggie, Patsy, and Bridie struggled to decide what clothing and personal items to pack for their new life in California. She divided her time between her house and Mom's. Without her and Annie's patient intervention, the task would have been overwhelming for the girls—Goliath-sized, as Annie liked to call it. Gracie helped each of them pack a small carry-on bag with pajamas, undergarments, personal items, and one change of clothing. Anything that couldn't fit into the three-by-two-by-two-foot trunk had to be left behind, destined to "find" a new home.

Gracie helped the girls sort through what they would need for their new life. Their heavy winter coats, sweaters, and snow boots were left behind—unnecessary in Southern California.

Meggie carefully made room in her trunk for her favorite books and the quilt Mom had made for her, though she had to leave behind several dresses and shoes she hated to part with.

Bridie, less concerned about what to take, packed her Shirley Temple doll, the sock monkey Mom had sewn for her, her rosary beads, and her First Communion missal, letting Gracie and Annie decide which clothing and shoes she should bring.

Patsy, as Gracie expected, used the extra space in Bridie's trunk for her favorite magazines: Modern Screen, Hollywood Reporter, and Silver Screen. Moving to Santa Monica, less than ten miles from Hollywood, Patsy announced that this was her big chance to become a movie star or, at the very least, marry one.

Gracie shipped the three trunks via the Railway Express Agency, not far from Tarrytown's commuter train station. She made sure the trunks would arrive in California around the same time the girls did, give or take a day. The week before, she had gone to the station to purchase their train tickets, ensuring everything was in order. Now, all that remained was getting the girls on the first leg of their four-day transcontinental journey.

~*~

June 25, 1941

Early Wednesday morning, Gracie and her three nieces boarded the train at Tarrytown to travel into midtown Manhattan. Each girl carried a small case containing the essentials to get them through the four days and three nights they would spend on the train. Gracie couldn't decide who was more excited, her nieces or herself.

The girls eagerly claimed facing bench seats. Dressed in comfortable cotton dresses and carrying a light jacket or sweater, Patsy sat beside Gracie while Bridie sat beside Meggie. After two long blasts of the train's steam whistle, it began moving with an initial lurch and sway.

"Girls, this is going to be a trip you'll remember for the rest of your life," Gracie said. "Meggie, you're in charge of your younger sisters. Bridie and Patsy, you are to do exactly as Meggie says." She patted Patsy's arm. "No arguing." She paused for effect and added, "Behave just as if Grandma Peggy were traveling with you. Use common sense. Stay together at all times. Never leave each other, even to use the restroom, without telling one another where you're going. The key to having fun will be cooperation and patience. Nobody gets their way all the time. Any questions?"

All the girls shook their heads.

Gracie handed each of her nieces a copy of her handwritten instructions summarizing the trip's logistics and the single train change. They had been over this before, but she so wanted the trip to go smoothly for them with no anxiety.

"Once we arrive at Grand Central Station, we'll have to find the boarding platform for the New York Central Railroad line that goes to Chicago. It shouldn't be too far because the same line operates this commuter train. Grand Central Station is big, busy, and so magnificent; just being inside is a treat!"

"The first leg of your trip to Chicago will take about a day. You'll spend the night on the train and sleep in a Pullman car. Your meals are already included in your ticket, and you'll eat together as a group.

"*Don't* ever get off the train until you arrive at Chicago's Central Station. The last leg of your journey departs from Dearborn Station, about one and a half miles away. You'll take a taxi to get there."

Gracie handed Meggie a small leather purse, jingling the coins inside. "Here's enough money to get you from Chicago's Central Station to Dearborn Station and then onboard the next train to Los Angeles.

"When you get off the train at Chicago's Central Station, you'll hire a porter to escort you outside where the taxis are lined up. Tell him you have no luggage because it was shipped separately. Porters are men whose job is to help people with their luggage and get them where they need to go. They wear uniforms and have name tags. They'll come up to you; you won't even have to look for them. Expect to pay the porter about fifty cents for his help.

"Next, you'll pay the taxi driver to take you from Central Station to Dearborn Station. The fare will be between twenty-five and fifty cents. Ask the driver how much before you get in the cab while the porter is with you. The porter will be happy to assist and ensure you aren't overcharged.

"Lastly, once the cab driver drops you off at Dearborn Station, you'll hire another porter to take you inside to the Atchison, Topeka, and Santa Fe Railway platform, sometimes abbreviated as AT&SF, for another twenty-five or fifty cents. Tell him you are taking the El Capitan train to Los Angeles. Your tickets, which you must not lose, have all the information about the specific lines and departure time.

"You'll stay on this train all the way to Los Angeles, where your father will be waiting once you get off. This part of the trip will last three days and two nights. Again, you'll share a sleeping compartment.

"The transfer between train stations in Chicago is the only tricky part. However, if you follow my directions, you should be fine. Chicago's Central Station and Dearborn Station are huge and busy. Hold hands and stay together."

Gracie paused. "Any questions?" Silence.

Meggie chewed her lower lip and studied the sheet in her hands intently.

Patsy said, "Piece of cake." She folded the written instructions Gracie had given her and stuffed them into her carry-on.

Bridie glanced from Meggie to Patsy and then back to Meggie. "Do you understand all this, Meggie?"

"Yes, I do. We'll be fine, Bridie," Meggie said with a smile, taking Bridie's hand reassuringly. "There's nothing to worry about."

"It's always okay to ask for help if you forget or are confused. Hang onto your tickets and these instructions," Gracie said.

"Let's talk about the great things you'll see on your trip. The passage between New York City and Chicago is called the 'Water Level Route' because the route is flat, making it a quick train trip. This route runs along the Hudson River and then follows the southern shorelines of the Great Lakes. You'll pass through five states outside New York: New Jersey, Pennsylvania, Ohio, Indiana, and Illinois.

"Once leaving Chicago, you'll pass through Missouri, Kansas, Colorado, New Mexico, Arizona, and finally California. Three different AT&SF trains leave out of Chicago's Dearborn Station for Los Angeles. They all have different tickets. If you look at your ticket, you'll notice it says 'El Capitan.'"

"Oh, how I wish I could go with you, girls. I've never been outside the states that neighbor New York!" Gracie reached into her satchel and withdrew three bound leather journals. "These are from your father to write about your experiences over the four days." She handed them each an Esterbrook fountain pen, each in a different color, so they wouldn't get the pens mixed up. Next, she pulled out a book for each of her nieces: *Thimble Summer* for Meggie, *Anne of Green Gables* for Patsy, and *The Story of Doctor Dolittle* for Bridie. "The pens and books are from me."

"Thank you, Aunt Gracie," the girls echoed in unison.

"Now, no one has an excuse to be bored! I look forward to getting my first letter from you, using those pens. I want to hear about the trip, especially Santa Monica. Your father says you'll love the place he has rented. It is very close to the beach."

TWENTY

June 1951 (Ten years later)

Meg, as she now referred to herself outside the classroom, stood a svelte five feet eleven inches—even without heels. She sensed the attention she commanded, whether at the front of her classroom or walking the halls, head held high. Her tailored, understated yet fashionable dresses projected the polished, professional image she aimed for, and her easy smile strengthened the connection with her students—something she deeply valued.

At twenty-three and a half, now in her second year of teaching, Meg stood at the front of her American Literature classroom at Marymount High School in Los Angeles. She held up Steinbeck's *The Moon is Down*, a slim, hundred-page novella, but her attention remained on the thirty girls seated before her, gauging their reactions.

The students, dressed in white Peter Pan-collared blouses tucked into pleated skirts and blue blazers, sat in neat rows. Meg couldn't help but remember sitting in this very classroom not so long ago, feeling the same excitement she now tried to instill in her own students. She knew well that her passion and enthusiasm mattered as much as the particular subject matter itself, drawing in even those who weren't particularly interested in the book.

She could easily spot who had kept up with the assigned reading of the hundred-page novella and who had fallen behind. The stragglers fidgeted under her steady gaze, betraying themselves with sidelong glances and the quiet rustling of notebooks—telltale signs portending last-minute cramming.

Meg couldn't imagine a more perfect job than teaching literature; she'd never gone anywhere without a novel in hand. She enjoyed working with the faculty and staff, many of whom had been there when she graduated near the top of her class at Marymount seven years ago.

Southern California had thrived during the years following the Second World War, a time when the respectability of being a career woman had taken root—a category Meg proudly placed herself in. She enjoyed the company of men, but her independence and single life, where she was the mistress of her own destiny, mattered more.

After high school, Meg enrolled at Marymount College in Los Angeles, run by the same RSHM sisters who had overseen her high school education just two miles away. They had also founded and operated Marymount College in Tarrytown, where her mother had studied for a year before marrying her father.

Meg often pictured her mother, vital and sharp—a woman worlds apart from the patient at Harlem Valley State Hospital—learning from the same RSHM sisters who had taught her and were now her colleagues. Their mission hadn't changed: preparing women for professional and personal success, with an emphasis on critical thinking, ethical decision-making, and a commitment to social justice.

Meg remembered reading *The Moon is Down* shortly after its release—just three months after Pearl Harbor had been bombed—and not long after it had been adapted into a Broadway play. It had been wildly popular at the time, although it hadn't remained so after the war. Now, years later, she chose the book for her students for its moral dilemmas, presented through the viewpoints of both the oppressed and the oppressors—ordinary people thrust into extraordinary circumstances. Given its brevity, she had saved it for the end of the school year.

Meg continued her lecture. "Steinbeck took great pains to avoid mentioning a specific country or military presence, but the general consensus is that he was writing about the Nazi occupation of Norway during the war.

"You were six or seven years old when President Roosevelt declared war on Japan the day after the bombing of Pearl Harbor. I was in eighth grade and remember that day vividly. Just six months earlier, my two sisters and I had taken the train from New York to Los Angeles.

"We were just getting used to living in Santa Monica when everything changed again. You may not realize it, but before the

Second World War, this area was mostly agricultural. As the war progressed in Europe, even before our country's formal involvement, Southern California became a hub for industry and technology, spurring dramatic growth.

"By the time the U.S. formally entered the war, we had already been sending warplanes, ships, tanks, weapons, food, and raw materials to Allied countries—Europe had been engulfed in conflict for twenty-seven months. The war changed life for Europeans dramatically, and while we faced rationing and sacrifice, it was nothing like the devastation Europe endured.

"The Nazis had bombed over a hundred cities—including London, Warsaw, Paris, Oslo, Belgrade, Moscow, and Athens—causing extensive damage, loss of life, and major disruption of daily life. Germany, as you'll learn when you study World History next year with either Sister Joan Catherine or Sister Frances Leo (who, by the way, are both fantastic teachers), had annexed or invaded a dozen countries by December 8, 1941."

When Germany had surrendered in Europe in the spring of 1945, Meg was herself a Marymount High School senior. Japan surrendered to the U.S. four months later as she prepared to begin her studies at Marymount College. Meg paused momentarily, remembering her uncle Thomas, who had died on the beaches of Normandy. *Eternal rest grant unto him, O Lord*, she prayed silently, before continuing.

"For your final exam next week, I will ask you to write an in-class essay on one of the main themes in the book on the blackboard behind me." A soft groan spread through the classroom as the students exchanged worried glances.

Meg feigned surprise and paused for effect, raising a single dark eyebrow. She knew the students would balk at the in-class aspect of writing their final essays.

A girl in the front row raised her hand.

"Yes, Mary?"

"Can we use our books as a reference during the exam?"

"No, but you can use a notecard crammed with as much information as you can fit. You'll turn in your books on your way into class."

A collective sigh of relief bounced off the walls as Meg grabbed a stack of blank notecards from her desk and began passing a handful to the first student in each row.

"Your best preparation is to have finished reading the book, reviewed any notes you've taken in class over the last month, and spent some time reflecting. You already know the topic. Use examples from the book to substantiate your points."

A few minutes later, a loud, clear, penetrating ring announced the end of class. When the bell stopped, the class of thirty girls waited for their teacher to excuse them.

"You may be excused," Meg said. "Have a good weekend if I don't see you at the graduation ceremony tonight."

The classroom was now empty. Meg erased the blackboard and gathered up papers from her other classes to grade over the weekend. Pausing with her index finger pressed to her lips, she ran through a mental checklist, ensuring everything was packed in her brown leather satchel before closing the latch. As she walked toward the door, she glanced back at the rows of desks. Sometimes, it felt like just yesterday that she had been sitting in the first wooden desk by the long row of windows.

"Miss Murphy, how about a ride home?"

A familiar voice pulled Meg's attention toward the door of the classroom. "Bridie, what are you doing here? I thought you'd be home polishing your speech for tonight."

Bridie, the valedictorian of the class of '51, wore a green and white gingham summer dress with a flared skirt and belted waist. The seniors had finished their exams earlier in the week and were no longer required to attend classes or wear uniforms. Meg had instructed Bridie to call her "Miss Murphy" while on campus. With Murphy being a common surname, even in a school of nearly 400 students, and Meg and Bridie having distinct appearances, their relationship wasn't immediately obvious. Not that Meg ever denied it, if asked, but there was no need to advertise. Meg was a private person.

"Any more polish and the shine will blind me," she said with a loud exhale. "I came to drop off a retirement and thank-you gift for Sister Rose Marie. She was the best science teacher ever! I rode the bus here but was hoping to ride back to the house with you."

"Of course, kiddo. I just need to stop by the office first, then I'm ready to go."

"Neat-o. I'll meet you in the parking lot by the car."

~*~

Usually, Patsy could tune out the clatter of forty other typewriters surrounding her as she and the other women converted scripts and notes into typed versions for the Metro-Goldwyn-Mayer production department. But today was different. Her fingers and head weren't working together. How could they with a pounding headache?

MGM had taken Patsy on after just one year of secretarial school, where she'd sharpened her typing and shorthand skills after graduating from Marymount High—not exactly at the top of her class, but enough to land her here. She was still waiting for the bigwigs on the 117-acre MGM campus to realize she was movie-star material.

One of 3,500 employees who kept the studio running smoothly, Patsy ate in the same cafeteria as the famous, the not-so-famous, and the completely unknown. Actors and actresses casually had lunch alongside production, technical, and costuming crews, studio operations, and administrative staff. Patsy was just another face in the typing pool.

That cafeteria, though—it served up far more than just food. Patsy wasn't naive. It buzzed with industry gossip, professional talk, and plenty of networking. She'd "networked" her way into dates with a few up-and-coming actors, including Rex Foster, the good-looking man she was currently seeing. Dating at MGM was as competitive as anything else. Patsy knew she was just one of many five-foot-five, bleached blondes with a 36-24-36 figure and bright red lips, all vying for attention with the same "assets."

After informing her supervisor that she wasn't feeling well, Patsy clocked out and walked to the main entrance. She waved to the guards in the brick security booth, who let her out. Passing under the huge wrought iron archway with intricate black and gold scrollwork, supported by impressive brick columns, she walked beneath the suspended plaque displaying "Leo the Lion" in his classic roaring pose.

She lit a cigarette while waiting at the bus stop on Washington Boulevard for LAMTA Line 33. After boarding and traveling west along Venice Boulevard, she transferred to the Santa Monica Line 5, which took her along Lincoln Boulevard. She got off the bus two blocks from home. Patsy crushed her cigarette with her red, two-inch peep-toe heels and spritzed herself and her red and white dress with the oriental notes of Shalimar to overpower the cigarette smell. The salty smell of the ocean air and the warm, gentle breeze made her forget her headache.

Walking the rest of the way home to 726 Pier Ave, Patsy opened the front door and immediately kicked off her heels in the entryway, even before she shut the door. Lupita, a petite Hispanic woman, rushed from the kitchen with flour on her hands.

"Patsy, you're home erlee today. Ehbreting okay? Not seek, are you?"

"I left work a couple of hours early with a headache. Nothing a quick nap at the beach won't fix."

"Plees remember deener is early tonight at faiv because Bridie's graduation is at seben. Also, Eddie is joining us for deener, too."

Patsy didn't know how her father and Eddie Hodges met—she'd never bothered to ask—but knew they were fast friends, even though the guy looked old enough to be her Dad's father.

"Right. How could I forget?" Patsy said sarcastically, dreading the whole ordeal. Patsy walked to the end of the hallway and into her bedroom, where she changed out of her work clothes and shimmied into her high-waisted bikini with its halter top.

~*~

Remaining in the front hallway, Lupita made the Sign of the Cross, leaving streaks of flour on her bronze forehead. "*Nuestra Señora, intercede por la protección de Patsy. Ella es joven y necia*," she prayed aloud. Our Lady, intercede for Patsy's protection. She is young and foolish.

She picked up the red heels, deposited them outside Patsy's closed bedroom door, and then headed back to the kitchen.

Lupita had worked for the Murphys for almost ten years now. Jamie had found her through the job board at St. Monica Church, even before his daughters had arrived from New York. Lupita remembered the years she'd spent in the fields alongside her husband in the Los Angeles Basin—before he passed and left her a widow. Twelve years alone, with no family in California, until she moved to Santa Monica not long before Jamie did, acquiring a second family to love and care for.

She had managed the Murphy household since then—shopping, preparing their evening meals, light housekeeping, and keeping tabs on the girls. Most evenings, Bridie helped her with the dishes so she could leave a bit early. Lupita cherished her place in the Murphy household—

an "adopted" *abuela* to Jamie's girls. She treasured her close relationship to Meggie, Patsy, and Bridie—although Patsy did try her patience at times.

Eddie Hodges, Jamie's *mejor amigo*, was no stranger to her either. She knew him well, as he was often invited to dinner on the weekends. Lupita liked Eddie's presence in the house. In some ways, he seemed her complement—an "adopted" abuelo for the girls—but for Jamie, even more so, a *figura paterna de confianza* (trusted father figure) who had helped him through the grief of losing his uncle, Fr. Jim, five years ago.

Jamie always insisted that Lupita sit down and join them at the dinner table. There was no point in refusing. At the end of grace before meals, Lupita always added, *"Gracias, Dios, por esta familia."* Thank you, God, for this family.

~*~

Marilyn Miller, Jamie Murphy's new secretary at Douglas Aircraft, eyed the clock on the wall opposite the bank of windows overlooking Ocean Boulevard. Four-thirty—her workday was over. She pulled out a mirror from her kiss-lock straw bag, examined her chin-length honey-blond waves, and applied a fresh coat of coral lipstick, which complemented her tanned skin.

Mr. Murphy was still on the phone. She could hear his deep, resonant voice through the door. She hated interrupting her boss, the head of the legal department at Douglas Aircraft, particularly when he was on the phone or in a meeting. But now she had no choice. He'd been crystal clear and authoritative earlier: "No matter what I'm doing, by four-thirty at the latest, *please* make sure that I walk out with you. I absolutely can't be late for dinner tonight!"

She stood and smoothed her orange peplum dress; the short, flared ruffle at her tiny waist emphasized her hourglass shape.

Marilyn didn't know Mr. Murphy's story. Was he married, divorced, or a widower? Few men wore wedding rings these days. He had three lovely daughters, whose trio of 3-by-5 senior pictures sat on his desk: two with dark hair and one with red hair. She'd made a point to ask him their names: Meg, Patsy, and Bridget and commented on how pretty they all were.

Her boss was professional and friendly enough but very tight-lipped about his family. But he did mention that the youngest, Bridie, was graduating tonight—that was why he said he had to leave early. Their mother must be very beautiful, Marilyn thought more than once, assuming she was still in the picture, with a niggling sense of envy.

After her first soft knock and then a second, louder one went unacknowledged, Marilyn entered Jamie's office suite. She stood in front of his large mahogany desk. His delicious chocolate-brown eyes looked up from his notepad, making eye contact with her, nodding his head, and giving her a thumbs-up. Was she supposed to stand here until he got off the phone? In other circumstances, it would be poor office etiquette to stay.

She studied his dark hair, now gray at his temples. *How unfair that men get more attractive as they age.* Mr. Murphy was the embodiment of such inequity. The man was still movie-star gorgeous. Whatever Jamie's exact age, he was the perfect age for her.

When Marilyn looked in the mirror, she saw only the beginning of soft lines forming around her sultry hazel eyes and the tiniest hint of a slackening jawline. She had never worried about such things until her fortieth birthday this year. Now, each year that ticked by decreased her chances of meeting an unattached "Mr. Right" (or even a "Mr. Acceptable"). *Where has the time gone?*

Marilyn knew from experience that work romances were a recipe for trouble and unemployment. But still, there was a subtle chemistry between her boss and her. Surely, Mr. Murphy felt it, too.

"Listen, Mac, we'll have to pick up this conversation again tomorrow. My daughter is graduating tonight. See if there is any flex in those numbers. We'll talk soon," Jamie said.

As soon as Jamie hung up the phone, he stood, stretched, and rewarded Marilyn with a broad smile.

As Jamie reached for his suit jacket from the coat tree by the door, Marilyn sensed a shift in his demeanor—he seemed more relaxed, ready to leave the office behind. She'd like to get to know this side of Jamie Murphy better—a whole lot better. He gave her a quick nod, and she led the way out.

"Thanks so much for helping me to cut that call short, Miss Miller. We are having an early dinner tonight to celebrate Bridie's graduation and her being named valedictorian. Are you ready to head out?" he asked her.

"Yes, I just have to grab my purse and sweater."

"Okay, let's go then. I'll lock up."

~*~

The moment Bridie stepped through the front door, the scent of dinner pulled her straight to the kitchen. Lupita had made one of her favorites: mole poblano—chicken drenched in a rich sauce of dried chilies, chocolate, almonds, raisins, cinnamon, and cloves—served with homemade tortillas. Peeking into the refrigerator, Bridie saw the *tres leches* cake waiting for tonight's dessert. Her mouth watered in anticipation of the sweet, creamy sponge cake. Beside it sat whipped cream, and the sliced strawberries resting in blue and yellow Tupperware bowls, their white lids snug on top.

Bridie grabbed a spoon from the drawer and cracked open the blue Tupperware lid just wide enough to sneak a taste of whipped cream.

After the delicious meal, Bridie and Meg had to head back to the high school to help set up for the evening's graduation. Bridie helped Lupita put away the leftovers but pleaded with her to leave the dishes until she returned after the ceremony. Of course, Lupita would hear nothing of the sort, shooing Bridie and Meg out the door: *'No se preocupen por eso, yo me encargo. ¡Ándale, váyanse tranquilas!"* Don't worry about that, I'll take care of it. Go ahead, off you go!

Fifteen minutes later, Meg and Bridie arrived on campus. As a staff member, Meg needed to help usher the crowd before joining the rest of their family. Sister Martha, the commencement coordinator, had asked Bridie to come early to assist with last-minute details.

Bridie looked out at rows upon rows of empty folding chairs, soon to be filled with expectant faces. She helped finish arranging the chairs into two groups, leaving space for an aisle between them. The Spanish Mission-style buildings, with their off-white stucco walls and red tile roofs, glowed softly in the fading light of early evening.

The temporary stage was set for the speakers and honored guests. The thought of standing behind the wooden podium, speaking into the free-standing microphone, made her stomach flutter—tonight's crowd would be large. At least she could sit with her classmates, blending in until it was time to step forward for her speech.

The chairs nearest the stage, marked off by twisted blue crepe paper, were reserved for the graduating class. Tall lights had been positioned around the area in case the ceremony stretched into the evening.

Bridie lifted her long robe to avoid tripping as she ascended the side stairs and stepped onto the platform. She adjusted the small step beside the podium, centering it to comfortably reach the microphone.

Her eyes scanned the crowd: her classmates—a sea of royal blue robes and mortarboard caps, each adorned with a blue and white tassel. Spotting her family was easy. Lupita jumped up like a jack-in-the-box, waving her arms and clasping her hands in a victory gesture, shouting, *"Mi niña, mi niña!"* My girl, my girl! To Lupita's left sat Meg and Jamie, and to her right, Eddie and Patsy—her treasured Santa Monica family, one and all.

Bridie lowered her head, silently asking the Holy Ghost to remove all fear and use her as His vehicle of truth and love. Then, she raised her head, folded her notes, and spoke straight from the heart.

> *Dearest Sisters of the Religious of the Sacred Heart of Mary, our amazing teachers, families, friends, and fellow graduates...*

Certain parts of her speech came as naturally to Bridie as breathing the air around her—they were part of the core of her being. She would recall her words many years later:

> *The lessons we have learned in our classrooms extend beyond academics—lessons we must strive to master throughout our lives: love of God, compassion for neighbor, gratitude for everything (for everything is a gift), kindness and forgiveness, a hunger for truth, and the pursuit of humility. True humility acknowledges our gifts, giving all credit to the Giver.*
>
> *God has a mission for each of us, and we must pursue it with courage and confidence, knowing we are not alone and that He equips us for the calling we have received. If we are truly humble, we need never fear our own failures nor the success of others. Everything we have is a gift—even our very lives.*

She would remember exactly how she'd closed:

> *St. Catherine of Siena wrote, "Be who God meant you to be, and you will set the world on fire." This is who we are called to be— women who will set the world on fire.*
>
> *Let's take this spirit and our wonderful memories with us as we begin the next chapter of our lives, ready to embrace the future with hope, gratitude, and a commitment to making the world a better place.*

... and the standing ovation that had followed as her classmates threw their caps into the air:

Thank you, and may God bless the class of 1951!

TWENTY-ONE

The Saturday after Bridie's high school graduation, Jamie drove her to the West Los Angeles Department of Motor Vehicles (DMV) office near Santa Monica. He couldn't help but feel a little nostalgic—it seemed like just yesterday when he was taking Meg to get her permit. He knew that learning to drive had taken a back seat to Bridie's studying and extracurricular activities for school and church. Besides, with Bridie catching a ride with Meg once she started teaching at Marymount had removed any sense of urgency, Jamie supposed. Overnight, it had become her top priority.

He'd been so proud of Bridie last night as he watched her give her speech, and he had no doubt she'd excel in the Bachelor of Science Nursing (BSN) program at the University of California, Los Angeles (UCLA), starting in the fall. He was pleased she planned to continue living at home, though she'd still have to commute to campus by public transit. After all, he still rode the bus to work each day—it wasn't so bad.

She'd mentioned that a driver's license would allow her to study on campus in the evenings instead of at the kitchen table, as she'd done throughout high school. Not that she ever complained. Jamie knew Bridie was more flexible and less bothered by interruptions than Meg. She always let Meg use the desk in their shared bedroom. He'd once joked that Bridie was "a fixture at the kitchen table," and she had simply replied, "Meg has six classes to prepare for and stacks of papers to grade—she needs it more." He admired so many things about Bridie.

On the way to the DMV, Jamie noticed Bridie watching him closely as he maneuvered the family's Chevy Bel Air. He figured she was trying to pick up tips for her own driving—always the student. The late morning "June gloom" haze had finally burned off as they drove inland, and the sun's insistent rays bounced off the car's maroon hood.

"Dad, did you remember my birth certificate?" Jamie briefly turned toward her, noticing her gray eyes widen.

"Yes, I've got it right here." He opened his blue-and-white seersucker jacket with his left hand, revealing the top half of a tri-folded document peeking out from his inner chest pocket. "See? Nothing to worry about," he said, turning his eyes back to the road.

"May I see it?"

Jamie's jaw tightened; he had known this day would come. Switching his left hand to the steering wheel, he fished out the document with his right and handed it to Bridie. He braced himself for the inevitable questions that he couldn't avoid forever.

He glanced over as Bridie's eyes scanned her birth certificate, issued by the state of Connecticut—not by the state of New York like Meg's and Patsy's. He had rehearsed what he would say, trying to be as truthful as possible without revealing the unpleasant details. What good would the whole truth accomplish? Absolutely nothing!

"Why does this say I was born in Danbury, Connecticut?" Bridie's eyes narrowed, and her head tilted to one side.

"Because you were, Bridie."

"Why not Tarrytown, like Meg and Patsy?"

"Because when you were conceived, your mother was already sick. By the time you were born, Katie was a patient at the mental hospital in Wingdale. The doctors thought it would be safer for both of you if you were delivered at a hospital with a proper maternity ward. As you can imagine, delivering babies wasn't common at Harlem Valley State Hospital. Danbury was the closest hospital, just fifteen miles away."

After a pause, Bridie asked, "Were you there when I was born in Danbury?"

"Yes, and so was your Aunt Eileen, your mother's sister. The two of us returned the next day and brought you home." Jamie didn't mention where home was.

"Did you see Mom?"

"Not the day you were born—she was still quite sedated—but the next day."

"Did Mom ever hold me?"

"I can't say for sure. Katie wasn't herself; in those days, she could become quite agitated."

"How come I didn't know I was born in Danbury before?"

"It just never came up, I suppose." Jamie pulled into the DMV parking lot and turned off the car. "Well, here we are. Ready, Bridie?" He was more than ready for this conversation to end.

Jamie opened the driver's door, but Bridie made no move to get out.

"The last time we saw Mom was when we went back for Great-Uncle Fr. Jim's funeral, when I was in the seventh grade. And we only had a short time at the hospital with her, then. Don't you think we should go back to check on her? Any chance we could fly back this summer?"

"I don't think it's possible this summer. But, yes, it's a good idea. You know Aunt Gracie goes twice a year to check on her."

"Yes, I know; I always read her letters. But that's not the same as seeing Mom myself. I miss her. Don't you, Dad?"

"Bridie, I can't begin to tell you how much I miss the woman I fell in love with... and married." Jamie's voice broke. He closed his eyes, willing the pain to subside and laboring to regain his composure.

Jamie felt Bridie's hand rest gently on his arm. "I pray for a miracle every single day. Someday, she'll come back to us. You'll see."

Jamie gazed into his daughter's gray eyes, which held a confidence and faith he no longer possessed. Katie's physical and psychological absence had gnawed a hole in his heart. The loneliness ran deeper than he cared to admit, leaving him more emotionally vulnerable than he even realized.

"Okay, let's go," Bridie said, a spark of determination in her voice. "Look out, world, here I come!"

~*~

After returning home with her learner's permit in hand, Bridie fixed a bologna and cheese sandwich for her dad and herself. She wrapped hers in wax paper and filled a thermos with ice cubes and water to take with her to the beach.

The house was unusually quiet. Her dad sat at the kitchen table, catching up on the news, reading the *Los Angeles Times* while he ate. Meg and Patsy were both out; neither had left a note saying where they'd gone, and Bridie doubted they were together. It wasn't like them to spend time in each other's company these days. Lupita had weekends off.

Lupita, Bridie thought. *Now that I've graduated, what'll happen to her?*

Bridie didn't want anything to change; she loved Lupita. But there was more, too. Dad worked long hours and often had work-related dinners. Lupita's presence had transformed their 1,500-square-foot 1926 Craftsman bungalow from a house to a home. She brought a unifying warmth to their family, whose members often scattered in different directions.

"Dad, are you going to keep Lupita on now that we're all old enough to take care of ourselves?"

Jamie sat back in his chair, wiping his mouth with a cloth napkin, laundered and pressed neatly by Lupita, just like always. "We've been capable of taking care of ourselves for a long time," he said. "Lupita can stay for as long as she wants, as far as I'm concerned. I consider her part of the family."

"Does Lupita know that?"

"Yes, and I told her that if she feels she wants to cut back her hours now that you've graduated, that's fine, too. But she said she has no plans to quit or reduce her hours."

"That's swell, Dad! You're the best! I'm headed to the beach, but I'll be home to fix dinner: hamburgers, potato chips, and carrots. If you see Meg or Patsy, can you ask if they plan to be home for dinner?"

"Sure."

Bridie refilled her father's coffee cup and placed the Sunbeam percolator back on the sienna-brown Mexican tile counter, reattaching its cord. She slid open the curtains above the kitchen sink, their fruit print of apples, cherries, and bananas coordinating with the cheerful buttercup yellow walls of the combined kitchen and dining room.

She walked over to Jamie and kissed him on the cheek. "I love you, Dad."

"I love you, too." He glanced up briefly from the newspaper, smiled, and then turned to the next page.

Leaving the kitchen through the arched pass-through, she entered the small living room and pulled down the bamboo shades inside the west-facing front picture window to shield the room from the day's heat. The sunshine outside was perfect for a day at the beach, but it wasn't ideal for keeping the house cool. The early afternoon light filtered through the gaps in the bamboo slats, casting a soft, warm glow across the room. The bold orange hibiscus flowers and green fronds on the cushions of the bentwood sofa and chairs added a tropical, airy feel to the space.

Bridie picked up the picture of her mother and father taken at their wedding, which sat on one of the glass-topped end tables. *Mom was so pretty.* In this photo, Katie looked radiant, not gloomy or empty. Bridie loved it when people said she resembled her mother.

As she walked through the narrow hallway, Bridie passed the bathroom she shared with her two sisters, then backtracked. She gathered up Patsy's curlers, placed them in a zippered bag, and stowed it under the bathroom sink. *Nice and tidy now.*

The door to Patsy's bedroom, opposite the bathroom, was left wide open. An assortment of Patsy's work outfits from the past week lay in a pile on the floor. Bridie stepped in, hung Patsy's clothes in the closet, organized her shoes, and made her bed. Patsy was messy, but it didn't bother Bridie as much as it did Meg. She cleaned up after Patsy as much for Meg—perhaps even more so—than for Patsy. After tidying up, she shut the door to Patsy's room.

Bridie shared a bedroom with Meg on the same side of the hallway as Patsy's room. Their father's bedroom was on the opposite side of the hall, the largest of the three bedrooms, with its own bathroom. Bridie and Meg's bedroom was small but just big enough for two twin beds, a single desk, and a chest of drawers. They shared a single closet.

After changing into her turquoise Catalina one-piece, Bridie pulled on a pair of tan pedal-pushers, donned a sleeveless floral-print shirt, and slipped on her flip-flops. She placed a beach towel and the detailed course description for her next four years in UCLA's BSN Program into a canvas tote bag.

By the time Bridie returned to the kitchen for her sandwich and ice water thermos, Jamie had moved to the living room sofa with his newspaper. She placed her lunch in her beach bag. Noticing her father's dishes on the table, she rinsed them and put them in the dish drainer to dry.

She grabbed her floppy sun hat from the hat rack by the door on her way out. "See you later, Dad."

"Have fun," he said, his eyes still glued to the paper.

Bridie headed down the seven blocks of Ashland Avenue to the beach. Her thoughts drifted back to the conversation on their way to the DMV that morning. She castigated herself for not considering her father's feelings. Of course, he missed his wife—even more than she missed her mother!

While Bridie didn't fully understand the love between a man and a woman, she remembered the words of her religion teacher, Sister Lucy: "Marital love is a physical, spiritual, and emotional bond created by God that, in some sense, models the communion of love within the Trinity."

Bridie couldn't count the times she had begged her father to tell her the story of how he met her mother. She never tired of hearing it. "Ah, the beautiful and charming Kathleen Mary Houlihan—love at first sight," Dad always said. "Your mother was my first date and only love." *Had the retelling of that story brought him joy or sorrow?* She had never considered his feelings, only her own.

Would she ever know and experience that kind of love? Bridie had never dated or had a boyfriend. Like most girls her age, she thought of such things, but romantic ideas were a distant second to her career goals. Her love for her mother was inextricably bound to her pursuit of a nursing degree. For Bridie, it was the key that would unlock the door to bring Mom home.

When she arrived at the beach, Bridie laid her towel on the sand, placed her bag to the side, and stripped down to her bathing suit. She removed her flip-flops and walked about a hundred feet to the shoreline, enjoying the smooth, warm sand massaging her feet. She looked northeast toward the Santa Monica pier, a beloved landmark extending approximately 1,600 feet over the Pacific Ocean, a half-hour walk from where she stood. The wooden structure consisted of two piers sitting atop concrete pilings, with only one of the original wooden pilings remaining.

The pier was a flurry of activity: amusement rides, food stands, and souvenir shops. These commercial attractions coexisted with casual fishermen casting off the end of the pier with rods and reels or simple lines and hooks. Bridie stepped closer to the cold, foamy waves, letting them lick at her calves. High tide was still about two hours away, and the currents were gaining strength, reaching higher up the sandy beach. She removed a slimy strand of seaweed that had wrapped around her ankle and waded out waist-deep just as the last wave retracted, dipping down to her neck. She let out a small gasp—the water was chilly but refreshing.

After her quick dip, she returned to her towel, dodging sunbathers and children running to and fro. Bridie pulled UCLA's nursing course description manual from her bag, but her thoughts returned to her father's conversation in the car, circling like the seagulls flying overhead searching for food scraps on the beach. *Mom was pregnant with me when she went to the hospital. How did I not know this?* Something felt off, a vague sense of things not adding up.

"Enough," she said aloud to herself.

She retrieved her sandwich and thermos from her bag. Lying on her stomach with her hat still on, she ate her sandwich while reading about the intensive four-year program that extended through the summers.

Her first two years would focus on classroom instruction and laboratory work in basic medical sciences, such as anatomy, physiology, biochemistry, and pharmacology. The final two years would combine classroom studies with clinical rotations in various medical specialties, including internal medicine, surgery, pediatrics, obstetrics and gynecology, and psychiatry, conducted in both hospital and outpatient settings.

Many two-year programs at other institutions offered preparation in basic nursing for a registered nurse. However, Bridie wanted a more in-depth education, particularly in pharmacology and psychiatry.

Bridie refused to accept that the only "progress" in her mother's condition was the relabeling of her diagnosis from dementia praecox to schizophrenia, following Eugen Bleuler's terminology. Dementia praecox had been such a negative diagnosis, implying inevitable dementia and hopelessness.

During Bridie's and her Dad's last visit with Mom five years ago at Wingdale, she'd seen a glimmer of something in her mother's ice-blue eyes—an intelligence bound by fear, perhaps—locked away in the shell of the person her father had fallen in love with. "Wishful thinking," Dad had said when Bridie shared her observation. But she disagreed.

A half-hour passed quickly. Bridie's fair skin would soon resemble a freshly boiled lobster if she didn't get out of the sun. She shook the sand from her towel and began packing her things into her beach bag. She pulled on her clothes and gulped down a few swallows of ice water from the thermos.

"Heading back to the house?" a familiar voice rang out.

Patsy stepped barefoot on the fine, golden sand toward Bridie. Her platinum blond hair, perfectly coiffed in soft waves, caught and reflected the sunlight like diamonds. Sunglasses, perched on her gently sloping, elegant nose, swept upwards at their outer edge and were adorned with rhinestones, creating a feline-like appearance. Her red and white polka dot two-piece bathing suit showcased a warm, radiant tan glistening under a layer of baby oil. Bridie could see why men were attracted to Patsy. Her sister was beautiful—though Bridie preferred Patsy's naturally dark hair—and could be just as charming when it suited her.

"I am. How about you, Patsy?"

"Yep, me too. Looks like you caught a few too many rays, little sister."

"It doesn't take much." Bridie shook the thermos, the ice rattling and clinking inside. "Want some water?"

"Yes, you're a doll." Patsy drained the thermos as they transitioned from the sandy beach to the sidewalk toward home.

"I got my learner's permit today."

"Congratulations! You waited long enough. I got mine at fifteen and a half."

"Better late than never. Hey, I learned something today I never knew before."

"Like what, brainiac? I thought you knew everything." Patsy winked.

"That I was born in Danbury, Connecticut. I just assumed I was born in Tarrytown, like you and Meg. Did you know that?"

Patsy hesitated before answering. "Maybe. Does it matter?"

"Well, kind of. That means Mom was pregnant with me when she went into the mental hospital."

Patsy remained silent as they strolled past several houses.

Bridie waited expectantly. "Well… did you know?"

"I might have overheard Aunt Annie say something to that effect. I'd ask Dad about it rather than me. I was just a little kid back then. Sometimes, our memories of things aren't accurate."

"I tried to ask Dad some questions, but I could tell it upset him. I guess it doesn't really matter. I'm just shocked that I never knew it before—like I was the only one in the family who didn't know."

"You could ask Meg." Patsy shrugged her bronzed shoulder.

"I suppose. Are you going to be home for dinner tonight?"

"Not if I can help it. I'm hoping to go out for dinner with Rex."

"Wouldn't he have asked you by now? It's not long until dinner."

"That's not his style, Bridie. He's more…" Patsy tapped her index finger to her lips. "…spontaneous."

"Well, you could have any man you wanted. Don't settle for less than you deserve. Rex Foster should treat you more respectfully. I don't care if he's a movie star or not."

"Who's giving whom advice on men, Miss Never-Been-On-A-Date?"

"I just know how I'd want to be treated."

~*~

December 21, 1951

Jamie sat at a round table, exchanging small talk with Colin Maddigan, head of the legal department for Douglas Aircraft's Long Beach operations, and his date. It didn't take long for the conversation to gravitate toward business.

Colin described how the Long Beach facility's transition to commercial aviation after the war had impacted his department. Jamie noticed Colin's date yawn several times while he shared details about Santa Monica's continued focus on military jets and its newest models, the F3D Skyknight and F4D Skyray, produced for the Navy. There was much to celebrate—beyond the holiday cheer, Douglas remained at the forefront of jet development, and business was thriving at all three of their Southern California plants.

Jamie knew well that the ongoing Cold War between the U.S. and Soviet bloc countries was the unfortunate reason for the government's high demand for military jets at both the Santa Monica plant and El Segundo, which was also the center of military jet research and innovation for Douglas Aircraft.

With El Segundo's central location, it made sense to host the Christmas party at their facility for the professional employees and their support staff. Several Christmas trees, decked with colorful lights, tinsel, red ornaments, and miniature airplanes, twinkled throughout the auditorium, which served as a banquet hall tonight. A live band played a blend of popular tunes and Christmas classics. Couples danced in front of the four-piece band, while others chatted and mingled around the room.

Though Jamie would have preferred to skip the drive tonight, he couldn't complain—Colin had driven twice as far. The real issue was the loneliness that ate at him, attending these events alone. His heart ached, a constant reminder of the female companionship he missed but would never fully regain.

Jamie had been unsure if he would attend when Marilyn Miller, his secretary, inquired earlier in the week if he planned to show up. Ultimately, he decided it was the right thing to do professionally.

The three of them gorged on the massive spread of food that graced a series of long, wide tables set end to end, covered with festive red tablecloths and draped with evergreen garlands. Appetizers like shrimp cocktail, deviled eggs, and stuffed mushrooms were followed by roast turkey with stuffing, baked ham with pineapple glaze, and roast beef with gravy, all served by men in white coats and tall white hats. Mashed potatoes, green bean casserole, candied yams, buttered rolls, Jell-O salad, Waldorf salad, pumpkin pie, pecan pie, Christmas cookies, and fruitcake followed. There was eggnog, punch, soda, coffee, and tea, though the open bar remained the main beverage attraction.

Just as they'd finished eating, Jamie saw Marilyn Miller wobbling her way to their table. *Oh, no! Marilyn looks plastered*, Jamie thought, a martini glass in hand.

"I guessh you 'cided to come to the company Christmas party after all," Marilyn said, slurring her words as she staggered unsteadily toward Jamie on her red high heels. She leaned to one side, spilling her martini—clearly not her first or second—onto her fitted black satin sheath dress with a side slit. A single strand of white pearls hung around her neck, drawing Jamie's and Colin's eyes to her exposed cleavage framed by a plunging V-neckline.

Jamie immediately stood up from the table, taking Marilyn's drink from her hand and carefully placing it on the table where he had been sitting with Colin and his female companion. He led Marilyn to the empty seat between himself and the woman, who took a sip of her Manhattan and shot Marilyn a disdainful glance.

"Well, who do we have here?" Colin said, raising an eyebrow at Jamie and flashing a lascivious grin.

"Marilyn is my secretary," Jamie said, a protective tone in his voice. "Marilyn, this is Colin, a friend from my law school days in New York."

Marilyn reached out her hand toward Colin, knocking over what remained of her drink onto the table without noticing. "Pleash'd to meet you."

Jamie quickly grabbed a napkin to mop up the spill, his face flushing slightly. Colin, still grinning, extended his hand to Marilyn. "The pleasure is all mine," he said with a smooth smile.

After righting her now-empty martini glass, Jamie gently touched Marilyn's bare arm to get her attention. "Marilyn, I'm going to get you some coffee."

"I think we should be heading back to Long Beach, Colin," his date said, clearly not thrilled with the newest addition to the table or Colin's behavior. "We have a half-hour drive back to Long Beach."

"Your wish is my command, darling," Colin said, planting a long kiss on her pouty, red lips.

Typical Colin. Will the man ever settle down? Jamie thought.

Once Colin and his date, who was at least ten years his junior, departed, Jamie tried to get Marilyn to drink another cup of coffee.

"Marilyn, you're in no shape to drive home. Did you drive yourself here?"

"Yes, just little ole me. All by myself." She stuck out her lower lip flirtatiously, batted her long eyelashes, and leaned in toward Jamie, resting her shoulder against his.

"I'm ready to call it an evening. How about I call you a taxi?" Jamie suggested.

"I jush live in Santa Monica. I'm fine to drive; it's only ten milesh away."

"I don't think so. I'm going to call you a taxi. A lot can go wrong in ten miles when someone's had too much to drink."

"Pleashe, no taxi. I need my car tomorrow."

"Okay, I'll drive you home in your car and take a taxi back here," Jamie said, his frustration evident.

Marilyn began to cry. "I'm sho shorry. Am I fired, Mishter Murphy? I jush had one too many."

"Of course not. You're a great secretary, which is why I want you to get home safe and sound. Come on, Marilyn, let's get you to your car."

Jamie grabbed Marilyn's clutch bag from the table and her red heels from under it, noticing for the first time that she was barefoot. He steered her out of the auditorium with some difficulty, eventually putting his arm around her to steady her, hoping to attract as little attention as possible.

When they finally reached the parking lot, Marilyn couldn't remember where her car was parked.

"All right, I'll drive my car. Where do you live?"

"2308 32nd, jusht off Pico. A yellow two-shtory apartment building, number 102."

Jamie knew the area; it wasn't far from his house.

When they arrived, Jamie parked on the street. "I'll take you back to get your car on Saturday. Just call me when you're up; I'll be around the house most of the day."

"All right," Marilyn said, seemingly to get a second wind.

Marilyn handed Jamie the key, and he unlocked the front door, holding it open for her. She pulled him inside, tripping over a rug just inside the doorway and rolling onto her back, laughing.

"Oops," she giggled.

Jamie stepped inside and helped Marilyn back to her feet. "Marilyn, I don't think you and booze mix well."

Once she was on her feet, Marilyn stood on her tiptoes and took Jamie's head in her hands. "Thank you for bringing me home." She slid her hands under his coat.

She kissed him softly at first, then more fervently. Jamie hesitated but eventually responded, his better judgment overwhelmed by the blaze of passion sparked by Marilyn's unanticipated, sensual touch—fueled by a decade of unfulfilled desire for physical intimacy. She led him to her bedroom and unzipped her little black dress, leaving him no room to second-guess his actions.

An hour later, Jamie arrived home, the scent of Chanel No. 5 still clinging to him, and lipstick smudged on his collar, wondering if Adam's first bite of the apple had tasted as sweet.

~*~

The next morning, Jamie rose early. He read the newspaper while sitting near the telephone on the sofa, not wanting his daughters to answer if it rang. When Marilyn didn't call until noon, it left him in an irritable mood all morning. He wanted to get the face-to-face discussion and his apology to Marilyn over with.

He couldn't deny what had passed between them, but he understood the encounter for what it was, and love had nothing to do with it. His commitment to Katie hadn't stopped him from greedily taking what Marilyn had offered in her uninhibited, inebriated state. The weight of his actions settled heavier now—he was no better than Colin Maddigan. Perhaps worse. Colin had no illusions about himself, while Jamie had believed he was above such behavior. He wasn't.

There would be consequences for his actions, both those he could foresee and those he could not. Working together every day, the line between their personal and professional lives had blurred disastrously. *Dear God, what have I done?*

He drove the short distance to Marilyn's apartment soon after she called. She answered the door barefoot, wearing tight yellow capri pants and a short-sleeved blouse printed with sliced lemons and beach umbrellas, tied at her tiny waist. Her broad smile only deepened the guilt twisting in his chest.

He asked if she remembered what had happened between them in the bedroom last night. Yes, she did ("I've wanted this for a long time, Jamie").

Jamie was apologetic ("I took advantage of you"), logical ("There's no future for us"), blunt ("I'm not in love with you"), and fully disclosed Katie's situation and his decision never to divorce her ("I still hope for a miracle").

"It may not have meant anything to you, Jamie Murphy, but it did to me," Marilyn sniffled. "Okay, so you're married, but your wife is in a mental institution and will probably never get out. Does your faith expect you to live like a priest?"

How had they ended up in bed again? Jamie's head spun as he thought about Augustine of Hippo's prayer: "Lord, give me chastity—but not yet!" This was not going to be easy.

They emerged from apartment #102 on Pico Boulevard an hour and a half later. Jamie then drove Marilyn back to the El Segundo plant to retrieve her car.

TWENTY-TWO

Early Spring 1952 (The following year)

Bridie stood at the southwest corner of UCLA's main campus. The loud clang of the pile driver and the steady roar of heavy equipment were almost deafening. How thrilling it was to be part of all the change surrounding her. By the time the state-of-the-art UCLA Medical Center was finished in 1955, she'd be ready to graduate with her nursing baccalaureate degree.

When Bridie was researching nursing degree programs during her senior year at Marymount, she'd learned that the Board of Regents had broken ground on the Medical Center in 1949, the same year UCLA had established the School of Nursing in the northwest corner of campus—at the opposite end of campus from where she now stood.

She found it somewhat amusing that her nursing classes were held in former military barracks and other repurposed military structures, while the future medical facility promised something so grand. Still, it was in those humble temporary buildings that she learned the basics of nursing, including her Fundamentals of Nursing class and practicum.

The rest of Bridie's first-year courses—anatomy and physiology, microbiology, chemistry, nutrition, psychology, and sociology—were held in either Romanesque Revival buildings or sharp-lined contemporary structures. The modern buildings were functional but lacked the poetic beauty of the older ones, with their graceful arches and intricate brick and stonework. She could almost "hear" the architectural dissonance between them when she walked through campus.

After her morning classes, Bridie needed this break before trading this perfect spring day for the confines of the library until her two o'clock lab. Squinting against the noonday sun, she studied the busy construction site, bounded by Westwood Avenue (where she now stood), the botanical gardens to the east, and Le Conte Avenue to the south. From her vantage point, Bridie could see the temporary building housing the School of Medicine, which had opened last fall with its inaugural class of twenty-eight medical students, just below the construction site.

She marveled at the scale of the undertaking, munching on the peanut butter and jelly sandwich she'd packed the night before. A dedicated biomedical library would soon be housed in the Medical Center. For now, medical books, journals, and periodicals were relegated to a corner on the third floor of the library—Bridie's home away from home. Bridie alternated between a study carrel and one of the sturdy wooden tables, where she laid out her books and reference material with her usual neatness.

"Too bad we won't be here to enjoy the facilities," a male voice called out over the construction racket.

Bridie looked behind her. She recognized the young man from her many hours in the library, although she had never spoken to him. He seemed to prefer studying in the same section of the library as she did, never straying far from the biomedical resources. She'd pegged him as a medical student from his textbooks and conversations with the medical resource librarian, on which she had occasionally eavesdropped—but only when she was bored, she'd told herself.

"Matt Ryan, first-year medical student," he said in a calm and approachable manner, extending his hand while stepping forward.

At close range, Bridie thought his hazel eyes hinted at a thoughtful, introspective nature. His brown hair was neatly trimmed, framing a still boyish-looking but handsome face. He was tall, like her father.

"Bridie Murphy, first-year nursing student." She shook his hand, offered a warm smile, and returned his direct, friendly eye contact. "You could do your internship here. The Medical Center is supposed to be finished by the time you graduate from med school."

"True. But I plan to do my residency out of state, either in Boston at Massachusetts General, in Baltimore at Johns Hopkins, or in New York City at the New York State Psychiatric Institute—one of the leading hospitals in psychiatric medicine."

"Sounds like you've done your research and know what you want. The weather won't be nearly as nice on the East Coast, but you probably know that, too," Bridie said, holding her arms out as if to embrace the glorious day.

"You got that right, Bridie."

"Well, microbiology calls. Nice meeting you."

"Headed back to the library?" He tipped his head toward the center of campus. "I've noticed that you study there frequently, even some evenings."

That Matt had noticed her before, just as she had him, sent an unexpected jolt of pleasure through her.

"Yeah, I prefer it to studying at the kitchen table at home. I don't have my own room."

"I'm headed that way myself. Mind if I join you?"

"Sure. Why not? You look pretty safe to me." Bridie shrugged with a wide smile.

"Very safe, but feel free to frisk me... Please," Matt teased, wiggling his eyebrows and trying to keep from laughing aloud. He turned so his back faced Bridie, held his arms out, spread his legs, and then faced front again.

"You pass inspection with flying colors," Bridie said, giggling. She liked how his smile reached his sparkling eyes, making them crinkle at the corners.

"You've been spending too much time in those old barrack classrooms."

Matt's pleasant smile revealed a set of straight, white teeth, adding to his easy charm. "But seriously, I prefer studying in the library, too. I rent a house in Westwood Village with three other graduate students—one of them a medical student like me. The other two, though, seem to have much more time on their hands than we do. It isn't always the best environment for studying."

"Westwood Village is a pretty convenient location. Sometimes, I take the bus home from there. Other times, on nice days like today, I walk a bit further to the Wilshire bus stop, which drops me off two blocks from home without needing to transfer."

"Where's home?"

"Santa Monica."

"Where's home for you, Matt?"

"I grew up in the West Adams neighborhood of L.A. Do you know it?"

"Historic homes, tree-lined streets, and pretty close to Loyola High School?"

"Yep, that's it. I went to Loyola, run by the Jesuits."

"I went to Marymount High School. My uncle Robert is a Jesuit, and my great-uncle was one too. He taught at Fordham until his death."

"Fordham's in New York, right?"

"Yes. My parents grew up in New York. We moved out here when I was in elementary school, but my dad's family is still back there."

"What brought your family to the L.A. area, Bridie?"

"The usual reason—my dad's job. How about you? Did you grow up in California?"

"Born and bred."

The front of the library, with its grand Romanesque façade of red brick and intricate stonework, came into view as they cut between Kerckhoff Hall and the Men's Gymnasium. Bridie was enjoying the conversation immensely and felt sorry that it would soon end.

"One last question," Bridie asked. "What made you want to become a doctor?"

"My oldest brother. He has schizophrenia. That has a lot to do with my decision to go into psychiatry."

Like the first vibrant crocuses, pushing up splashes of purple, yellow, white, and blue through late winter snow, the bloom of hope unfurled in Bridie's heart. She had prayed for someone to help her understand what, if anything, could be done to help her mother get well. Could Matt be that person?

"How about you? What motivated you to become a nurse?"

"My mother. She has schizophrenia. I hope to become a psychiatric nurse. How old was your brother when he got sick?"

"Nineteen, in his first year of college, during finals week, right in front of Royce Hall. He was arrested, naked as a jaybird and completely out of his mind."

"I'm so sorry for him—and for your whole family."

"Yes, quite the tragedy. A life full of potential was cut short."

"Where is he now?"

"Still at Metropolitan State Hospital in Norwalk. Here we are already."

They had arrived outside the library.

"Could we pick up this conversation another time? Maybe over lunch or dinner? It sounds like we have a lot in common. I'd like to hear more about you and your mom."

"I'd love that, Matt. You know where to find me, most days, anyway." Bridie hoped she didn't sound too eager. They said goodbye at the bottom of the red brick steps leading up to the library's main entrance.

After opening the heavy wooden door under the stone archway, Bridie glanced back at Matt. He hadn't moved and was still watching her. She smiled and waved goodbye. A tingling, pleasant feeling, as gentle as a butterfly flapping its wings, infused a lightness to her step as she made her way up the staircase to the third floor, where her studies awaited her.

~*~

Jamie sat opposite Patsy at the kitchen table. She was still wearing her pajamas and looking rather peaked, he thought. She'd declined the cup of coffee that he'd offered to pour her and had passed on the glazed donuts that he'd brought home from Winchell's on Third earlier that morning. In retrospect, he should have realized something was wrong.

After her bombshell announcement, Patsy now had Jamie's full attention. His newspaper was already folded, his half-eaten donut abandoned, and his coffee sat untouched, growing cold.

"A June 6th wedding? It's already May 3rd, Patsy. That doesn't leave much time for planning," Jamie said, his mouth drawn tight and his neck flushing red.

He had expected a quiet Saturday morning after Bridie and Meg left for the beach—the younger to study, and the older to grade student essays, lugging a large beach umbrella. He'd planned to leave a note in the afternoon saying he'd gone to work for an hour or two but would instead head to Marilyn Miller's apartment, as they'd arranged. Jamie already had plenty on his plate without a June wedding materializing out of nowhere.

"I have no idea how one goes about planning a wedding. Other than arranging for your great-uncle Fr. James to marry your mother and me, I just showed up. She and her sister Eileen took care of everything."

"There's nothing to worry about, Dad. Rex and I are planning a civil ceremony at the West Los Angeles County Clerk's Office."

"You can't be serious." Jamie's eyes widened in disbelief.

"Rex isn't Catholic and refuses to go through all the rigmarole required for a Catholic and non-Catholic to marry in the Church. But really, Dad—not to sound disrespectful—I'm surprised you care so much. You haven't been to Mass since Christmas."

"Well, I do care, Patsy. And my failings don't excuse you from doing the right thing."

Jamie hadn't heard Patsy come in last night. He suspected that she didn't always spend the night with a girlfriend, as she claimed. Since she'd turned twenty-one, he hadn't pressed her about where, when, or with whom she spent her time, even though she still lived under his roof.

"Even if Rex were agreeable—which he's not—it can take months to go through all the steps to get married in the Church. I can't wait that long." Patsy paused, then said softly, "Dad, I'm pregnant, almost three months."

Jamie's first reaction was anger toward Rex and disappointment in Patsy. But he quickly remembered the mercy his mother had once extended to him and Katie in a similar circumstance. He forced himself to respond calmly, though gravely concerned.

"Pregnant? I'm confused. I didn't think you were still seeing Rex," Jamie said, recalling the drama, the flood of tears, and how he'd gone into her room to cheer her up. He'd never liked Rex during the few times he had come around. Jamie knew Rex was all about Rex—hardly husband material. Jamie had been proud of Patsy for breaking up with the jerk after discovering he'd been two-timing her with an actress from the set of his latest movie.

"Well, I wasn't. When Betty Rydell dumped Rex, he came crawling back to me. By then, I'd found out I was pregnant and, of course, took him back—gratefully, I might add."

"Now things are starting to make sense." Jamie's demeanor softened, his thoughts drifting back to when Katie had hidden her pregnancy from him before their marriage nearly twenty-four years ago. "Do you love Rex? Does he love you, Patsy?"

"Does it really matter, Dad, now that there's a baby involved?"

"Yes, it does matter. Very much so. You can't weather the storms in marriage without love. And believe me, darling, there'll be tornadoes, hurricanes, blizzards, tsunamis, droughts, and wildfires amidst the idyllic, clear blue skies. Are you really ready for motherhood? There are options other than marriage, you know."

"Don't you suggest an abortion, too. Rex assured me that the studio has connections with doctors willing to perform abortions, though illegal, right here in Los Angeles."

"I would never suggest an abortion! But have you thought about returning to Tarrytown and living with one of your aunts for a while, then giving the baby up for adoption? Wouldn't that be better than spending your life with a man you don't love or who doesn't love you? A man who doesn't even want his own child?"

"Didn't you marry Mom because she got pregnant with Meg?"

"I absolutely did not! Who told you that?"

"Meg told me. But you can thank your big-mouth sister Annie for telling Meg when she and Bridie lived there after you first moved out to California. I swear, Annie gets some sort of pleasure from gossiping and shocking. I'm no saint, Dad, but at least gossiping isn't my vice."

"I'd already proposed to your mother when she conceived Meg. Your mother didn't even tell me she was pregnant until our wedding night, fearing that I'd feel pressured into marriage—which I wouldn't have. Although, for her sake, had I known, I might have pushed the date up earlier. I must talk to Meg. Does Bridie think that?"

"I don't think so. But Annie hinted that Bridie isn't your child... though she didn't come right out and say it."

"Look, Patsy, we're both adults here. I'll be completely honest with you. During the early years of your mother's institutionalization, when I couldn't imagine things could get any worse, I found out someone had violated her." Jamie's voice broke, and he ran his hands through his still-thick hair, trying to buy time to regain his composure.

"Only with time and your grandmother's wisdom did I come to understand the gift of that innocent, beautiful baby, no matter how she was conceived. At first, I wasn't sure I could love Bridie as my own, but it turned out to be the easiest thing in the world once I let go of my anger and embraced God's grace. It's an undeniable case of God bringing good out of evil. Your half-sister, Bridie, became the better part of worse.

"And that's where *true* love comes into play. Real love is more than an emotion; it's a day-to-day decision: for better or worse, for richer or poorer, in sickness and in health, until death do you part."

The sting of hypocrisy pierced Jamie's conscience—his affair with Marilyn Miller felt like a snake biting its own tail, a self-inflicted wound now bearing its consequences. *What has happened to me? Who am I to give advice? How could I have been so foolish?*

He took a deep breath, struggling to steady his emotions before continuing.

"Do you love Rex? Does he love you? Do you feel safe with him— that he won't leave you when the inevitable storms roll in?"

"I think so. But maybe I just want to believe that." Patsy shrugged, tears trickling down her cheeks.

"Whatever you decide, Patsy, I'll support your decision. Please, don't feel that I judge you. I stand upon no high moral ground. Have you told your sisters or Lupita?"

"Meg and Bridie don't know. I wanted to tell you first. I think Lupita's figured it out. She hasn't said anything, but she keeps encouraging me to eat."

An hour later, Jamie called his old friend Eddie Hodges. He hadn't seen much of Eddie over the last five months, not since he'd been "seeing" Marilyn outside of business hours. Eddie sounded delighted to hear from him.

"Yes, now is fine. I look forward to catching up. Drop by the house anytime this afternoon. I'm free until six tonight," Eddie said.

~*~

Upon hearing the doorbell ring, Eddie Hodges placed the crossword puzzle from today's newspaper on the end table next to his rosary and tucked his pencil behind his ear. Easing out of his green-corduroy upholstered recliner, he stretched his back and muttered, "A seven-letter word for the rapid repetition of a single note with a middle 'm,'" as he made his way to answer the door.

"Ah, Jamie, I was hoping it was you. Come in, come in," Eddie said, his voice carrying the familiar rasp that had come with age and decades of smoking. At seventy-six, he had grown accustomed to the sound.

Jamie handed Eddie a six-pack of Michelob and followed him into the two-story house just off Ocean Avenue near Palisades Park. The furnishings, wallpaper, and draperies were from another era. While the interior decor was dated, the home had a timeless panoramic view of the Pacific Ocean and a glimpse of the Santa Monica Pier.

Eddie and his wife, Maybell, had built their dream house here many years before she passed. The house hadn't changed; not a single knick-knack had been moved since Maybell had arranged them. Over the last eleven years, Eddie had gotten a bit rounder around the middle and his pate shinier, but like his home, he remained impervious to change.

"Ah, I see you came prepared," Eddie said, eyeing the beer. "Just what I needed to wet my whistle. You want one too?"

"Absolutely," Jamie said with less enthusiasm than usual.

Eddie studied Jamie's long face. "Take a load off; it looks like you're carrying one."

"Never one to beat around the bush, are you, Eddie? One of the many reasons I'm here. Several loads, actually."

"Should I dust off my old counseling shingle?" Eddie chuckled, his teasing brown eyes always quick to catch on, though perceptive enough to know when his friend needed more than jokes."

"Probably," Jamie said. Just as Eddie turned to walk the six-pack into the kitchen, he noticed Jamie picking up the nearly finished crossword puzzle from the end table between his recliner and what had always been Maybell's. A moment later, Eddie returned with two icy mugs—always kept in his freezer for company—now filled with beer.

"Tremolo," Jamie said, pointing to the remaining space as Eddie handed him a cold, foamy mug.

"Thank you kindly, my boy. I'm musically illiterate, I'm afraid." Eddie filled in the remaining spaces in the crossword puzzle.

Eddie held up his mug toward Jamie, and the two men clinked their mugs together. "To life," Eddie said. Jamie repeated the toast half-heartedly, and they took a long draw.

"Okay, spill," Eddie said, "and I don't mean the beer."

"My life is a mess. It's hard to know where to start."

"I figured something was wrong. I haven't seen you at St. Monica's for months, though I've seen Bridie and Meg often enough. I'd hoped you'd decided to go to Mass at a different time and that our paths just hadn't crossed. Besides, I've occasionally been going to St. Anne's Spanish Mass with Lupita. I hoped you'd tell me what was happening when you were ready. And here you are."

"Lupita?"

"Yes, we've been dating since the first of the year. I finally got up the nerve to ask *la encantadora mujercita* for a date. We've been seeing each other ever since. In fact, we're going out for dinner tonight."

"That's great, Eddie. Lupita is one of a kind, a bright bit of sunshine. Ha, I thought she was interested in you. You couldn't do much better than our Lupita."

"I never expected to feel like this again. You know, Jamie, the heart never grows old—love is the fountain of youth."

"We haven't been missing each other at church, Eddie. I stopped going. It felt too hypocritical."

"Don't tell me you lost your faith. I don't believe that for one minute."

"No, but I lost my bearings. I've been having an affair with my secretary since mid-December last year. I've tried to end it several times but never quite succeeded."

"She got drunk at the company Christmas party, and I drove her home, afraid she'd get in a wreck and kill herself or someone else. I wasn't drunk and knew full well it was wrong and could never go anywhere, but I couldn't seem to refuse what she was offering. She wants to get married, even though that was never an option. I'll never divorce my Katie."

"Many a man's downfall has been his desire for a woman," Eddie said soberly. "I remember being tempted once. Only by the grace of God did I not fall. I never doubted my love for my dear wife, but after twenty-five years of marriage, I felt like life was passing me by—like a beautiful woman waving goodbye from a red sports car. I was flattered by a younger woman's attention. You could say it was my version of a midlife crisis."

"Sadly, Marilyn's not even my type; she was just available. I realized this morning that I can't see Marilyn anymore. I must set a better example for my girls. I'm here to ask you to hold me accountable."

"Jamie, you're in a hard place. If you're serious about ending your affair with Marilyn, you can't be working with her every day, especially if she doesn't want things to end. It's playing with fire, and you're bound to get burned. Repeatedly. She needs to transfer to a different office, or you need to get a new job. Otherwise, you're just fooling yourself."

"Besides that, you need to darken the door of the confessional and return to Mass. You can't do this on your own. Yes, I'll be here for you, but you need stronger medicine than I can provide. You'll need supernatural power. When we recognize our weaknesses and confess our sins, we can follow the way the Holy Ghost leads anew. The old 'when I am weak, then I am strong, through Him.' Don't cut God out of your life when you need Him the most. The Church isn't a museum of saints; it's a hospital for sinners who acknowledge their brokenness and dependence on God who never abandons them, no matter what they've done."

Eddie paused, swallowing a gulp of beer. "Sermonizing always makes me thirsty," he said, winking.

"By the way, Jamie, Monsignor Conneally has confessions starting at three this afternoon."

"I was thinking the same thing. No time like the present, as they say."

"It's only two. You have plenty of time to get there. How about I meet you at ten o'clock Mass tomorrow morning? And we can go out to breakfast afterward?"

"You're on," Jamie said.

TWENTY-THREE

May 1952

Patsy still hadn't told her sisters that she and Rex were getting married in two weeks. Her father had nudged her to tell Meg and Bridie, but he wasn't going to push it—it was her choice, after all. He'd only reminded her that if she wanted family or friends at the courthouse, she'd have to let them know soon. But she was resolute—she didn't want anyone there. Truthfully, she didn't even want to be there herself. Still, the die was cast; her fate was sealed.

Over the past two weeks, she'd seen Rex only a few times, and only to firm up the details of their "wedding." Ha—what a joke, some wedding. Rex was a shadow on what should have been a sunny day—present, yet lacking warmth. They hadn't made love in weeks. In the past, sex had made her feel desired, even loved. Now, though, the very thought of it with Rex was enough to turn her stomach.

They'd filed California's requisite paperwork with the courthouse, including the health certificate certifying that neither she nor Rex had tested positive for syphilis. Yet, nothing felt right about their upcoming marriage.

Patsy wore no engagement ring to offer the slightest clue that she was soon to be wed. Rex hadn't even mentioned a ring for her—and that hurt. She knew that a civil ceremony didn't require rings for a legal marriage and told herself there'd be time for that later.

And all this secrecy that he demanded. Would it really hurt Rex's career if word got out at MGM that they had married? She tried to give her future husband the benefit of the doubt—but he made it difficult.

Although Patsy was near the end of her first trimester, her slim figure and great muscle tone concealed her pregnancy reasonably well.

However, the waistbands of her slacks and skirts felt constricting. She'd lost weight because the smell of food made her nauseous, and when she did eat, it was hard to keep it down. Only Lupita and Bridie had noticed that Patsy was eating like a bird.

Her skin had broken out with mild acne like she was fourteen all over again. She was dog-tired—a battery down to its last spark, struggling to keep its charge, with no energy left to antagonize Meg, her favorite pastime not so long ago.

She knew next to nothing about caring for an infant, and the idea of motherhood was terrifying. It wasn't as if she had a mother she could turn to for guidance. Lupita, the closest thing to a mother figure for Patsy, had never had children.

On Saturday evening, Rex didn't come by as he had promised. Patsy was too hurt, tired, and angry to bother calling him to ask why. She didn't trust him anyway. Borrowing the family car, she promised to return in an hour, though she knew it could take longer if she had to chase Rex down.

She headed south to Rex's apartment on Venice Boulevard. Halfway there, she changed her mind and found herself in the empty parking lot at St. Monica Church. She sat in the car for a few minutes before slipping inside and lighting a votive candle. Patsy knelt in front of a side altar in the right transept, slightly hidden at the back of the alcove.

Would God bother with her, given her long hiatus? Thinking she might have better luck with the Blessed Mother, who had also found herself pregnant before moving in with Joseph, she began with a Hail Mary. Perhaps Mary could put in a good word for her to her Son. It couldn't hurt, she thought. After an Our Father and a Glory Be, she made the Sign of the Cross and sat silently, the groaning of her heart whispering prayers she couldn't formulate.

The next day, Patsy stayed home from Sunday Mass, as usual, but noticed her father had gone with Meg and Bridie and seemed in better spirits than he had in months.

Patsy still hadn't decided what to wear for her dreaded wedding. Late Sunday night, she stood in front of her open closet. She slid the hangers along the rod, her eyes scanning her best suits and dresses, hoping something would stand out so she could avoid buying anything special.

A peach-colored rayon suit caught her eye—a fitted jacket with a nipped-in waist and a matching mid-knee skirt that flared gently at the hips. Next, she found her beige shell in her bureau drawer, shocked at how neatly everything was arranged and folded. *Bridie's work*, Patsy thought, smiling and shaking her head in disbelief at all her little sister did for her. *Unacknowledged and without thanks.*

She tried on the outfit and looked at herself in the mirror mounted on the wall. She could leave the jacket unbuttoned, and the shell hid the skirt's unfastened button above the back zipper. She could even remove her jacket if the day were miserably hot. This was not how she had imagined her wedding—not caring enough to purchase a new dress or suit for the "big day."

Having made her decision, she crawled into bed and felt herself dozing off.

Patsy was jolted awake by a terrible cramping. She ran to the bathroom and sat on the toilet, bending over with her arms wrapped around her lower abdomen. She pulled over the small garbage can nearby in case she threw up, too.

An hour later, amidst the blood, clots, and gray-pinkish bits of tissue, she saw an object about an inch and a half long floating in a pool of crimson water. Her hand shook as she fished out the fetus, its tiny umbilical cord attached and face perfectly formed. There was no mistaking it—a human person in miniature—her miscarried child. The arms and legs were well-formed, and the fingers and toes were separate and clearly defined. The thin, translucent skin showed a network of underlying blood vessels.

Although she hadn't wanted to have a baby, a tsunami of uninvited emotions flooded her psyche: shock at seeing the fetus, grief and sadness at a life cut short, guilt and self-recrimination that perhaps she had caused her child to die. All this, and yet an undeniable sense of relief.

She didn't know what to do with the fetus but didn't want to flush it down the toilet either. It was so clearly a baby, just not fully developed. In her mind, Patsy heard the commanding, resonant voice of Sister Carmel Therese, her twelfth-grade religion class teacher: "Human life begins at conception, and the soul is present from that moment."

Patsy tenderly swaddled her tiny baby in toilet paper and carried it into the kitchen to find something to place her miscarried child in. She spied an empty Peter Pan peanut butter jar with a screw-on lid in the kitchen cupboard. Lupita never threw anything away. *That'll work for now*, Patsy thought. Once back in her bedroom, she placed the child in its glass sarcophagus at the back of her closet. *Tomorrow, I must bury my baby. But where?*

She imagined Rex, even now, trying to figure out how to weasel out of their wedding. Patsy would save him the trouble. She wouldn't marry him on June 6 or ever, even if he were the last man on earth. As for the baby, she'd let Rex know she had miscarried but would wait for him to call her—if he ever did.

By morning, the worst of the cramping was over. Patsy was still bleeding, though now not much more than the first day of her period. Having not slept after she had lost her baby, she'd watched as dawn's rays announced the new day through the slatted wooden blinds in her bedroom window.

Before anyone else got up for the day or Lupita had arrived at the house, Patsy went back downstairs. She left a note for Dad and Lupita on the kitchen table: *Not feeling well. Staying home today.* She called into work to let her supervisor know that she would be out for a few days.

Work. Something had changed in her. Working at MGM in the typist pool and trying to turn male heads felt as repulsive as seeing Rex. Patsy didn't wish Rex ill, but she saw him for what he was. She no longer had to make excuses for him. She had been nothing special to him, just available. *How could I have been so stupid?*

Seeing Rex in a clear light had brought into sharp focus her own values and choices. Nothing felt right about her life. What had changed, and why? Yes, she was ashamed of herself on many levels, but this was something deeper. She was grieving for a baby she hadn't wanted, but that wasn't all. She hesitated to look within, afraid of what she might learn about herself.

By mid-morning, Lupita knocked on Patsy's bedroom door.

"Come in," Patsy said. She lay in a fetal position on her bed, facing the door through which Lupita had just entered, Patsy's splotched face awash with tears.

"Patsy, whass wrong? Do you wan' to talk abou' eet?" Lupita wore a bright red cotton housedress trimmed in peacock blue, fuchsia pink, and candy-apple green rickrack.

"You'll hate me if I tell you," Patsy said, still in her pajamas. She turned away from Lupita. "I already hate myself; I don't need anyone else to join the club."

Lupita sat on the bed next to Patsy. She gently rubbed Patsy's back. "You talk like a *chica loca*. How can I hate you? I love you as eef you are *mi propia hija.*"

"Promise?" Patsy turned back to face Lupita.

"I promeese*,*" Lupita said, making a Sign of the Cross to sanctify her promise. The diminutive woman's hair was still thick and wavy, with strands of gray intermixed with her natural dark color. She had fastened it back in a low bun. Her brown eyes, framed by crow's feet, reflected concern.

Patsy explained that she had been pregnant and was supposed to marry Rex this Friday afternoon at the West Los Angeles courthouse. She hadn't told anyone but her father. She had lost the baby during the night and pointed Lupita to the closet where she had placed the tiny body in the jar.

"I lost *mi tres bebés* through meescarriage. I know how you feel. Should you see a doctor? To make sure everything is okay." Lupita smoothed Patsy's platinum hair away from her face, her dark roots starting to show.

Patsy shook her head and wiped her eyes. "I'm okay. I always wondered why you never had children, Lupita."

"But I deed have children. The tree of them are in heaven, waiting for me to join them. *Mi esposo*, Miguel, and I buried them in a cemetery in México where my family is buried. I never got pregnant again. Miguel is buried in the Catholic Cemetery in Culver City, Holy Cross Cemetery. I visit his grave on the *Día de los Muertos* and always walk through the "Garden of Angels" section where *bebés* are buried, even those meescarried."

"I want to bury my baby, even though it's so tiny. Will you go with me to Holy Cross Cemetery?"

"Of course. We can call today and go dere when you feel up to eet."

"Thank you." Patsy took Lupita's hand in hers. "I can't make sense of my jumbled emotions, Lupita. I didn't want to be a mother or have a baby. But I feel such a sense of... something. Loss, I guess." A lone tear careened down Patsy's cheek, landing in the corner of her mouth.

"I lay awake all night worrying that, somehow, I caused my baby's death because I didn't want them. But I never wanted my baby to die. That's why I wouldn't go along with the abortion when Rex pushed it."

"*Mia querida* Patsy, no woman has the power to weesh her pregnancy away. Eef they did, I probably wouldn't be here being number thirteen of *mi madre's* fifteen children. But every child has a God-given purpose, whether we understand eet or not, including a child that never draws a breath outside the womb or with only a short time on thees earth. *Mi madre*, may her soul rest in peace, always said, '*Todas las cosas ayudan a bien, incluso las malas, a los que aman a Dios.*' All theengs work together for the good, even the bad, for those who love God." I suspect your *bebé diminuto* has already begun eets work in your life.

~*~

Jamie looked up at the sound of two staccato knocks on the metal frame of his office door. Marilyn stood just outside, peering in without crossing the threshold. Since he'd ended their relationship, she always knocked and waited for permission before entering his inner sanctum.

"Come in, Marilyn," Jamie said, setting aside the papers he was reading.

It was her last day, and Jamie couldn't help but notice that Marilyn was dressed to stop traffic. Her leopard-print sleeveless silk blouse, with its plunging neckline, drew attention to the movement of her full bosom with every step. A black fitted pencil skirt with a slit halfway up the back hugged her hips, while three-inch black heels with peek-a-boo cutouts and ankle straps completed the look—a look that had once drawn him in.

She placed a manila folder on Jamie's desk. "Here's the documentation explaining how I've organized your filing system, Mr. Murphy—for your new secretary." Since their split, Marilyn had stopped calling him by his first name.

"Please, have a seat for a moment," Jamie said, gesturing to one of the leather chairs in front of his desk. Marilyn complied—polite but palpably distant.

Jamie rose, walked to his office door, shut it, and returned to his high-backed black leather chair. Once seated, he bowed his head and closed his eyes. He folded his hands as if in prayer, pressing them against his lips, gathering his thoughts before finally speaking.

"Marilyn, I'm deeply sorry for how things turned out between us. I appreciate all the work and dedication you've shown as my secretary. As your boss, I take full responsibility for what happened and wish I had been a better man. If I could go back and change things, I would in a heartbeat. Maybe someday, you can forgive me."

"It takes two to tango, Mr. Murphy. I took the lead in our 'dance' long before I enticed you to take your first step. Even so, I appreciate your apology." She paused before adding, "I'll never understand your faith or your wife's hold on you. It seems like your God would want you to be happy." Marilyn shrugged, her mouth twisting in a mix of disappointment and resignation.

"God wants me to be happy, yes, but not by grabbing at fleeting pleasure. I lost sight of what really mattered and let myself get swept up in the moment. I made choices that hurt both of us." Jamie's voice was steady, clear, firm, and contrite.

Jamie couldn't explain everything to Marilyn; she wasn't ready to hear it. Without the foundation of faith and Christ as the model, how could she understand that true happiness required love in its purest form—a love that often demands self-denial and resisting temptation, two things he had failed at spectacularly?

Even Christ had faced temptation in the desert but didn't give in. Temptation was inevitable, but surrendering was a choice.

Jamie had learned much about himself through the ordeal of his affair and, afterward, about God's mercy. He had fallen, but forgiveness and grace awaited him, just as the father had awaited the return of his prodigal son.

"You're a mystery, Mr. Murphy, but I doubt I'll ever forget you. If I were a woman of prayer—and we both know I'm not—I'd pray that someday your wife returns to you whole and healthy and that I find a man who loves me like you love your Katie." Marilyn pursed her lips, her eyes shining with what Jamie thought were unshed tears that she quickly blinked away.

"Don't sell yourself short, Marilyn. You deserve a man who'll love and honor you; expect nothing less."

"Well, on a brighter note, my new job is a promotion and pays better, so I suppose things have worked out for me professionally," Marilyn said, forcing a half-hearted smile.

"I have no right to offer advice, but be careful. You're a beautiful woman, and you know it. I'm afraid your new boss might not be above taking advantage."

Colin Maddigan. Jamie considered the many years he'd watched Colin play the field, always at the expense of his ever-changing female companions. *Women can be so easily deceived when it comes to matters of the heart,* Jamie mused. Marilyn had given sex to get love, while he had offered a cheap imitation of love to get sex. A dangerous combination in a broken world. Jamie prayed she wasn't jumping from the frying pan into the fire.

"I'll be sure to let Mr. Maddigan know you said that," Marilyn replied.

"Please do."

~*~

June 1953 (One year later)

"I got the article, Bridie, all the way from Paris," Matt said with a bright smile, his voice victorious. His face had lost its hints of boyishness over the last year, replaced by chiseled lines and strong angles.

Matt pulled out a chair, settling in next to her. Bridie sat at their usual wooden table for four, a panoply of books spread around her like a fortress in the corner of the third floor of the UCLA library. Her pharmacology textbook lay open in front of her, its pages filled with diagrams of drug classifications—her attempt to study dissolved as she focused on Matt and his fantastic news.

Matt placed the journal, *Annales Médico-Psychologiques*, on top of the diagram she had been trying to commit to memory just moments before.

"Hey, how about a 'Hello, it's nice to see you'?" Bridie whispered, turning towards him, pretending to be irritated but not the least bit so.

Matt kissed her lightly on the lips. "Does this work?"

"Yes, it does. It's nice to see you, too," Bridie said, feeling a warm sense of contentment.

"The article starts on page 112," Matt said, opening to that page.

Bridie read the article's title silently: *38 cas de psychoses traités par la cure prolongée et continue de 4560 RP—chlorpromazine.* Then she translated it for Matt: "Thirty-eight cases of psychoses treated by prolonged and continuous treatment of 4560 RP—chlorpromazine." The article hadn't been published yet in English or outside France.

Matt had learned about this newly discovered drug during a lecture hosted by the UCLA School of Medicine, delivered by Dr. Heinz Lehmann, a visiting psychiatrist from McGill University in Quebec. Bridie had listened closely as Matt enthusiastically shared the details of Lehmann's lecture about six months ago.

Lehmann had advocated for the use of chlorpromazine, which had been successfully used in France since early 1952 by Pierre Deniker and Jean Delay for the treatment of psychosis and schizophrenia. The two French psychiatrists, authors of the article, were now familiar to Bridie. Deniker and Delay had presented their findings at a professional meeting in Paris a year ago and published their results six months later in the *Annales Médico-Psychologiques*.

Bridie couldn't believe that now she had this very article in hand, thanks to Matt. He'd pestered Lehmann, enlisted the help of a librarian at UCLA, and forked over the $20 to make it happen. It seemed like the miracle she and Matt had been waiting for.

Still, there remained significant hurdles to the drug's use in the United States, as Matt had explained to Bridie after Lehmann's lecture. "The use of medication runs counter to the prevailing practices outside Europe," he'd said. "Psychiatrists in the United States emphasize electroshock therapy and psychoanalysis, both of which had proved disappointing or fruitless with psychotic or catatonic patients."

But there was a ray of hope. According to Matt, Lehmann had said that Dr. Robert H. Noce, a psychiatrist at the State Hospital in Modesto, California (92 miles east of San Francisco), had received special permission a month ago to begin a trial of chlorpromazine on a select group of patients. And, according to Lehmann, Dr. Noce was already seeing impressive results.

Bridie's eyes scanned the six-page article. "I'm not sure my four years of high school French are enough for a word-by-word translation. There are many terms in this article I don't recognize."

"Well, your French has to be better than my four years of Latin. I think the Jesuits were trying to turn us into priests at Loyola."

Matt left the article with Bridie and headed to his next class.

Bridie slowly read through the article, piecing together an amazing story:

Chlorpromazine had been developed by the French pharmaceutical company Rhône-Poulenc in 1950, initially as an antihistamine, and by 1952, it was licensed for use in France.

Henri Laborit, a French surgeon, had discovered that a strong dose of chlorpromazine reduced surgical shock by allowing the use of much lower amounts of anesthesia during surgery. Additionally, chlorpromazine significantly reduced patients' pre- and post-surgery anxiety. Laborit hypothesized that this effect was due to its impact on chemicals in the brain and suggested that chlorpromazine might have psychiatric applications. Laborit's brother-in-law, Dr. Pierre Deniker, and his colleague, Dr. Jean Delay, explored this possibility by administering chlorpromazine to thirty-eight psychotic patients at Sainte-Anne Hospital.

She marveled at how Delay and Deniker observed remarkable improvements in patients who had previously been unresponsive or extremely agitated, often aggressive. The medication offered remission from hallucinations, delusions, and anxiety. Patients who had existed in a vegetative state could now engage in conversations. Some were released in less than a year. The improvements persisted as long as the patients continued their medication.

The time flew by, and two hours later, when Matt returned, Bridie hadn't moved.

"Matt, this seems like the miracle we've been hoping for! I can't translate every word, but I get the gist of it. We need to pray that this drug becomes available in the U.S. and that doctors here are willing to prescribe it."

~*~

Mid-November 1953 (Six months later)

Bridie sat at the kitchen table on Saturday morning, nibbling her breakfast, her attention divided between her cinnamon toast and the front page of the *New York Times*. She flipped to the next page, searching for something specific—news Matt had mentioned about chlorpromazine being submitted to the Food and Drug Administration (FDA) for approval.

The paper always arrived a few days late, but she was sure the story would appear soon. And there it was! Her heart leaped as she found it on the second page: "New Drug Submitted for FDA Approval:

Potential Breakthrough in Mental Health Care."

She read the entire article twice. Smith, Kline & French, an American pharmaceutical firm, had petitioned the FDA for approval of chlorpromazine (or Thorazine—the requested trade name, if approval was granted). Even though approval wasn't guaranteed, and the process could take a long time, chlorpromazine had cleared a major hurdle.

Bridie felt certain this was the answer to her prayers. It took all her self-control to let her father sleep in. She closed her eyes and whispered a prayer of thanksgiving for this crucial first step, asking that chlorpromazine be swiftly approved and that this drug might finally bring her mother home.

TWENTY-FOUR

March 1954 (Four and a half months later)

Bridie eagerly began her clinical practicums at Los Angeles County General Hospital, sixteen miles east of the campus, during the spring semester of her third year in the nursing program. The practicums accompanied her classroom studies in Medical-Surgical Nursing II, Obstetric Nursing, Psychiatric Nursing, and Community Health Nursing. This was the semester she had most anticipated, particularly because of the psychiatric nursing class and practicum.

Her nursing focus remained on helping her mother and others suffering from serious mental illness. Bridie quickly realized that textbook learning could only go so far. Honing her nursing skills required interacting with actual patients, especially in the psychiatric ward. Understanding, patience, and building trust were essential to patient care—qualities in which Bridie excelled.

While some student nurses quickly realized that psychiatric nursing was not their calling, Bridie's experience only strengthened her sense of purpose. She encountered patients from all walks of life and socio-economic backgrounds, each at different stages of psychiatric distress—psychosis, severe depression, extreme agitation, and mania.

Although the county hospital was not a dedicated mental health facility, it provided short-term stabilization and some longer-term inpatient care. As a student nurse, Bridie's duties were straightforward but essential: walking with patients, assisting with hygiene and grooming, helping with meals, monitoring patients' behaviors, moods, and interactions, and reporting her observations. She also had the opportunity to observe group therapy sessions, where she gained deeper insights into the complexities of mental illness.

While Bridie's duties often involved routine tasks, there were moments when her work became deeply personal, bringing her face-to-face with the raw human suffering behind psychiatric illnesses. One such moment occurred with Mr. Clark, an elderly gentleman on the psychiatric floor who had tried to take his own life after losing his wife of sixty years.

"Mr. Clark, I know you weren't hungry, but look how well you've done!" Bridie wiped the applesauce dribbling from the man's downturned mouth to his chin. The skeletal-looking man seemed lost in his grief, barely able to muster the energy to eat.

"I'm proud of you for trying." Bridie gazed into his eyes, pools of sadness, and gave up on spoon-feeding him any more of his lunch. She resisted the urge to hug the poor old fellow, who looked as if he desperately needed one. Instead, she held his hand briefly.

"I just want to sleep, if you don't mind," Mr. Clark murmured, closing his eyes as if to shut out the world.

"Of course, Mr. Clark."

Bridie gently cranked his hospital bed into a flat position, watching as the tension in his frail body eased ever so slightly. As she walked to the end of his bed to pick up his chart, she couldn't help but feel a pang of worry. He hadn't eaten much, she noted—less than a quarter-cup each of applesauce and cottage cheese.

She jotted down the minimal intake and paused momentarily, her pen hovering over the paper. The weight of Mr. Clark's sorrow seemed to fill the room, and Bridie wished she could do more for him— something beyond what the clinical notes could capture. But for now, she could only ensure he was comfortable and hope that tomorrow might bring a little more light into his life.

As the bed groaned and creaked into a flat position, snippets of an animated conversation between two men reached Bridie's ears: "chlorpromazine" and "FDA approved yesterday." Her attention piqued, she carefully plumped Mr. Clark's pillows and quickly finished charting, noting the date and time: March 27, 11:36 a.m. With a sense of urgency fueled by the overheard conversation, she clipped the chart back onto the end of Mr. Clark's bed and exited the room with purposeful strides, her mind racing with questions.

Two doctors were conversing in the hallway just outside Mr. Clark's room. Bridie recognized them both, though she'd never had the opportunity—or the need—to speak with either psychiatrist before. Nursing students typically interacted with the charge nurses, not the doctors. She had noticed that the older of the two seemed a bit cranky and stiff while the younger man had an easy smile, making him more approachable in Bridie's eyes.

"Excuse me, doctors," Bridie said, stepping forward with a mix of determination and nervous energy as she interrupted their conversation. "Did I overhear you say that Smith, Kline & French received FDA approval for Thorazine yesterday?" Her heart pounded in her chest, and her grey eyes flashed intensely, reflecting the significance of what she thought she'd just heard.

The older doctor, balding and bespectacled, looked indignant at being interrupted by a student nurse. In contrast, the younger doctor, with a relaxed posture and a bright, attentive gaze, seemed intrigued by Bridie's enthusiasm and unexpected knowledge.

"I mentioned that chlorpromazine received FDA approval yesterday," the younger doctor clarified, "but I didn't specify who submitted the application or the trade name. I'm impressed you know both." He smiled, his eyes briefly flicking down to Bridie's name tag. "It seems UCLA is doing a great job keeping their nurses on top of things."

"Oh, it's not just UCLA, although the School of Nursing is wonderful. I have a personal interest in the drug. I read the press release when Smith, Kline & French submitted their application to the FDA last year. If you'll permit me one more question, and pardon my impertinence, how long after FDA approval does it usually take for hospitals to start using a new drug like this?"

The older doctor cleared his throat and responded with a tone of authority. "There has never been a drug like chlorpromazine—Thorazine—as it's the first of its kind. We plan to proceed cautiously, observing its use and effects elsewhere before fully integrating it into our treatment protocols."

"Dr. Noce at Modesto State Hospital has been using chlorpromazine on a trial basis since last year," Bridie added, her tone respectful yet confident. "Did you, by chance, hear his talk last October at the American Psychiatric Association meeting? And France has been using the drug under a different name for several years."

The older psychiatrist sighed. "There is no permanent cure for serious mental illness, like schizophrenia, outside of psychoanalysis, Miss..." The doctor paused, glancing at her name tag. "Miss Murphy, but it may have value if it helps to relax patients and reduce the extreme agitation or anxiety that often leads to compulsive behavior—a surface symptom of their illness."

The younger psychiatrist discreetly rolled his eyes at the mention of psychotherapy as a cure and now chimed in, "Miss Murphy, state hospitals tend to be the earliest adopters, given their budgetary constraints and the vast numbers of seriously mentally ill patients they care for.

"A colleague of mine at Norwalk State Hospital mentioned that they are very interested in trying Thorazine, especially after seeing the results at Modesto State Hospital. Norwalk is about a half-hour east of here. Are you familiar with it?"

"Oh yes, I've been there with a friend whose brother has been a patient for several years. He has schizophrenia, like my mother. We both have high hopes for Thorazine."

"It is early, and knowing which patients will likely benefit is hard. What I'd like to know is if the drug stops hallucinations or just makes the patient care less about what is disturbing them," the younger man said. "It's a very different treatment modality from what has been available. I, for one, would like to see an end to lobotomies, insulin shock therapy, and electroshock therapy for those with schizophrenia. By the way, I did hear Dr. Noce's talk and am not without hope." He nodded ever so slightly to Bridie.

Bridie had seen the effects of both lobotomies and insulin shock therapy, though not the procedures themselves. There had to be a better way.

The hours between Bridie arriving home after work and her father walking through the front door felt like an eternity. She had already informed her family about the new drug that, she prayed, might bring Katie home to them.

The moment Jamie stepped into the living room, Bridie rushed to him, her excitement barely contained as she shared the news about Thorazine.

"Bridie, I don't mean to dampen your hopes, but your mother has been institutionalized for twenty-five years. Even if this Thorazine were a miracle drug that could make her well enough to come home, the world has changed so much. That alone might be more than she could bear."

"Dad, it's okay to have hope and to pray for Mom's healing. God hears the cries of our hearts, even when we're too afraid to voice them for fear of disappointment." The late afternoon sun emerged from behind the clouds as she spoke, filling the room with brilliant light.

Tears welled in Jamie's eyes as he enfolded Bridie, a full foot shorter than he, into his arms. He kissed the top of her head, her apricot curls so reminiscent of Katie's. "Dare we hope to be delivered from this valley of tears?" he whispered.

~*~

June 3, 1955 (The following year)

The warm afternoon air buzzed with excitement as family and friends gathered to celebrate the graduates of UCLA's School of Nursing and Medical School in a combined commencement ceremony. Jamie, with his Kodak Brownie Hawkeye hanging from his neck, Patsy, and Meg stood with Lupita and Eddie outside Royce Hall, a stunning Romanesque Revival building famed for its twin towers, intricate brickwork, and grand arched windows.

Arriving an hour early might not have been necessary, but here they were, mingling with other early birds, all vying for front-row seats and the perfect spot for capturing memories.

Bridie and Matt were already inside, sheltered from the sun, receiving last-minute instructions alongside their fellow graduates, all set to receive their degrees today. Matt had picked Bridie up earlier at the Murphy home for the commencement ceremony and had invited Jamie and her sisters to join them afterward for a reception at the Ryan household—the first time their families would mingle.

When the trio of oversized oak double doors finally opened, the crowd surged into the spacious lobby, flowing through the six auditorium doors like a river rushing through a narrow canyon, eager to claim the best seats.

As they entered, Lupita's eyes widened in awe. "The ceiling *es magnífico!*" she exclaimed, her gaze drawn upward to the opulent array of square moldings adorned with rosettes and medallions, covering every inch of the ceiling in a harmonious mix of Romanesque and

Byzantine styles, featuring golds, yellows, sky-blues, and earth tones.

"Well, we won't have to sit in the balcony," Jamie said, soaking in the grandeur and size of the auditorium, "although it might be interesting to see that ceiling up close."

The combined graduating class included thirteen women receiving their Bachelor of Science in Nursing, along with twenty-six men and two women earning their Doctor of Medicine degrees. The School of Nursing had grown from an initial class of fifteen women in 1949 to a total enrollment of sixty by the spring of 1955. Meanwhile, the Medical School's enrollment had blossomed to over a hundred students within its first four years

The first five rows of center seats were reserved for the graduates, marked off with light blue and bright gold ribbons. Even with each graduate bringing a dozen or more supporters, the auditorium's main floor, with its 1,800 seats, along with the 483 seats in the balcony, would remain far from filled.

Bridie's little cheering section found seats near the front, close to the aisle, ensuring a clear path for Jamie to capture Bridie receiving her diploma on film for posterity. Jamie sat between Meg and Patsy, while Patsy sat beside Eddie and Lupita, holding hands.

Jamie took Meg's hand in his right and Patsy's in his left. "I'm so proud of all of you girls," he said, his voice heavy with emotion. "God has blessed me beyond measure through my children. My life may not have unfolded as I once envisioned, but here I am, surrounded by truth, beauty, and goodness."

Almost as if giving a benediction, he gestured toward the chiseled inscription—*Education is an ornament in prosperity and a refuge in adversity*—above the elaborate proscenium framing the stage when he said, "Truth." He squeezed his daughters' hands briefly as he continued, "Beauty," and finally, raising his palms heavenward, he added, "Goodness.

"Do you know who said that?" Jamie asked his daughters.

"Who, Dad?" Meg asked while Patsy narrowed her eyes in concentration.

"Good ole Aristotle," Jamie said with a smile. "Wise words then and now, on many levels. A woman can always take care of herself with a good education."

"Wow, Dad, how did you know that was Aristotle?" Patsy asked, intrigued. She had traveled from the Motherhouse of the Religious Sisters of the Good Shepherd in St. Louis to attend Bridie's graduation. She wore a novice habit, distinguished by a white veil instead of the black one worn by professed sisters. Her wimple covered her short, dark hair, leaving only the skin of her face and hands visible.

Three years ago, after miscarrying her baby, Patsy had experienced a profound metanoia—a deep spiritual and psychological transformation that changed her worldview, as if she had been reborn. She left her job at MGM, abandoned her platinum locks for her natural dark hair, and began volunteering full-time at the House of the Good Shepherd near Echo Lake Park in Los Angeles.

The mission of the religious order was to provide training, rehabilitation, and shelter for women and girls in crisis, including those facing unplanned pregnancies or domestic abuse. Over the next year and a half, Patsy discerned a vocation with the Sisters of the Good Shepherd, eventually entering the order as a postulant. Six months ago, she transitioned to the novitiate and received her habit.

No one was more pleased (or more shocked) by Patsy's total transformation than Meg. After five years of teaching English, Meg submitted her resignation at Marymount High School and was set to enter the doctoral program in English at UCLA in the fall.

"You'd be surprised what your old man knows," Jamie said, winking at Patsy before turning to include Meg in the conversation. "I came across Aristotle during my seminary days while studying Aquinas and again in law school at Fordham," Jamie explained. "Aristotle believed that we can discover moral and ethical truths through reason alone, which shaped his views on education. Aquinas built on this idea, teaching that God's eternal law provides the foundation for moral behavior. Aristotle also argued that living a virtuous life is the key to happiness and fulfillment."

"Aristotle got that right," Patsy said, radiating joy, her sharp-tongued, sarcastic attitude long buried in the past. The self-condemnation, competition, and anxiety from which it had sprung were now rechanneled into a well of compassion she drew upon in her work with confused, frightened, and sometimes hardened women.

Patsy whispered to Jamie, "I learned that the hard way."

Jamie, now fifty-one, replied softly, "We both did."

The musicians in the orchestra section began the opening measures of "Pomp and Circumstance," with the trumpets leading in bold, clear, melodic notes. Soon, the horns joined in, adding fullness to the sound.

Everyone stood and turned to face the graduates, who processed down the aisle in two lines—doctors on one side, nurses on the other—bedecked in their academic regalia. Nurses wore mortarboards with gold tassels, while the doctors donned tams and green velvet hoods to signify their medical degrees. As the violins and violas joined in, their harmonies enriched the music, while the timpani underscored the stately character of the day.

Bridie led the nursing graduates, having placed first in her class. She glanced over at Matt, who led the doctoral graduates. Even from Jamie's seat, the unspoken exchange of affection between the two was evident, filling him with nostalgia for the time when his love for Katie was new.

He suspected Bridie would be the only daughter to marry and bring him grandchildren. Meg loved her books and seemed content with the single life, while Patsy was devoted to the Good Shepherd and His ewes and lambs. Jamie had no doubt that Patsy would take her final vows as a bride of Christ within the next five to seven years.

As Bridie passed down the aisle, making eye contact with her family, Jamie felt a pang of grief for Katie's double loss—her inability to know her remarkable daughters and her apparent disconnection from life itself. The last time Jamie and Bridie visited Katie, she didn't recognize them, as usual.

His mother had been prophetic when she referred to Bridie as "Katie's last gift to you" some twenty-two years ago. Through his faith, family, and friends, Jamie had found solace and gratitude for the blessings he had received. He marveled at the Almighty's ability to bring good out of evil. And her name was Bridie.

~*~

March 1956 (Nine months later)

The house was as dark and quiet as a tomb when Jamie arrived home after work. He missed Lupita's vivacious spirit, as well as the tantalizing aromas and heavenly taste of her cooking. But his loss was Eddie's gain now that Lupita and Eddie were married.

He hung up his raincoat and flipped on the living room and kitchen lights. Although the day had been wet, the temperature was a pleasant sixty degrees. It would still be cold in South Nyack, New York, where Bridie now lived. After passing her state boards in both California and New York, she accepted a position at Rockland State Hospital, one of the largest psychiatric hospitals in the country. The hospital was located in Orangeburg, New York, on the opposite side of the Hudson River from Tarrytown.

Dr. Nathan Kline's pioneering research on a new class of drugs targeting schizophrenia and manic depression had drawn Bridie to apply for a position in his research unit at Rockland. Bridie was an ideal fit, well-versed in the peer-reviewed literature on Thorazine and Serpasil, both recently approved by the FDA and central to Kline's work. Rockland's psychiatrists were at the forefront of psychopharmacology, and Bridie was passionate about these new medications that promised to revolutionize mental health treatment.

Jamie didn't miss the harsh New England winters, but he did miss Gracie, Annie, their families, his brother Fr. Robert, and now Bridie. He had even thought about moving back. Sometimes, he felt like an albatross around Meg's neck.

Walking into the kitchen, he removed his necktie and noticed a note from Meg on the counter.

> *Dad – Some of us grad students are going out for dinner tonight.*
> *I grabbed some Chinese takeout for your dinner since it was my*
> *night to cook, and I knew you'd skip dinner altogether if left to*
> *your own devices. It's in the fridge. Love, Meg*

Opening the fridge, he peeked into the takeout boxes to see what Meg had brought home: kung pao chicken, pork fried rice, and egg rolls—all his favorites. How wonderful not to have to figure out what to eat for dinner or go out alone on a Thursday night. Besides, he was bushed.

He grabbed a bottle of Michelob from the fridge and the bottle opener from the kitchen drawer. After flipping the lid and gulping several mouthfuls, he picked up the New York Times from the mail Meg had brought and laid it on the counter. As he sifted through the rest of the mail, a large envelope caught his eye; the return address read South Nyack.

Jamie opened the 9-by-11-inch ochre envelope and found a brief note along with, unsurprisingly, two journal articles: one from the *American Journal of Psychiatry* and another from the *Journal of Clinical*

Psychiatry. He immediately skipped past the article summaries to the personal part of Bridie's note.

> *Dear Dad,*
>
> *As I mentioned when we last spoke on the phone, Harlem Valley State Hospital is now using Thorazine for many of its patients. Here at Rockland, Dr. Kline is having good success with a newer antipsychotic, Serpasil. Please reach out to Mom's doctors again—this time in writing—since they are still not giving her any antipsychotics. Could you send me a copy of your letter? Pretty please? I plan to meet with her doctor again, armed with your letter and my research experience.*
>
> *By the way, Matt's brother has been released from Norwalk State Hospital and is doing reasonably well. Thorazine does have side effects, particularly weight gain, but compared to a life spent in a mental hospital, it's an easy choice.*
>
> *Speaking of Matt, his internship at New York-Presbyterian Hospital (NYP) in Manhattan is going well. I hardly see him with his busy schedule—he's on call seven days a week, often working 24-36 hours at a time. He's already been accepted into a four-year residency at the New York State Psychiatric Institute (NYSPI) starting in the fall. Both NYP and NYSPI are affiliated with Columbia University and are renowned for their excellent patient care, research, and pioneering medical treatments.*
>
> *Love you bunches,*
>
> *Bridie*
>
> *P.S. How do you like my new car? It's pink and white! I love, love, love it! Thank you so much!*

Jamie studied the Polaroid snapshot Bridie had taped to the back of her note. If he squinted his eyes, she could almost pass for Katie. She stood beside a 1953 Chevy Bel Air, an ear-to-ear smile on her face.

Even though Bridie's apartment in South Nyack was only six miles north of Orangeburg, Jamie knew that getting to work wasn't easy for Bridie. Public transportation options were limited or nonexistent in the counties west of the Hudson River. Visiting Katie in Wingdale was even more challenging—it required crossing the George Washington Bridge into Manhattan and then taking the train to Wingdale.

Once Jamie became aware of these transportation issues, he enlisted Gracie's husband, Chuck, to help find a solution. Chuck located the perfect car for Bridie, and Jamie wired the cash. With the Tappan Zee Bridge opening last December, Bridie could now drive from South Nyack to Wingdale in just an hour and a half.

Jamie needed to give his brain a break. He decided to read the articles Bridie sent later. Instead, he took his beer and the newspaper—whose subscription he'd maintained for the last fifteen years—to the table and sat down. The paper was dated February 25, only five days behind. There was always a delay, but the *New York Times* kept him connected to his roots.

As he flipped through the pages, several items that hadn't appeared in the *Santa Monica Evening Outlook* caught his interest, particularly an article on Thorazine. The article touted the drug's effectiveness in treating severe mental disorders like schizophrenia, emphasizing its impact on psychiatric treatment by providing relief to patients who had not responded to other therapies.

The statistics impressed Jamie: "...between 1955 and 1956, the number of patients in New York State's mental hospitals fell by roughly 500, compared with an increase of approximately 2,500 during the previous year. The state mental hospitals, bursting at the seams, had experienced an average rise of 2,000 patients annually during the last decade. Thorazine holds the promise to reverse this trend."

This was the eleventh article about Thorazine he'd read in the *New York Times* over the past fourteen months. He continued cutting them out, just as Bridie had started. Across those eleven articles, "experts" hailed Thorazine as a potential miracle drug, while others claimed it was harmful, causing a mix of nightmarish side effects—permanent involuntary movements, shuffling, weight gain, and sedation, among others. Some psychoanalysts even challenged the idea that Thorazine could truly help the mentally ill. Bridie had told him, "I've seen patients that these new medications have helped tremendously, as well as others they haven't. But more are helped than not. Isn't it worth a try, Dad? Mom deserves that."

Finally, he had been moved to agree with Bridie. Katie deserved a chance. What was there to lose? What had stopped him before? The answer was clear if he were honest: fear of failure and dashed hopes.

PART FOUR – HOPE'S REWARD
(1956-1959)

TWENTY-FIVE

May 1956 (Two months later)

Bridie eased her pink and white Bel Air into the Harlem Valley State Hospital parking lot. She was early for her one o'clock meeting with Dr. Glen Strong, her mother's psychiatrist. With a deep breath, she gathered her thoughts, steeling herself with a final pep talk. *You can do this, Bridie. Stay composed and professional. No tears, no angry outbursts.*

She had two strikes against her: Bridie was only twenty-three and men easily dismissed what women said when they became emotional. She couldn't afford a third strike; she needed a home run. So much rested on the outcome of this meeting—the final, arduous steps to reach the summit after a lifelong climb.

"Have faith that right makes might," she reminded herself, recalling the line from Abe Lincoln's 1860 Great Hall Speech. The quote, from a relatively unknown candidate at the time, had propelled him to the presidency. Convincing Dr. Strong to start her mother on Thorazine might be a long shot, but Bridie knew right was on her side.

She picked up the folder from the passenger seat and double-checked the contents. First was the copy of the letter her father had written to Dr. Strong almost two months ago—still unanswered. Her eyes scanned the page, focusing on the key sentence: "I request that my wife, Kathleen Murphy, be allowed a trial on Thorazine." Bridie knew all too well that the silence was as good as a refusal.

After tucking her father's letter away, she reached for the next one from her supervisor, Dr. Nathan Kline, the Research Director at Rockland State Hospital. For the past eight months, Bridie had worked directly under his supervision in the research unit for patients with severe mental illnesses. Dr. Kline had already gained considerable professional recognition for his innovative approaches in psychiatry. Surely, a letter from him, noting their success in treating patients with schizophrenia using Thorazine or Serpasil, would carry some weight.

She reread the closing lines of Dr. Kline's letter: "Bridget Murphy, RN, is an invaluable and highly competent member of my research team." Bridie hoped these words would help establish her credentials to discuss her mother's case with Dr. Strong.

Bridie knew that her mother had not been given either of the neuroleptics now authorized for use in the U.S., Thorazine (chlorpromazine) or Serpasil (reserpine). Neither drug was perfect— both had serious side effects—but they held the potential to work miracles for some severely ill patients, offering them a chance to return to their families. And that was exactly what Bridie wanted—for her mother to come home.

Her work schedule and visiting her mother on Sundays governed the rhythm of Bridie's life, leaving little time for anything else. She saw Matt when his intensive intern schedule allowed, but those moments were rare. Nothing, however, was harder than visiting her mother.

Women like her mother, whose mental illness was deemed incurable, were assigned to the back wards of Harlem Valley State Hospital. From what Bridie had seen during her visits, her mother's life consisted of uniformity, isolation, and hopelessness—waking up and retiring in a sparsely furnished room at the same time each day, eating tasteless meals at fixed hours, wandering down the long, sterile corridors, and, if lucky, going outside in groups like animals for fresh air.

During her weekly visits, she had never seen anyone else visiting the residents in the back ward, where her emotionally blunted, lethargic fifty-year-old mother simply "existed." She wasn't surprised—"lifers" had few visitors at state hospitals, even at Rockland.

She whispered a quick prayer: "God, grant me the serenity to accept the things I cannot change, courage to change the things I can, and wisdom to know the difference." Making the Sign of the Cross, she then placed the letters back in the folder and headed inside for her meeting.

~*~

The front desk receptionist, dressed in a straight black skirt, white blouse, and black pumps, escorted Bridie to the second floor. The thin, wrinkled woman cleared her throat loudly to gain the attention of the two men in white lab coats seated at a table in the small meeting room.

"Doctors, Miss Bridget Murphy," she announced with a pinched mouth, her tone as stiff as her posture.

Both men stood, pushing their chairs back with a loud screech against the simple wooden table in the center of the sterile, white-walled room. Four matching chairs surrounded it, their straight backs and hard seats designed more for utility than comfort. The single window, covered in bars, was open, letting a comfortable spring breeze drift into the room. As Bridie entered, the two men exchanged furtive glances.

"Door closed?" the receptionist asked, sniffing as if the air itself were beneath her.

"Yes, please," said the corpulent man, wiping his sweat-covered face with a large white handkerchief, inexplicably at odds with the comfortable room temperature.

"Miss Murphy, welcome. I'm Glen Strong, and this is Dr. Al Schuler, the Medical Director here at Harlem Valley." Dr. Strong, the taller and younger of the two men, had a full head of wavy brown hair that he pushed back with a hand as he made the introductions. A friendly smile played at the corners of his mouth, and his clear brown eyes conveyed openness.

"Dr. Schuler was one of the first doctors to oversee your mother's care and treatment when she was first admitted."

At the mention of his name, Dr. Schuler gave a slight nod of his bald head. He had to be in his early seventies, but something beyond his advancing years had imparted a pasty, gray pallor of ill health to his skin. Yet his gray eyes, though burdened with large, puffy sacs beneath them, still appeared sharp as they searched Bridie behind his round eyeglasses.

"Please be seated, Miss Murphy," Dr. Strong said, waving a hand toward the two empty wooden chairs on the opposite side of the table. Once Bridie was seated, the two men resumed their seats.

~*~

Dr. Schuler remained silent, his mind a tempestuous sea where waves of past memories crashed against the sharp rocks of the present. He recalled the first and only time he had met his daughter, nearly fourteen years ago. *Bridie, she had called herself then.* Hundreds of times, he had replayed that tender scene: an angelic child begging to walk with her mother outside on a summer's day. Her gray eyes, an innocent, feminine incarnation of his own but almond-shaped like her mother's, had indicted him then as they did now.

Little Bridie, all grown up and just as lovely as her mother, he thought. He still looked in on Kathleen Murphy at odd times, manufacturing excuses to visit her ward. He never touched her, though he still desired her, even in her madness. His fingertips remembered the feel of her body.

The girl began, "Thank you for agreeing to meet with me, Drs. Strong and Schuler. As I mentioned in my letter requesting this meeting, I'd like to discuss Kathleen Murphy's treatment options with you today on behalf of my father."

"Please proceed, Miss Murphy," Dr. Strong replied.

"I presume you have both read the letter from my father, James Murphy, sent two months ago," Bridie said as she handed the letter to Dr. Strong.

Dr. Strong glanced at the letter. "Yes, I'm familiar with your father's request," he said, passing it to Dr. Schuler, who scanned it briefly before setting it aside on the table.

"But I'm also representing what I believe is my mother's best interest, both as her daughter and as a registered nurse in the research unit at Rockland State Hospital, working with Dr. Nathan Kline and many schizophrenic patients who were previously considered hopeless."

Bridie handed Dr. Strong the letter from Dr. Kline, which Schuler had neither seen nor expected.

Dr. Strong's eyebrows raised slightly as he leaned forward, his eyes widening as they scanned the letter's content. When he finished, he handed Kline's letter to Dr. Schuler.

As Schuler read, his mouth tightened, and he began blinking, buying time while his mind raced.

Bridie spoke next. "I don't claim to be a psychiatrist or a medical expert. However, as part of the research unit at Rockland State Hospital, I've had firsthand experience with patients suffering from active psychosis, catatonia, severe depression, and chronic schizophrenia, like my mother, Kathleen Murphy. I believe she is a textbook case of schizophrenia: blunted affect, anhedonia, emotional dysregulation, social withdrawal, depression, and anxiety. At Rockland, these patients are on trials of Thorazine or Serpasil—Serpasil more recently, as that is Dr. Kline's current area of research. Many are responding positively."

The girl paused before she resumed speaking. "Many patients have been discharged from Rockland after continued pharmaceutical intervention with these new antipsychotics—some in weeks, some in months, and others in a year or two. Most, if not all, still need supervision, particularly to ensure they continue taking their medication, as the side effects can be unpleasant. Yet, being reintegrated into family life is always better than a lifetime of institutionalization.

"Sadly, some of our patients have been abandoned by their families. But let me assure you, my mother's family hasn't written her off. I love my mother and am committed to caring for her until she draws her last breath."

A mix of pride and angst stirred within Schuler. His daughter worked with Nathan S. Kline, the innovative, influential, and outspoken proponent of pharmacological treatments in psychiatry. It was a testament to her competence and intelligence, traits she had clearly inherited from him.

Dr. Schuler bid his time, gathering his thoughts, as he waited for Bridie to finish her impassioned monologue. He recalled the confused look on Dr. Strong's face when he'd overruled the trial of Thorazine that Strong had approved for Katie when her husband's letter had arrived. But Strong knew his place and had not dared to question his authority as medical director.

Schuler was confident in his authority and secure in his knowledge of how the hospital operated. Kathleen was a ward of the state of New York, and he, as medical director, was ultimately in control of whether she would be allowed a trial of Thorazine. While the family's wishes would be considered, they weren't binding, especially if the medical staff believed a different course of treatment—or none at all—was in the patient's best interest. Moreover, even if Kathleen received the medication and responded well, she could not be discharged unless her doctors determined that institutionalization was no longer necessary.

"Miss Murphy, I do appreciate and sympathize with the cogent presentation of your points," Dr. Schuler said, his voice slow and thick, like dripping honey. "But as you know, your mother has been institutionalized since December 1929. The world has changed dramatically. I believe life outside the institution might be too much for her to handle."

Dr. Schuler's forced smile quivered slightly as he looked down at the pen he rolled between his hands. *Putting Kathleen Murphy on a neuroleptic was too risky—what if it restored incriminating memories? His ruin could be just a dose away.*

"But how can we know if my mother can experience improvement and adjust over time unless we try pharmacological intervention, Dr. Schuler?" Bridie's eyes moved deliberately between Schuler and Strong, unsettling him with her calm determination. "I have another option I'd like you to consider."

"Another option?" Dr. Schuler's gaze intensified as he studied the articulate, attractive young woman seated before him. His irritation surged, a dull ache forming at the base of his neck, spreading upward as his jaw tightened.

"If you're reluctant to put my mother on either Thorazine or Serpasil, I plan to initiate a transfer to Rockland State Hospital. I understand that medical directors at Harlem Valley and Rockland must agree to a transfer. Although Dr. Kline is not the medical director at Rockland, he has assured me that Dr. Lurie would be amenable. I'd hate for my mother's case to gain public attention, but I'm not above seeking that route if we can't move forward with her treatment plan."

This is getting more complicated by the second, Schuler thought. "Miss Murphy, surely, that won't be nece—"

The words caught in his throat as a sudden, searing pain and suffocating pressure shot through his chest. His narrow, blue-tinged lips parted in shock, his gray eyes widening in terror. He gasped, trying to draw breath, but the pain was relentless, merciless. With a final, desperate shudder, his body collapsed forward, his forehead striking the table's surface with a dull thud. His breath escaped in one last, ragged sigh, then all was still.

~*~

Early October 1956 (Five months later)

Bridie waited for Matt at the northeast entrance to Riverside Park, their usual meeting place. The park stretched from 72nd Street to 158th

Street along Manhattan's western edge, offering scenic views of the Hudson River and the rugged New Jersey Palisades—a twenty-mile expanse of sheer cliffs running from Jersey City to South Nyack. The park was just a ten-minute walk from the New York State Psychiatric Institute (NYSPI), where Matt was in the first year of his four-year residency.

Standing by the railing, gazing into the Hudson, Bridie pondered the best course of action, hoping Matt could offer professional guidance. She hadn't wanted to bother him during his first rotation last month. Matt had described his first rotation in emergency psychiatry as a "trial-by-fire baptism," and she remembered how exhausted he'd sounded explaining that "every patient was in acute crisis" over the phone.

She checked her watch. Matt should have been here by now. He'd assured her that his current rotation in outpatient psychiatry was significantly more predictable because the patients were stable and no longer hospitalized.

The fall Sunday afternoon was unseasonably warm, though the breeze off the Hudson still nipped at Bridie through her overcoat. The trees, in their kaleidoscope of autumn colors, formed a lush canopy overhead, filtering the midday sunlight into dappled patterns on the ground. The sounds of lapping water against the embankment and the soft chirping of birds filled the park.

Now that her mother was a patient at Rockland State Hospital, Bridie saw her every workday—not as her attending nurse, but as her daughter. She was finally getting to know the mother she had always loved. The process was bittersweet. Each visit brought them closer, but she knew building her mother's trust would take time.

On Sundays, Bridie attended Mass and met up with Matt if his schedule permitted. If not, she often spent the day in Tarrytown with family, just fifteen minutes away from her apartment in South Nyack, thanks to the Tappan Zee Bridge.

Bridie jumped when she felt a set of arms wrap around her waist. "Matt, you scared me!" She spoke more sharply than she intended.

"Sorry, I didn't mean to startle you." He pulled her close, and she found the familiar comfort of resting her head on his chest as her body relaxed into his embrace. "I've missed you so much, Bridie," he murmured, kissing the top of her head.

"I wanted so much to see you these past weeks, Matt, but I needed time to sort things out before dragging you into my mess."

"That doesn't sound like my girl." Matt held Bridie at arm's length, his eyes searching hers. "Do I see storm clouds in those beautiful eyes? What's going on? Is this about your mother? We both knew her road to recovery would be long and steep."

"Yes, but it's not what you think. Mom is progressing well enough. Her psychiatrist switched her from Serpasil to Thorazine, and bits and pieces of her memory are returning, mostly from her early life, before she got sick. Dad talks with her psychologist, so he has a rough idea of Mom's life before her breakdown. It's just... I didn't..." Bridie struggled to finish her thoughts as tears streamed down her cheeks.

"But that all sounds good, so why the tears?" Matt gently wiped away her tears, brushing her cheeks with his thumbs.

"Mom entered Harlem Valley State Hospital in December 1928. I was born in April 1933. See the problem? My mother had already been institutionalized for three and a half years before she became pregnant with me." Bridie's voice trembled as she blurted out, "I'm some other man's child. Not Dad's."

"Are you sure? Isn't there some way that they could have—"

"Matt, please! We both know that isn't possible. But that isn't the biggest problem. How do we address this with my mother? Eventually, she'll figure out that some horrible person raped her when she was out of her mind. I'm frightened of how that realization will impact her recovery and, honestly..." Bridie gulped air like a drowning person, "...how it'll impact her relationship with me."

"You read your mother's medical records to learn this?"

"Yes. When I saw the admit date, I paged frantically through the chart and found an entry from September 1932: 'Tubal ligation delayed, patient found pregnant, father unknown.' Then, in April 1933: 'Patient delivered in Danbury General Hospital.' I had always assumed my mother was pregnant with me when she got sick. Poor Dad... he had so little time with her."

"I could never understand why Meg and Patsy had no memories of Mom, only of me as a baby. How could they? Mom was institutionalized when Patsy was a newborn, and Meg was only a year old."

Matt hugged Bridie closer. "That's a whole lot to carry alone. Have you spoken with your father about this?"

"Eventually. The shock was overwhelming at first," Bridie

admitted, her voice trembling. "But then I realized... maybe everyone else already knew, and perhaps I was just the last to figure it out.

"I didn't want to hurt Dad's feelings or risk him thinking I was angry with him for not telling me because I wasn't. He even offered to fly out to be with me so we could talk in person, but we ended up having a long conversation over the phone. He told me that he had his lawyer draw up papers threatening the hospital with a lawsuit if they aborted me. He saved my life, Matt.

"He's always been my hero, but now more than ever," Bridie said, wiping her eyes. "I can't believe how much he's done for me. He said he didn't tell me because he didn't want me to feel unloved or unwanted. Do I wish things had been different? Of course! For Mom, for Dad, for me.

"He told me about my aunt Eileen, who had never been able to have children and wanted to adopt me. I knew Eileen had died of breast cancer, but I didn't realize the timing—that I had lived with her for several months after I was born until she could no longer care for me. Dad said they agreed to wait a year to make my adoption final, but then Eileen was diagnosed, and I came back to him, where I'd always belonged.

"He told me that I was Mom's last and most precious gift...to him." Bridie's voice broke as she sobbed in Matt's embrace.

"I've had a great life, Matt. But how do I reconcile that my beautiful, wonderful life was at the cost of terrible evil inflicted upon my mother?"

"You're asking the hardest question, Bridie—how can a loving God allow evil and suffering?" Matt gently lifted her chin, placing his hands on her shoulders. "It's something we all wrestle with. I don't have all the answers, but I do know this much: God brings good out of even the hardest things. Look at you, Bridie—you've already done so much to help your mom.

"I don't just love you; I admire you. You may not be Jamie Murphy's biological child, but God chose him to be your father and you to be his daughter. We can only see the tangled threads, but God sees the whole tapestry. It's not easy to walk by faith instead of sight, though in the end, trusting His plan is really all we have."

"Does it change your feelings about me, knowing that I'm the child of a rapist?" Bridie's bottom lip quivered.

"You are a child of God. And no, it doesn't change my feelings for you. I'd marry you right now if only you'd agree."

"Not until you finish your residency. Besides, maybe you'll meet someone else." Bridie laughed through her tears.

"That won't happen, silly girl. I'm nuts about you."

"But, Matt, how do we handle this situation with my mother?"

"It's hard to sit in ambiguity, and definitely not your style, Miss Bridget Murphy. But what choice do you have? Your mother's recovery, the counsel of her psychologist, the passage of time, and prayers will provide the answer you seek. Not today. Not tomorrow. But all in good time."

TWENTY-SIX

JOURNAL OF KATIE HOULIHAN MURPHY
(Selected Entries)

August 1, 1958

Today marks a new beginning. After spending more years at Harlem Valley State Hospital than I can count and the last two years at Rockland State Hospital, my doctors have told me that I'm set to be discharged in two weeks. The thought of leaving after so long feels unreal—although the passage of time was not something I was able to fully grasp until I started taking this new medication. For so long, my life was lost to me. Confined by the hospital walls and its grounds, my days blended into nights beneath the same gray ceiling.

When I started taking Thorazine in July '56, a fog seemed to lift from my mind. It wasn't until it was gone that I'd even realized it had been there—although, reading what I just wrote, it hardly makes sense to me. The chatter of tormenting voices quieted, and the haunting visions dissipated like smoke in the wind. The world outside of me became something I could cautiously approach, like the hesitant steps of a child learning to walk.

The madness that once plagued me felt as real as the pen I now hold and the notebook open before me. What a gift to run my fingers over the paper, feeling its smoothness and knowing that the page is real. Thanks to my medication, the persistence of my remarkable daughter, Bridie, and the dedicated work of my doctors at Rockland, I'm told that I'm ready to leave this hospital. Am I really ready to leave this place? I desperately want to believe my doctors, even as my hands tremble while writing these words.

I know there is no cure for my illness; the best I can hope for are periods of stability and a reasonable quality of life when my symptoms are well-managed by Thorazine. Trading the torments of my illness for its side effects is a small price to pay to come home to everyone and everything I love. I eagerly embrace whatever joy I can find. The sunlight streaming through the window warms my face. I feel many emotions jockeying for first place. Yes, I'm frightened, but more than anything, I feel <u>hopeful</u>. At least tonight.

~*~

August 8, 1958

Jamie moved back to Tarrytown several months ago from California to make my transition home easier. But "home" is no longer the house where we all lived together on Elizabeth Street. It feels strange to think of us living anywhere else. He told me they sold the old house after Mom died—my dearest Peggy. In some ways, the past has caught up with the present: Jamie now practices law in the same building in White Plains where we first met, back when I worked for Mr. Kennedy. Now, Jamie works with Mr. Kennedy's son, Bryan, who is also a lawyer.

I've decided to keep writing in my journal when I get home, at least for a while. Dr. Kahn, my psychologist at Rockland, encouraged me to start journaling in the fall of '56. Writing helps me put my feelings into words and untangle my thoughts. When I look back at my older entries, I can see my progress, just as Dr. Kahn promised I would.

There are so many kinds of doctors now for people with problems like mine: psychiatrists and psychologists. One prescribes medicine, while the other seems to just listen as I talk. It's helpful to be able to share how I feel with Dr. Kahn without holding anything back. I'm trying hard to become who I'm supposed to be, but I hardly know who that is.

I remember when there were only doctors. The world has moved on without me, evolving while I remained trapped in time. But my doctors are helping me find my way out.

I'm filled with a mixture of hope and trepidation about the future. Hope because I'm finally stepping back into a life I thought I had lost forever. Trepidation because I know how fragile my progress is and how much work still lies ahead. I pray that I'm ready to face it, taking one day at a time, trusting that with each step, I'll find my way.

Tonight, I'm feeling a bit overwhelmed. My progress feels like it's moving at a snail's pace. How much work lies ahead just to feel relaxed around Jamie when he comes to visit me—without worrying that I might sound crazy or do something wrong?

~*~

August 15, 1958

Jamie brought me home from the hospital today. I <u>really</u> looked at him today instead of being so focused on myself. Hair, once so dark, is now salt and pepper, with distinguished gray at his temples. His chocolate brown eyes are still as warm and kind as when we first met.

He is still so handsome, but I've lost my looks. I'm self-conscious about how much my appearance has changed—I never realized how vain I was as a young woman.

How can my Jamie still love me? When I look in the mirror, a stranger stares back at me. My red hair has lost its brilliance and faded. My face is lined with wrinkles, especially around my eyes, and the weight I've gained on this drug—I hardly recognize myself. Any semblance of youth has vanished.

I wanted to see the house where I lived with Eileen and Frankie after they got married, so I asked Jamie to drive through White Plains before taking me to our new home in Tarrytown. The trees and shrubs have grown into giants compared to when we lived there. More brutal testimony to the passage of time. I felt overcome with deep sadness— so many lost years.

Jamie said Frankie is still alive, but they've lost contact. Eileen died of breast cancer so young, just like Mam. White Plains looks familiar but different, too. The downtown area has changed so much—new stores line the streets, and sleek, modern cars fill the roads. The bustling energy, the vibrant mix of people, and the noise make my head spin.

I know how Rip Van Winkle must have felt upon awakening from his long nap to find everything changed. Thankfully, Tarrytown hasn't changed nearly as much as White Plains. It still feels like a village. I didn't want to drive by the house on Elizabeth Street—not yet, anyway.

When we arrived home, Jamie surprised me by carrying me over the threshold. As if he could read my mind, and sense my insecurities, he told me that I'm still beautiful and that he loves me. He hasn't changed—he is still the Jamie that I fell in love with. He made me laugh and cry at the same time.

The house Jamie found for us is small but charming. My needs are simple now: a peaceful place to recover and rediscover who I am.

I'm not ready to see anyone just yet other than Jamie and Bridie. I'm most comfortable with them. But Meg and Patsy are coming soon. Will they be embarrassed by me? I'm nothing like the woman Jamie married. I hope they don't expect me to look like the woman in our wedding photo that Jamie has displayed in the living room.

~*~

September 6, 1958

Meg and Patsy are visiting over the long Labor Day weekend. I could hardly believe my eyes when I saw them standing before me as grown women, no longer the little girls I remembered. I was so overwhelmed; I could hardly speak.

My heart raced as Meg and Patsy walked into the room, their faces wearing tentative smiles that barely concealed the anxiety of meeting a stranger they call Mother. We all felt the strain, the tension thick between us. As they stepped forward, we collided in a tight embrace, a wave of shared emotion crashing over us. Our communal sob filled the air, a mixture of overwhelming joy and deep, gut-wrenching sorrow. I felt every missed moment—their first steps, first words, their entire childhoods and teen years slipping away, gone forever. As I clung to them, the weight of those lost years wrapped around me like a suffocating shroud, pressing down on my chest.

Meg towers over me and has Jamie's coloring—dark hair and brown eyes—and is every bit as striking as her father. Her voice, clear and confident, fills the room when she speaks, each word precise and eloquent. I wonder if she finds her mother a bumbling fool. I feel lost in conversation these days. Writing is easier for me than speaking; it lets me sort through my feelings and find the right words.

Patsy is more of a blend of Jamie and me. She's stunning, even in her religious habit, she has soft features and a serene demeanor. She moves with a quiet grace, her presence gentle and reserved. Patsy is shorter than Meg but taller than Bridie, who's even shorter than me. (How does that happen? Bridie must take after Mam.)

All my girls are so accomplished. Jamie has done such a good job; it is obvious how much they all love each other.

~*~

September 13, 1958

Even a week after Meg and Patsy's visit, I'm still trying to sort through my feelings. They were so cautious around me, trying not to do or say anything that might upset me—it was both heartwarming and heartbreaking. I saw a wariness in their eyes, as if they're unsure of who I am or what I might do. I can't blame them. I ache for the life we might have had—together—had things been different.

On my good days, I find solace in small things: the smell of freshly brewed coffee in the morning, the flowers Bridie brings on her weekly visits to Tarrytown from South Nyack, Jamie's dimpled smile as he greets me returning home at the end of his workday ... things that ground me in the present and point me toward a future filled with hope, even as snippets of my past torments threaten to pull me back to what I can only describe as a living hell.

As I putter around my new home, with its cozy corners and cheerful rooms—emptied of strangers lacking purpose—I know I should feel grateful, and God knows I do. Yet, I can't shake this feeling of being out of place, like a puzzle piece that doesn't quite fit. I just want to feel normal again—whatever that truly means.

Jamie has been wonderful, always knowing when I need space and when I need to be pulled back into the fold of our new life. He's been cooking dinner most nights, something he never did before. It's his way of helping, I suppose, but it also makes me feel like a stranger in my own kitchen. I want to cook for him, to reclaim some sense of normalcy, but every time I try, my hands shake too much, and I end up making a mess. It's humiliating.

I keep telling myself to be patient, and to take things one day at a time, just as Dr. Kahn taught me. But it's hard. It's hard to be patient when I've already lost so much time.

~*~

October 5, 1958

Sometimes, I find it hard to fully trust my senses and perceptions, even though the hallucinations have mostly disappeared now. There are moments when doubt creeps in, and I wonder if the reality I perceive is genuine or a figment of my imagination.

Today, I asked Jamie if the couple pushing a baby carriage outside on the sidewalk reminded him of us walking Meggie. I was worried it was a product of my imagination. Thankfully, Jamie saw them, too. I find myself questioning if my daughters were ever really standing in front of me and whether this house I live in, or the neighborhood where it stands, truly belongs to Jamie and me.

Jamie has been my rock. His patience and understanding are unwavering, and he never pushes me to take on more than I think I can handle. I have my own bedroom; maybe that'll change someday. I can't say at this point.

The colors of fall are so beautiful, even though they signal the coming gloom of winter. Winter's promise is the glory of spring. Death and rebirth, death and rebirth ... the change of seasons mirrors my life. Just as spring does not look back to winter but forward to summer, I must look ahead, beyond mourning for a life unlived, and embrace the spring and summer to come.

Jamie suggested that his brother, Fr. Robert, officiate a renewal of our wedding vows at Transfiguration Church, where we are now parishioners. Robert is a Jesuit priest (this does not surprise me) and has been a missionary in the Philippines since 1946. When he returns home for a visit, I think I would like that at some point—when I am ready.

Simple tasks like shopping, cooking, housework, and even relaxing are now learning experiences filled with modern conveniences I can scarcely comprehend. Automatic washers, dryers, dishwashers, and television sets—all these advancements are bewildering yet fascinating.

I hope, like Old Rip van Winkle, to make peace with the changes in the world and within myself.

~*~

November 1, 1958

I have never shared this with Jamie (nor anyone else), but I don't even remember being pregnant with my daughter, Bridie. Sometimes, a vague and disorienting dream leaves me bewildered upon waking. Perhaps it's a blessing that certain memories remain locked away. I ask God only to restore the memories I can handle.

Other than Jamie, it is with Bridie that I feel the strongest sense of connection, like memories itching to be born but still held at bay. I suppose it's because she looks so much like I did at her age, although her eyes are gray, not blue, and she has a cleft in her chin that came out of nowhere. Something about gray eyes—I can't quite grasp it.

Bridie's presence is soothing and calming, like someone brushing my hair with a thousand gentle strokes.

~*~

November 15, 1958

I've been taking more walks outside and going shopping with Jamie. I've noticed how unkind and unforgiving people's attitudes can be—a sideways glance of disdain, whispering that stops as I draw near, a look of confusion (or perhaps sympathy) as their eyes travel from me to Jamie and back again. People like me were once hidden away, stigmatized, and forgotten.

Well, we're still stigmatized, but maybe that will change someday. Schizophrenia wasn't even a word I'd ever heard until I started getting well, and it isn't something most people can (or are willing to) understand. It's easier simply to judge. But in their defense, most people can't understand what they haven't experienced, and they fear the unknown.

I pray that people will become more compassionate toward those with mental illnesses, that scientists will develop better medicines, and that those who need help will not be ashamed to seek it. I still struggle to shake off years of shame and isolation.

Inventions and discoveries have leaped forward in ways I could never have imagined. That Jamie worked in the aerospace industry—his word for it—makes me so proud. How does he find the patience to teach a dinosaur like me? Telephones connect instantly across distances without switchboards, televisions broadcast moving pictures, and there's even talk of space travel. It all seems like science fiction brought to life. Jamie showed me a magazine article about a satellite called Sputnik that the Russians launched into space last year, and this year, the U.S. launched one called Explorer. The idea of humans sending objects into space is both thrilling and terrifying. What's next?

~*~

December 25, 1958

This morning, I unwrapped my Christmas gift from Jamie. I immediately recognized the gray and black dress and the T-strap heels. I had completely forgotten that I once modeled this outfit as a mannequin for Macy's in Manhattan. Jamie reminded me that he'd promised to buy me that dress when he graduated from college, but he returned the next day and bought both the dress and the shoes I had worn.

That Jamie has held onto that dress all these years means so much to me—not because of the dress itself, but because of the love it symbolizes.

But, of course, the dress doesn't fit. Accepting my body now is an exercise in humility, especially with that irritating clicking sound and the protruding motion I make with my tongue that I can't control. I can't blame people for staring at me when I go out in public—I'd stare at myself, too.

Lord, grant me the serenity to accept the things I cannot change, as the prayer goes.

At least the T-strap heels still fit. Eileen would have loved them. I miss her so much—her style and her hats. I wonder what happened to all those hats!

~*~

January 20, 1959

Meg and Patsy can't visit often, but we write letters back and forth. Meg tells me about her dissertation research, the undergraduate classes she teaches, and how I "will simply adore Southern California" when I visit someday. She still lives in the house where Jamie and the girls stayed when they moved to Santa Monica. Patsy, or Sister Mary Clare, shares stories of her life at the convent and the shelter where she works in St. Louis. She is such an inspiration to me. Both Meg and Patsy are remarkable women. I have missed so much of their lives, but I strive to focus on the present.

Bridie has been a constant presence. She understands my struggles in a way that others cannot. Her gentle guidance and medical knowledge are invaluable, helping me differentiate between reality and lingering doubts. She provides a desperately needed balance, keeping me anchored to the shore of reasonable expectations. She has a special fellow, Matt Ryan, who is in his third year of internship at a mental hospital in Manhattan associated with Columbia University. This handsome young man is going to be a psychiatrist. He and Bridie just became engaged, and they plan to marry when he finishes his fourth year of residency.

~*~

February 15, 1959

When I was a child, I loved the book *Alice in Wonderland*. I recently checked it out from the Warner Public Library and am rereading it, having revisited that story many times in my head over the last few months.

Some days, I feel like Alice—trapped by disorientation, apprehension, fear, and frustration, as if I'm falling down the rabbit hole or sitting at the Mad Hatter's Tea Party. On my better days, I hold a tiny golden key that opens a small door leading to a beautiful garden, though I cannot walk through it just yet. Just as Alice was initially too big to enter the garden, which symbolized beauty and tranquility for her in a chaotic world, I feel the same way.

As I reread Carroll's classic, I imagine the garden as a symbol of my fully restored relationship with Jamie, for which I hold the golden key. Fear stops me from opening the door.

When Jamie first brought me home from the hospital, he said I was always welcome to share his bedroom, but he correctly anticipated that I wasn't ready for that. He has never pressured me, and we still have separate bedrooms.

It isn't that I'm not physically attracted to Jamie—he is even more handsome in middle age if that is possible. Rather, it's about being comfortable in my own skin and having the confidence to reach out to him. It's not easy, but his love and patience give me strength. I want to turn that golden key and open myself fully to Jamie.

Most evenings, we sit together, discussing our days and hopes. He tells me stories from the years I missed, painting a picture of a life I am slowly assimilating into again.

I'm praying about all this, trying to lean more on the Lord and not myself, trusting Him with my today and tomorrow.

~*~

March 30, 1959

Tonight, as I sit by the window watching the pink and golden-hued sunset, I feel a sense of tranquility and inner peace. The world is not the same as the one I left behind, and neither am I. I'm adapting to my new "normal" and my limitations. But I am here, living and breathing, surrounded by the people I love. My moments of doubt and fear are becoming less frequent. I'm learning to trust myself and others again and to believe in the reality and goodness of my life.

The journey ahead is long, and there'll be many obstacles, but that is the nature of life itself, is it not? I'm filled with hope and joy. I'm emerging from the shadows, step by step, reclaiming my life and my place in this ever-changing world. With golden key in hand, I am nearly ready to enter the garden.

TWENTY-SEVEN

April 4, 1959

Jamie began getting ready for bed as soon as Katie finished her evening bath ritual. The floral scent of her bath powder lingered in the air. He rinsed off his razor and placed it beside his buff-colored shaving mug, which held a disk of soap and his well-worn shaving brush.

Normally, he shaved in the morning, but on weekends, he shaved only on Saturday night. He recalled how decades ago, Katie used to love it when he shaved just before bed, back when they still shared the same bed. Now, after forty years of battling his heavy beard, he was just tired of shaving and gave himself a day off.

He grabbed his Old Spice aftershave from the mirrored medicine cabinet and splashed some between his hands. The scent of nutmeg and citrus filled the room as he patted the astringent onto his clean-shaven face. The amplified sting alerted him to a small nick on his jawline.

After brushing his teeth, he checked his reflection in the mirror. A pensive, lined, fifty-five-year-old face stared back at him. Time marched on, but at least now he wasn't completely alone—though, in some ways, he still felt the absence of the intimacy he and Katie once shared.

Jamie turned off the bathroom light and walked down the hallway to his bedroom. He switched on the bedside lamp, casting a warm glow over the half-finished novel that would, as usual, serve as his bedtime companion. Clad only in pajama bottoms, he paused by the bedroom window, where the silvery moonlight bathed his firm, fit body. After a moment, he drew the floor-length drapes closed, sealing out the night.

The weekends were his best times with Katie, but tonight, she had seemed preoccupied, as if something was on her mind. She hadn't shared what it was, and he hadn't asked.

Now sitting on the edge of his bed, Jamie recalled Katie's delicate profile from earlier that evening as she read *Alice in Wonderland*. He had pretended to read his novel, but instead, he had been studying her. Katie—absent for more years of his life than present—yet she had shaped his world profoundly.

In the solitude of his room, his thoughts turned to the other key events that had framed his life: the deaths of his parents and beloved Uncle Jim; two world wars, each claiming a brother—first Danny, then Thomas twenty-three years later; and the harsh years of the Great Depression. He'd married the woman of his dreams, only to face his own "great depression" when he lost Katie to mental illness—and she had lost herself.

But there had been many blessings, too. Maybe he hadn't always been lucky, but he had been blessed many times over. He thought about the "gift" of Bridie, her unwavering commitment to Katie, and how instrumental she had been in bringing Katie home. Brilliant Meg and compassionate Patsy. Each had crafted successful, fulfilling lives for themselves, a testament to his sainted mother's influence (certainly not his).

Gracie and Annie had stood by him all these years, helping when he asked, as best they could, and Robert, always through his prayers. Gracie and Annie's families had never left Tarrytown. Gracie spent time with Katie, taking her shopping and helping her put together a new wardrobe—one that was both flattering and in line with the current styles. Even Annie invited them over for dinner monthly and seemed to have mastered her tongue—at least in his presence.

Jamie remained close to Eddie and Lupita, his "adopted family." God had brought them to his little family almost as soon as he'd stepped off the plane in Los Angeles—even before his daughters had arrived by train. He still felt their love embracing him across the miles. He so looked forward to their visit this summer when they would finally meet his Katie.

While working at Douglas Aircraft, he had enjoyed a successful career and a generous salary, which gave him a sense of direction, especially around the time of Mom's death, when he felt lost and near the breaking point. Even though his affair with Marilyn Miller seemed like the greatest failure of his life—something he deeply regretted—it had taught him humility. He knew just how selfish he could be and had come to understand the folly of living as a natural man, unregenerated in Christ.

He fell to his knees, facing the crucifix hanging above his bed—an icon of Christ's suffering and sacrifice, an image of divine love personified. Jamie's own suffering had taught him the true meaning of love and how closely it was intertwined with sacrifice. He realized that God's arms had always embraced him, even when he had felt abandoned. It was he who had walked away, not God.

Jamie was a different man now, just as Katie was a different woman. He felt guilty for wanting more from her emotionally and physically than she could give, but he was still a man. And Katie was still a woman, one to whom he remained deeply attracted despite the wear and tear of time. He prayed for an unconditional love for Katie, a selfless devotion with no expectations.

He thought he heard a soft knock at the door but dismissed it as the radiator—nights were still cold. But no, there it was again. "Katie?" Jamie said, rising to his knees and opening the bedroom door.

"May I come in, Jamie?" Her voice trembled slightly.

"Please do. You never need to ask permission, Katie. My bedroom is your bedroom too... that is, if you want it to be." His words were gentle and inviting.

"I do want that." Katie moved tentatively toward him, wearing a simple white cotton nightgown gathered at the neck with a drawstring. Her movements, slightly shaky, appeared almost timid as she placed her arms around him.

"Does this mean what I think it means?" The last thing Jamie wanted was to misinterpret her actions, to presume more than she was ready for.

"I hope so... if you still want—"

"Of course I do, Katie. Nothing will ever change that. Are you sure?" he whispered.

Katie answered with a slow, steady nod.

For so many years, Jamie had dreamed of this night, never certain it would come. They had navigated the turbulent waters of her return, rebuilding the fragile bond that time and circumstances had nearly severed. Now, as he held her close, Jamie felt the distance between them vanish.

When they lay down together, Jamie felt a reverence in their movements, an unspoken understanding of all they had endured. Their reunion felt like a tender dance of rediscovery—joy and sorrow intertwined. Afterward, a peaceful silence enveloped them. He stroked Katie's still-wavy hair, feeling contentment return.

"I love you, Katie Houlihan Murphy," he said, his voice steady. "I always have, and I always will. We're made for each other."

Katie moved her hand to his mouth, tracing his smile, feeling for his dimples. "That's always been one of your best lines, Jamie Murphy."

She nestled closer, her head resting on his chest. "I love you too. Thank you for never giving up on me."

As Jamie closed his eyes, love and gratitude filled his heart. He silently prayed, trusting that the Lord would guide them through whatever lay ahead.

Acknowledgments

A historical novel blends fact with fiction—an impossible task without critical human and published resources. I'm fortunate to have received invaluable guidance, encouragement, and expertise from several individuals, all of whom have made this book better and given me the confidence to tell Katie and Jamie's story.

My deepest appreciation goes to Dr. Raymond Biersbach, who generously shared his experiences working with schizophrenic patients at Greystone Park Psychiatric Hospital in Morristown, New Jersey, where he served as the Administrator of Psychology from 1988 to 2004. His insights and detailed account of the hospital's history were invaluable to me.

Greystone Park was originally known as the New Jersey State Lunatic Asylum when it opened in 1876. It was later renamed the New Jersey State Asylum for the Insane and, finally, Greystone Park Psychiatric Hospital, reflecting society's growing sensitivity to the plight of the mentally ill. Built according to the Kirkbride model, the hospital was initially designed to accommodate 350 patients. Over the years, the facility underwent several expansions, eventually housing more than 7,700 patients, leading to severe overcrowding. The historic building was demolished in 2015 and replaced by a new facility on the same campus.

I am profoundly grateful to J.M. Hamlett for meeting with me and trusting me enough to candidly and articulately share her story of postpartum psychosis. J.M. is a blessing to many women through her courageous efforts to increase awareness of this rare condition.

Gregory S. Foxley, my alpha reader extraordinaire, read every line of my first draft, providing invaluable and extensive feedback. He ensured that my character, Jamie Murphy, thought like a man—not a woman. The fact that he is an ex-seminarian and an English major was the icing on the "critique" cake. His generosity and expertise in sharing his time and wisdom enriched every page. Thanks also to Mia G. Ready, my patient beta reader, for her thoughtful feedback and support.

Thanks to my editors Patrice MacArthur and Ellen Hrkach, who never fail to make my work shine. It was Ellen who encouraged me to rewrite the novel from omniscient POV to third-person limited POV. Along the way, she provided cheerleading and technical support in equal measure. More than any other person, I am an author due to Ellen, whose encouragement dates back to 2016. Thanks also to my proofreader, Ben Hrkach, for working quickly and skillfully to excise any remaining issues.

Hannah Linder blew me away with her cover design. Hannah makes me want to write books just to see how she brings my story to life through her artistic vision. Okay, this may be a slight exaggeration, but she is totally amazing.

To my church friends—Kendra, Jane, Marie, Julie, Cindy, Grace, Susan, Rebecca, Tina, and Sharon—who read my books and encourage me to keep plodding (and plotting) along: thank you! To Clare, Bernadette, Suzanne, Elizabeth, and Carole, many thanks for your support. Julianne, Bart, and Linda, like a fine wine, you just get better with age. And to my husband, Neal, who lends an indulgent ear as I brainstorm aloud during dinner, you're the best!

With gratitude, I acknowledge my local library's interlibrary loan service for books, as well as online resources like the Internet Archive, PubMed, and EBSCOhost (accessed through my local public library's portal) for out-of-print books and for access to peer-reviewed journal articles. I definitely get more than my money's worth from my tax dollars!

Author's Notes

My novel begins in 1927 and concludes in 1959, with Katie Murphy returning home after nearly thirty years in mental hospitals. During the twentieth century, terms like "insane asylum" were gradually replaced by "mental hospital" and later, by "psychiatric hospital" or simply "hospital," reflecting society's evolving perceptions of mental health care.

As my novel ends, a seismic shift in the care of individuals with severe mental illness has already begun. This shift was driven by 1) the development of the first effective drugs, such as Thorazine, making outpatient care a possibility, 2) the soaring costs of continuing the current model of long-term institutionalization, and 3) a growing public awareness of the horrific conditions in many state-run mental hospitals. Ultimately, these factors spawned the deinstitutionalization movement that would take place over the next thirty years.

Hundreds of thousands of people were institutionalized during the first half of the twentieth century, and many never left, especially if their condition was considered incurable or socially deviant. Commonly, those with mental illnesses, intellectual disabilities, and severe physical deformities were isolated from the rest of society.

For example, prevailing medical "wisdom" counseled parents whose babies were born with Down Syndrome to institutionalize them at birth. This only began changing in the 1950s with the formation of parent advocacy groups like the National Association for Retarded Children, now called The Arc, which rejected the idea that children with disabilities should be hidden away and ultimately led to the Education for All Handicapped Children Act in 1975.

Despite some limited expansions, state mental hospitals and institutions for people with disabilities became severely overcrowded. Harlem Valley State Hospital had 2,000 patients when it opened in 1924 and 5,800 when it closed in 1958. Rockland State Hospital accommodated 5,700 patients when it opened in 1931; by 1958, it housed 9,000 patients.

During and after the Great Depression, dwindling budgets at both the state and federal levels couldn't keep up with the patient load. The cost for such care and custody far exceeded what society, through their elected government representatives, was willing to pay.

When we read about the "barbaric" methods used to "treat" and "restrain" those with mental illness in the past, we have to remember what the options were—nothing any stronger than being strapped into warm baths (called hydrotherapy) or subjected to a cold shower. No medications were available, and overcrowding and understaffing were rampant. It was a vicious circle. There were dedicated doctors, nurses, and attending staff—but not all.

Unable to calm psychotic patients who became violent and combative, long stints in isolation rooms, electroconvulsive therapy without anesthesia, and physical restraints—including, but not limited to, straitjackets—were common practices. Insulin shock therapy, despite its long-term metabolic issues and lack of evidence supporting its efficacy, was used between the 1930s and 1950s.

Lobotomies were common between the late 1930s and 1950s. However, with the advent of antipsychotic medications and growing public awareness of their severe consequences—highlighted by Rosemary Kennedy's 1941 procedure—lobotomies began to fall out of favor. Rosemary's lobotomy, performed at the request of her father, was intended to help with her mood swings, outbursts of anger, and impulsive behavior. However, it left her with permanent cognitive impairments.

Nowadays, many people are unaware of the eugenics movement in the United States during the twentieth century, with Margaret Sanger being one of the best-known proponents. In 1921, Sanger founded the American Birth Control League, and in 1942, her organization was renamed Planned Parenthood Federation of America. In her 1919 article "Birth Control and Racial Betterment," Sanger wrote, "No woman can call herself free who does not own and control her body." Sanger's words, now shortened to the familiar refrain: "My body, my choice," are used to justify abortion at any stage of gestation for any reason.

In the 1927 case of *Buck v. Bell*, the Supreme Court ruled in favor of a Virginia statute that permitted forced sterilization of those deemed "unfit," including those with intellectual disabilities and mental illness, for "the protection and health of the state."

The last known forced sterilization in a New York State mental institution occurred in 1963; New York officially banned forced sterilizations in 1979. In California, the last forced sterilization in a mental institution occurred in 1979, when their eugenics program, which had been in place since 1909, was officially terminated.

The frequency of female patients being raped or sexually abused by staff or male patients in mental hospitals and "homes" for the "mentally defective" is unknown. Specific records are difficult to obtain and are typically non-existent, for obvious reasons—it is a failure in protocol. However, it is widely accepted that such abuses did occur.

Pregnancies resulting from these assaults would be terminated using a broad interpretation of "medically necessary" for the female patient or resident. These procedures were consistent with the prevalent eugenic philosophy and served to protect the institutions from negative scrutiny. States like Oregon, California, and Virginia which had very active eugenics programs, frequently sterilized women before being discharged.

Albert Q. Maise published his article, "Bedlam 1946," in the May 6, 1946, edition of *Life* magazine. His article drew national attention to the overcrowding and inhumane treatment. (It is easy to access this online via Google Books, pp 102-118). The heartbreaking images testify to the consequences of more than a decade of decreased funding (while the population of patients grew) and an "out of sight, out of mind" societal mentality.

As public awareness of the harsh realities inside these institutions grew, deinstitutionalization gained momentum. Between 1955 and 1980, 80% of the State Mental Hospitals were closed as part of the deinstitutionalization movement. Most state hospitals were in serious disrepair, and the cost of maintaining was beyond what most states were willing to or could pay.

With antipsychotics, patients previously kept locked up for life could be released with a short supply of medications to outpatient care. This assumed there was community-based medical and psychological support to ensure the discharged patients took their medications and had a place to go home to. However, many did not. Unfortunately, this transition to deinstitutionalization often lacked the necessary support systems.

Without adequate community support, there was a rise in homelessness among those with severe mental illnesses. We continue to see this impact today, with an estimated 20-25% of the homeless population suffering from severe mental illness.

In 1963, President Kennedy signed the Community Mental Health Act to put federal monies in local coffers to help revitalize a flagging system. Then, in 1981, President Reagan signed the Omnibus Budget Reconciliation Act, severely cutting back federal funding for community outpatient centers.

Although a work of fiction, my novel was influenced by several specific events that I can now point to, including my own family history. The earliest was a short article published in the early 1970s, which described how, during the first half of the twentieth century, husbands could easily commit their wives (against their wills) to mental institutions for almost any reason, with little medical oversight. The fact that I can vividly recall where I was, when I read it, and with whom, speaks to the surge of adrenaline that accompanied my reading, embedding the gist of the article into my memory.

After conducting my research for this book, I suspect that the short article, which appeared in *Parade Magazine* was prompted by the national interest in the legal proceedings that Kenneth Donaldson had brought against the superintendent of a mental hospital in 1967. Involuntarily committed by his father for delusions, Kenneth spent fifteen years as a patient, never receiving any treatment at the Florida hospital. The case of *Donaldson v. O'Conner* eventually made its way to the Supreme Court in 1975, curtailing the ability of families, doctors, and medical institutions to commit non-dangerous individuals to mental hospitals without due process involuntarily.

Later, I learned that my grandmother, a former Miss White Plains beauty queen, had been committed to a mental institution in her late twenties. This article immediately came to mind. My grandmother "Kaye" was diagnosed with dementia praecox. She spent the rest of her life in Harlem Valley State Hospital until she was transferred to a nursing home, where she died of breast cancer.

My aunt recalled snippets of her mother's illness: her mother fearfully crouched in a bedroom closet to escape the snakes that she imagined writhing on the bedroom floor. My aunt, then a very young child, pretended they were playing hide and seek. "Kaye" was in psychosis—not playing a game. My mother was just a baby then; her "mommy" became a photograph taken of "Kaye" at age nineteen, at the time of her wedding.

Schizophrenia is a severe mental illness that affects approximately 1% of the world's population. It is a complex and multifaceted disorder with genetic, environmental, and neurodevelopmental factors interacting dynamically. In a November 10, 1988, editorial, the journal *Nature* described schizophrenia as "arguably the worst disease affecting mankind."

Several years ago, a relative had a complete psychotic break after experiencing mania due to an underlying bipolar disorder and ended up in a state mental hospital. After twelve days of unremitting psychosis, an antipsychotic was added to their medications. Within several days, the psychosis was gone. Although not cured— Bipolar I Disorder with mania is a lifelong condition—but they would learn to manage this by adjusting their medications with professional help and by "listening" to their body and brain.

In 2020, Robert Kolker published *Hidden Valley Road: Inside the Mind of an American Family.* The non-fiction book tells of a Colorado Springs family, with seven out of ten children being diagnosed with schizophrenia. The book does a great job of pointing out how mental illness impacts the whole family and how, historically, mental illness had often been blamed on the mother's parenting style. In this case, there was a genetic link on the paternal side.

My issue with Kolker's book is the way he characterizes neuroleptic drugs (antipsychotic medications used to manage psychotic conditions such as schizophrenia, bipolar disorder, and treatment-resistant severe depression). There is no happily-ever-after for people with severe mental illness, such as schizophrenia, because that would require a cure. Instead, their illness can be managed, and they can enjoy productive, rewarding lives *if* they stay on medications and take them as prescribed.

Only when one fully appreciates the poor quality of life of those like "Kaye" with ongoing psychosis decades ago—neuroleptics are seen in their proper light: a godsend. This is not to underplay their side effects—they are unpleasant and can have serious health repercussions that must be managed. But what is the alternative?

Sadly, most people with serious mental illnesses like schizophrenia, schizoaffective disorder, and certain types of bipolar disorders don't realize that they are ill because the part of the brain that performs self-reflection doesn't work correctly. This is one of the reasons it is difficult for those with serious mental illnesses to stay on their medication, and in many cases, they prefer how they feel without it. They don't know they can experience a better quality of life once their brain's neurotransmitters are balanced.

The stigma of mental illness, although not as extreme as during the time period of this novel, is still alive and well, remaining a hurdle for the individual who suffers, as well as their family. While a person may feel no shame in taking an antibiotic for, say, a bladder infection, the same person is reluctant to take medication to rebalance the neurotransmitters in the brain. We take medicines for other parts of the body, but how about the organ—the brain—that runs the show? It is as if all one has to do is "will" or white-knuckle the brain's biochemical or organic issues away.

In my late forties, my circadian rhythms went on strike. I never slept more than an hour and a half or about four hours cumulative a night. I also had a killer headache 24/7. Elimination of caffeine, trying melatonin, and prescription sleeping pills had no effect. This torture went on for a year and a half.

My CT scan revealed no brain tumor. Finally, I went to a clinic that used SPECT scans (Single Photon Emission Computed Tomography) to image the parts of my brain that were in overdrive and which parts weren't pulling their load. The scan revealed an overstimulation of my limbic system, consistent with a diagnosis of anxiety, and decreased prefrontal cortex activity, consistent with depression. Although I didn't feel depressed, I could agree that I was extremely anxious about *not sleeping!* I wasn't worried about anything—my brain simply wouldn't turn off. My neurotransmitters were out of balance.

My excellent psychiatrist prescribed an efficacious cocktail: a small dose of an antipsychotic, an antidepressant, and a low dose of an antiseizure medication. For the next seven years, I wasn't pleased with the morning grogginess but learned to live with it: a small price to pay for sleeping. While I couldn't fix my sleep issue on my own, I was fortunate to know that something was wrong with me, unlike "Kaye" or most people with serious mental disorders. Eventually, my brain reset, my SPECT scan was perfect, and my brain was happy.

Before researching my novel, I was unfamiliar with postpartum psychosis. I wondered if this could have been a triggering issue for "Kaye." Postpartum psychosis is a condition that is not widely recognized until it affects someone close to us, underscoring the importance of raising awareness about this serious mental health issue.

I started by watching TED Talks given by survivors of postpartum psychosis. There are many excellent choices. Here are two:

- Teresa Twomey, "Breaking the Silence on Postpartum Psychosis" (youtube.com/watch?v=W7gyRpTkSP0)
- Rachael Watters, "Understanding Postpartum Psychosis" (youtube.com/watch?v=8qgV7Yug-xs)

A simple Google search will provide a myriad of sources on postpartum psychosis. Here are two reliable and useful resources:

- Postpartum Support International (postpartum.net/get-help/postpartum-psychosis-help)
- Center for Women's Mental Health at Massachusetts General Hospital (womensmentalhealth.org and then type postpartum psychosis in the search window)
- Action on Postpartum Psychosis, U.K. (www.app-network.org)

I found books written by people who had experienced psychosis essential to "get inside" Katie Murphy's mind. Here are my favorites:

- Catherine Cho, *Inferno: A Memoir of Motherhood and Madness*. 2020.
- Clifford Whittingham Beers, *A Mind That Found Itself: An Autobiography*. 1908.
- Charlotte Perkins Gilman, *The Yellow Wallpaper*. 1899.
- Lori Schiller and Amanda Bennett, *The Quiet Room: A Journey Out of the Torment of Madness*. 1994.
- Bethany Boik, *Diary of a Schizophrenic*. 2016.

Selected books that helped me understand the state of psychiatry as the novel begins include:

- Kraepelin, Emil. *Dementia Praecox and Paraphrenia*. 1919.
- Bleuler, Eugen. *Dementia Praecox or the Group of Schizophrenias*. 1950. Originally published in 1911 in German.
- Kirkbride, Thomas Story. *On the Construction, Organization, and General Arrangements of Hospitals for the Insane with Some Remarks on Insanity and Its Treatment*. 1854

Selected books that were medically helpful regarding Schizophrenia and Postpartum Psychosis include:

- Kurtz, Matthew M. *Schizophrenia and Its Treatment: Where is the Progress.* 2016.
- Hutner, Lucy A. *Textbook of Women's Reproductive Mental Health*, Chapter 16. 2021.
- Ross, Marvin. *Schizophrenia: Medicine's Mystery – Society's Shame.* 2008.

Books for those who want more information on the deinstitutionalization movement and its consequences:

- Torrey, E. Fuller. *Out of the Shadows: Confronting America's Mental Illness Crisis.* 1997.
- Mechanic, David. *Mental Health and Social Policy: Beyond Managed Care.* 2007.

Useful Statistical Resources:

- *Annual Report of the New York State Department of Mental Hygiene (1928-1932).* State of New York, New York State Department of Mental Hygiene, Albany, NY.
- *Annual Report of the New York State Department of Mental Hygiene (1958).* State of New York, Albany, NY.
- Substance Abuse and Mental Health Services Administration. *Current Statistics on the Prevalence and Characteristics of People Experiencing Homelessness in the United States.* U.S. Department of Health and Human Services, 2011.
- U.S. Department of Health and Human Services, and U.S. Department of Housing and Urban Development. *The 2020 Annual Homeless Assessment Report (AHAR) to Congress.* U.S. Department of Housing and Urban Development, 2020.
- Cox, J. L., Murray, D., and Chapman, G. "Postnatal Depression: A Comparative Study of Incidence and Prevalence." *British Journal of Psychiatry,* vol. 163, 1993, pp. 27-31.
- O'Hara, M. W., and McCabe, J. E. "Postpartum Depression: Current Status and Future Directions." *Annual Review of Clinical Psychology,* vol. 9, 2013, pp. 379-407.
- Osborne, L. M. "Recognizing and Managing Postpartum Psychosis: A Clinical Guide for Obstetric Providers." *Obstetrics and Gynecology Clinics of North America,* vol. 45, no. 3, 2018, pp. 455-468.

- Raza, S. K., and Raza, S. "Postpartum Psychosis." *StatPearls*, StatPearls Publishing, 2024. Accessed June 26, 2023.

Articles on early twentieth-century medical treatments, such as those for breast cancer, biopsies, mastectomies, the introduction of forceps, twilight anesthesia, the prevalence of midwifery, and the treatment of burns in the 1920s, are too numerous to list in full. Several examples follow.

- DeLee, Joseph B. "The Prophylactic Forceps Operation." *American Journal of Obstetrics and Gynecology*, July 1920.
- Martin, Hayes E., and Edward B. Ellis. "Biopsy by Needle Puncture and Aspiration." *Annals of Surgery*, July 1930.
- Halsted, William Stewart. "The Results of Radical Operations for the Cure of Carcinoma of the Breast." *Annals of Surgery*, Nov. 1894.
- Bourne, Randolph (first published anonymously). "The Handicapped – By One of Them." *Atlantic Monthly*, Apr. 1911.
- Terman, Lewis M. "The Sterilization of Defectives." *The Scientific Monthly*, Mar. 1924.
- Sanger, Margaret. "The Eugenic Value of Birth Control Propaganda." *The Birth Control Review*, Oct. 1921.

Final Note: The scientists and medical professionals depicted in this novel, with the exception of Dr. Albrecht Schuler, Dr. Glen Strong, Doc Collins, and Dr. Jacob Cohen, were pioneers in the surgical treatment of breast cancer, the field of psychiatry, psychopharmacology, and psychiatric neuroscience.

Reading Group Discussion Questions

1. **Multi-Generational Households:** The Murphy house on Elizabeth Street was home to several generations of Murphys until Peggy's death. This arrangement was common in the U.S. during the Great Depression, World War II, and the post-WWII housing shortage. Why do you think we are seeing a resurgence of multi-generational living today? Do you view this trend as positive or negative?

2. **Stigma of Mental Illness:** How did the novel portray society's general attitude toward mental illness? Was this stigma a factor in Jamie's decision to move across the country after Peggy's death? Have societal views on mental illness improved since then?

3. **Eugenics Movement in the U.S.:** Were you aware of the eugenics movement in the twentieth century? How does it compare to Nazi Germany's plan to exterminate the Jewish population? In what ways has eugenics impacted today's culture and values?

4. **Health Care Advocates:** In the novel, Bridie is a courageous and relentless advocate for her mother's health care. Is the role of a health-care advocate still important today? Why or why not?

5. **Sharing Painful Truths:** In Chapter 25, Bridie finally discovers that she was conceived in rape. Do you think Jamie should have told Bridie sooner? Should he have told Katie the details of Bridie's conception?

6. **Reconnection After Separation:** When Katie is finally discharged from the mental hospital, she is essentially a stranger to Meg and Patsy. Do you think they would have been able to reconnect with Katie after so many years apart? Would it have been easier for Katie to reconnect with them? Why or why not?

7. **Christian Worldview:** The novel shares nuggets of Christian theology through characters like Peggy Murphy, Fr. James (Unc) Gleason, Eddie Hodges, Lupita, Jamie, and Matt Ryan. Which moment of insight or advice did you find most memorable or impactful?

8. **Good from Evil:** The novel suggests that God can bring good out of evil, with Bridie being a striking example. Are there other examples of this theme in the novel? Can you recall examples from your own life where something positive emerged from a bad or painful experience?

9. **Stress and Schizophrenia:** Research links schizophrenia to significant life stressors or trauma, particularly in childhood. Did Katie experience a stressful childhood, and were there early signs in the novel indicating her vulnerability to mental instability?

10. **Role of Women:** How does the novel contrast the opportunities available to women in the early twentieth century with the opportunities women have today? Can you provide examples?

About The Author

Denise-Marie Martin is a retired scientist with a diverse research career. Her favorite experience was working in bioinformatics—a discipline that combines biology, computer science, and mathematics to interpret large genomic datasets. She has an impressive portfolio of scientific publications, numerous awards, and nine patents. She also worked as a mathematics instructor at both the secondary and college levels.

In retirement, Denise-Marie has turned her analytical mind and creative spirit to writing fiction. *The Better Part of Worse: A Novel of Hope* is her second novel. Her debut novel, *Tangled Violets: A Novel of Redemption*, was an award-winning finalist in the Christian Inspirational category of the 2022 American Fiction Awards.

A wife, mother, and grandmother, Denise-Marie is actively engaged in her faith community. She and her husband reside in the picturesque Pacific Northwest.

~*~

Denise Marie loves creating stories that engage and connect with readers. She'd love to hear your thoughts and feedback. Your reviews and ratings assist others in finding her books. Thank you for reading her novel and sharing your experience. You can get in touch with Denise-Marie through her website denisemariemartin.com, where you can also subscribe to her newsletter.

9 781735 238890